THE REVOLUTIONARY'S COUSIN

CINDY DAVIES

ODYSSEY
BOOKS

Published by Odyssey Books in 2019

www.odysseybooks.com.au

A Cataloguing-in-Publication entry is available from the National Library of Australia

ISBN: 978-1-925652-70-3 (pbk)

ISBN: 978-1-925652-71-0 (ebook)

Cover design by Simon Critchell

For all the women who have come to a new country as migrants or refugees and made a new life for themselves and their families in a foreign land.

AUTHOR'S NOTE

Although *The Revolutionary's Cousin* is a sequel to my first novel *The Afghan Wife*, it stands alone as a story. It is a work of fiction, but I have referred to some real people and places.

Youri Egorov, the concert pianist, actually existed. He escaped from the USSR during the cold war, but sadly died in New York in 1982. The Dead Dog Saloon in South Carolina is a colourful establishment, which I visited a couple of years ago. The New York subways are in a much better condition than they were in 1980. My description of them in the novel dates from then, not now.

I've included a glossary at the end of the book that contains the Persian words I've used in the text. Dress restrictions in Iran have eased somewhat since 1979 and not all women wear a chador. However, every woman must still adhere to the Islamic dress code and wear a headscarf in public as well as a long-sleeved, three-quarter length top and full-length pants.

The Fairly Meadow Migrant Hostel was an actual place and I taught English there from 1979 to 1981. The hostel was opened in 1951 to deal with an influx of migrants and refugees to Australia post WWII. It was still open in 1979, when my character Zahra arrived and it closed in 1982. The land it occupied is now part of the University of Wollongong.

The characters in this book, however, are purely fictional. Zahra's story is not based on any particular person I met while I was teaching at the hostel.

For the sake of the story, I altered the Illawarra train timetable and only allowed the express train from Wollongong to Sydney to stop once. Gulf Air no longer flies to Sydney but it was an important carrier in 1979.

Devotees of *Jane Eyre* might find that incidents from the novel have been updated and eased into my own story. This reflects my abiding admiration of Charlotte Brontë's work.

CHARACTER LIST

THE AFGHAN FAMILY

Zahra Ghafoori—A widow who worked as a companion to the late matriarch of the Konari family in Tehran. Zahra's mother was Iranian, her father Afghan.

Mahmoud Ghafoori—Zahra's deceased husband.

Ahmad Ghafoori—Zahra and Mahmoud's five-year-old son.

Firzun Khan—Zahra's first cousin. He and Zahra were brought up together in the family house in Afghanistan.

THE KONARI FAMILY

Abbas Konari—Karim's father and former employee of an American oil company in Tehran. He and his wife Esmat have recently moved to the USA.

Esmat Konari—Abbas's wife and owner of a department store in Tehran as well as a fashion label and a number of fashion boutiques in Iran's major cities.

Karim Konari—Their son, a thirty-four-year-old architect, educated in the Iran and the USA.

Soraya—Karim's younger sister who lives in Boston, USA.

Nadir—Soraya's husband and father of their two sons.

Nasim—An old friend of the family. Nasim's husband Rashid was executed by the new regime in November 1979 for 'crimes against the State'. Nasim now lives in Los Angeles with her parents.

Tahmineh—Housekeeper to the Konari family in Tehran. She lives in an apartment at the back of the Konaris' house with her husband, and niece Shirin.

Amir—Tahmineh's husband, a driver and odd-job man.

THE O'ROURKE FAMILY

Lawrence O'Rourke—Businessman and British immigrant to the USA and the Caribbean.

Beulah O'Rourke—Lawrence's part-Creole wife.

Lauren O'Rourke—Lawrence's twenty-four-year-old daughter, a psychologist.

Seamus O'Rourke—Lawrence's twenty-six-year-old son who works in the family business.

THE ASHRANI FAMILY

Leila Ashrani—An Iranian widow who befriends Zahra in Sydney.

Hamid Ashrani, also known as Harry Ashton—Leila's younger son who lives in the United States.

Mehran Ashrani—Leila's older son who has lived in Australia for a few years.

Tula Ashrani—Mehran's wife.

Darius and Lili—Their young children

OTHER CHARACTERS

Nousha Kashani—Firzun's 'fiancée'.

Nigel Palmer—Harry's partner.

Bahram—Karim's business partner in their architectural firm.

PROLOGUE

Tehran, Iran, November 1979

The large house was so quiet that Zahra could hear the rain spattering intermittently on the bedroom windows behind the heavy drapes. In the distance the *azan-e-magreb*, the evening prayer call, echoed through Elahiyeh, the elegant suburb of Tehran where she had lived for over two months. Finding it impossible to think straight about her future with her five-year-old son Ahmad jumping on the bed and chattering, she sent him down to the kitchen to play cards with the housekeeper's niece. Alone with her thoughts, Zahra folded pillowcases and tablecloths and put them in boxes to be shipped to the United States. Her employers, the Konari family, like so many Iranian families, had left hastily after the Ayatollah Khomeini had seized power.

Her thoughts wandered to her cousin Firzun, the self-styled revolutionary. He had survived the failed raid he had led to free the American hostages held at their embassy, only to be killed in a random bomb blast ten days ago. His leg had been injured during the raid and he walked with a cane. That was all they found after the blast—that and, she shuddered, part of his leg.

She remembered their visit to Iran as children sixteen years ago. Foolishly brave even then, Firzun was determined to have an adventure. She had always done what he wanted, always followed.

Zahra put her hand on the pile of linen and stared ahead remembering ...

The Tower of Silence, Yazd, Iran, 1963

'Vulture, look out!' her cousin yelled.

Zahra crouched low, her arms over her head as the bird swooped toward the ground. She heard the beat of its wide wings as it rose with a deep throated squawk, carried aloft on the warm currents of the desert air.

Firzun ran across the baked earth of the circular tower and yanked her arms away from her head, pulling her roughly to her feet.

'It scared me,' she wailed.

'Don't be a baby, Zahra. You're eleven years old.'

'It's getting dark ...'

'Turn around and look!' Firzun ordered. 'The fire worshipers leave their dead bodies here. Then he and his friends come and eat them.'

He pointed to the vulture, now an ominous moving silhouette against the red blaze of the setting sun. Firzun threw his arms out and ran around the tower squawking like the bird. He stopped at a shallow pit in the centre.

'The vultures pick the bodies clean, then the priests throw the bones in here. Come and look!'

Zahra peered into the shallow pit, but when he touched her arm she turned too quickly and lost her balance. With a shriek, she fell into the subterranean charnel-house. The soft earth clung to her hair and clothes like the fingers of the dead. She put her hands out to push herself up and felt something rigid and smooth. The empty eyes of a whitened skull stared back at her. Paralysed with fear she screamed out to her cousin. As he dragged her out, the bird returned and circled overhead. She saw its golden throat feathers lit by the setting sun, its hooked beak hungry for prey. A mournful cry came from deep in its body. It was so close that Zahra could hear the beat of its wings as it headed toward the desert and the distant mountains.

She gripped her cousin's hand and threw her head back, gasping for breath. 'Quick, it's getting dark!'

Bright shards of light from the setting sun lit a pathway for them across the tower. She ran toward the wall with Firzun, desperately sweeping the clinging soil and white powder from her long cotton shift and pants.

'It's lime. Don't touch it,' he gasped as they ran.

He squeezed through a hole in the ancient wall that was hardly bigger than his fourteen-year-old body. She blinked, trying to clear her vision as they stumbled down the steep trail to the road. She risked a look back at the dumpy mud-brick tower silhouetted against the darkening sky. Several vultures now circled over its looming stillness, making her shudder and take to her heels. They ran through the scrub and clinging branches toward the blinding lights of her uncle's car as it skidded to a stop.

'I told you to wait at the farm,' he yelled as they scrambled in. 'Stupid Afghan kid!' her uncle spat at Firzun. 'You're nothing but trouble.'

1

IN THE DEAD OF THE NIGHT

And now her cousin Firzun, the 'stupid Afghan kid', had gone forever. Apart from her son Ahmad, he'd been her sole family here in Iran. There would be no escape together to Australia as Firzun had planned. No more lies as he'd used her dead husband's identity and made her pretend to be his wife. She was truly free—and alone.

She finished her work and joined her son and the other servants in the kitchen for the evening meal. As she ate, she only half-listened to the talk around the table.

'Remember, Karim *Agha* is leaving tomorrow to close up the family's beach house on the Caspian Sea—such a shame,' Tahmineh, the housekeeper, remarked. 'He's taken a lot of responsibility, finalising everything for his parents—such a good son!'

At some point, Zahra thought, Karim will have to tell the housekeepers about our unofficial engagement. Everyone who knew the Konari family would be shocked and his mother would be furious, Zahra was sure of that. The wealthy son of a prominent family marrying one of his mother's employees! *I'm a well-educated woman,* Zahra reminded herself, *even though I haven't got any money. Karim and I love each other. He's vowed to marry me as soon as he can in America and I trust him.*

After she'd wished everyone goodnight, she put Ahmad to bed in the elegant guest room Karim had insisted they occupy after his mother left. Zahra read a few chapters of her book, then got ready for bed herself.

She'd finally fallen asleep, but the car bomb that had killed her cousin and the terrible aftermath she'd witnessed haunted her dreams. Often in her nightmares, she was running away from her former husband, then from the bomb blast. Sometimes she saw her husband lying dead in a bomb crater and she woke up calling for help. In her dreams, her dead cousin was limping toward her, leaning on his cane. She could hear it tap-tapping on the ground.

Zahra woke abruptly and sat up in bed, her heart racing. She forced herself to breathe slowly and looked across at the other bed. Ahmad was sleeping soundly, his dark hair framing his calm face. She remembered now that she was in the Konaris' house. She was safe.

She leaned back against the pillows, the scenes of the last two months replaying in her head.

On the eve of the failed raid at the American Embassy three weeks ago, Karim had begged her to leave Firzun and go with him to America. She'd refused, letting him think that Firzun was her husband, but now Firzun's death had changed everything. *We're free at last, me and Ahmad,* she thought as she closed her eyes.

A sudden noise jolted her senses. The sound from her dream—the sound that had woken her—a faint tapping like Firzun's cane, was *in the house.* She sat up again, fear squeezing her heart, her ears straining for the faintest sound.

There it was again—tap, tap, tap. Someone was knocking on the door of the empty bedroom next to hers. She switched on the bedside lamp and the sound stopped abruptly. She slipped out of bed and pulled on her robe. Were there intruders in the house? A chill flowed through her body. Was it the Revolutionary Guard, the paramilitaries who'd ransacked her friend's house further along the street? Would they burst in and arrest her, then drag Karim down the stairs and throw them both in prison? Catatonic with fear, she was torn between protecting her son and getting to Karim. She'd heard him come in before she'd fallen asleep. But the only way to his apartment on the next floor was across the landing. And someone —*something*—was out there. Firzun's spirit back from the dead? She tried to shake off the thought.

The plush carpet deadened her footsteps as she walked nervously across the room. She heard the knock again, but this time it was on her bedroom door.

'Zahra, are you there?' a voice said softly.

'*Khoda!* Oh my God!' She could hardly breathe. It was *his* voice —her dead cousin's—calling to her from the grave! 'Go away!' she croaked, not sure if she was asleep or awake.

She stepped back, hands over her mouth as the door handle turned slowly and quietly. When the door swung open she gasped, transfixed with terror. Fear, like a slow freezing trickle of water, ran down her skin. A figure stood in the doorway, backlit by the soft light that burned all night on the landing. Firzun! The white *shalwaar kameez* he was wearing on the day he was killed glowed in the dim light. His dark hair was massed round his face like a shadowy halo.

'*Waiee!*' she gasped. He caught her before she collapsed on the floor. She felt him walking her along the landing, then through the passageway to her old room above the kitchen. When she woke fully, she was sitting on a bed. Firzun stood quietly watching her. In the dim light, his features looked soft and indistinct. She struggled to stand up, to escape from the nightmare.

'Go away—go away!' she gasped.

'Zahra, it's me, Firzun. I'm alive,' he whispered.

She shook her head. *It's a dream. I've got to wake up!*

'I'm not a ghost, I survived. Touch my arm.' He held it out to her. 'No!'

He grabbed her arms and shook her. 'You're not dreaming. I hid in a cellar. I'm alive,' he repeated.

She *was* awake! She grasped his forearms. When she clenched her fingers around them she burst into tears. He sat her down on the edge of the mattress, then fetched a towel from the bathroom. She snatched it with trembling hands, covered her face, and sobbed into it. When the storm had passed, she jumped to her feet and beat his chest angrily with her fists.

'Ashraf said you were DEAD!' Her voice broke as he caught her wrists. 'He found your cane. He even said he'd seen your leg ... How?'

Firzun took a deep breath. 'It was a mistake! Listen, Zahra, I was getting our tickets for Australia at the travel agency, remember? They got a phone call—a warning. I told Ashraf to get you away. I thought I could stop the car bomb. I ran up there and dropped my cane. I made it back to the cellar just in time ...'

Zahra sat down again. 'They brought injured people into the mosque courtyard. I saw them collecting ...'

'Body parts, I know,' he said quietly. 'Ashraf came looking for me. He found the bits of my cane.' He shrugged. 'I've been laying low. If the authorities find out I wasn't killed, they'll be after me.'

Zahra's fear turned to fury. She'd gone to her cousin's funeral, buried him as her 'husband', said prayers for his soul in the mosque. And all the time he'd been *alive!*

'Get *out*,' she hissed. 'Ahmad and I are going to America with Karim. I've made a promise to him. He thought you were my husband and with you dead I was a widow and free!'

'He didn't waste much time, did he?' Firzun retorted. 'Well, I'm alive, Zahra, and we're sticking to the plan. Your husband, Mahmoud, *is* dead, remember? He was an ugly violent animal, he deserved what he got. I've got his passport and we're leaving for Sydney. I fixed up refugee visas for us months ago, remember? We'll live in a migrant hostel ...'

'No!' she cut in. 'I'm not going with you!'

'Listen to me, Zahra.' He pushed his face close to hers. 'I need Mahmoud's identity to get out of Iran. And you and Ahmad are coming with me, understand?'

She steeled herself. 'I won't do it Firzun.'

His eyes glittered in the dull light, making him look malevolently alive. 'Okay, Zahra, if you don't come with me, I'll turn Karim over to the Revolutionary Guard. They don't like rich people *or* traitors, and in their eyes he's both.'

'You're contemptible ...' She reached out to hit him, but he caught her hand. 'He's innocent,' she spat. '*You're* the guilty one. *You* organised that suicidal mission to free the hostages at the American embassy. People died because of you. *You* dragged Karim into it. You're lucky to be alive and now you're on the run again!' Her voice broke into a sob.

He recoiled from her torrent of words and looked away. She knew she'd hit her mark. He was the commander who'd led his troops to their death. He said nothing. She wasn't fooled, he was a charlatan and she knew he'd try to manipulate her. This time she'd be strong and refuse him.

'I know, may God forgive me,' he answered soberly. 'Zahra, if I'm caught I'll be executed.'

The words hung in the air between them.

'You'd turn Karim in to be executed though, wouldn't you?' she whispered.

His shoulders sagged and his head drooped. 'If you want to stay with him, that's your choice. But remember how I saved you in the mountains on the way here from Afghanistan?'

He'd played his last card, or so she thought. Yes, he'd saved her from her violent husband. At first, he'd told her it was an accident, then an honour killing. No one treated a member of Firzun's family like that!

In turn he made her promise to protect him from his enemies in Iran and kept his secrets. But she'd suspected that he had another agenda. He knew he might need to escape from Iran, and masquerading as her husband meant he'd be able to do just that.

And now he was asking her to make another, greater sacrifice. He wanted her to give up Karim and a new life in America. When she didn't answer, her cousin leaned forward.

'I've got Mahmoud's passport. It'll be easy,' he urged. 'The authorities won't recognise me.'

She hesitated, then shook her head. '*No, Firzun.*'

'Zahra, you owe me your life, remember?'

'It's too dangerous.'

'Since when has danger ever worried me?'

'It worries me.'

She grabbed his arm. He was asking too much, she told him. He could get out quicker on his own. He could go south and then cross the mountains into Turkey. He had a passport and friends; why did he need her?

'I won't do it,' she repeated.

He narrowed his eyes and put his face close to hers, enunciating each word. He would take Ahmad with him instead. She could please herself. Ahmad wouldn't understand 'dead'; he'd think Firzun had gone away and come back.

'He's *my* son. You can't!' she countered. 'They'll ask about his mother at the airport.'

'No, they won't,' he sneered. 'Fathers have more rights than mothers in Iran these days.'

She jumped up and ran toward the door, ready to rush back to her room and save her son. Firzun got there before her and leaned on it, facing her.

'You wouldn't be able to stop me, even if you came to the airport screaming and pleading to get him back.'

'I could tell the Revolutionary Guard who you really are.'

She tried to push him aside but he grabbed her wrists.

'How? What proof do you have that I'm *not* your husband?' he asked with a laugh.

'Karim knows who you are,' she said desperately. 'He could identify you.'

Firzun laughed again. 'Your Persian boyfriend! Do you really think he'll marry you? When he gets what he wants, he'll dump you before he goes, or even when you get to the States. Then what will you do?'

'He *loves* me! He's an honourable man,' she insisted, twisting out of his grasp.

Firzun went on: had she told Karim the truth yet? That they'd buried her first husband in the mountains? That she'd lied when she'd told Karim he had died of a heart attack in Afghanistan? How would Karim feel if he knew that everyone, even his best friends, had lied to him? Firzun warned her not to call out and wake 'her lover' or try to get him to help her. This was between *them*. Either she came with him, or he'd take her son right now. Ahmad was his second cousin—*his* blood too, he reminded her.

She wanted to spit in his face. She hated him; she was sorry he hadn't been killed, God forgive her. He had the upper hand and he knew it. He had Mahmoud's passport, which proved he was the boy's father, and under shari'a law he had every right to take her son.

Once again, her cousin was living on his wits. Using every black-mail tool he could. Yes, she owed him her life, but if she went with him she knew she would lose her chance of happiness with another man forever. How could she ever repay Karim for her treachery, for breaking all the promises she'd made about their future together? But maybe there was a solution that meant she could still be near him.

'Let's go back to Afghanistan instead.'

'For God's sake, you know we can't! I'm a wanted man there too.' Firzun opened the door slightly and turned to her. 'The flight to Sydney leaves late Monday afternoon. Be ready. What's Karim up to?'

'Family business. He's leaving early tomorrow and will be back on Tuesday night.'

Firzun took her face in his hands and told her to say nothing —*nothing*. Let Karim Konari think everything was fine. This was life and death for him; he was her cousin—her blood—had she forgotten? There were spies everywhere, he had to get out fast.

'Are you with me, cousin?'

She nodded reluctantly. *What choice have I got?*

'God protect you, Zahra. I knew you wouldn't desert me.'

'You threatened to take my son, Firzun. You left me no choice.'

'I'm desperate, cousin. Now listen carefully.'

His instructions went on and on. Tell the housekeepers she was going home to Afghanistan. She was using money her husband had left her. Take a taxi to the airport and don't let the housekeeper's husband take her and Ahmad. He'd meet her just inside the door of the Tehran International Terminal. The plane left at three.

'Get there by noon.'

'But what if you're not there?' she asked.

He tutted irritably. 'I *will* be. I'll be dressed like a cleric. Keep an eye out. I'll use my cane as a prop and get sympathy for being an injured holy man.'

She braced herself for more. She would be questioned and searched in the women's area. Make sure Ahmad called him *Baba*.

'I'm a *Haji*, remember? I'll look holy and religious.' He laughed.

She glared at him, resenting his sudden change to an ebullient mood. 'You've got no right to get respect for going on the Hajj to Mecca,' she snapped. 'You've never been!'

'Hey! If I shave the beard off, I won't look like the photo in Mahmoud's passport, will I?'

'But you're limping. Won't they be looking out for an injured man?'

'I'm dead and buried.' He shrugged, irritating her even more. 'I've covered my tracks well.'

She changed the subject and pointed to his travel bag. Would he be glad she'd kept it? Probably not. He picked up the Mickey Mouse backpack next to it.

'That's a surprise gift for Ahmad from Karim.' She moved forward to take it from her cousin.

'It's a surprise gift from *me* now,' he told her as he shoved it into his own bag. 'Ahmad can have it if he remembers to call me daddy.'

God forgive me, I hate you sometimes.

He ordered her to get him some food from the kitchen, then he'd be gone. He fixed her with his black eyes and told her to shut her mouth from now on.

'I'm your husband Mahmoud, in Iran *and* when we get to Australia. If the authorities know that Firzun Khan is alive, they'll arrest me and then *you* for harbouring me!'

His words had the desired effect; she felt terrified as she cautiously opened the door. He followed her down the back stairs to the kitchen. After she'd parcelled up some food from the fridge, she asked him how he'd got in the house. He dangled a key in front of her, said he'd found it under a stone.

'The housekeeper's husband doesn't know she hides it.' He shook his head and tutted. 'Women and secrets! *Yours* was a big one —leaving for America with your employer's rich son.'

'That's none of your business, Firzun,' she said sharply.

'Don't think you can marry your Persian boyfriend tomorrow and dump me, Zahra,' he said. 'New regime—shari'a law. Widows can't remarry for over four months.'

Furious with him, she dragged the door open, resisting the urge to push him out. He grinned ghoulishly at her through the glass as she shut the door in his face and tested the lock. The faint moonlight caught a glint of the silver key as he shoved it under a large stone. He raised his hand in a peremptory wave as he sauntered off down the shadowy path toward the cover of the trees.

After he'd gone, she ran silently up the stairs and stood in her bedroom, her thoughts swirling in dizzying eddies through her brain. She couldn't do this to Karim, could she? She covered her face with her hands. He'd been her rock after the bomb blast and supported her at the terrible funeral for the victims. The funeral that she had believed included her cousin. Karim had arranged everything for a smooth trip to America for her and her son. He'd held her close and told her about the wonderful life they would have in New York.

There would be no departure for America now, but if she defied Firzun and confided in Karim, he might turn her cousin in. That was something she just couldn't risk.

2

ZAHRA'S DECISION

Zahra gripped the handrail to steady herself as she walked down the dark back stairs to the kitchen for breakfast. Before she pushed open the door she closed her eyes and wondered, not for the first time, if she'd been dreaming. Had Firzun crept into the house last night. Was he really alive? Her head swam when she remembered her cousin standing in her bedroom doorway like a baleful ghost.

When she opened the kitchen door, she caught her breath. Tahmineh, the housekeeper, was standing in front of the open fridge with her hands on her hips. She turned to Zahra full of questions and speculation about the missing food. To Zahra's relief, she concluded that Mr Karim must have helped himself to it during the night.

'Are you ready for your trip to our village today?' she asked Ahmad as she poured Zahra a large glass of tea.

'He's really looking forward to it,' Zahra reassured her.

'There's nothing like country air for young boys!'

'Are you all right, Zahra Khanoum?' Tahmineh asked.

'I've decided we'll go back to Afghanistan soon,' Zahra said slowly, hating herself for lying to the other woman. 'I have a few things to talk over with my husband's mother. I won't mention it to Karim yet, though.'

'Very sensible.' Tahmineh wiped her hands on her apron and adjusted her headscarf. 'Your husband's family must be devastated about the loss of their son.'

They would be if they knew what he'd been up to. She hadn't written to Firzun's mother, her Aunt Mina, about her son's death yet. But now he was alive—she caught her breath, still unable to believe it—now he was alive he could write to his mother himself. It was Aunt Mina who had slammed the door in Zahra's face when she'd run away from Mahmoud's violence and asked for shelter. *Hateful woman!*

'Yes, I'm looking forward to going home,' she replied with a faint smile.

According to Tahmineh, Karim had left early this morning for Ramsar to pack up the holiday home there. Unknown to the housekeeper, Karim had come to say goodbye to Zahra before he went. He knew she wasn't going to the village, so he'd arranged to phone her to check that she was alone in the house. He would come back—if she wanted him to. He looked into her eyes.

'It will be a consummation of our love,' he said as he kissed her lips lightly.

Zahra had said yes, but she knew she couldn't go through with her promise. She would never forget the savage way her husband had treated her in the bedroom. She hated lying to Karim about being married to Firzun. But if she could bring herself to make love to Karim it would be another, even worse deception. She was about to escape from Iran with her cousin. She couldn't give herself to Karim and then leave with no explanation.

The housekeeper's voice broke into her thoughts. 'You're welcome to come with us to our village, Zahra. But maybe you need a rest from the shock you had when that bomb went off. How

terrible that you were there ... and your husband killed like that ...'
Tahmineh wiped a tear away with the corner of her apron.

It would take Karim *Agha,* the housekeeper went on, at least four hours to get to Ramsar. It often rained in the mountain passes and it was never a pleasant journey. She sat down opposite Zahra at the kitchen table.

'You must eat,' she said, pushing a plate of fruit toward her.

Tahmineh continued to chatter about her favourite subject, the recently deposed Shah of Iran. He'd had a palace at Ramsar, she told Zahra. Karim's parents Esmat and Abbas Konari had often been invited there to dinner. How beautiful the Konari family villa was, right on the beach ... how sad that it had to be closed up. How would the shah and his family, now exiled in the USA, cope with being refugees?

And what was the future of their beloved Iran now that the Ayatollah Khomeini and his Islamic Council were the rulers? And what about those poor Americans held hostage in their embassy for three weeks? When would that end? Would President Carter send the shah back to be tried—for what? Or would it all end in disaster? To Zahra's relief, Tahmineh's listing of Iran's current problems finally petered out.

Zahra shook her head; these were terrible times. Everyone seemed to be on a wanted list—not just her cousin, but maybe even Karim. He'd told her recently that he no longer felt safe in his own country.

'The house feels bleak now that sir and madam have gone to America and the old lady has passed,' Tahmineh said mournfully. She poured Zahra another glass of tea. 'And then there's your husband ... God be merciful.'

I have to get away before Karim calls, Zahra thought. *I'll go to their village with them.* She smiled at Tahmineh and told her she'd come after all. She quickly got herself and Ahmad ready, then helped to pack up the rest of the food the Konari family had donated. They were leaving in half an hour, the housekeeper said.

When Karim rings, the house will be empty, Zahra thought, *but what can I do?*

'Esmat Khanoum has even bought milk powder for my family!' Tahmineh said as she loaded up the boxes. 'It will save my family so much money! It's hard to phone and thank her now she's in the United States with Abbas Agha and poor Nasim.'

Nasim. How will I ever forget my first friend in Tehran? Zahra thought. Now Nasim was in the United States with her parents, a pregnant young widow after her husband had been executed by the authorities. Zahra thought about Firzun—how incredibly lucky he was to have her, his human shield.

'Who knows when the family will ever come back?' Tahmineh was saying. 'They said we can use the car as much as we need to. We can even take it to our village and keep it there when we move in December.'

Zahra nodded. Karim's parents had always treated their employees well, including her. But that might change when Karim told them about their engagement. She checked her watch; they were running late—it was already nine-twenty. What if Karim rang while they were still here and asked to speak to her?

In a sudden burst of energy, Tahmineh sealed the final boxes and got her husband Amir to put them into the car. Zahra glanced at the kitchen clock: nine-twenty-five. In the atrium, she helped Ahmad into his outdoor shoes, then pulled hers on. She hurried him out to the car and they slipped into the back seat. Tahmineh was behind her and just closing the front door when the phone started ringing.

'Just a minute!' Tahmineh called out.

Amir looked over from the driver's seat. 'Leave it!' he said.

'It might be important!'

Tahmineh shuffled off her outdoor shoes and went back into the house. It seemed an age before she reappeared and closed the front door.

'It was Mr Karim,' she said breathlessly, manoeuvring her bulk into the passenger seat of the car. 'I told him we were all just leaving for the village. He said he'll call later.'

As Amir steered the car down the driveway and out the high gates, Zahra leaned back and closed her eyes. What would Karim think of her? She'd broken her promise to him about today and worse was to follow.

3

YASMIN

Karim put the greasy phone down slowly. What was going on? Why had Zahra changed her mind? He tried to think kindly of her but couldn't help feeling annoyed, not to mention sexually frustrated. Maybe Ahmad hadn't wanted to be separated from his mother and that's why she'd gone with him to the village. Karim walked up to the counter in the cafe and gave the owner a few coins for the phone call.

'Can I get you a coffee, sir?' the man asked.

He shook his head. He didn't fancy a fiddly little cup of Iranian coffee made by the shy young woman who had peered round the plastic curtain when he came in. What he needed was a double strength cappuccino from an American diner, followed by a large hamburger.

So, he thought irritably as he walked to his car, *she doesn't want me—yet. When she's got a ring on her finger she'll do it, but not till then.* He took off his leather jacket and threw it on the back seat of the station wagon. He was in no man's land on the edges of the city. It had started to rain; the locals were watching him as if he were an extra-terrestrial. Zahra had turned him down. Damn! He really did *not* understand women.

As he manoeuvred the heavy station wagon back onto the highway, his mind wandered from Zahra to his American first wife Nancy. That was pure lust, he realised now; he must have been crazy to marry her! When she had packed up, emptied his bank account and told him she had someone else, he had been angry and humiliated. His friends had warned him before he married her, but he ignored them.

He didn't need to be warned about Zahra though—everything about their relationship was perfect. He would marry her, inherit a son, and probably have a few more children. Poor Zahra. Her cousin Firzun had married her out of pity. He remembered sharing a meal with him once; he could hardly believe that now. Firzun told Karim 'in confidence' that Zahra's first husband had died suddenly from a heart attack a couple of years ago. Even though Firzun was Zahra's cousin, he had married her.

'It's an Afghan thing,' Firzun had told him casually. 'In my country, widows are a burden on the family.'

Karim was determined to help Zahra. She had been widowed twice now, and needed protection and loving care. He planned to take Zahra and her son to America. Once there, they'd get married. He wanted her to be an equal partner in the marriage, to make joint decisions with him about their future. He shrugged to himself—was he living in fantasy land? What did he really know about Zahra? How could he have imagined himself in love with someone he'd only known for eight weeks? He was going down the same road again. He had hardly known Nancy when he had married her and that had ended in a bitter, acrimonious divorce.

He felt annoyed with Zahra. Tahmineh had told him that she was sitting outside in the car. She could easily have come back into the house and spoken to him. Why hadn't she? Well, he'd be back in Tehran in a few days and she could explain everything then.

He was in mountainous country now. The rain was coming down in sheets and the wipers thwacked backward and forward across the windscreen. He pushed his *Top Hits of 1979* tape into the stereo deck. A friend had sent it last week from the States. Given that there was a crackdown on everything American now, he was surprised it hadn't been confiscated at the post office. Finally, the cassette tape got going. As the bends got tighter on the treacherous road, he joined in the chorus of the song 'YMCA', belting out the words at the top of his voice. It stopped him thinking about the steep ravines on either side of the bitumen.

After crawling up the mountain for hours, he began the long, winding trek down the treacherous muddy roads into Ramsar. It was seven o'clock when he manoeuvred the station wagon onto the driveway of the beach house. The outside lights were on and a warm glow showed through the blinds of the downstairs rooms. He eased the heavy vehicle into the garage and parked next to the smaller convertible his parents used in the summer. A warm smell of casseroled meat greeted him as he pushed open the door from the garage. He propped his umbrella against the wall; he didn't want to get in trouble from the housekeeper for getting drips on the highly polished ceramic tiles.

'I'm here!' he called out.

Peri Khanoum, the housekeeper, came out of the kitchen. She bustled and fussed just like her counterpart in Tehran, greeting him with a torrent of words. She told him where everything was and that his bed was made up. She asked about his parents, gave condolences about his grandmother's passing. She had laid the table in the kitchen; did she need to stay and serve his food? After he thanked her and said he was fine, she pulled on her black chador and wrapped a black head covering over her other headscarf. She promised that she and her husband Sami, who was hovering in the background while she talked, would return tomorrow morning. She bid Karim a quick goodbye and took off into the night, followed by her husband.

Karim stood in the large modern kitchen, recovering from the tirade, and looked around. How Zahra would have loved this house, he thought. He helped himself to the salad Peri had left him and tore some bread from the warm loaf she'd taken from the oven. The lamb casserole was delicious—there was enough to feed a family of six.

As he ate, he thought again about Zahra. His plans for a future together were well advanced in his mind. They would live in his apartment in New York. He had already decided to buy a beach house in Florida for winter breaks. He smiled to himself. Ahmad and Zahra would be amazed when they saw the ocean for the first time.

He rinsed his plate and put it in the sink, helped himself to an apple from a bowl of fruit, and wandered into the main living room. The rain had blown out to sea and from the clear black sky a full moon dappled the water as it washed onto the beach near the house. No lights shone from the neighbouring houses. They were all closed up for the winter.

As he looked round the living room, a wave of nostalgia overwhelmed him. The beach house had belonged to his grandmother, and now it was his. In her will, his grandmother had left an apartment in Tehran to his sister and the beach house to him. Even though it wasn't hers, his mother Esmat had redecorated the whole house a couple of years ago. His grandmother never saw the makeover; she had been too sick to travel at that stage. Esmat had ordered several large white couches for the main living room and scattered blue and white striped cushions on them. She had the walls painted 'a nice ice-blue white', cleared out all the antiquated dark furniture, and replaced the drapes with shutters and blinds. The Persian prayer rugs and pictures of 'dead people' came off the walls. Now the place was full of family photographs in white frames and large canvases with a seaside theme. Esmat had also furnished the basement area as a recreation room and small gym for Karim.

'I know you're into a fitness regime in the States,' she had commented to her son.

On the second floor, all the bedrooms had a theme. A Disney-themed bedroom for his nephews when they came from the States with his sister, and a Scottish-themed room for him.

He pushed open his bedroom door. The incongruous picture of a Highland stag on the opposite wall never failed to startle him. Out of the corner of his eye, he saw Mary Queen of Scots watching him from her wooden frame. He had objected to tartan wallpaper and instead had settled for 'splashes of the Highlands', as his mother put it. Two wooden chairs, 'exact copies of the throne of the Scottish kings', sat on either side of the large patio window. Bright red Stewart tartan cushions were scattered everywhere. At least he got his own way about a white bedspread, albeit with a tartan overlay at the end, and a plain headboard.

The room, which had once irritated him and made Nancy shriek 'My God, how kitsch!' when she'd seen it, was now a welcome sight after his rain-drenched journey. He plucked a small lace-edged tartan placemat from the phone and picked it up. To his dismay the line was dead. He felt unreasonably disappointed. He wanted to speak to Zahra and get an explanation before he went to sleep.

The lines to Tehran were still down the following morning. He had a lot to do and the time passed quickly. He sorted through the boxes mechanically. So many decisions: ocean shipment to America, store here, take back to Tehran. By lunch time he was exhausted. He felt that the whole weight of his parents' choice to emigrate to America now rested on his shoulders. He looked around the vast spaces of the beach house, wondering whether to put it up for rent. In the end, he decided to phone his father when he got back to Tehran and discuss it with him. Maybe he should sell it or simply lock it up. If things changed for the better in Iran, they could all come back and resume their former lives.

The rain cleared by the afternoon and the air felt surprisingly warm. He needed a Band-Aid for an annoying cut on his hand that wouldn't stop bleeding. He drove into town and found a parking space easily—the rain had kept everyone indoors. As he neared the pharmacy, a sharp memory reared up. He remembered coming here a few years ago with Nancy, then his girlfriend. Men had stared at her in the street, partly because of her long blond hair, but mostly because of her hot pants and bikini top. Karim had tried to persuade her that even though Iran, at the time, was quite a free-thinking country, this wasn't the city. Women wore a long beach dress over their beach gear when they went shopping. She had laughed in his face and told him not to be so prudish, this was the age of feminism and they could all get ...

The pharmacy was quiet. The male pharmacist was counting pills into a bottle, and a couple of chador-clad women were checking the shelves behind the counter. One of them raised her hand to her forehead and brushed away an invisible strand of hair. With a shock he recognised her. Her name was Yasmin—they had been in lustful love with each other for a whole summer sixteen years ago, when they were both eighteen. He'd first met her here, in this same pharmacy. After he got to know her better, she told him how she was moving to live with an aunt in Tehran where she'd got a place at university.

'It's my last summer *ever* in Ramsar. I'm never coming back!' she had announced one evening after they'd made love in a secret room at the back of the shop.

They had met secretly, but then his mother found out he was 'messing with the local girls'. A week later, incandescent with, he'd thought at the time, a disproportionate rage, she sent him back to Tehran. He spent the end of that miserable hot summer in the family home studying. The following year Yasmin no longer worked in the pharmacy. He had only seen her once after that when he was walking along the street with Nancy. She'd flicked him and Nancy a quick look, then crossed over.

He remembered how, when she had worked there, she used to wear neat white overalls with her name embroidered on the pocket. Now she wore the ubiquitous black chador and black headscarf with only her face showing. Her spectacular thick black hair had been scraped out of sight. As she reached to put something up on the shelf, the light caught her wedding ring and at the same time she turned and saw him.

'Hello, Yasmin,' he said quietly.

She came up to the counter. Their eyes met briefly, then she blushed and looked away. When she glanced up again, she spoke softly with the slight lisp he remembered.

'Hello, Karim, how are you? What can I help you with?'

'I'm well, Yasmin, and you? I need some Band-Aids. I'm packing up the beach house and I've cut my hand.'

'Packing up!' She laughed nervously, a small coughing sound.

'My family's gone to America and I'm following them soon with my fiancée.'

She looked straight at him, her dark eyes with their thick lashes alive with interest. 'You mean the American lady ...' She lowered her voice to a whisper. 'My friend said she would sunbathe ... topless.'

'No, this is a different fiancée.' He couldn't resist teasing her. 'Band-Aids?'

'Oh, yes!'

She hurried away from the high counter and came back, not with a box as he'd expected, but a strip of six.

'Since the regime took over, you know, it's been hard to get boxes,' she told him. 'They used to come from America, but ...'

'Okay, they'll do.' He handed over a banknote. 'So, you're a qualified pharmacist now?'

She looked down. 'I didn't go to university. I got married instead. It's what my parents wanted.'

No surprises there, he thought. Even sixteen years ago, when the shah's education reforms were in full swing, it was unusual for a village girl to go to university. Pity really, she was very clever. He had grappled with his maths and had to resubmit some assignments before his university place was confirmed. She'd done them for him, and at twice the speed he could. Their eyes met briefly when Yasmin handed him his change and she stroked his palm surreptitiously with her finger. An electrical charge shot through his body at her touch.

'I hope you're happy,' he said, trying to keep his face impassive.

She smiled and shrugged. He wasn't sure what that meant.

'I've got a family now. My daughter's fifteen—she wants to be an architect.' Her eyes held his, then she looked away. 'Our son is two years younger.'

'Well, wish them luck,' Karim said cheerfully. 'Nice catching up, Yasmin.'

'*Khodāfez*, Karim *djan*,' she whispered.

He left the shop quickly. He needed fresh air to rid himself of the steamy memories that seeing Yasmin had stirred up. He strolled round the familiar town. His route took him past the deserted royal palace with its wedding-cake style façade. The Shah and Empress of Iran had stayed here nearly every summer with their family until this year. What a terrible come-down to be stateless in America. In all the anti-shah protests, he hadn't thought of the human face of this tragedy. Exiled with his wife and four children, the refugee former monarch was being treated for cancer in an American hospital. The prognosis for his survival was a well-guarded secret.

At least his own parents were in a better situation, he reflected. Unlike him, they had become American citizens years ago. His father was employed by an American oil company and when Karim was studying there, his parents had lived in the States for two years.

It was good to walk after being confined to the house and Karim set off at a brisk pace down the tree-lined boulevard that led from the palace. Eventually he turned back and retraced his steps to the car to head home. As he pulled into the driveway, he glanced up at the mountains that surrounded the town. Clouds obscured the tops and a mist was rolling in. Large drops of rain were already hitting the car roof.

He opened the garage with the remote control and steered the car in. He was glad that most of the packing was finished and the boxes were stacked ready to go. Above the noise of the rain and the closing garage door, he heard the phone ringing. He flung open the door, took off his outdoor shoes, and grabbed the receiver. Before he could speak, Tahmineh's voice asked if it was him.

'I was just about to hang up!'

'Is everything all right?'

'Yes, sir, everything's fine. I'm calling about Zahra's trip home.'

He frowned. What was the woman talking about?

'Sorry, I don't understand ... Did you say Zahra's going home? You mean Herat, Afghanistan?'

Tahmineh confirmed it. 'Zahra and Ahmad are very excited. They are leaving tomorrow,' she said in a rush. The flight was at three o'clock, but Zahra would leave the house at twelve, just in case. She had a lot to talk over with her family, of course, but then Mr Karim would understand that, wouldn't he? He managed to stop her for a second and asked to speak to Zahra.

'Well, actually, I rang you about clothes, sir,' Tahmineh said in a lowered voice. 'Can she have some of the things from your mother's department store? From the boxes here?'

'Yes, of course,' he said quickly. 'Can you bring Zahra to the phone, please?'

'Certainly, I won't be a minute.'

Karim leaned on the wall, unable to think straight. Afghanistan? What was going on? He heard a shuffle and voices near the phone, then Zahra came on the line.

'Hello, Karim.'

'Zahra. Is this right? You're going to Afghanistan tomorrow?' When she didn't reply, he said sharply, 'Zahra! When are you coming back?'

'I ...' She hesitated. 'I'm going to speak in English, Karim—the housekeeper's listening. Something's happened, I have to go home.' She paused and he heard her take a breath. 'I'm not coming back,' she rushed on. 'I'm sorry, Karim, it's family business, that's all I can say. I've got to go. I do care about you. It's all in the letter I've left you.'

'Letter!' he shouted in his own language, then lowered his voice. 'If Tahmineh hadn't called, I'd never have spoken to you again! What about us, the plans we made? I was just about to book our tickets. We were going to Istanbul to get an American visa for you and Ahmad ... Next stop New York!'

'I'm sorry,' she repeated quietly, still speaking English. 'I can't go with you.'

'*Why*? What's happened?' His voice echoed in the empty beach house.

'It's a family thing. I don't have a choice.'

'I'm coming home tonight, Zahra! For God's sake, you owe me a better explanation than that.'

He slammed the phone down and leaned against the wall, feeling stunned. What the hell was going on? She'd dumped him— why? He rushed round the house making sure everything was turned off and locked. Unbidden, the words of the Beatles' song 'Yesterday' floated across his brain.

What family business? She didn't have any family in Afghanistan as far as he knew, but then what *did* he know about her? Firzun had once rattled off something about her parents being dead, no siblings, Firzun's mother her only relative. Maybe she had to go back to see her, mourn with her over the loss of her son.

Okay, so maybe Firzun's family had put pressure on her and she had to go home. She might have *mentioned* the possibility. Maybe she'd told them about their engagement, and they'd ordered her to come back. *Well*, he thought, *her home city's only a couple of hours' flight from Tehran. If I can't stop her going, I'll follow her there. But damn it! Why didn't she phone and tell me herself?*

He heaved a few remaining boxes into the station wagon. When he'd finished, he pulled his outdoor shoes on, grabbed the car keys, and pushed the button to open the garage door. *How could she do this to me?* he thought angrily as he revved the engine.

The rain lashed the streets and ran down the gutters in torrents. The car felt heavier and more cumbersome with the weight in the back. He gritted his teeth and guided it carefully toward the town. As he drove through the deserted shopping centre, a movement caught his eye. A woman was standing at the taxi rank. Her umbrella had blown inside out and she was struggling to right it. He slowed down; the woman's wet chador clung to her body outlining her full breasts. He recognised her immediately: Yasmin. He rolled to a stop, trying not to spray her with a wave of water from the gutter.

She backed away when she saw the car and continued to struggle with the umbrella. He jumped out of the driver's seat and called to her above the sound of the wind.

'Yasmin! Get in!' He stepped across the surging gutter and on to the footpath.

Yasmin bundled her clothes around her and he took her arm. He scanned the street quickly as he helped her into the passenger seat. He had no idea what the penalty was for picking up women from the footpath and he didn't want to find out.

'Thank you, thank you, Karim! I was so frightened. I missed the bus.'

She dumped her umbrella and handbag on the floor at her feet. She had brought the wet night into the car with her, so he turned up the heater. He glanced sideways at her as she released her luxurious hair from her sodden headscarf. He shivered slightly, remembering her hair from their crazy teenage years.

'Do you still live in the same village?' he asked, forcing himself to look at the road.

'Yes.' She sounded nervous.

'I'm on my way back to Tehran. I passed your place on the way here. I can drop you off.' Even to himself, making the four-hour drive on a night like this sounded insane.

'Oh! It's a long way to Tehran and it's raining!'

He didn't reply, just swung the station wagon toward the mountain road. They travelled in silence while she wriggled and adjusted her wet clothes, then put her hands under her hair and fluffed it out.

'Oh! Karim, look!'

Ahead of them, a mudslide blocked the approach road to the mountains. There was no way he would get past it.

'The road's blocked,' she said. Stating the obvious was a habit of hers, he remembered suddenly. 'It's the one to my village and the Tehran highway.'

He stopped the car, yanked on the handbrake, and leaned his head on the steering wheel.

'They'll probably clear it tomorrow morning,' Yasmin ventured, but she didn't sound too hopeful.

'Damn!' he muttered through gritted teeth.

She leaned over and stroked the back of his neck. He jerked his head up and turned to her.

'I can't get you home tonight, Yasmin,' he said. 'Is there anyone you can stay with?'

She stroked the back of his neck again. 'Maybe with you?' she whispered softly.

4

THE PERSIAN GARDEN ROOM

The rain beat down on the car's roof as Yasmin's words hung between them. Karim stared out the windscreen wondering what to do next. The last thing he wanted was for Yasmin to stay in his house. He had enough complications in his life without a former girlfriend showing up, and a married one at that.

'Have you got a friend you can stay with in town?' he asked hopefully.

She pushed her hair back with both hands and combed her fingers through it. She turned and smiled at him.

'Only wealthy people live in town,' she said with her little hiccup laugh. 'I have a friend who lives near the bus station, but we can't go there. My friend's neighbours would see the car and ask questions.'

She shrugged, put her head on one side, and bit her lower lip. Karim doubted that anyone would be looking out their windows on a night like this, but you never knew. The windscreen wipers swished back and forth as the silence stretched out between them. *What choice have I got?* He put the car in gear and turned it round.

As they approached his beach house, he felt her relax deeper into the passenger seat. He swung the car into the driveway and waited impatiently as the garage door rolled open. At least she could get out of the car and into the house without anyone seeing them. As the roller door closed, she struggled out of the passenger seat.

'I have to call my husband,' she said breathlessly.

He nodded; the thought of a husband in the picture made him feel jumpy. It was risky having her here, but she wasn't safe on a dark street at night. As he opened the door into his home, he asked her again about the friend she'd mentioned. She shook her head, her eyes wide with apology.

'She's not nearby.' She smiled.

'All right, Yasmin, but, you know, I'm not really comfortable with the two of us here alone in this house.'

'I know, but I'm a good girl.' She took his hand and squeezed it.

Oh my God, that's what she said the first time I kissed her. She was nothing of the sort, she was a sex goddess.

Yasmin took off her wet chador and scarf and spread them over a chair near the fuel stove. She shrugged out of her thin-looking winter coat and put it on another chair. He dragged his gaze away from her voluptuousness as she eased her fashionably long cream jumper down over her black skirt. She was wearing mesh tights and calf-high boots.

'The phone?' she queried with a coy look.

'Oh, yes, here in the entrance.' He opened the kitchen door.

Her voice drifted through to him, making him feel edgy. He turned on the radiators to warm up the house.

'You must be hungry,' he said when she returned to the kitchen. 'I'll heat up this lamb casserole for you.'

She made a fuss: he shouldn't be cooking for her.

'I always cook for myself in the States,' he answered with a smile.

He told her to sit near the stove and observed her covertly. She looked cold in her cheap clothes, he thought sadly.

While she ate, he made himself a cup of coffee and a sandwich.

He couldn't face more lamb casserole. Perhaps it wasn't too late to phone his housekeepers and get them to come and fetch her. Then he remembered that they lived in a mountain village too. Karim, feeling agitated, watched her as she got up and rinsed her plate in the sink. She dried it carefully and placed it on the benchtop. If he got anyone else involved, there'd be gossip. Yasmin's husband would know she'd been alone in the house with him. He was stuck with his decision.

'Well, it's getting late,' Karim began, then glanced at the kitchen clock. Surely it wasn't only eight o'clock? It felt like midnight.

He waited as she gathered her things together, then led the way upstairs to the Persian Garden room. He felt more and more apprehensive as she squeezed past him into the room. His own bedroom was only two doors down the hall from hers. If only his mother had put gothic padlocks on all the bedroom doors in keeping with the Scottish theme!

Yasmin loved everything. The flowery room, the guest nightdress and gown, the ensuite bathroom with the scented soaps. She assured him she could make up the bed herself. She indicated the pink sheets neatly laid on the floral bedcover. The housekeepers were due to pack up the bedrooms tomorrow. Karim would have to leave them a note to explain why the Persian Garden room had been slept in.

He hovered at the door, not wanting to cross the threshold in case she got the wrong idea. She looked at him expectantly and he gave her a distant smile and wished her good night. When he got to his own room, he wished he had a dungeon-sized padlock. He considered pulling the replica of King Malcolm's throne across to block the door, but he was too tired. He showered quickly, threw his towel over a chair, and fell naked into his bed.

He half woke from a deep sleep. In his dream, Zahra was standing by his bed stroking his face. Suddenly he was wide awake.

'It's only me, Karim,' Yasmin whispered, leaving her hand on his cheek.

He flicked on the bedside lamp. The light glowed eerily through the thistle pattern on the shade. Yasmin was kneeling next to him in her long white gown. Her black hair cascaded over her shoulders. He backed away from her, pulling the sheet up to cover his chest. She looked for all the world like Lady Macbeth. Feeling trapped in his nakedness, he grabbed his robe from the end of bed and shrugged it on with difficulty.

'Remember when we were teenagers?' she whispered.

Will I ever forget? I was crazy about you! My mother nearly killed me when she found out about us!

'We were young kids, Yasmin, teenagers,' he said firmly.

He got out of the other side of the bed and walked round to her. Taking her gently by the arms, he helped her to her feet. Before she could snuggle into his chest, he turned her toward the door.

'This can't happen, you're a married woman ...'

Even as he said the words, he thought what a hypocrite he was. He had tried to seduce Zahra only a couple of weeks ago, before she was widowed.

'But I just thought, for old time's sake ...' Yasmin said breathlessly. 'Fate has thrown us together.'

He led her back to her room. In the dim light of the landing, she looked as beautiful and voluptuous as she had at eighteen. He would never forget their wonderful time together. Why shouldn't he make love to her again right now? Who would ever find out? After all, Zahra had dumped him.

'It's not a good idea, Yasmin,' he said resolutely.

She reached up and kissed him on the mouth, making his senses reel. He pushed her away gently and opened the door to the Persian Garden room.

'Goodnight, Yasmin,' he asserted.

She ran her hands through his hair and kissed him again. Then she smiled and slipped into the room. She closed the door quietly in his face. He shuddered and went back to his room as fast as he could.

By the time Yasmin made an appearance the next morning, Karim had been pacing the kitchen floor for what seemed an age. If the housekeepers showed up early, he would ambush them somehow and send them out on an errand. Yasmin smiled at him, an intimate unsettling smile.

'Thank you for everything, Karim,' she said quietly. 'Last night is another secret we share.'

'Nothing happened, remember ...' he began, feeling edgy again.

She moved closer and put her fingers on his lips. 'I've waited so long to see you again,' she said wistfully. 'When I saw you with that American girl, it nearly broke my heart, especially ... Anyway, I do understand that we can never be together again. I'm married and you have a fiancée.' She glanced around the kitchen. 'I've always wanted to see inside this house.' She picked up an apple from the bowl on the bench top. 'May I?'

Karim nodded mutely as she took a bite.

'*Khodāfez*, Karim. I can go to my friend's place for breakfast.'

'I thought ...' he began, but what was the point?

She smiled eerily, condescendingly. 'She can be trusted.'

Oh my God!

'Yasmin,' he said firmly, 'you mustn't tell anyone that you stayed here. For your own sake.'

Yasmin nodded, and to his relief she tied back her hair and wound her black headscarf over it.

She commented that now the rain had eased he should have a fast trip home. When he looked puzzled, she pushed a stray lock of hair out of sight. She bent her head to tie the strings of her chador and told him casually that the council had resurfaced the other road.

He was completely taken aback and asked her to explain. She told him that no one used the old road he was trying to get onto last night. There had been so many mudslides that the council had opened a new road last year. It was a couple of kilometres to the west. When he remonstrated that she might have told him, she said she thought he knew. Of course he didn't know, he'd been living in New York for two years! He had come here down the old road.

'I was so overwhelmed when I saw you, Karim *djan*,' Yasmin replied huskily. 'It wasn't my place to say anything. The weather was bad, remember?' She smiled again and touched his arm as she passed. 'Thank you for a wonderful time.'

She flicked open the lock on the outside door, then turned and blew him a kiss. He watched her flit across the garden in the pre-dawn light to the anonymous safety of the beach. He was furious with her and himself. If he had known about the other road, he could have seen Zahra, maybe spent the night with *her*. His mind raced with calculations. If he left at once and the new road was good, he would get to Tehran by midday easily. All he could think of now was getting out of Ramsar.

He wrote a hasty note and a cheque and left them in an envelope for the housekeepers. He was beyond caring what they would think when they saw that someone had slept in the Persian Garden room.

The sun was rising over the sea, the rain had cleared, and the day promised to be bright and sunny. He decided to go home, grab his passport and an overnight bag, tell his Tehran housekeepers where he was going, and get a taxi straight to the airport. Too bad if they thought he was crazy. It would be easy to get a last-minute seat on a plane to Afghanistan. Not many people wanted to go there, he was sure of that. Zahra could explain herself while they were travelling.

5

AIRPORT

Zahra ran quietly up the stairs to Karim's apartment, but once inside she hesitated. Where could she leave the letter without the housekeeper finding it? She walked across to Karim's freshly made bed. The housekeepers wouldn't come in here again today, she thought as she slipped the envelope under Karim's pillow. Back on the landing, she paused. *How can I do this to him? He's a caring, considerate man. He gave me $200 after the US embassy raid when he thought I was in danger. He's offered to take me and Ahmad with him to the States. He wants to marry me.* But everything had changed.

'*Just remember, blood's thicker than water, Zahra. You and Ahmad are coming with me. You've got no choice!*'

Firzun's words had filled her with dread, in the same way his threat to take her son had scared her. She knew what he said was true. Whatever the personal cost to her, she had no choice but to accompany him. Everyone knew him as Firzun, and Firzun was officially dead. She had to keep his secret and no one, including—*especially*—Karim, must know that her cousin was alive. Or that he was going to impersonate her dead husband and use his passport to leave the country. She didn't want Karim to be involved; this was a family matter. If Karim found out Firzun was alive, she wasn't sure what he would do. If he called the authorities, it would be a death sentence for her cousin. She hadn't wanted to tell Karim she was leaving. Hearing the hurt in his voice had upset her a lot. If it hadn't been for Tahmineh worrying about clothes, she wouldn't have had to tell him at all.

Zahra checked her watch and a shiver ran down her spine. She had to leave in less than an hour, and Tahmineh was still piling clothes on the bed. She had sorted things for Ahmad and herself for the Afghan winter. But, unknown to the housekeeper, they were heading south to an Australian summer.

Finally, the large blue suitcase was closed and stood waiting for her at the front door. The taxi arrived on time and the driver beeped the horn impatiently until the locked gates swung open. Still protesting that Amir could have driven them to the airport, Tahmineh hugged Zahra and Ahmad. Her young niece Shirin sobbed loudly as she said goodbye. Amir heaved Zahra's suitcase into the taxi and shook her hand. Tahmineh held a copy of the Koran over Zahra's head and insisted that she honour the custom and pass under it three times before her journey.

I'm lying to these good people, to everyone! Zahra thought miserably. *But what can I do?*

She glanced up at the house. Her life had changed dramatically in the months she had lived there. What she was about to face—getting safely out of Iran and settling in a new country—would be even more challenging.

'*Khodāfez*—may God protect you on your journey,' the housekeeper said, sniffling. When Zahra turned and waved, she saw Tahmineh and Shirin throwing water after the vehicle—another custom. With an effort, she shifted her overnight bag onto the seat next to her and told Ahmad to sit down. A terrible thought made her catch her breath. What if things went wrong at the airport and Firzun was arrested? She'd be returning down this same road in a police car, on her way to the women's prison.

The taxi moved through the heavy traffic and she knew in her heart that this was probably the last time she'd ever see Tehran. *If I don't get arrested.* They swung past Azadi Square and the Azadi Tower monument. A short time ago, her life had nearly ended here during an ill-fated women's march. She would never forget how Karim had fought his way through the crowds to rescue her. And now she was deserting him.

The sky had cleared at last and the sun shone on the white peaks of the Alborz Mountains that ringed Tehran. Eventually the taxi turned away from the busy city streets. Zahra got her last glimpse of office buildings with huge posters of the Ayatollah Khomeini plastered on their sides. They passed billboards advertising soap and washing-up liquid. The few women in the pictures were dressed like her in black chadors, their hair scraped away under black headscarves tied tightly under their chins.

When the taxi slowed, she looked out of the window. They were already at the airport. Zahra scanned the terminal apprehensively; she had no idea where to go when she got out of the cab. 'Wait inside the main door,' Firzun had instructed, but there were several doors.

'We're here,' the taxi driver announced as he double-parked the vehicle outside the terminal building.

'How much?' she asked, fumbling in her purse.

'Paid already by the *Agha*,' he said.

Amir had paid her fare! She pushed away her feelings of guilt about lying to them. The driver heaved her suitcase onto the footpath and turned away respectfully as he held the door open for her. She struggled out of the taxi, clutching her smaller bags in one hand and trying to help Ahmad with the other. She was convinced that at any moment her bags would be torn from her by the pestering porters. One of them rushed at her with a luggage trolley.

'You want help, *Khanoum?* I've got your case. Only ten *tomans*, ten!' he said, holding up his hands, fingers spread wide.

She fumbled in her purse and handed him the money. He seized her suitcase and swung it onto the trolley. To her dismay, he disappeared into the terminal building with it. She grabbed Ahmad's hand and pulled him along as she ran after the porter. She was hurrying to catch up with him when she heard a familiar voice.

'Give me that and clear off,' Firzun barked.

'Another ten *tomans, Haji*—the *Khanoum* only paid half.'

'Get out of here!' Firzun waved his cane and the man ducked and ran for the door.

'Why did you encourage him?' Firzun glared at her as he swung his own bag onto the trolley. 'We're trying to keep a low profile,' he added.

'You're the one yelling and waving ...' Zahra began, but he interrupted her.

'No problem with lover-boy?' he sneered.

'If you mean Karim, he's in Ramsar.'

'Try to look a bit more modest, Zahra. Don't glare at me like that. I'm a respectable religious man, remember? *And* your husband.'

She glanced at him fearfully.

'I could pass for Mahmoud, couldn't I? Just like the passport photo, eh?'

She looked away. This whole idea was crazy! Supposing someone who knew them showed up at the airport? Someone who knew he was Firzun Khan, not her dead husband Mahmoud Ghafoori? Their whole cover could be blown in an instant. She checked her headscarf to make sure it hadn't slipped to expose strands of hair while she was saying goodbye and adjusted her chador over her long coat.

Firzun kneeled down next to Ahmad, who'd been watching the throngs of people coming and going.

'Listen kid, I've got something for you, but you only get it if you call me Daddy, understand?'

Ahmad shrieked with delight when Firzun produced the bright red backpack with a picture of Mickey Mouse on the outside. Zahra felt a stab of indignation. This was Karim's gift for Ahmad. He'd intended to give it to Ahmad when they all left together for the States, and here was Firzun using it to bribe her son!

'You can have it soon. I'm Daddy—remember?'

'Yes ... *Daddy*,' Ahmad said hesitantly. 'Can I have it now?'

'No!' Firzun snapped. He turned to Zahra. 'Look confident, not like some agitated village woman. I'm a pious, God-fearing man and you're my wife.' He took a copy of the Koran out of his bag. 'It won't harm me to be carrying this. Just keep your mouth shut and do as you're told.'

'You're even beginning to sound like Mahmoud,' Zahra retorted.

He lowered his voice. 'Zahra, getting out of here is life or death for all of us. Trust me.'

He pointed the way forward and she took Ahmad's hand. Firzun stopped suddenly at a large board suspended above them. She watched as times and destinations rattled round in illuminated yellow letters. She scarcely had time to read a destination before the letters moved again.

'We're on a Gulf Air flight to Bahrain at three o'clock. We change there for the flight to Australia,' he said, squinting at the letters. 'Okay, I can see it, let's go!'

He walked away and she scurried along in her flowing chador, desperately trying to keep up with him. When they got to a roped-off area, he jerked his head slightly to the left and raised his eyebrows. She looked past him at the armed Revolutionary Guards in their green uniforms. They were standing at several official-looking desks and their eyes scanned the waiting passengers. One scratched his beard, his glance insolent; another adjusted his rifle; and a third fingered his low hanging bullet belt.

'Not too much to worry about,' Firzun said under his breath. 'They're just kids.'

Zahra looked round fearfully. In addition to the Revolutionary Guards, there were armed police and soldiers everywhere, their eyes watchful. They were men, not teenagers. Were they looking for them ... for Firzun? She glanced away quickly. If they escorted him out of the line, she'd be arrested too. What would happen to Ahmad? Would they take him to an orphanage? Her heart raced, she could hardly breathe, and she jumped when Firzun nudged her.

'They're checking tickets and passports here. Stop looking so worried,' he muttered.

Beads of sweat gathered under the edge of her headscarf as she took her place in the line behind him. She dabbed her forehead, running her fingers under her scarf as casually as she could. Ahead of them, a smartly dressed official in a dark uniform was examining passports and tickets. He stared closely at each person before raising a rope barrier to let them through. Next to him an armed Revolutionary Guard looked over people's heads. Another official walked along the line, peering at everyone.

Zahra moved Ahmad closer to her and gripped the handle of the trolley to stop her hands trembling as they inched forward. She hardly dared look at the official, who waved his fingers impatiently for their documents. Her agitation increased as he flicked slowly through the pages of the passport Firzun handed him. He stared at Firzun, then back at the passport. *He's noticed something. Has the passport photograph fooled him?* Her nervousness increased when the man made no comment. He returned the documents to Firzun with a brief nod.

'Look at me, *Khanoum*,' the man ordered.

She glanced up quickly. To her relief he returned her passport to Firzun with a brief nod and waved them through.

'Stay behind me. This is the Gulf Air check-in line,' Firzun said.

When they got to the counter, another voice asked her to look up. She raised her eyes. A pleasant-faced man with neat dark hair and a moustache checked her passport. A sign behind him said *Gulf Air* in English and Arabic. Underneath the logo and also embroidered on the pocket of the man's uniform was a large bird. Its wings were outstretched behind its body as though it was just about to land. Zahra allowed herself to hope—maybe they really *would* get on a plane and escape from Iran.

'Just one suitcase?' the man asked with a professional smile.

Firzun nodded; his only luggage was his black overnight bag. He lifted Zahra's case onto the conveyor belt. The Gulf Air employee leaned down and fastened a label onto the handle.

'It'll go straight through to Sydney,' he said to Firzun. 'But you'll need to identify it before you board the plane here.'

Zahra watched her case as it juddered down the conveyor belt. Would it really be waiting for her on the other side of the world when she got there—*if* she got there?

Firzun pushed the trolley aside as they walked away. 'We've got our boarding passes to get on the plane. Just a few more checks and we'll be on our way. Say nothing and keep Ahmad quiet.'

She unzipped her bag and stowed her documents carefully inside. Firzun had shown her dead husband's passport twice to officials and no one had queried the photo. She felt a rush of anticipation. They were nearly through!

The midday prayer call was echoing round the suburb of Elahiyeh as Karim drove down his street. With any luck, Zahra hadn't left yet and they could go to the airport together. He heaved the station wagon off the road and up to the gates of his house in Maryam Street. He flicked the remote control on the car keys and the gates juddered open. With a sigh of relief, he steered the car into the driveway. Karim leapt out of the driver's seat as the gates closed behind the car. He breathed in and wrinkled his nose. The air in Tehran smelled of diesel fumes and the honking traffic assaulted his ears.

'Has Zahra gone?'

'Welcome, sir. She went about half an hour ago,' Amir answered. 'She said her flight was at three o'clock.'

Karim hurried past him into the large atrium. 'You didn't drive her?'

'She insisted on taking a taxi, sir.'

Karim ran to his father's study and grabbed his passport from the safe. The startled housekeepers were still in the atrium when he returned. He asked Amir to call him a taxi, waving away the suggestion that he should take him. A taxi would be faster than Amir's careful driving.

'I'm going to Afghanistan. I'll be there for a few days,' he told the astounded couple. 'If you unload the station wagon, I'll help you sort things when I get back. The taxi?'

'Of course, sir,' Amir said smoothly. 'I'll call one right away.'

'The boxes are all marked,' Karim said quickly. 'I'll call you.'

'Have you eaten ...?' he heard Tahmineh say as he closed the front door.

He collected his overnight bag from the car then checked his watch again, desperately hoping that Zahra and Ahmad hadn't already gone through to the passenger area. His mother had told him that when they'd left it had taken *forever* to get through the airport checks. The new regime was ponderously bureaucratic. But he was in the taxi and on his way now. He was determined to get on the plane with Zahra and Ahmad.

The taxi raced through the city streets, dodging other traffic and ignoring the honking and curses. Posters of the Ayatollah Khomeini glared down from several buildings. *I'll be glad to get away from those wherever I end up.* His taxi joined others that had parked haphazardly blocking the car park entrance. As soon as he could he jumped out, paid the driver, and slammed the door.

He strode into the international terminal, glad that the proposed new airport, twenty kilometres out of the city, was still on the drawing board. He looked around, wondering which airline Zahra would be flying. He was annoyed with himself that he hadn't asked Amir before he'd left. He walked along quickly, keeping his eye out for her. It wasn't an easy task. The place was swarming with chador-clad women.

He wondered how many more international airlines would

suspend flights to Iran if the hostage crisis dragged on. The Pan Am desk was shut, and so was British Airways, but Air France and Gulf Air were still operating and he knew Gulf Air flew to Afghanistan. He stood at the board watching the destinations flick around, but nothing came up for Herat. He waited until the letters went around a second time. Zahra's destination still didn't show up. He looked around, feeling puzzled, when he spotted a uniformed Gulf Air employee. When he asked about the flight, it took him a minute to absorb what the man told him.

'Taken off?' Karim repeated.

'There's only one flight a day to Herat at noon.' The man checked his watch. 'It left on time as far as I know.'

She's gone. I've missed her! Karim stood in the middle of the terminal as people pushed past him. He felt totally deflated. If only Yasmin had been quicker getting out the house. If only she hadn't come at all. If only he had left earlier, driven faster. He looked around, uncertain of what to do next. Then a thought struck him: how could she have caught a midday flight? She'd left his house half an hour before he got there according to Amir. He set off for the Gulf Air desk. Maybe the employee was wrong.

A group of people ahead of him veered right suddenly. In the cleared space, he saw a couple and a young boy walking away from the Gulf Air check-in desks. The man wore a long dark sleeveless vest over his *shalwaar kameez,* matching white pants, and a crocheted cap over his thick hair. He was carrying a battered bag. He held an old leather-bound book in one hand and supported himself with a cane. As Karim watched, the man turned and looked casually over his shoulder. Their eyes locked. After an initial look of surprise, the man smirked insolently straight at Karim.

'Firzun.' The name escaped Karim's lips and he had to steady himself on a nearby wall. He was dumbfounded. How could Firzun be here? He was *dead.* The chador-clad woman and child turned around too. Zahra and Ahmad! The boy twisted away from his mother and ran toward him.

'Uncle Karim!'

Karim kneeled down and hugged him. He looked over the child's shoulder and met Zahra's horrified gaze. Firzun took her elbow and walked over.

'Time for a chat,' he said calmly, indicating a quiet corner.

Karim stood up unsteadily and followed the other man. He leaned against a wall, feeling like he'd been punched in the stomach. Firzun was here. Alive! He was walking and talking and as bellicose and confident as ever. It beggared belief, but it was true.

'I hid in a cellar before the bomb went off,' Firzun said before Karim could speak. 'Then I laid low in Nasim and Rashid's house.'

'You bastard,' Karim spat.

Firzun had hidden in a house two doors away! The house that the Revolutionary Guards had trashed after they arrested and then killed his friend Rashid. The house had been boarded up; how like Firzun to get in somehow.

Karim turned angrily to Zahra. 'Did you know he was alive?'

Her cousin answered for her. 'A couple of days ago.'

Two days! Was he lying?

'I took Zahra to your *funeral*.' Karim badly wanted to hit the other man. 'While you were hiding out like the rat you are.'

Firzun laughed. 'Did you expect me to hand myself in?'

Karim leaned forward and grasped Zahra's wrist. 'Okay, Firzun, that's enough. She's coming home with me. I can give her a better life than you ever would.'

Zahra eased her hand from Karim's grip as Firzun took a step closer to him.

'A better life,' he sneered. 'I've already done that. What do *you* know about her life, eh?'

'I know she should be with me, not you.'

'Want to rescue her, do you?' Firzun laughed. '*I* saved her from being killed by her first husband.'

Zahra grasped Firzun's arm. 'Please, *please*, don't.' She turned to Karim. 'I've left a letter in your apartment. It explains ...'

Both men ignored her.

'You know nothing about the real world,' Firzun spat at Karim. 'All you know is luxury and privilege.'

'Which I've offered to her,' Karim retorted.

Zahra looked around in alarm. 'Keep your voices down.'

Two Revolutionary Guards in smart green uniforms walked by and glanced suspiciously at them. On seeing Firzun in his religious clothes, the men touched their foreheads.

'*Salaam, Haji,*' one of them said politely.

He returned the greeting, solemnly moving his head slightly to the side. '*Salaam,* brothers.' He touched his forehead piously as they moved away.

'You damned hypocrite,' Karim muttered.

Firzun glared at him. 'Mind your own business, *Agha* Karim,' he snapped. 'Zahra owes me. That's why she's here.'

Karim looked at Zahra as she grabbed her cousin's arm again.

'No, Firzun,' she urged. 'Don't tell him.'

'It's about time he knew. Her first husband beat her up, regularly. I got her out of it the only way you can in our country.' Firzun drew his finger across his throat.

Karim felt sick. 'What about her husband's heart attack and your story about marrying Zahra out of family loyalty?'

'Yeah, well ... but he's certainly dead. I'm her second husband and we're getting out of Iran. Now move aside, we've got a plane to catch to Australia.'

'Australia! I thought you were going to Afghanistan?'

'Not yet.' Firzun extended his hand with the patronising smile of a cleric to a sinful worshiper. 'Bye, Karim,' he said sarcastically in English. He jerked his head at Zahra. 'You gave her such big ideas,' he added. 'She's an Afghan wife, *my* Afghan wife. She knows her place—family first.'

Karim ignored Firzun's hand. He turned to Zahra, trying not to sound desperate. He told her she had a choice, she could divorce

Firzun. She kept her head bowed, refusing to look at him. She took a step back and reached out, moving Ahmad to her side.

'People are looking at us,' she whispered.

Karim moved towards her.

'Please, Karim, don't make it harder. I *have* to go with him.' She looked up and met his eyes.

'You've got a choice, Zahra,' Karim said desperately.

Firzun took Zahra's arm and told Karim to stop grandstanding. They were going to Sydney whether he liked it or not. They would be safe there. When Karim retorted that the regime would get him wherever he went, Firzun laughed.

He took a step closer to Karim. 'If you try and stop me, I'll take you down as well, understand?'

Karim understood all right. He had been a reluctant participant in Firzun's abortive attempt to free the American hostages. *He's probably still got my rough sketch maps of the embassy compound somewhere. In case he needs to blackmail me, like now.* He made a last desperate attempt to change Zahra's mind. He told her she was a pawn in Firzun's game of self-preservation. She was crazy to trust him.

She looked straight back at Karim. 'I have no choice,' she said quietly. 'He's my husband.' She gave him a searching look. 'Say goodbye to Uncle Karim, Ahmad.' She nudged her son and glanced up at Karim.

'Bye bye, Uncle Karim. Why aren't you coming?' Ahmad asked.

'Let's go!' Firzun took Zahra's arm.

'Zahra, please ... write to me.'

'For God's sake, shut up and clear off,' Firzun hissed, glancing round. 'People are looking. Zahra, get the kid.'

As Firzun steered her away, Karim willed her to look back. She turned once and met his eyes. She was frowning and pressing her lips tightly together. He felt totally bereft when Ahmad turned and waved and he saw the child's lower lip tremble. He watched them until they were out of sight, then he turned and walked to the exit in a daze. His head was pounding with questions. Why had she led him on like that, then deserted him for her useless cousin-husband? Could he believe anything she had said to him?

He felt shattered. He had nothing to look forward to but a lonely journey to the United States and his lonely apartment in New York. His Iranian friends in America had told him they felt uncomfortable now because of the hostage drama at the Tehran embassy. His life was fast fading to black.

6

I'M MAHMOUD NOW

Had Karim understood? Would he ever understand that she had no choice? Zahra sniffed back her tears. Firzun looked at her irritably as he released his grip on her arm.

'Forget about him,' he muttered to her in *Dari*. 'I'm Mahmoud now, remember?'

His use of their own language startled her. During her time in Iran she'd become used to speaking Persian. Now he was using their own language again, manipulating her to identify with him, to push his point about family loyalty. She owed him her life; it was true that her violent husband might have killed her eventually.

Her chance of happiness, of being with a man she loved and who loved her, had vanished forever. She would never see Karim again. He wouldn't come to Australia to find her because he believed she was married to Firzun. But she wasn't, she *wasn't*. She had to continue with the lie until she got her cousin out of Iran. One day, when she was settled in her new country, she would write to Karim and tell him the truth.

'Okay,' Firzun's voice cut across her thoughts, 'we've got our boarding passes to get on the plane. Next they'll check our passports against their lists. Say nothing and keep Ahmad quiet.'

He took her elbow and guided her to the escalator, which clicked relentlessly upward. When she saw a Revolutionary Guard watching her, she looked away quickly. She stepped onto the escalator and realised too late that Ahmad was on a step below her. She motioned him to step up and nearly tripped as the escalator got to the next floor. Her clothes got in the way, her bag was heavy, and she felt hot under her headscarf. She had to move quickly to keep pace with Firzun. He hurried ahead of her, in spite of his cane and his limp.

He stopped at a closed double door. Revolutionary Guards and soldiers stood on either side of them, scanning the passengers as they walked through.

'Passports, boarding passes, *Haji*.' A Revolutionary Guard held out his hand.

He checked their documents carefully before opening the door and waving them through. They joined the back of the line, and Zahra could see two men sitting in separate glass cubicles under a huge poster of the Ayatollah Khomeini. The line of people moved forward at a snail's pace as the uniformed men examined passports.

'Not many people,' Firzun whispered.

'Is that good?'

'No, they've got more time to question us,' he replied. 'Stay calm.'

She didn't feel calm as Ahmad fidgeted and wriggled and tried to twist his hand out of hers. She kneeled down and told him to be good and keep quiet. They shuffled forward slowly and were almost at the counter when a commotion broke out behind them. Someone pushed Zahra in the back and tried to squeeze past her. Zahra turned around, getting the full blast of the woman's shrill voice in her face.

'Let me through, I'm late!'

A couple of Revolutionary Guards strolled over to the line.

'What's the problem?'

'My plane's leaving soon! This man's in my way.' The woman pushed Firzun's arm.

'Wait your turn!' One of the guards glared at her. 'Can't you see he's injured?' He looked across at Firzun. 'Apologies, *Haji*. Please come this way.'

Zahra swallowed hard. *Stupid woman! She's drawn attention to us. Now we're being escorted by a Revolutionary Guard.* She glanced at her cousin; if Firzun was worried he was hiding it well.

'Bless you, young man,' he said.

She looked up briefly. The Revolutionary Guard smiled at Firzun.

'Follow me, *Haji*,' he said. 'Tell me about your injury.'

'I tripped and hurt my leg at the *Hajj*. You know how crowded it gets there,' Firzun lied. 'Allah be praised it isn't permanent.'

'Allah be praised indeed, sir.' The young man smiled. '*Ensh'allah* I will visit the holy place next year,' he concluded proudly.

He escorted them past the line of people. The Revolutionary Guard was tall, young, and fit. If Firzun made a slip, Zahra reflected, this pleasant young man could have him in a headlock against a wall in a minute. The two men had stopped in front of her and she glanced up; they'd arrived at a cubicle attached to a small office. A surly official silently put out his hand for their documents.

'*Khodāhāfez*. God give you a good journey!' their youthful escort said formerly and shook Firzun's hand.

'*Ensh'allah!*' Firzun replied. Moving his copy of the Koran delicately under his left armpit, he shook the guard's hand, smiling and nodding.

Hurry up, Zahra thought, watching the passport control officer turn each page of their passports with studied sloth. She looked away, feeling sick with nerves.

'*Khanoum*, look up!'

Their passports were open at the photograph pages. The man looked intently at Firzun. Would he see that the passport photograph wasn't Firzun? Zahra's knees felt weak when the official put the passport down and stood up. Was he about to call the Revolutionary Guard back and have them arrested? But he was looking down at Ahmad.

'Mahmoud Ghafoori, is that you?' he asked Firzun. 'And the boy —your son Ahmad Ghafoori?'

'Yes.'

'Mummy,' Ahmad whispered loudly.

'Shush!' Zahra glared at him.

He looked back at her shocked. She thought he was going to cry; instead he pouted and put his head down. The official's voice made her jump.

'*Khanoum*! What's your name?'

'Zahra Ghafoori.' She glanced at Ahmad, willing him to keep quiet. To her relief, he was still pouting. The man snapped his fingers at Firzun as he sat down.

'You got some documents at the border, where are they? They've got to match up.'

Firzun rummaged in his bag. Was he stalling for time? Had he lost some vital papers? He pulled out a couple of crumpled sheets. The man took them with an irritated grunt.

'I can hardly read these,' he said. 'Which border crossing is this?'

He frowned when Firzun answered.

'That's closed now. I'll have to check in the office.' He hauled himself to his feet, still peering at the yellow papers. Firzun said nothing.

'Hello,' Ahmad said as the man turned to go. 'My name's Ahmad.'

'Well, young man, you should look after your daddy. He's injured.'

Before she could stop him, Ahmad blurted out, 'He's not my daddy!'

Zahra held her breath but the man hadn't heard. He was already heading for the glass-walled office. He stepped around another man at a desk, who was eating rice from a large bowl. She saw their official searching through a filing cabinet.

Firzun kneeled down to Ahmad's level, supporting himself with difficulty on his cane. 'Ahmad, see that man over there with the big gun? If you don't shut up, he'll take you away.'

'No!' Ahmad looked terrified.

'Stop it. You're frightening him,' Zahra snapped at Firzun.

'Keep him *quiet*, Zahra. He could blow everything,' Firzun muttered.

Ahmad buried his face in her clothes, not daring to look around. She kneeled down and hugged him. She wouldn't let anyone take him away, she told him. Firzun was joking, but he had to keep quiet. The child nodded and sniffed back tears.

She watched nervously as the emigration official conferred with his colleagues in the office. The man who was eating put his fork down, stood up, and looked across at them. Zahra clutched Ahmad to her side. The officials exchanged a few more words and the other gestured to a different filing cabinet. The second man sat down and resumed his lunch. After several minutes the emigration officer emerged from the office. He told them they were lucky he had found the copies. He clipped the papers together, put them to one side, stamped the passports, and handed everything to Firzun.

'Have a good journey, *Haji*. Next!'

Ahmad was close to tears as they filed through the gateway. As they passed several armed soldiers, he started to cry. When they got to an open area, Zahra searched her pocket for a handkerchief and cleaned him up as best she could. It was all too much for Ahmad and he held the handkerchief over his face and wailed loudly. He moved from one foot to another and said he needed the toilet.

Firzun stopped and walked back. 'Zahra, shut him up, for God's sake! Take him to the women's room over there.' He pointed with his cane. 'We've still got another check to go through and a bag search.'

'Firzun, he's only five. He's hungry and he's tired,' she told him, feeling overwrought and hungry herself.

To her relief the women's room was clean and pleasant and smelled of fresh flowers. After he'd used the toilet, she told Ahmad he could have his backpack soon. But he must promise to keep quiet and not talk to everyone. Ahmad nodded despondently and she felt a stab of guilt. This was her fault; she'd chosen to help her cousin, and now her son was suffering.

Zahra took off her scarf, combed her hair and looked at her reflection in the mirror. Her face looked pale and drawn, even without the tight head covering. She tied her hair back and splashed water on her face, wishing she could put some lipstick on her lips to reduce her pallor. The new regime had banned all make-up, and women from the Decency Police patrolled the streets. They picked on young women and cleaned off the make-up in public while they screamed in the other women's faces. Zahra shuddered, glad it had never happened to her.

She re-tied her headscarf and checked for stray hairs. Her face, surrounded by the unflattering black covering, felt completely naked. Suddenly the door of the ladies' room swung open and a tall attractive woman swept in. Like Zahra, she wasn't wearing make-up, but she looked flushed and angry. She opened her handbag, reached in, and pulled out a cosmetic bag. She opened the bin and threw the bag into it.

'This is all Max Factor stuff,' she announced. 'I've just found out that this damn regime won't even let you leave the country with cosmetics. I'm throwing everything out myself so they can't get their hands on it!'

'Where are you going?' Zahra asked tentatively.

'Paris,' the woman answered. 'What about you?'

'Sydney.'

'Australia! How weird.' The woman smirked at Zahra in the mirror. 'Isn't that where kangaroos hop down the main streets?' She laughed. 'Paris is a lot more civilised than *Australia*. Good luck! *Bye*,' she said brightly in English. With another laugh she opened the door and was gone.

Zahra supervised Ahmad's laborious hand washing, feeling completely deflated. She knew very little about the country she was going to. Surely it wasn't true that wild animals ran down the city streets? Maybe Firzun knew. She decided not to throw her own make-up bag in the bin. Let the officials take it off her; it might give them a sense of power over her.

Outside the women's room, Firzun frowned and looked pointedly at his watch. If he was nervous he was hiding it well. He fumbled in his luggage and handed the new backpack to Ahmad.

'Thank you!' Ahmad shrieked with delight.

'*Daddy*,' Firzun corrected. 'There's a truck in there for you as well. He's not a bad kid, Zahra, he's just got a big mouth,' he concluded.

'He's a child,' Zahra remonstrated, but Firzun was already ahead of them.

Zahra followed him down a broad passageway with shops on either side. Ahead of them she saw a large sign: *Passengers Only*. Several distressed relatives milled around closed double doors saying final goodbyes. Firzun pushed through the crowds and handed their documents to an airport official. He checked them, nodded, and indicated the doors with his head. Once through them they were in a wide corridor with windows down one side. Through the grimy glass she could see planes lined up like cars in a car park.

'That's ours.' Firzun pointed.

A white plane with *Gulf Air* painted on the side in blue letters stood waiting on the tarmac. Their plane—had they nearly made it? She clutched Ahmad's hand. Another official ordered them to separate into lines for men and women. She lost sight of Firzun as she was jostled forward.

'You, woman with the boy, how old is he?' a voice called out.

Zahra looked up in alarm. A heavy-set woman in a black chador that swirled around her ankles motioned her forward. She asked again how old Ahmad was and told Zahra if he was seven he had to go with his father. Satisfied with the answer, she ordered Zahra to follow her.

I've been singled out—why?

The woman stopped suddenly at a thick vinyl curtain and pushed it to one side. She ordered Zahra to put all her bags on a table and open them. Two young female officials in the small stuffy room stood to attention and exchanged glances when they saw Zahra's escort. Zahra opened her handbag and unzipped her overnight bag. She heard the other women murmuring to each other as they examined make-up bags they'd confiscated.

'How could she afford that stuff?'

'Rich old husband,' another giggled as she dumped a silver cosmetic bag into a large bin.

The heavy-set woman glared at them. 'You two—get on with your work and mind your own business.' She turned to Zahra. 'Are you carrying any weapons or drugs?'

'No, of course not,' Zahra replied.

'Yes or no is sufficient,' the woman said sharply. 'Documents.'

She peeled off one of her black gloves and held out her hand. She turned the pages of the passport slowly, checking the photographs. She stared straight at Zahra, then at Ahmad, before wordlessly returning everything to Zahra's trembling hand.

'Empty your handbag.' She pointed to the table.

The woman sifted through the scattered contents with her thick fingers. She pushed a packet of tissues, Zahra's purse, and a comb to one side. In a swift movement, she swept up Zahra's cosmetic bag and dumped it in the bin. She clicked her fingers at Ahmad.

'Backpack!'

Zahra helped him take it off. Ahmad glanced fearfully at the large woman, who picked up the little bag and glared at the Mickey Mouse logo. She stood up straighter, her lips a colourless line in her sallow face.

'This is American propaganda. It will have to be destroyed,' she said firmly.

Zahra was furious both with herself and Firzun. *Why did I let him take the backpack? It was Karim's gift to Ahmad.* Of course the authorities would grab this 'American propaganda' with its silly Mickey Mouse picture. She would never forget the raid on Karim's house by the Department of Religious Affairs. They took all of Ahmad's Mickey Mouse books. They hated Disney and anything fun for children, she thought angrily. There was no chance of saving the backpack, but maybe she could salvage something.

'There's a toy truck inside. It was a gift ...'

The woman opened the backpack and took out Ahmad's truck, which was still in its box. She banged it down on the table.

In spite of all the warnings to be quiet, Ahmad whispered desperately, 'It's my truck, when I ...'

'Well, you'd better look after it!' the woman interrupted, sternly pushing it at him.

She picked up the backpack and frowned again at the logo. Then she dumped it in the bin on top of the confiscated cosmetics.

Ahmad gasped, his face crumpled, and he wailed loudly. 'That lady took my bag.'

'Keep him quiet, madam.'

'You've got your truck, Ahmad,' Zahra whispered and put her finger to her lips. Large tears ran down his face. He tried to wipe his nose with the nylon sleeve of his yellow parka. The woman ignored him and told Zahra to empty her overnight bag. She obeyed, watching with mounting irritation as the official shook out every garment including Ahmad's little jeans and t-shirts.

'Are you taking any Iranian money out of the country? Any antiques?'

'No.' Zahra looked up from wiping Ahmad's face.

The woman tutted and picked up Zahra's purse. She rummaged quickly through the notes and small change, then dumped it back on the pile. Zahra watched her in petrified silence. A trickle of sweat ran down between her breasts and over the two hundred American dollars Karim had given her a few weeks ago. She'd hidden the money in her bra.

'*Take it, Zahra,*' Karim had urged her when she'd tried to refuse his money. '*You'll need it one day.*'

What if the horrible woman took her away to another room and searched her? If she found the dollars she would confiscate them, then interrogate her about where she got them. Zahra's hands trembled. She gave Ahmad a quick hug and stood up. She clutched bunches of her chador in her fists. *Please God, get me out of here!*

The official shot questions at her. Her place of birth, her son's place of birth, why they were in Iran, where her husband had worked, their reason for leaving. She switched to *Dari* to make sure, she told Zahra, that she was from Afghanistan and not an Iranian trying to escape the law. Zahra tripped over her answers as the questions hit her like machine-gun fire.

Next came questions about drugs, and Zahra's stomach clenched with panic. Was the woman trying to break her down? If she carried on much longer, Zahra doubted she'd be able to hold out. She'd confess everything: how she found drugs hidden in the old van when they had crossed the border into Iran. She might even tell them about her husband's death at the hands of her cousin. Maybe confess that it was Firzun who had organised the abortive attempt to free the American hostages. The questions stopped suddenly and Zahra looked up. The woman was staring at her with expressionless hard brown eyes.

'Are you travelling with your husband?'

'Yes.'

'Come with me. Bring the boy. Take your purse, leave everything else,' she ordered.

The official pushed past the younger workers. She pushed aside another vinyl curtain and pointed at the waiting men in a large room.

'Which one is your husband?'

Zahra's heart lurched as she indicated her cousin. 'The man with the cane—the *Haji*.'

Firzun was chatting amiably to a couple of Revolutionary Guards, who were leaning forward to see the small book he was holding. *He's discussing passages from the Koran with them while I'm being interrogated—hypocrite!* Zahra thought furiously.

The woman sniffed. 'He seems to be instructing our young people from the Holy Koran,' she said righteously. 'You're fortunate to have such a husband.'

She dropped the heavy curtain, pointed to Zahra's clothes, and told her to collect them. She motioned to one of the younger officials.

'Get the backpack,' she ordered. 'If his father approves, I suppose he can have it.' The younger woman smiled at Ahmad and handed it over. Zahra's interlocutor turned away without saying goodbye. She snapped her fingers and the young woman leapt forward, pulling aside the heavy curtain. Her boss marched out into the main airport.

'Bitch,' the girl said under her breath as she dropped the curtain. Her colleague sniggered.

Zahra shoved her things into the bags with shaking hands and Ahmad waited, clutching his backpack and truck to his chest. Neither of the young women moved when she struggled to pull the heavy curtain aside. At the end of the large room, Firzun half turned, looking casually for his wife but didn't move to assist her. Zahra had only just stopped shaking by the time she joined him.

Firzun nodded goodbye to the Revolutionary Guards, who shook his hand and touched their foreheads as they left.

'What kept you?' he asked as if she'd been deliberately dawdling.

She told him everything including that the woman spoke *Dari*.

Firzun let his breath out through his teeth with a hissing sound. 'Okay, you got through, but they might still be watching you,' he remarked.

The comment did nothing to calm her nerves.

'Why aren't they watching *you*?' she asked angrily.

'I'm a *Haji* and an Islamic scholar, remember?'

'*And* a scholar?' She laughed nervously, but he shushed her.

'Control yourself, we are still being watched,' Firzun muttered. 'We'll only be safe when the plane's out of Iranian air space.'

He helped Ahmad put his truck away and slipped his backpack over his shoulders. Zahra knelt and wiped Ahmad's face again.

'So he's still got Mickey Mouse,' Firzun said casually. 'Like I said, being a *Haji* has its benefits.'

Zahra glared at him. 'Mostly for you.'

He held his hands out in a *so what* gesture, then pointed to a café with *Women Only* written on the window and told her to get a cup of tea. He promised to come and get her in good time. She turned to go, but he called her back and told her that she had to identify her suitcase on the tarmac before she boarded the plane.

'What?'

'They blow up unclaimed baggage, remember?'

'I've had enough, Firzun ...' she began.

He gave her a withering look, took her arm, and escorted her to the café. He shoved some banknotes into her hand.

'I'll be back in half an hour, be ready.'

She watched him limp away leaning on his cane. He adjusted his bag over his shoulder and held the copy of the Koran in his other hand. He knew what he was doing, she reflected. What was the point in getting annoyed with him? He would get them on the plane and out of Iran.

Zahra sat down thankfully at a table in the café and ordered tea and sandwiches. What a relief to get away from the tension that flowed from her cousin like radio waves. While Ahmad ate hungrily he ran his truck up and down the table. Zahra looked out of the cafe window at the people scurrying past.

Not long now. Not long before I leave Iran and Karim forever, she reflected as she ate the small chicken sandwiches. But Karim was already a memory, an opportunity she had turned away from. In her mind's eye she saw her Iranian friends, Nasim and her husband Rashid. She remembered how they used to sit together on their sofa, so happy and young, and her eyes filled with tears. Rashid was dead, executed by the new religious regime in Iran. Nasim was in America with her parents, a pregnant widow who wasn't yet thirty. *And I'm heading for what?* Zahra thought. *A future in a foreign country I know nothing about.*

Her reverie was interrupted by a voice at her elbow. 'Would you mind if I join you?' A woman in her fifties was already pulling out the third chair at the table.

'My name's Leila,' she said as she sat down. 'I feel very conspicuous sitting alone. I'm a widow,' she added as Zahra shook her hand. '*Mashallah!* What a beautiful child, what's your name?' Leila smiled.

'Ahmad,' he replied shyly. He pointed to his backpack. 'This is Mickey Mouse.'

'He looks like a funny person,' Leila said.

Ahmad nodded vigorously. 'He's my best friend.'

Zahra indicated his sandwiches and juice, and he carried on eating, still smiling at his backpack.

'Did they say anything in the bag search about Mickey Mouse?' Leila asked. Before Zahra could answer, Leila rushed on. 'I thought they were going to steal my handbag. As for that tough one—I put her straight!'

She asked where Zahra was going and was thrilled with the reply.

'We'll be on the same plane,' she said. 'I've been there before, you know ... with my late husband. My son and his family have lived there for three years. I can't wait to see them.'

Zahra felt as if a great weight had lifted from her shoulders. Leila knew about Australia! Maybe she could fill in the gaps.

After Leila had ordered tea, she turned to Zahra. 'Well, Sydney is a beautiful city and Australia is an amazing place ...' she began.

7

KARIM GOES HOME

By the time he got home from the airport, Karim's frayed nerves were at breaking point. He'd suffered one shock after another. Firzun was alive and Zahra wasn't going home to Afghanistan. She was helping her cousin get out of Iran and escape to Australia, halfway across the world.

Karim closed the front door and leaned against it, trying to make sense of what had happened. He felt exhausted and angry with himself. What madness had taken hold of him? He'd actually tried to drag a woman away from her husband in a public place. He'd upset Ahmad, made a dangerous scene ... and for what?

He crossed the silent atrium, pushed open the door, and looked into the deserted kitchen. As usual the housekeepers were having their afternoon nap. In the small dining room, he picked at the lunch plate Tahmineh had left for him and tried to think straight.

He could afford to fly to Australia tomorrow, first class if he wanted. And then what? Hang around harassing Zahra? A wave of indignation washed over him. He wasn't totally to blame—she was complicit. Had she really only found out that Firzun was alive two days ago? For all Karim knew, she could have been taking food to him at Nasim and Rashid's house. In fact, Karim thought, as he walked slowly up the stairs, she might have known he was alive almost immediately. Had it all been a sham? Going to the funeral, running off to the mosque to say prayers for Firzun's soul? By the time he got to his apartment, Karim was convinced that he was the victim of an enormous hoax perpetrated by both Zahra and Firzun.

She was playing me, he thought bitterly. That's what Nancy had done, played him for a fool. At least he hadn't let Yasmin get the better of him. He tried to feel glad that Zahra was no longer in his life, but he couldn't. His heart ached whenever he thought of her. He would never forget meeting her for the first time at Nasim's house years ago. She was a gauche kid of seventeen and he was twenty-three. He had found her attractive even then and he still did.

He stood at the patio windows in his apartment, watching the trees at the far end of the garden as they swayed wildly in the wind. Rain spattered against the panes. Maybe the flight to Dubai would be cancelled because of the wild weather. But where would Zahra and Firzun go if that happened? They had to get out of Iran as quickly as possible. A vision of Firzun, piously dressed and holding a Koran, crossed his consciousness and he clenched his fists. How the hell did he think he'd get out of the country? He was officially dead. The authorities must know that by now. The names of the victims had been intoned at that awful mass funeral. Then how ...? Suddenly it came to him in a flash.

'My God! What a gamble,' Karim shouted, his words echoing around the large room.

Firzun was using Zahra's first husband's identity. He was leaving as ... he didn't even know the man's name. That explained why she'd had to go with him. She was his human shield, his ticket out. *No wonder she lied to me. What an idiot I've been! Why didn't I think of that before?*

And what about the letter she had left him? Would that be full of lies too? He looked around his apartment. He had to find it before the housekeeper did. He wanted answers, he needed to feel better about himself. He found it easily under his pillow.

> *Dearest Karim,*
>
> *By the time you read this, I'll be gone, not to Afghanistan, but to Sydney, Australia with Firzun. Amazingly he survived the bomb blast, God be praised. He took refuge in Nasim and Rashid's house only two doors away. He visited me here late on Friday night. I was terrified, I thought I'd seen a ghost. I have to go with him or he'll be arrested for his counter-revolutionary activities. I know it will be hard for you to understand, but he's my husband and my cousin, a blood relative. I have no choice, but I will miss you and so will Ahmad.*
>
> *I did love you. Please believe me, Karim, although I'm sure you think that I have cheated and wronged you. I am truly sorry. Peace be with you, dear one. I hope that you will find happiness and love in your new country.*
>
> *Zahra.*

Karim re-read the letter several times, imagining her bending over the page as she wrote, maybe wiping away a tear. Hardly, he thought angrily. She hadn't mentioned the identity switch or the tremendous risk she was taking for Firzun. She could be arrested and imprisoned and he would be executed for crimes against the State. Wasn't she worried about Ahmad being sent to an orphanage, for God's sake?

Why hadn't she confided in him? He could have helped somehow. She obviously didn't trust him. He crumpled the paper in his hand and sat down on the bed, his energy spent. '*I did love you*'— past tense. He didn't believe her. If you loved someone, you put your trust in them. She had betrayed his. He lay back on the bed feeling exhausted.

The sound of heavy rain on the roof woke him up. He jumped up quickly and walked to the window. Clouds had gathered over the tops of the mountains and the wind was even stronger. He knew their flight was due out at three o'clock. He checked his watch: three-fifteen. The plane would be taxiing down the runway now. He imagined Ahmad's excitement and Zahra's trepidation. She'd told him she was scared of flying. Had they really done it and left Iran? He hoped for her sake that they had. Though God knows why he gave a damn.

Karim picked up the crumpled letter from the floor and put it in the drawer next to his bed. He showered quickly, and as he dressed he remembered Firzun smiling piously at everyone in the airport and felt wildly irritated again. He wouldn't be surprised if Firzun told people he was injured on a pilgrimage to Mecca. He could hardly tell the truth, that he was shot in the leg during that stupid raid to free the American hostages. What a disaster that was—Firzun was lucky to be alive. In fact, it was he, Karim, who had saved him, got him into the truck and to the hospital. Ungrateful bastard!

Even without Firzun's threats at the airport, Karim knew that his own time in Iran was running out. The authorities were still investigating and arresting anyone who was involved in the embassy raid. And he was one of them. Eventually he was pretty sure the Revolutionary Guard would crash through his front door like they'd done at Nasim and Rashid's house.

The afternoon was closing in and the shadows were darkening on the mountains. Perhaps he should check out Nasim and Rashid's place for the last time. Make sure Firzun had covered his tracks. He grabbed a torch and ran down the outside steps from his apartment to the garden below. The sodden grass sucked at his shoes and he nearly slipped a couple of times. He remembered finding his way through here in the dark on the night of the raid. As he got nearer the fence he squinted, looking for the loose paling.

He and his housekeepers had boarded up Nasim and Rashid's place after the Revolutionary Guards had been through and trashed it. He'd left a space to get in if he ever needed it, like now. That's probably how Firzun got in too, he thought.

Once inside, he shivered. The house smelled damp and it was eerily quiet. A sudden gust of wind rattled the outside boards and whistled mournfully through the gaps. Gloomy thoughts haunted him as he walked carefully through the trashed rooms.

Surprisingly, Firzun hadn't covered his tracks. In a corner of the small breakfast room, Karim found a pile of tumbled bedding and discarded cups and dishes, encrusted with old food. The room looked and smelled like a rat's nest. He dragged the pillowcase off the pillow and tossed the crockery into it. He scooped up Firzun's mud-caked clothes and rolled them up in the bedding. He turned his face away in disgust from the sharp smell of body odour. Yanking open the door, he dumped the linen and crockery outside in the hall-way. Who had brought food here for Firzun? Zahra?

He swung the torch round and something caught his eye. He moved closer and kneeled down, frowning. A pile of small hessian bags had been thrown into a corner. He picked up one of them and looked at it, trying to remember something.

'Yes!' he said out loud.

His friend Sami had done his National Service on the Afghan border. He was an expert on drugs and the Mujahideen.

'They hide little bags of resin in boxes of fruit—that's how they get it over the border,' Sami had said, smirking. 'Slippery Afghans!'

So Firzun was a drug smuggler, just as Karim had suspected all along. Firzun had financed his counter-revolutionary activities by importing and selling drugs—no surprises there. He crushed the hessian bags in his hand and flung them back where he'd found them. Another gust of wind rattled the windows. A door slammed somewhere upstairs and he jumped. His imagination was in over-drive. Were the ghosts of the young men Firzun had led to their death haunting the house? He swept up the bundles he had collected and climbed out of the desolate building the way he'd come in.

Karim tramped home through the garden deep in thought. Had Firzun taken heroin with him on the plane? Surely he wouldn't be that stupid? Another slippery Afghan. *My God, I hate that man!* Karim thought, clenching his fists.

He finally got to his kitchen garden and threw the pillowcase of rubbish in the garbage bin. He yawned; wakened by Yasmin in the middle of the night and second-guessing Firzun had exhausted him. He was ready to leave, he thought grimly as he dialled his travel agent's home number. Within half an hour he was booked on a flight to New York in three days' time.

8

DESERTION

Zahra's new acquaintance and fellow traveller Leila launched into her life story. She was going to live with her son and his family in Sydney, and did Zahra know that it took over twenty hours to get there? Zahra was taken aback; up to this point she had been too distracted to think about the actual journey. Leila produced photographs of her family: a smiling couple at a beach, in a park, near the Sydney Opera House ...

Zahra only half listened as the other woman told her about her husband's early death.

'I blame the regime,' Leila said, dabbing her eyes. 'My husband had a heart attack after he lost his job in a government department. They harassed him, insisted that he pray five times a day at work. They said he should retire and move over for younger people who were more committed to the regime.'

Zahra wanted to ask more questions about Australia, but Leila had moved on to a recount of her younger son's life. He was 'making a lot of money' in the United States. Her son in Australia said he couldn't wait to see her. Leila stopped talking abruptly and looked past Zahra. She wished Zahra a hasty goodbye and got up. Zahra turned around and saw Firzun outside the window gesticulating at her to hurry up. No wonder Leila had rushed off, Zahra thought. Firzun looked like a member of the new Islamic regime with his clipped *Haji* beard, long Islamic clothes, and crocheted cap.

She collected their things and took Ahmad's hand. As soon as they joined him, he jerked his head to the left, then limped ahead of her down endless wide corridors. She pulled Ahmad along, trying to keep up with Firzun. He stopped abruptly, turned, and pointed.

'Get your stuff out,' he said when she caught up with him. 'This is the final check. Don't mess up.'

Zahra felt sick with nerves as she waited behind her cousin. At the desk, the official moved deliberately and with agonising slowness. He turned each passport page carefully, examined the photograph, stared at Firzun, looked back at the picture, and put his head on one side.

'Can we go now?' Ahmad's plaintive voice floated up to him.

The man looked down and smiled. '*Mashallah!*' he remarked, handing Firzun his passport. 'You have a fine son, *Haji*.'

Firzun bestowed a benevolent smile on Ahmad. The man flicked quickly through the other two passports and waved them toward a door. To Zahra's surprise, Firzun held it open for her.

'This is the departure lounge,' he muttered as she sat down. 'Ensh'allah, we'll be out of Iran soon.'

Firzun suddenly grabbed her arm and yanked her to her feet.

'They've just called our seat numbers, let's go!'

Firzun swung through the door ahead of her. The other passengers were already jostling to get to the pile of suitcases that had been dumped on the tarmac. Two men were pushing steel steps up to the front and the rear of the aircraft. This was it! Once they were in the air, they'd be out of Iran forever.

'Pick out your suitcase. I'm getting on board,' Firzun said, hoisting his battered black bag over his shoulder.

She followed him, struggling with her son and her hand luggage. Gusts of cold rain blew across the tarmac and she hugged her clothes close to her body. Before she could stop him, Ahmad ran across to the scattered luggage and was back in seconds. He'd found the suitcase, he said, and she had to tell 'the man'. She let Ahmad pull her across and she pointed to her case. A dour-face baggage handler nodded and heaved her bag into the hold.

Close up, the white plane with its blue lettering looked enormous and she felt a sudden surge of excitement. She took Ahmad's hand, pushed through the group of searching people, and toiled up the steel steps. A smiling young woman directed them toward their seats. Firzun was sitting in an aisle seat with his leg stretched out. He struggled to his feet as the air hostess helped Zahra stow her overnight bag and Ahmad's backpack in an overhead locker.

'You'll have to put your leg under the seat when we take off, sir,' the woman remarked.

Firzun grunted a reply and motioned to the window seat. 'Ahmad can sit there,' he told Zahra.

Zahra struggled with the seat belts, only half-hearing the announcements. She looked over Ahmad's head and out the window. Two Revolutionary Guards were standing at the exit door from the departure lounge. They held submachine guns against their bodies and were looking directly at the plane. At her. She nudged Firzun and indicated the window.

'Relax!' he muttered. 'It's standard procedure when a plane leaves.'

But the plane didn't leave. It sat on the tarmac. One of the guards took a walkie-talkie from his belt and spoke into it. He turned to his colleague and said something. Zahra's heart pounded as she watched them. Would they run across the tarmac and up the stairs? Then charge down the narrow aisle and drag Firzun out of his seat? Her breath came in short gasps. Her whole body was tense; she dug her fingernails into her palms and clenched her fists. An announcement came over the loudspeakers, something about the crew and cross-checking. Ahmad leaned up and closed the window blind. She pulled his hand away and opened the blind just as the ground crew were wheeling the steps back from the plane. It started to move backward very slowly. The Revolutionary Guards were still there, watching. One of them waved and the other gave a half salute at the plane, then they both turned and disappeared through the doors. The plane revolved gradually, paused, then bumped along the runway. With a sudden roar it picked up speed. In an instant, Zahra was looking down on the buildings of Tehran, dwarfed by the majestic Alborz Mountains that surrounded the city.

'We've done it!' Firzun murmured. He had his head bowed and didn't look at her.

But *what* had they done? Zahra asked herself. They'd left a trail of destruction and misery in their wake. Men had died because of the abortive raid on the American embassy that Firzun had led. She was culpable as well. She had encouraged then rejected and hurt Karim, a man she truly cared for. He would have found her letter by now. Would he check his watch and think about her when the plane took off? She felt miserable and dejected. He had probably blotted her out of his memory already.

As the aircraft rose higher, the clouds parted and she saw the brown landscape far below. The map on the TV monitor showed that they were flying south toward the Arab states. She wondered if she would ever see her own country again. Memories flooded Zahra's mind of her days as a teacher and the faces of her students as they listened to her. She recollected shopping in the bazaar hundreds of kilometres to the east; of visiting her women friends in their homes. She had delighted in new babies, commiserated with losses. All the familiar, sometimes silly, sometimes terrifying things in her life had become memories in an instant.

'Seat belt please, madam.'

The voice woke her up and she roused Ahmad, who'd been asleep with his head in her lap.

'Bahrain, United Arab Emirates,' Firzun announced as the plane landed with a jolt. 'We change here for the flight to Sydney.' He waved his boarding pass at her. 'Stay near me when we get off. I've got to check the gate number, it's not on here.'

Holding Ahmad firmly by the hand, she followed her cousin off the plane.

After consulting an illuminated board, he turned to her. 'Gate 43—that way.' He pointed with his cane. 'Okay?'

She looked up at him and saw his mouth open slightly as he looked beyond her. His gaze fixed on something or someone ahead of them. He stopped abruptly and stared intently at the milling airport crowds. He looked from left to right, then turned around quickly and scanned the crowds behind them.

Zahra paused with him. 'What is it?'

'Nothing. Look, I'll meet you at the gate, it's straight down there.'

'But ...'

He put his hand on her arm and his black eyes met hers. 'Just *go*, Zahra.'

He limped away without another word. She stood for a moment, trying to get her bearings, then followed the signs past glittering jewellery shops and down endless corridors. When she and Ahmad arrived at Gate 43, she saw Leila, the woman she'd met in Tehran airport. Without her chador and scarf Leila looked smart and Western. She waved Zahra over to her.

'There's a ladies' room over there.' She pointed. 'I'll mind Ahmad for you. You can take your chador and scarf off now.'

Zahra thanked her, grateful to be alone for a few minutes. When she emerged from the restrooms, she saw Firzun walking toward her.

As soon as she saw his face, Zahra knew something was wrong. He had the same hunted expression he'd had when she'd left him in Antaz the morning the bomb exploded. He walked alongside her toward the lounge without speaking. When she asked him if anything was wrong, he brushed her question aside. He was fine, he told her.

'Did you see something?' she asked.

'Not something ... someone ... maybe.' He went quiet and Zahra looked at him in alarm.

'Are you going to tell me more?'

'Can't,' he said shortly.

She changed the subject. 'I met Leila again. She's looking after Ahmad.'

'Listen,' Firzun muttered, ignoring her comment, 'we don't have to board together. I'll see you on the plane.'

She felt alarmed. After they had taken off from Tehran, he'd said he was safe at last. A terrible thought struck her. Had someone followed him? Is that why the Revolutionary Guards in Tehran had made a phone call, to confirm that Firzun was on the flight? A trickle of fear ran down her spine. Could he be arrested here in the United Arab Emirates? No, it's a foreign country, she told herself. He had an Afghan passport. He hadn't broken the law here. She turned to ask him a question, but he'd slipped away.

She walked over to where Leila was sitting with Ahmad.

'He's been very good,' the other woman said, smiling. 'You know they have showers in Singapore airport? Why don't we meet when we get off the plane and go to the shower rooms?'

Zahra nodded; it sounded like a good idea.

'We're boarding now. Is your husband ...?' Leila looked around.

'He had to visit the bathroom,' Zahra said hastily.

When their seat numbers were called, she shuffled onto the plane with the other passengers. Their new seats had more leg room and faced a wall with a television screen on it. She settled Ahmad in the middle seat. Eventually people stopped walking past. Everyone was on board, but where was Firzun? She was straining to see up the aisle when she heard an announcement, first in Arabic then in English.

Could passenger Mahmoud Ghafoori please make himself known to the cabin crew?

A young stewardess tapped Zahra's arm, then kneeled next to her seat with a worried expression in her brown eyes.

'Your husband hasn't boarded the plane and we're due to leave,' she began.

She stood up quickly as Firzun fell into his seat on the other side of Ahmad with no apology. The stewardess walked up the aisle and nodded to the huddle of cabin crew. Zahra saw one of them roll her eyes. Next to her, Firzun was breathing heavily.

'Where *were* you?' Zahra hissed.

'I had some business to fix up,' he answered, pulling his seat belt around his body and fastening it.

'I was worried ...'

'No need. It's sorted.'

'What is?'

The plane was moving down the runway and gathering speed.

He turned to her and met her frightened eyes. 'We're safe now. Someone was following me. I gave him the slip—that's why I nearly missed the plane.'

'Who? How do you know?'

Zahra felt a creeping fear rising in her chest. He told her he'd recognised the man. He knew what he was and what he'd become. She had no idea what this meant and asked him to explain.

'It's a long story, Zahra.'

'We've got a long flight ahead of us. Tell me, for goodness sake.'

Firzun hesitated and tightened his lips as he looked sideways at her. Then, with a sigh, he explained that the person he'd seen at Bahrain Airport was an old adversary from his university days in Tehran. His name was Ali Esmaeili. In the hotbed of Tehran University politics, he'd been Firzun's worst enemy. He was a religious, reactionary zealot. Firzun had watched, via newspapers and television, Ali's rise through the ranks of the Revolutionary Guard to a prominent position in the new regime. And now here he was, someone who could recognise him and reveal that he wasn't dead and he wasn't Mahmoud Ghafoori. That's why he'd had to be given the slip.

Zahra shuddered and put her arm round Ahmad, who was

watching the television screen. Firzun had nearly missed the plane! *My God! I would have been on my way to Australia alone with my son if he had!*

Day had changed to night and back to day again by the time they landed in Singapore. Firzun pored over a map of Changi Airport before they landed. When they disembarked, Leila was waiting for Zahra as she'd promised.

'Gate 30, in an hour,' Firzun said abruptly before he limped away.

'I know my way around this airport,' Leila assured her. 'My husband and I stopped here two years ago,' she said sadly. 'When you're ready we'll find a coffee shop.'

Back at Gate 30, Leila left her with a brief smile when she saw Firzun leaning against a pillar. He was still wearing his long white tunic, pants, and crocheted cap.

'I had a shower too,' he commented.

'Why didn't you change?'

'It's what Mahmoud was wearing in the passport photo, remember?' His eyes glinted at her through the gold-rimmed glasses with clear lenses.

'So Ali Esmaeili hasn't followed you here?' she asked.

His eyes flicked past her briefly, then back. 'Not sure. I haven't seen him though.'

His answer didn't reassure her much, but before she could ask him any other questions, their seat numbers were called and they shuffled aboard.

'Ahmad can stay in the middle.' Firzun lowered himself into his seat.

'Are you in pain?' Zahra asked.

Her cousin shrugged but didn't answer.

Their journey from Tehran to Sydney had taken more than twenty-four hours. Zahra had slept fitfully with Ahmad shifting against her. When the captain announced they were beginning their descent into Sydney, she tapped Firzun on the arm.

'Our papers are in order, aren't they?' she asked quietly as the crew handed out immigration cards to the passengers.

'Of course,' he muttered, filling out his card. 'We got out of Iran and we didn't have any problems at Bahrain or Singapore, did we?'

Apart from you being followed in Bahrain.

Zahra didn't comment but fumbled with her seat belt and Ahmad's as the cabin crew made their final checks. She stretched up, trying to see out the window, and glimpsed a vast forest, then a river glinted in the evening sunshine. The plane dipped and she saw Sydney Harbour. The evening sunshine dappled the water, which was dotted with tiny boats. Leila had told her to watch out for the Harbour Bridge.

Someone called out in English: 'There's the Opera House!'

Zahra leaned up in her seat again. The graceful white building with its curved roofs was far below, near the water's edge. She glimpsed the Harbour Bridge before the plane swung out over the ocean then back toward the airport. With a roar and a jolt, it landed, the ground raced past, and the plane slowed then stopped. Firzun had said that someone from the Immigration Department would be waiting to meet them. *What if my English isn't good enough to talk to native speakers?* she thought nervously.

'*Welcome to Sydney,*' a voice said over the loudspeaker. Zahra caught something about the time—six-fifteen in the evening—and the temperature—22 degrees Celsius, 71 degrees Fahrenheit. It was Tuesday 27 November. The seatbelt sign went off and suddenly everyone was on their feet, pulling down bags and pushing into the aisles. Zahra took her bag and Ahmad's backpack from the overhead locker and helped him put it on. As they waited, she grew nervous again. Why weren't they opening the doors? Would another announcement ask Firzun to identify himself as Mahmoud?

Finally, they started moving and she ushered Ahmad ahead of her as she struggled down the narrow aisle with her bags. The crew smiled their farewells as she stepped into an enclosed corridor. To her relief, the uniformed men they passed weren't armed. Firzun had already limped ahead of them and he turned impatiently, motioning her to move faster. Her eyes felt dry and tight, and Ahmad was dragging his feet, slowing her down.

'This is passport control, give me yours,' Firzun ordered when she joined him in a long queue. 'We go through here together, then we'll pick up your suitcase.'

They shuffled forward to the row of glass booths manned by uniformed men and women. Her hands felt clammy, her nerves on edge, but Firzun seemed totally relaxed. He stepped forward, motioning her to follow, and handed over the passports. The immigration officer opened the passports at the photographs and looked up at them. Her hands were trembling and she gripped her shoulder bag close to her side. She held her breath as he checked the visas.

'G'day, son!' the man called cheerfully. He leaned out of his seat to look at Ahmad, then he stamped the passports and handed them to Firzun.

'Welcome to Australia.' He smiled, motioning them through the narrow space at the side of the booth.

When Firzun returned her passport and immigration card, their eyes met briefly and she nodded without speaking. They'd made it! They were in Australia.

'This way.' Firzun took her elbow. 'The suitcases will come out down here.' He pointed. Just after they got to the open arrivals area, the carousel started moving slowly. Ahmad was fascinated and stepped closer before Zahra pulled him away. In the distance, she saw a man in uniform with a dog on a lead.

'They're looking for drugs. The dog can sniff them out,' Firzun told her.

He took her elbow and manoeuvred her to a clear space at the back of the crowd.

'You didn't bring ...?'

'Of course not, stop worrying. Look, he's got someone. They've only got one dog.'

Zahra frowned; how did he know that? Was he making it up to stop her worrying? She glanced across to where a man in a uniform was talking to the owner of the suitcase, while the dog sat quietly near it.

She turned back to Firzun. His face was tense and he looked down at the ground, then straight into her eyes.

'Zahra, listen to me carefully. That guy in Bahrain, the one I gave the slip? I thought I'd lost him, but he's *here*. I saw him in the passport line ahead of us. He was travelling first class. He disappeared through another exit. He'll be waiting for me in the arrivals hall.'

She stared at him, wide-eyed. 'Are you sure it was him?'

'Oh yeah, it was Ali Esmaeili all right.' Firzun paused and touched her arm. 'Zahra, I have to get away from here!'

'What?'

'I can give him the slip again. I have to disappear for a while.'

'Disappear?' She shook her head. 'What do you mean?'

'You'll be okay. The immigration people will find you and take you to the hostel.' He nodded as if everything was organised.

'What! Don't leave me, I need you. Where are you going?'

She felt terribly afraid. Was he going to dump her here ... at Sydney airport?

'Nousha's family. They'll hide me.'

'I don't understand. You've got to come to the hostel with us. You said ...'

He glanced over his shoulder. 'Look, like I told you, I saw Ali at passport control.'

She gripped his arm. 'You're imagining things. You can't just abandon us.'

'I'm not *abandoning* you.' Firzun shook her off. 'I'm in danger, for God's sake!'

People were jostling them, pushing past with their suitcases.

She grabbed her cousin's arm again, harder. 'Please Firzun, don't do this,' she begged, but he twisted away from her.

'Zahra, he's a professional assassin. The regime—they've sent him to kill me.' He looked around desperately. 'Get your suitcase. I'll be in touch.'

Ahmad tugged her sleeve. 'There it is! I saw your suitcase, Mummy.'

She turned and told him to wait a minute. When she looked back, Firzun had gone and Ahmad was already running toward the carousel.

'There!'

He rushed forward before she could stop him. She hauled the case off the carousel and dragged it across to a trolley. Ahmad jumped up next to it. Zahra stood for a minute, anxiously scanning the crowd for Firzun, but she couldn't see him.

'Can you see cousin Firzun?' she asked her son as she struggled with the cumbersome vehicle.

'No, Mummy.'

She pushed the trolley toward the exit sign, determined to catch up with her cousin and stop him. She saw him at the customs check. He was already well ahead of her and his hand luggage had been searched. She saw him push his things back into his holdall. She called out to him, but he ignored her. To her dismay he limped away in the direction of another set of exit doors. An official stopped her and asked for immigration cards. She fumbled in her bag. When she looked up again, Firzun had gone.

The official waved her through and she heaved the trolley forward and through the door. She was at the top of a slope leading down to a brightly lit arrivals area. The noise and harsh lights were overwhelming. Her hands felt slippery with sweat. She lost her grip and the vehicle veered away from her into the side rail. She wiped the handle with her sleeve and gripped it harder. Manoeuvring the trolley down the incline was impossible. The wheels jammed twice, people pushed past, and the noise from the hall below was deafening.

She reached the bottom of the slope and scanned the area looking desperately for Firzun in his white clothes and crocheted cap. Ahead of her a set of automatic doors opened and closed constantly. A figure caught her eye—a familiar-looking stocky man in jeans, black t-shirt, and baseball cap. He was limping quickly toward the exit. She put her hand to her throat. Firzun! He'd abandoned his Islamic clothes and his cane. He must have changed in Singapore and worn his cleric's clothes over his jeans and t-shirt.

'Firzun, stop.' Her voice came out as a strangled terrified whisper.

The automatic doors opened. In an instant he was hurrying across a busy road. Then the doors closed. She didn't see anyone following him. *Khoda! I've got to get him back.* She pushed the trolley through groups of hugging, smiling people.

'Too fast, Mummy, you're going too fast!' Ahmad called. He was running to keep up with her. He grabbed the handle of the trolley, slowing her down.

'Quick, get on,' she told him.

He scrambled up, unbalancing the vehicle even more. When she got to the doors, they flew open for her too. She felt cool air on her face and blinked in the bright light. She pushed the trolley forward, looking round desperately. There was no sign of Firzun. Cars rushed past on the road and through a car park. She had no idea what to do.

'Zahra! Hello again. Welcome to Sydney.'

She turned and saw Leila.

The woman's smile disappeared. 'Oh my dear, you look terrible! What's happened? Is it the boy?'

'My husband,' Zahra began. 'He's gone. He's left me.'

'What? *Left* you? Oh, my goodness!' Leila turned to the young man next to her. 'Mehran, you've got to help her.'

'Did you say your husband has left you?' Leila's son asked in Persian.

'Yes, he just walked away—disappeared!'

'Maybe he's getting you a taxi.'

Zahra shook her head. 'No, he told me he had to go.'

She stopped. How could she tell anyone what Firzun had said about an assassin following him? It sounded unbelievably dramatic, even to her.

Leila glanced at Mehran in alarm.

'Was he meeting someone?' the man asked. 'A friend with a car? Maybe I can find him.'

A friend with a car. Firzun had mentioned Nousha's family. Had everything been arranged from Tehran? Had Firzun *expected* to be followed?

'He's deserted us.' She stared wildly at Leila. 'I don't know what to do.' She tried to control the tears that were rising in her throat.

'Come on,' Leila said gently. 'Let's go back inside. My son will sort this out. Weren't the Immigration people meeting you?'

Zahra looked down at Ahmad standing quietly by her side. *Brave little boy.* She swallowed hard and tried to pull herself together, for his sake. Leila kneeled down and gave Ahmad some sweets. He accepted them wordlessly.

'I'll try and find someone from Immigration,' Mehran told them.

He was back within minutes with a flustered, fair-haired woman.

'Have you just arrived on a flight from Tehran?' she said breathlessly to Zahra.

'Yes, they have,' Leila's son answered. His English was clear and precise.

'Hello, I'm Kathy Graham from the Australian Department of Immigration.' She glanced at a list on her clipboard. 'I'm looking for

Mahmoud, Zahra, and Ahmad Ghafoori.' She looked expectantly at the group.

When Leila's son explained what had happened in his fluent English, Kathy was taken aback. She asked if Zahra's husband had said where he was going.

'She says he's abandoned them. She doesn't know where he's gone,' Mehran answered for her.

'Thank you for your assistance.' Kathy smiled at him. 'I can sort it from here.'

'Take this, Zahra *Khanoum*.' Mehran handed Zahra a small white card. 'Call me anytime if you need help.'

Zahra pushed the business card into her pocket and stammered her thanks. Leila hugged her, said goodbye, and shoved more sweets into her hands.

'God protect you,' she whispered in Persian.

'Thank you,' Zahra sniffed.

'This way!' Kathy said. 'Can you speak English?'

'Yes,' Zahra answered as she turned the trolley around and followed the other woman.

'I'm sure he'll be back soon,' Kathy reassured her as they walked along.

He won't, Zahra thought.

They joined a group of weary-looking people. At the head of the group, a large man dressed in a blue shirt, shorts, and long socks nodded to Kathy.

'Found them okay?'

'Sort of,' Kathy replied. 'Anyway, hello again everyone!' she said brightly. 'Just follow Ron, our driver, to the coach. I'll be with you in a minute.'

After the group had started to shuffle off, Kathy turned to Zahra. 'I'll have a quick look around for your husband. What was he wearing?'

'Jeans, black t-shirt, and a cap.'

'Right, don't worry.' Kathy smiled. 'I'll ask them to look out for him at the airport. You just follow the others. I'll see you on the coach.'

As she trudged behind the group of new immigrants, Zahra felt angry with herself for not anticipating Firzun's treachery. She and Ahmad had served their purpose, she thought bitterly. He would probably lay low at Nousha's place. Firzun had casually tossed out some information about his fiancée in Sydney before the bomb blast. With Nousha's family's help, her cousin was going to fix himself up with another new identity, Zahra thought angrily. If someone *had* followed him, they wouldn't find him at the hostel. But he had only told *her* half his plans.

Finally, the group stopped by a large coach. She was too distracted to take her case off the trolley and jumped when the driver told her he'd get it, then swung it into the hold.

She helped Ahmad up the steps and found a seat. *What's going to happen to us now?* She felt a rising panic. *Where are we and where are we going?* Firzun hadn't been around enough to give her any details of the arrangements he'd made for them in Sydney. Just that they would go to a migrant hostel. She didn't even know where it was. Why hadn't she insisted on more details? She was furious with herself for trusting him. This was how he'd repaid her loyalty, by dumping her!

Another terrifying thought struck her—the Australian police. They would want to know where her husband had gone, surely? Would they take her to a police station and yell in her face? Keep her in jail and question her till she told the truth? She shuddered. Nasim had told her some terrible things about how the Iranian police had treated young women after the revolution. Would the Australian police do the same things? Hit her and make her undress?

She had to do something—but what? Could she go back to Tehran, tell Karim everything, and beg him to forgive her? She was still at Sydney Airport. Her mind was in overdrive as she tried to work out what to do. She had two hundred American dollars; would that be enough for a one-way fare? Perhaps they would let Ahmad travel free because he was only five. In addition, she had gold coins and jewellery. Maybe she could change them somewhere. Then she might have enough money to get back to Iran or maybe Afghanistan. She started to get up, but the coach was reversing out of the parking bay. She looked around desperately and fell back into her seat. She couldn't get off now. She was trapped. There was no way back.

9

FAREWELL MY COUNTRY

During his final few days in Tehran, Karim couldn't get Zahra out of his mind. Every time the phone rang, he felt edgy, wondering if it was the authorities telling him one of their 'servants' had been arrested. His house was Zahra's last address in Tehran. When no call came and no one thumped on his front door, he assumed they'd got out of Iran and arrived in Australia. They were probably staying in a smart hotel in Sydney while Zahra's despicable cousin disposed of his smuggled drugs.

Karim pushed on with the work of organising the final packing in his family's home. The day before he left, he stood in the echoing atrium of the house. His life in Iran was over. After Tahmineh and Amir had helped him lock up, he was sure he would never see this house again. He was grateful for their promise that they would come back from their village and check on it now and then. There was little hope that people like his parents, supporters of the former shah, would ever be able to return to their own country while the Ayatollah Khomeini's regime was in power. Karim didn't want to come back either. It was a sad thought.

He wandered from room to room, haunted by recent memories.

As he walked up the wide ornate staircase, he could have sworn he heard Ahmad's voice shouting excitedly from the garden. He reached the top of the stairs and fancied Zahra was there on the way to read to his grandmother. He pushed open the door to his grandmother's room. Her bed was still there with the blue coverlet in place. He opened the drapes and looked across at the view of the mountains that she'd had from her sickbed. He felt overwhelmingly sad. The late afternoon sun caught the harsh browns and blues of the crags and he could see a faint dusting of snow on the high peaks. He remembered the excitement of seeing the first snow. How he and his sister had begged to go skiing and snowboarding.

He closed the drapes and went out onto the landing. When they were children they used to watch guests from here as they arrived for one of his mother's famous soirées. He was always dressed in a child-sized dinner suit and his younger sister in a frilly party dress. The women milling around below in their short cocktail dresses had glittered with jewellery. The men had stood in groups in the ubiquitous evening dress of the wealthy middle-class business man. This assembled cream of Tehran society often included the many Americans who worked alongside their Iranian counterparts like his father.

Oil, Karim reflected as he stood on the silent landing, was the source of Iran's, and the shah's, enormous wealth. But that world had vanished almost in the blink of an eye. He shook his head. Why hadn't anyone seen it coming? Why had they thought the Ayatollah would run a democratic government?

The lucky, wealthy people like his parents had managed to leave. But what about people like Yasmin and her family? He didn't think life would be better for them. While she was eating her meal in the kitchen, Yasmin told him that her children's school curriculum had changed to include two hours' Koranic study a day. Her fifteen-year-old daughter was forced to wear strict Islamic dress too. She was glad she had a son; at least he'd have some freedom. Her mother-in-law thought the new curriculum was a good thing, but Yasmin and her husband weren't so sure.

Karim frowned, unable to shake the uncomfortable feeling he had each time he thought about Yasmin. He felt selfish and privileged when he reflected on her life—bright intelligent Yasmin, forced to wear a chador and veil. She was stuck in a dead-end job and doomed to live in her home village for the rest of her life. Her children were being educated contrary to her wishes and she'd told him how helpless she felt about it.

He ran up the stairs to his apartment; he had to pack for his departure tomorrow and he was going out tonight. The long evenings of saying goodbye to old friends and their endless political discussions saddened him. Very few of his old crowd was still in Iran. The ones who were left made noises about emigrating but didn't. A massive brain-drain was already underway, Karim reflected. His friends were professionals—doctors, lawyers, architects like himself. Their wives were also professional women. The new regime thought women should stay at home, so most of them had lost their jobs or been demoted. Everyone was reluctant to go, but most felt they had no choice. What an enormous vacuum they would leave behind, Karim thought sadly.

The next morning, he stood at the door waiting for Amir. The ocean shipment had gone the previous day, his cases were packed, and he was ready to leave. The house was a bare shell with a few pieces of furniture in each room. His mother had insisted on that. 'We might even be back next year!' she'd said cheerfully on the phone when he had called her in the States. He doubted it but agreed with her. It was always easier to agree with *madar djan*.

Tahmineh was predictably distraught when it was time to say goodbye. Karim was upset too. He couldn't remember a time when Tahmineh and Amir had not been in his life. As he hugged her, the enormity of what was happening enveloped him like a huge wave. This was finally it; he had to leave. He could no longer live in his own country and he was here on borrowed time. Eventually the regime would find out about his involvement in the raid on the US embassy and armed guards would show up at his front door and arrest him.

After he and the housekeepers had locked the double front door for the last time, Tahmineh insisted on holding the Koran over his head while she prayed for him to have a safe journey. The gates swung open and a taxi came slowly up the drive and stopped outside the house. The housekeepers climbed into the station wagon he'd given them, waved sadly, and headed out the gate first. His taxi followed, then he pressed the automatic button to close the gates of his home for the last time. He watched as they closed slowly over the final chapter of his life in Tehran. The chapter, he thought ruefully, where he'd met and lost Zahra.

As he was driven to the airport, he consoled himself with the thought that his parents' housekeepers had their lives sorted out. They were going to take over running their family's village shop. There would always be a job with his family, he told them, when they returned to live in Iran. But that was never going to happen, he thought wearily.

Getting through emigration was a gruelling experience. It had cost him quite a lot of cash in 'tips' to be able to take his antique books with him. Finally, every item in his hand luggage was tipped out, rifled through, and pushed to one side.

'Can I go now?' Karim asked, trying to keep the impatient edge from his voice.

'Yes.' The man glanced contemptuously over his shoulder as he walked away. Karim heard him mutter *and good riddance* under his breath.

At last he was on the plane. He settled in his comfortable first-class seat with a sigh, relieved that at least Air France was still flying into and out of Tehran. It was the airline that had flown the Ayatollah Khomeini from Paris to Tehran in February, Karim reflected ruefully. He remembered seeing the cleric being helped down the steps by the Air France captain. How ironic! There was no liberty, equality, or freedom in Iran at the moment.

The jet took off in a high wind and low cloud. He squinted out the window, trying to see familiar landmarks for the last time. He could just make out snow on the higher peaks of the Alborz Mountains. His eyes were riveted on the landscape below as a terrible sadness engulfed him. He had been home for only a couple of months—terrible months. His friend Rashid was dead, his other friends scattered as migrants and refugees to foreign countries. Zahra was out of his life forever. How foolish and impulsive he had been to imagine a future with her. In his heart, he knew his mother would never have accepted her. Zahra had been a companion to his grandmother, but in his mother's eyes she was a servant.

I did care for her, I really did, he thought. *Maybe I'm fatally flawed.* His impulsiveness with women in the distant—and recent—past, he reminded himself, had led to nothing but disaster. His mother could find him a wife now; he knew that's what she wanted to do.

The captain's voice shook him out of his reverie.

'Ladies and gentlemen, our course will take us over the Caspian Sea to take advantage of the tail winds. We will then turn west for Turkey and Eastern Europe and land in Paris in eight hours' time.'

The flight attendant appeared at his side and delivered his coffee. Karim glanced out the window as he sipped it. He blinked in the harsh bright light and caught his breath. They were flying over Ramsar already. Below him the city lay spread out on the edge of the Caspian Sea. The sky had cleared and the water was a brilliant blue. White crested waves broke on the shore. *Goodbye Yasmin,* he whispered.

Thousands of feet below, Yasmin was battling with her broom

against the leaves that kept blowing into the shop. Her boss had told her to go out and clear the footpaths because the customers were complaining. She squinted up at the hard blue sky where the sun caught a silver plane high above her. She knew it was the midday flight leaving Ramsar and bound for Tehran. She watched as the plane turned south. In her imagination, it was an overseas flight and she was on it with Karim. She stopped brushing and indulged in a daydream of walking arm-in-arm with him down a fashionable avenue somewhere in Europe.

She had found the money when she got to her friend's house last week. Karim must have put it in her bag when she was in the shower. It was more than she earned in a year working at the pharmacy. She had felt ashamed, not because it made her feel like a prostitute—it didn't. He had stopped her from being unfaithful, after all. Rather, she was ashamed that she was so delighted to see Karim again. She sighed. *He still cares enough for me to help me out financially*, she thought with a smile.

The children needed new shoes and there was a medical bill for her husband that she couldn't pay. She would make a lamb casserole for them all. She smiled, remembering how Karim had listened so attentively when she told him how things were. She was mesmerised as ever by his beautiful hazel eyes with their flecks of gold. As for the money; she decided to tell her husband that she was owed back-pay or something. She would eke it out gradually, buying them little treats now and then.

'Dignity is a luxury for poor people, Yasmin,' her grandmother had often told her.

In the foothills of the mountains, Yasmin's husband Bijan saw the glint of silver in the sky too. He turned back to digging the vegetable patch using his good arm. His other arm, bandaged from wrist to shoulder, hung useless at his side. Every day he thanked God that

Yasmin had married him, useless and ugly though he was. His family was surprised at the size of the dowry her parents offered. After all, Yasmin was beautiful and had plenty of choices. When her parents approached his parents, everyone was amazed and even more so when Yasmin agreed to marry him at their first meeting. He adored their daughter Emagine, the light of his life. She was born well before their first wedding anniversary, but he didn't care.

Bijan was grateful to Yasmin's employer, the pharmacist, too. He'd stood up to those pumped-up teenagers who called themselves the Revolutionary Guard of Ramsar. Last week, they visited every local shop, throwing their weight around. They told the owners that the new government said women weren't allowed to work and had to stay home. He and Yasmin laughed when she told him how her boss had pointed to the 'ladies personal items' high on a top shelf. He needed women employees to deal with those, the pharmacist said. Yasmin wiped tears of laughter from her eyes when she described the armed teenagers tripping over themselves in their embarrassed rush out of the shop. They never came back.

Bijan thought fondly of his wife and his daughter, with her unusual gold-flecked hazel eyes. They were inherited from a long-dead grandmother, Yasmin had told him. Two years after Emagine's birth, his wonderful son Sadeq was born. Now Yasmin had to work long hours to put food on the table for them all because he was an invalid husband. She never complained—she was the sweetest, most wonderful wife a man could wish for. Bijan nodded to himself; he loved her with all his heart.

———

When Karim changed planes in Paris, he noticed that the sky outside was darkening. It felt like a curtain was being closed on his life. When it reopened, he would be forced to continue with his other life, away from his beloved country for ever.

A flight attendant touched him lightly on the arm. 'Can I get you anything, sir?' she asked.

He looked up. Her eyes were a startling blue.

'Erm ... thank you, no.'

He tipped his seat back and raised the foot rest. It was good to be on the plane with absolutely nothing to do after the workload and stress in Tehran. There was plenty to keep him occupied in New York. For a start, his apartment had been closed up for over two months. Then he had to get back to work with Bahram, his partner in their architectural business. Bahram's latest fax had worried him. The business was slowing down, apparently, and orders had been cancelled with only vague reasons given. Then there was *madar djan*, his mother Esmat. She had phoned him in Tehran before he left. She demanded that he call her immediately when he got to his New York apartment.

10

THE MIGRANT HOSTEL

When the coach stopped at the airport doors where she'd last seen Firzun, Zahra felt sick. He was nowhere in sight now. The only person who got on the coach was Kathy, the immigration officer. Zahra saw her shake her head at the driver. She walked down the aisle and told Zahra that she had asked the police at the airport to keep a look out for him. If he was still missing by tomorrow evening, she would make an official report to the police. Unfortunately, they couldn't wait for her husband any longer, Kathy added. They had to consider the other new arrivals. Zahra nodded mutely.

'You must be exhausted,' Kathy said. 'Let's get you to the hostel and sort out your room.' She paused, looking slightly uncomfortable. 'Zahra, tomorrow morning we will need to ask you more questions about your husband. Just relax now, though.'

'Thank you.'

Relax! How could she do that after what Kathy had just said? What did she mean by 'we'? Were the authorities, the Australian *police,* going to question her? Maybe they were so terrifying that Kathy had taken pity on her and warned her in advance.

She was angry with herself for getting involved in her cousin's dangerous life again. But she had been forced to agree to his crazy plan, she reminded herself, because he had threatened to take her son away. Now she was stuck here, alone, at the other end of the earth. Her life, which could have been so wonderful with Karim, was in ruins.

'Look Mummy!' Ahmad tapped her arm. 'There's Uncle Karim's car!' Ahmad knocked on the window and waved.

A silver sports car, similar to one Karim owned, was meandering slowly through the car park. Was she imagining it or was that Firzun in the passenger seat? No, Firzun was long gone. He had known exactly where he was going when he left her. He had obviously arranged for someone from Nousha's family to pick him up. Maybe even phoned them from somewhere en route. She wondered if his fiancée's family knew about the assassin. *Stupid, stupid me! Why on earth did I trust him?*

She put her hand on Ahmad's arm. 'Uncle Karim isn't here, Ahmad.'

Ahmad watched until the car was out of sight, then sat down suddenly in his seat. Zahra glanced at him. He looked very small and just a little lost.

Kathy's voice on the speaker above her head broke into her thoughts. 'Good evening, everyone, and welcome to Australia. It's seven-thirty on Tuesday 27 November,' she announced. 'I know you've travelled a long way and crossed datelines so I'll keep this short. My name is Kathy Graham and I'm from the Australian Department of Immigration. We're on our way to the Fairy Meadow Migrant Hostel, near a town called Wollongong. It will take us over an hour to get there. Your rooms are ready and there's a hot meal waiting for you.'

'I just want a shower and a bed,' a woman sitting in front of Zahra remarked.

Zahra gripped her hands together in her lap. She hardly dared breathe. What was Kathy going to say next? That 'a husband' had gone missing and if anyone saw him ...

'Please say *yes* when I call your name,' Kathy continued.

To Zahra's relief, when she got to *Ghafoori* Kathy called out 'Zahra and Ahmad'. Zahra answered quickly and turned to look out the window. Thank goodness Kathy didn't call Mahmoud's name.

She realised that the coach had picked up speed. It was now travelling along a wide road. Ahmad stood at the window, mesmerised by the passing cars. Kathy touched her lightly on the arm and she turned away from the window. More questions? Zahra wondered nervously as the woman perched on the seat opposite Zahra.

'Sorry—I have to ask ...' she began slowly. 'Did your husband say anything to you before he left?'

Zahra shook her head. How could she tell Kathy what Firzun had said? An assassin? Who would believe that here? They hadn't experienced a revolution. As for Nousha and her family, Zahra didn't even know their last name. Maybe that was a lie too. Maybe Nousha didn't exist; he might have met someone else entirely.

'We'll do everything we can to find him,' Kathy assured her. 'You and your little boy will be looked after. When we get to the hostel, you can have a shower and something to eat. Then a good night's sleep.'

As Kathy made her way back up the coach, several people stopped her and asked questions. *At least I'm not the only person on the coach with problems.*

'Look to your left everyone,' Kathy said over the microphone. 'We're passing Botany Bay.'

Zahra looked out the window. The reflection of the setting sun dappled the water of an enormous bay. People ambled along the shoreline of the white sandy beach. Young mothers with children were leaving the beach and waiting to cross the road. Ahmad looked up at her and she smiled at his eager face. For a brief second, it crossed Zahra's mind that life without Firzun might not be so bad. Six months ago, she had barely known where Australia was. Now she was here, looking at Australian beaches and suburbs.

Ahmad kneeled on his seat and gazed out the window, eagerly absorbing everything he saw. Surely they would have a better life here than in Afghanistan? she thought. In her own country she had been trapped in a violent marriage. Here in Australia, Ahmad could go to school and learn English.

They would have good food and hopefully one day they'd live in a nice house. The houses they passed looked clean and solid and the people on the footpaths were well-dressed. They didn't look scared like the people in Tehran or poor like so many in Afghanistan. Ahmad smiled at her and sat down. Then he lay across her lap and fell asleep. The coach engine droned and the voices of the other passengers got fainter as Zahra drifted into a doze.

She woke up as the coach slowed at the top of a steep hill and she looked out of the window. Below her was a carpet of glittering lights and the white tinges of surf on the black ocean. The coach began to descend slowly from the plateau and down a winding mountain road.

'Not long now!' Kathy announced brightly.

The low buzz of conversation on the coach got louder. They passed a row of shops, closed now for the night, then the driver swung the vehicle through a wide gateway. He edged it along a lit path bordered by lawns and stopped outside a single-storey brick building. Zahra swallowed hard. *This is it. What will they do to me?*

'Here we are!' the driver announced. 'Don't forget to take all your belongings from the coach. Collect your cases later.'

Zahra waited in line behind the other passengers as they struggled down the steps with their hand luggage. As she got to the top step, a dark-haired man turned around. He picked Ahmad up and lifted him down carefully.

'*Mashallah!*' he said with a smile. 'God protect him,' he repeated in English.

'Thank you, you're very kind.'

'Where are you from?' the man asked as she stepped onto the ground.

'We're from Afghanistan. I speak Persian and English.'

'I thought you might be Turkish like us,' he began. 'Is your husband with you?'

Zahra shook her head. 'No.'

Ahead of them a woman turned and called to him. The man gave Zahra a small bow and joined his wife and family. The Turkish woman turned around again and looked straight at Zahra. She understood the look. It was a warning—keep away from my husband.

So now I'm a single mother with a child and other women think I'm a threat. Zahra gripped her bags to her body. *Firzun has turned me into a social outcast.* But Ahmad was pulling on her hand as if he couldn't wait to start his new life. She followed the group into a large, brightly lit room. Overhead fans did little to clear the stuffiness in the air.

Another wave of anxiety swept over her. Supposing the authorities had found Firzun at the airport and the police escorted him here? Would they be waiting inside the building, standing on either side of her cousin? Waiting to question her? She glanced around anxiously. He wasn't there, of course. He had gone forever this time. She sat down wearily in a plastic chair at the back of the group. Ahmad lay across her knee. His eyes fluttered shut and he sucked his thumb.

Her own eyes kept closing as she listened to the droning voice of a man who introduced himself as Clive, the hostel manager. He told them about meals, room cleaning, and crockery. *I know that word, I can't remember what it means.* While he was talking, Kathy went from person to person collecting passports. The manager assured them their documents would be locked in the hostel safe. Tomorrow they could come and deposit any valuables as well. Finally, Clive handed around an information sheet, then picked up a clipboard and read out names. People shuffled forward and collected their room keys and directions. Zahra was the last person to be called. She shook Ahmad awake.

'Zahra.' Kathy's voice sounded as if it was coming from far away. 'I'll take you to your flat.'

Zahra nodded. She just wanted to sleep.

'I'll take her,' Kathy told the hostel manager as she collected Zahra's keys. 'Can you manage your suitcase, Zahra?'

Zahra picked it up and followed Kathy wearily down a paved path. Ahead of her she could just make out some low brown brick buildings. Tall trees cast shadows across a lawn at the side of the path. Her suitcase felt heavier and heavier as she walked. A breeze sprang up and the cool evening air revived her. Kathy stopped suddenly at a door and unlocked it.

'Here we are! Number five,' she announced brightly as she opened the door. 'You've got an English family next door.'

She waved her hand in front of her face as a blast of hot air escaped from the room.

'Phew! It must have been closed up for a while.'

Zahra stood uncertainly on the threshold and looked inside at the bare brick walls that still held the heat of the day. Kathy strode across the black and white tiled floor and opened a window on the opposite wall. The cool breeze filled the room, stirring the thin curtains.

'Come in, come in ...' Kathy encouraged. 'This is your new home. Put your things down and I'll show you around.'

Zahra put her luggage on the floor near a large cupboard. Before she had time to take in her surroundings, Kathy beckoned her to follow down a passageway to the left of the front door.

'You've got two bedrooms, a single one here ... then a double, and a bathroom,' she announced, pushing open doors.

'There's no kitchen—it's a fire hazard. But you've a little sink there, an electric jug, and some cups. All meals are in the dining room near the administration block.' Kathy waved her hand in the direction of the door. 'The meal times are on your information sheet. They're still serving dinner if you're hungry.'

'I don't think we'll ...' Zahra answered, longing to be alone with Ahmad.

'About tomorrow ...' Kathy went on. 'As I said, someone will want to talk to you about your husband.'

'The police?'

'Er ...' The other woman hesitated. 'Maybe just someone from the Immigration Department, for the moment.'

She handed Zahra her door keys.

'I'll fix up a meeting. Is eleven o'clock okay? Go to the administration block, where we've just been.' She pointed out of the window. 'I can organise an interpreter for you if you'd like.'

Zahra thought quickly—she didn't want anyone else involved in her private life.

She shook her head. 'Thank you, but my English is good enough.'

'There's a kindergarten where you can leave your little boy.' Kathy opened the door and smiled again. 'I'm sure we'll find your husband. I won't see you tomorrow—I'm on airport pickups. Well, goodnight and welcome to Australia.' She shook Zahra's hand. With another smile she closed the door.

Zahra stared at the door. *So much information!*

'I've found my bed, Mummy!'

Ahmad pulled her into the first bedroom. It was sparsely furnished with two single beds, a night table, and a small wardrobe. She turned back the green and blue striped top cover and sniffed. The linen smelled clean and fresh. She pressed the mattress; it was hard and didn't give under her hand. She lifted the bottom sheet to find the mattress was covered in thick olive-green vinyl.

Ahmad emptied the contents of his backpack on to one of the beds and threw his parka off. She left him rummaging through his things and looked in the double bedroom. The mattress was as hard as the one on Ahmad's bed. Night tables with small lamps stood on either side of the bed. There was a wardrobe and a woven rug like the one in the other room.

Back in the living room, Zahra had a quick look through the spyhole in the front door. What if she saw Firzun out there in the silent grounds? Or the assassin, Ali Esmaeili? She saw a few people walking toward a brightly lit building. Europeans, she thought thankfully. She turned and looked again at her new flat. It was sparsely but adequately furnished. The big cupboard that she opened gingerly was a wardrobe with drawers underneath. She recoiled from the strong smell of disinfectant.

Ahmad was bouncing his bottom on the yellow vinyl couch that stood against the wall. 'It's very nice,' he told her.

He put his cars on the coffee table in front of the couch and continued to explore the room.

'Look, we've got a table!' He pulled out one of the chairs and sat down, running his hand across the green Formica surface.

'I've found some biscuits, Ahmad.' She handed him a packet, which he opened carefully. Zahra looked through the other things in the sink area. A white ceramic jug with a blue lid sat on a shelf next to the small sink unit. Curious about the jug, she flicked open the lid, surprised to see an electric element in the base. Inside the tiny fridge she found two bottles of water and a small carton of milk. Next to the basket of biscuits was another with teabags, sachets of sugar, and instant coffee. She picked up one of the green cups from the shelf below the sink.

'Crockery!' The forgotten word came back to her.

Ahmad came up to her. 'I had a wee-wee,' he announced.

She took him back to the bathroom and helped him wash his hands with the piece of hard soap in the washbasin. The bathroom, with its utilitarian white tiles, seemed tiny after the one she'd had in Karim's house. Shower, toilet, and basin were all crammed into a long narrow space. She touched the rough bath and hand towels that were neatly folded over a rail. Catching sight of her face in the mirror, she was shocked. *I look terrible!* She ran her hands over her face and patted the dark shadows under her eyes.

'Where's cousin Firzun?' Ahmad asked as he dried his hands.

'He's gone away for a while.'

Ahmad said nothing and ran ahead of her into the living room, jumping over the small rug with both feet. She filled the heavy jug and made tea for them in the green cups, letting Ahmad eat all the biscuits.

She wouldn't go to the dining room tonight. She couldn't face a mass of strangers, she thought as she took their nightclothes out of her small bag. The big case could wait till tomorrow.

She was dropping with exhaustion by the time she finished showering Ahmad and put him to bed. He fell asleep instantly. She showered and got into the other single bed. If Ahmad woke up alone in a strange room in the middle of the night she knew he'd be frightened. He had never slept in a room by himself in all his short life.

Although she was desperately tired, Zahra couldn't sleep. Incidents from the past two months chased through her mind. Her main thoughts were of Karim, of being held securely in his arms. But Karim already belonged to another place, another time. Now she had to face an uncertain future alone with her son. Surely it couldn't be worse than her life had been in Afghanistan with Mahmoud?

Tomorrow another ordeal lay ahead. The authorities were going to question her in English about Firzun. She had to remember to call him Mahmoud, the name he had used to enter Australia. She had to get her story straight, to pretend she had no idea why her husband had abandoned her. *I mustn't say anything about the assassin. No one would believe that for a minute.* And if they did believe her, the Immigration Department would alert the Australian police. Then they might suspect she was covering up for her husband.

Firzun was a stupid, risk-taking fool! Why had he left her? What was going on? She sat up in her hard little bed. She was wide awake and her mind crystal clear. He had arranged to be picked up. It had crossed her mind before, but now she was certain. He'd had every intention of dumping her from the minute they'd left Iran. The story about the assassin was rubbish! As usual there was another agenda.

Surely, he wasn't stupid enough to bring drugs into Australia?

He'd denied it at the airport, but had anything he'd said been the truth? She knew he had a supplier in Afghanistan. She knew about the opium resin he'd smuggled into Iran when they had crossed the border in the old van. She'd found it herself, hidden in boxes of fruit. *Is that why he dumped me at the airport? Is that why the authorities want to question me? But they'd searched him and let him go.* Zahra clenched her fists. *I must keep calm tomorrow. I mustn't let the Immigration people have an inkling of this—they might think I'm a drug smuggler too.* She lay down on her hard pillow, trying to block her feelings of dread about the coming day.

11

NEW YORK

Karim pushed open the door of his New York apartment and stood
back for the concierge's assistant to drag his luggage across the
threshold. He waited in the entrance while the man took his cases
into the bedroom. Shafts of morning sunshine filled the room and
caught swirling dust motes in its beams. He thanked and tipped the
assistant. After he'd closed the heavy door, Karim slipped off his
shoes and walked along the short passage into the sunlit room.

He'd been surprised to hear from the captain's announcement
that the temperature in New York was expected to climb to sixty-six
degrees Fahrenheit. He crossed to one of the high rectangular
windows and opened it. A temperature like that was almost unheard
of in New York at the end of November. He'd expected snow and
Santas. Instead, as he looked out across Central Park, he saw bare-
headed early morning joggers and cyclists in light jackets and sweat
pants.

He turned away from the window and ran his hand abstractedly
across the keys of his baby grand piano, reflecting that it was almost
as good as the one he'd donated to the Conservatorium of Music in
Tehran. He smiled to himself as he looked around the familiar room.

When he was a student, he'd spent many happy weekends here with his Uncle Cyrus. His mother's brother had lived in the States since he was a young man. Karim missed his uncle—fifty-seven was too young to die. Like Karim, his uncle had been married and divorced in his twenties and never remarried. *Will that be my fate, too?* Karim wondered. Last month he had turned thirty-four. He had a string of affairs and a disastrous marriage behind him and now he was alone.

He was glad that his housekeeper had lit a fire in the fireplace despite the mild temperature. It made the place much more welcoming to a homecoming single traveller. He smiled up at his uncle's portrait and greeted him.

'Hi Uncle, I'm back. Thanks for leaving me this place in your will.'

His uncle had loved Persian carpets. 'They remind me of home,' he used to tell his nephew. The most spectacular one was in this room. Cyrus had had it specially made in Isfahan and shipped over to New York. Karim stepped onto it and curled his toes into the pile, admiring how the light picked out the sheen of the silk and the bright blues and reds. He sank down in one of the large leather sofas facing the opposite wall where the bare trees of Central Park were reflected in the large gilt mirror. He should be happy, he told himself, but he wasn't. He was miserable and restless and he missed Zahra.

She would have loved this apartment, he reflected, especially the small library with its divan sofas. Karim got up and padded restlessly from room to room. He had refurbished his bedroom in his own style. The white walls were a perfect background for the vibrant colours of the modern paintings. His large bed stood on a bright red Persian carpet on the stripped wooden floor. Cy had approved heartily. When his uncle died, Karim kept this smaller room, leaving Cy's larger bedroom and another room for guests.

His housekeeper Rusika had folded away his summer clothes in the closet. Now piles of woollen sweaters were stacked neatly on shelves. He showered quickly and changed from his travelling clothes into jeans and a sweatshirt. Rusika liked to unpack his suit-cases. She got annoyed if he did it and messed up her system. He opened his hand luggage and gently took out the rare books from his library in Tehran. He carried them through the apartment and put them on the shelves of his New York library. He touched a few of the spines and felt sad. These books, he thought mournfully, repre-sented his homeland ... and his identity.

He wandered into the small galley kitchen—he didn't cook much, and if he wasn't going out, he ordered his meals from the restaurant in the basement of his building. *I'll have to get used to eating alone again.* It was a dreary thought. His bachelor uncle had rarely entertained and the original dining room had become the library.

While he made himself a cup of coffee, Karim's thoughts strayed again to Zahra and what might have been. They would have lived together in this apartment with little Ahmad. He could have taken Ahmad across to the park at the weekends. He'd intended to enrol Ahmad in a kindergarten to learn English. He would have paid for him to go to a good school. *How close I came to remarrying!* He thought of his first wife Nancy. She'd calculated the value of the apartment and its contents in one glance when she'd first seen it.

Karim carried his coffee into the living room. Before he could sit down, the phone rang.

'Hello, Kar ...'

'Karim *djan*, I'm so glad you got here safely,' Esmat interrupted. To his surprise, his usually controlled mother sounded relieved. 'I wish you'd called me sooner. I was so worried ...'

'I was just about to, *madar djan*.'

'I'm coming to New York to see you,' she announced. 'It's very boring in Boston.'

'When?'

'Tomorrow. Your sister Soraya is driving. We're going Christmas shopping and we'll stay with you. Tell your housekeeper to make up the beds.'

He assured her he would. He didn't bother asking why his sister and mother, nominally Muslim, needed to do Christmas shopping. It was a waste of his energy.

His mother questioned him briefly about his exit from Iran and his flight. He could tell she was only half listening to his answers and she interrupted him mid-sentence.

'Good, we'll be there at about midday.' She paused and her voice softened. 'I'm glad you got here safely, son.'

'So am I, Mother. Take care. Love you.'

As he walked back to the kitchen with his empty coffee cup, he thought of how much he had missed his easy-going sister. There were some good things about leaving Tehran, he reflected as he rinsed his cup and left it to drain. His mother had suggested a few times that he modernise his kitchen, but he liked the polished wooden cupboards and black and white tiled floor.

He glanced at his watch, surprised that it was already eleven in the morning. That meant it was seven in the evening in Tehran, and the following day in Sydney. He felt spaced-out, tired, and restless after his long flight. He decided to get out of the apartment and try to shake off his jetlag. He pulled on his leather jacket and his favourite boots and headed for the elevator.

'Nice day, sir. Very mild for the end of November,' the uniformed doorman of his building commented. Karim smiled and nodded, blinking in the bright daylight.

The traffic noise assaulted his ears after the cocooned silence of his apartment. Was it really the end of the month? What had happened to November? What had happened *in* November? Drama, that's what. Firzun's abortive attempt to free the American hostages from their embassy. His beloved grandmother had died. Finally, he reflected as he walked along in the sunshine, he'd fallen in love with a married Afghan woman. She'd become a widow, and then within days her husband had resurrected himself. Karim had left his own country, Iran, for good because he disliked—no, loathed the people running it. Hopefully December would be quieter.

He turned out of his building on Central Park West and walked toward Columbus Circle. The mild weather had brought people out in droves. A tour bus passed him and people on the top deck snapped pictures of the apartment buildings. A sudden wave of desperation and sadness swept over him. Zahra's face was always with him—her beautiful expressive face, her almond-shaped dark eyes with their long lashes. She wouldn't look at him at the airport. When she had glanced over her shoulder at him, he had been sure that Firzun had coerced, or more likely, threatened her into leaving with him.

His mind had wandered so much that he was surprised to find himself at Columbus Circle and being swept across the road by the Christmas crowds. He didn't want to be anywhere near shops or shoppers. Ignoring the red-robed Santa who rang a handbell as he passed, he headed for the gates of Central Park.

The vegetation was wintery in spite of the warm day; the trees had long since shed their leaves but the grass was still green. Tourists were getting into horse-drawn carriages for a trip around the park. He strolled past rock ledges where kids climbed and shrieked. He slowed down when he saw an old lady sitting on a bench reading a book. In his confused state he thought it was his grandmother, Rezvan Khanoum. He started to walk toward her, then stopped suddenly, feeling foolish when she looked up. Of course it wasn't his grandmother—she had died in Tehran a month ago.

He turned away and walked along the road, feeling as if a fog had descended on his brain. He forced himself to look around, to breathe in the fresh air. Then an image of Firzun came into his head. His rage toward the other man threatened to engulf him. He thought again of his last sight of Zahra at Tehran Airport and Firzun's smirking face. He wished he'd given in to his impulse to hit him.

'Hey, watch out!'

The front wheel of a bicycle hit his right leg, but he kept his balance and stepped quickly onto the footpath. The female cyclist wasn't so lucky. Karim turned back, brushing his jeans. The rider had come off her bike and was struggling under it.

'I'm so sorry! Are you all right?'

He ran to help her to her feet. Her beret had fallen off and her crinkly red hair flew wildly round her face.

'No, I'm not! Where the hell did you come from?'

'Sorry, I just didn't see you.'

'It's okay. Get the bike, would you? I think I've sprained my ankle or something.'

He picked the bike up from the gutter and looked at the rider. She was in her early twenties, he thought. Her face was pale and she pressed her lips together in pain. She was standing on one leg and balancing the toes of her left foot tentatively on the ground.

'I think I've twisted my ankle. Can I lean on your shoulder?' she said, biting her lip.

'Sure. May I?'

She nodded as he put his arm around her back and helped her onto the footpath. She kept her injured foot off the ground, then tested it gingerly.

She smelled good, Karim noticed, and her hair brushed his cheek as she leaned against him. He was careful to keep his supporting hand only lightly on her slim waist.

'Look, I'm really sorry,' Karim repeated. 'I'm a bit jetlagged.'

'I thought you were the damned Phantom, appearing from nowhere like that. Ouch!' she exclaimed as her foot touched the ground.

He helped her toward a nearby bench, guiding the bicycle with difficulty using his left hand. As she sat down, their eyes met briefly. Hers were light green and she was frowning with pain. He was relieved that after she'd sat down, the colour came back slowly into her pale face, making it glow pink.

'You have really unusual coloured eyes!' She smiled at him again. 'Where're you from?'

'I'm from Iran—Persia. I'm Persian.'

'Oh wow, Iran! Has anyone harassed you in the street yet?'

He shrugged. 'I only flew in this morning. How's the ankle?'

'Not so bad.' She tapped her sneaker gently on the ground.

'Stay there for a few minutes,' he suggested. 'Is this a hire bike?'

'Yes, from over there.' She pointed to a green-painted shed near the entrance gates.

He returned the bike and came back with the deposit. She was still sitting on the bench and had rolled her sock down to inspect her ankle.

'You'll need to get some ice on it,' Karim said as he handed her the money. 'Do you live nearby?'

'No, but I can get a cab home. It's not a problem.'

Her green eyes met his again. She smiled—an American smile of perfect white teeth. When he'd helped her to her feet, he was surprised that she was almost at his eye level.

'My name's Lauren O'Rourke.' She pulled off a glove and extended her hand. 'I'm a psychologist—I just graduated,' she added.

Her smooth hands were fine-boned and the nails were painted a delicate shade of pink. Her handshake was firm and confident. He doubted that she had much experience as a psychologist. She couldn't have been more than twenty-three years old.

'Karim Konari, erm, architect,' he answered.

It felt good to smile again at a woman. The regime in Iran had all but forbidden any contact with women, even smiling.

'Karim,' she repeated and raised her eyebrows slightly as he released her hand. 'Karim, from Persia.'

He nodded. 'I'm afraid it's not a good place for Americans at the moment,' he said apologetically.

'No, I guess not.' She leaned forward and brushed specks of dust off the bottom of her jeans and drew her green jacket closer into her body.

'Could I buy you ... I mean, would you like a coffee?' he asked. 'Can you make it across the street to a coffee shop?'

She hesitated, then smiled again.

'You know what, Karim? I'd love a coffee. I may need help getting up from here and crossing the road though.'

He extended his arm and she pulled herself up. Linking her arm unselfconsciously through his she let him take the lead. She was still limping and she leaned lightly on him as they waited for the lights to change. He felt his body relax as if a huge burden was slowly sliding away. He looked sideways at Lauren.

She reminded him of Nancy. His ex-wife had had the same air of confidence. But he didn't want to remember *her* right now. He just wanted to live in the moment with this woman, Lauren, hanging on to his arm at the cross-walk as if she'd known him all her life.

'I know a place nearby where they make really good coffee,' he said.

'McDonald's? Surely not! You're wearing handmade boots if I'm not mistaken.'

He laughed. 'Give me credit for a bit of class.'

People often missed this French restaurant, he told her. It was an old-fashioned type with lace curtains at the windows. She smiled at him again as they took their places at a small white-clothed table. Karim didn't miss the look the waiter flicked over him. When the other man addressed her by name and spoke in French, he realised she was a regular customer. She answered almost reluctantly in the same language but quickly switched to English.

'Just coffee, Jean-Claude, *Merci*.'

Karim looked up at the waiter. 'Madam has twisted her ankle. Could you bring us some ice?'

'Certainly, sir.' The waiter returned quickly with a soft ice pack. He fussed around Lauren as she put her foot on a chair. Karim removed his scarf and secured the ice pack around her ankle with it.

'I spent a year in Paris before college. I get kind of good service here,' she half apologised.

Karim nodded but said nothing. Her father ran an import-export business, she went on. She left Karim in the dark about exactly what was being imported and exported. He noticed she wasn't wearing any rings.

She saw his glance and said hurriedly, 'Almost. He was a nice guy, with an unpleasant mother. He broke my heart,' she concluded with a half-smile. 'So, what about you?'

'Divorced, no kids,' he replied.

He told her how things were in his country—the repressive regime, the withdrawal of basic rights, the arrests. And now the American hostage situation.

'I studied at MIT, and I've lived in the States on and off for eight years, since I was twenty-five. I had to go home for family business,' he explained.

He told her he didn't want to live in Iran under the present regime and that his family had emigrated as well.

'It's good you've got family here,' she replied. 'Everyone needs family support if they can get it. Things sure sound bad in your country.'

He kept everything as general as he could as he related snippets of his life in Tehran. While he was speaking, he could see Zahra in his mind's eye—choosing a book in the library, walking out the front gate with Ahmad. He remembered observing her covertly as she read to his grandmother in her perfect Persian. Already Tehran felt like a foreign place, where people did things differently. If he ever saw Lauren again, Karim decided, he might tell her more. But for now, this was enough.

She listened attentively, her foot still propped on a chair. She'd passed her coat to the waiter to hang up for her and removed her beret. In this light, he thought, she looked like a woman in a Pre-Raphaelite painting. Her auburn hair fell forward over her shoulders. He noticed that the tips touched the nipples of her breasts, which swelled beneath the pale green sweater she was wearing. He could imagine her playing tennis in the summer and skiing expertly in the winter. Things he used to do before he became an alien in his own country, and maybe eventually in hers. She came from a wealthy family like his, he realised. Like his *used* to be.

As they talked, he relaxed back into his American persona. Lauren chatted about familiar places, plays and movies they'd both seen. He felt as if his Persian self was slowly drifting away as it always did. His Persian soul was only revitalised when he saw his family or old friends from home. But for now, he had to put on his American identity cloak and speak English. After all, he was a graduate of MIT. He had spent the last eight years of his life working here as well as in Iran. His ex-wife was American. Now he wondered if his recent application for citizenship would be rejected because of his nationality. He looked across the table at Lauren.

'So, are you going to tell me about the bad guy who broke your heart?'

She stirred her coffee, then shrugged. 'Why not?'

They had met two years ago, and his name was Max, she began. He was an art dealer and a few years older than her. He came from a very old family, very *prestigious*. His ancestors from way back were Dutch, early settlers in the New World—when New York was New Amsterdam. The wedding had been arranged for the following spring, April 1980. Then out of the blue, something happened; he broke off the engagement and got a job in Europe.

'I think his Mom was *really* happy. She never liked me, or my family,' Lauren ended bitterly.

'Mothers can be very powerful,' Karim commented.

'When you trust someone, that's when it hurts the most.' She looked across at him and held his gaze. 'You really *do* have the most remarkable eyes. You know, like honey flecked with gold.' She smiled. 'I guess plenty of women have told you that.'

The comment rang a warning bell in his brain. It was exactly what Yasmin had whispered to him when they were teenage lovers. *Karim djan, you have flecks of moonlight in your eyes.*

'So, you're alone in New York?' Lauren continued when he didn't reply.

She was wrong, he thought. He had plenty of friends in New York, and family in Boston. Though the only person he really wanted to be here would never arrive. So yes, he was alone.

'Do you like music?' Karim asked, wanting to move the conversation away from himself.

'Sure.' She sat up straighter in her chair. 'Have you heard of Youri Egorov, the Russian pianist?'

Karim nodded.

'Well, he's performing at Carnegie Hall soon.' Lauren smiled.

'Really? The guy who defected from the Soviet Union?' Karim asked, and she nodded. 'I saw his debut concert at the Lincoln Centre last January.'

'So did I!' Lauren exclaimed. 'We were at the same concert, how about that! I've got a spare ticket for his concert on 19 December. I'd love you to come ...' She stopped abruptly. 'I'm sorry, we've just met, forget I said that.'

'I'll be there,' Karim heard himself say. 'Just give me your number.'

He reached into his wallet and slid his business card across the table. She gave him hers. Their two cards crossed halfway. Like ships in the night, he thought. Maybe, he reflected, his personal ship was about to change course.

12

FAIRY MEADOW MIGRANT HOSTEL

Zahra opened her eyes the next morning and stared at the ceiling, trying to remember where she was. In a sudden rush she remembered the events of the previous day. Firzun had abandoned her at the airport! She was alone with Ahmad in a migrant hostel in a place called Fairy Meadow, in Australia. She sat up suddenly—she was going to be interviewed today by the authorities. They'd want to know where Firzun had gone. But what could she tell them? She had no idea where he was. She got out of bed, opened the curtains a fraction and peered out. The bedroom faced some trees and an open lawn area, which was dappled with early morning sunlight. A flock of white parrots with yellow crests screeched and swooped overhead, startling her. When she opened the curtain, the room was suddenly flooded with sunshine. Through the trees she could see the administration building where she was going to be interviewed later that morning. She felt sick with anxiety.

She left Ahmad sleeping while she showered then dressed quickly in light cotton pants and a long-sleeved floral blouse. Her fingers shook as she fastened the buttons, and when she looked in the mirror her reflection stared back at her, anxious and exhausted.

She took a deep breath, tied her hair back, and dabbed some make-up on her pale face.

Her thoughts were running in circles. With no husband, would the authorities here send her back to Afghanistan? At the airport that's all she could think of—to run home. But she knew it wouldn't be that easy. Where would she live in her home city? Her husband Mahmoud had rented out their small apartment and she had no proof that he was dead. The authorities in Afghanistan wouldn't believe she was a widow unless she had a death certificate. She knew that Firzun's mother, her Aunt Mina, would slam the door in her face as she'd done many times before. She wouldn't be welcomed back into the family house. Mina would think Zahra had run away from Mahmoud and brought disgrace on the family. So Zahra would live in limbo in Afghanistan, a widow who had never buried her husband. She wouldn't be able to remarry. There was nothing and no one there for her back home, she thought despondently.

She wondered whether to contact Karim at his sister's address in the US. But if she told Karim what had happened, he probably wouldn't want anything to do with her either. She'd lied to him after all, initially when she'd pretended to be married and later when she'd found out Firzun was alive.

Her total possessions amounted to less than two hundred American dollars. She'd spent some money on make-up in Singapore at Leila's insistence. She had some gold jewellery and a few gold coins. She had Iranian money, but that would be worthless in this affluent Western country. What could she do? Beg the authorities to let her stay in Australia? Why would they do that? She would be a drain on their society, a deserted woman with a son. If they did find Firzun, they'd probably put him in prison for deserting her. That's if the 'assassin' didn't find him first.

Zahra felt mentally wrung out by the time they were ready to go to the dining room for breakfast. She opened the front door and closed it again. She had no idea where the dining room was. When Kathy had shown her to her flat last night, she'd waved vaguely toward the window and said, 'The dining room's over there.' But where?

'Can I play with that boy?' Ahmad asked from where he was standing at the window.

Zahra glanced out. A young couple and their son were walking along the path in the sunshine. All she had to do was follow the other people and she would find the dining room. She opened the door again cautiously, then stepped back inside. She just didn't have the nerve to meet all the other people in the hostel. *We have to eat,* she admonished herself. She tried again, got Ahmad to go first, then pulled the door shut behind her. A few people were strolling along and a couple of them smiled and said good morning. Trying to look confident, Zahra took Ahmad's hand and followed them.

When they got to the huge sun-filled dining room, it was noisy and busy. Zahra watched what the other people did and picked up a tray. Above the place where the food was being served she noticed a portrait of the Queen of England. She was puzzled—was Australia still a British colony? She didn't think so.

She selected fruit, toast, and tea, and milk for her son. Ahmad insisted on getting a bowl of multi-coloured loops. She found a table a long way from everyone else in the cavernous space. She didn't want to mix with the other residents. She was sure everyone knew about her already: the woman whose husband had dumped her at the airport.

She watched Ahmad as he ate, and the food and hot tea restored her spirits a little.

'Excuse me.' A young woman pulled out a chair at their table and sat down. 'Are you Mrs Zahra Ghafoori?'

'Yes,' she replied nervously. *Who on earth is this?*

'Hello, Ahmad!' The young woman smiled at him, then turned to Zahra.

'Do you speak some English, Zahra?'

'Yes, I do.'

'I'm Leanne, the kindergarten supervisor. We're expecting Ahmad at kindergarten this morning while you have your interview.'

Did everyone know everything here? Zahra thought nervously. 'He can't speak any English ...' she began.

'We'll manage,' Leanne said. 'Just tell him we've got lots of trucks and trains and a toy house.'

When she told Ahmad that he was going to kindergarten, he looked worried.

'I want to stay with you, Mummy.'

Leanne understood Ahmad's anxiety. 'He'll be fine!' she assured Zahra. 'If he's got a backpack or a favourite toy, he can bring that. The kindy's next to the administration block. See you later.'

Leanne was right, Ahmad loved the kindergarten as soon as he saw it. After she'd signed him in, Zahra helped him hang his Mickey Mouse backpack on a peg with a picture of a kangaroo. She lingered with him as long as she could. Before she left, she hugged her son hard, then checked her watch. It was still only nine-thirty and her interview was at eleven o'clock.

She walked slowly back to her flat and unpacked her suitcase, stowing their things in the disinfected wardrobe and the drawers below. By then, the time had crawled round to ten-thirty. She wandered through the sparsely furnished flat, made their beds, and went into the bathroom. When she checked her make-up in the mirror, she stared at her face for a long time. She looked like she felt —wretched. She looked at the time again and took a deep breath. It was still early but she decided to go anyway.

As she walked along the path to the administration building, she clenched her fists nervously. What were they going to ask her? She would stick to the truth as much as she could and say that her 'husband' Mahmoud had abandoned her and Ahmad at Sydney Airport. She didn't know why and she didn't know where he was.

She pushed open the glass door into the reception area, surprised to see a few other people milling round the reception desk. They looked worried too and were asking questions of one of the clerks. When Zahra walked slowly up to the counter and gave her name, another young clerk consulted an appointment book on the desk in front of her.

'Take a seat, Mrs Ghafoori. They're on their way.' She smiled.

Zahra sat down on one of the chairs in the waiting area, trying to pull her thoughts together. All she could think about was that she was about to tell a string of lies. Her head ached and her mouth felt dry.

She looked up when she heard the outside door click open. A man and woman came in, deep in conversation with each other. The woman was wearing a pale grey suit with a white shirt. Her blond hair fell across her face as she talked to the man and she pushed it back impatiently. The balding man was also formally dressed in a dark suit, striped shirt, and tie. The sight of them made Zahra feel sick with dread. They were probably her interlocutors, looking both formal and formidable. At least they weren't wearing uniforms or carrying guns, she thought.

The pair didn't notice her. They said something to the clerk, who indicated Zahra. The blonde woman nodded without turning around, and Zahra watched as the couple disappeared into an office behind the reception desk. She tried to breathe deeply to slow her thumping heart.

'Won't be long now,' the clerk called out to her.

Zahra swallowed and smiled. She tried to say 'thank you', but no words came out. She picked up a magazine from the low table in front of her and leafed through the pages.

'Mrs Ghafoori?' The clerk beckoned her toward the office. 'They're ready to see you now. This way, please.'

Zahra got up reluctantly and followed the woman. A headache throbbed behind her eyes and her legs felt shaky.

'Can I get you a drink of water or something?' the clerk asked.

'Yes, water, thank you.'

She was ushered into the small room where the smartly dressed couple sat behind a large desk.

'Good morning, please take a seat Mrs Ghafoori,' the blonde woman said, indicating an upright chair.

Zahra sat down hesitantly. The empty wooden desk stretched like a desert between them. When the clerk put a glass of water in front of her, she picked it up and took a sip. *Are they watching me? Can they see my hand shaking?*

'Well, Mrs Ghafoori er ... can I call you Zahra?' The woman rushed on without waiting for an answer. 'My name's Sally Hosking and this is my colleague Greg Frost. We're from the Australian Department of Immigration. We are here to ask you a few questions about your husband Mahmoud Ghafoori.'

Zahra nodded. She put the glass down and waited.

She heard the door open behind her and a delicate floral perfume filled the room. Another woman sat on a seat next to her. She greeted the two people behind the desk, then turned to Zahra and introduced herself as Caroline, the Migrant Women's Liaison Officer.

'I'm a social worker,' she said with a smile. 'My job is to help and advise the women who live here in the hostel.'

The compassionate look on Caroline's face relaxed Zahra a little.

'If you get upset, or if you don't understand something, let me know and we can stop the interview,' she said gently.

'Thank you.' Zahra nodded. The feeling of dread in her chest rose slowly into her throat.

Greg looked straight at her. 'You said you don't need an interpreter, Mrs Ghafoori—Zahra, is that correct?'

'Yes, I taught English in Afghanistan.'

Her hands felt damp and clammy and she wiped them surreptitiously on her trousers. *Just start the questions and let me go. Firzun put me in this position,* she thought angrily. *He must have known the authorities would question me about his disappearance.* She looked at the two people opposite. They were consulting a folder that lay open on the desk between them.

I've only been in this country for a day and they've got a folder about me! Do they know about Firzun and his covert activities in Iran? Have the Iranian authorities been in touch with them?

'Can you tell us your full name please?' The woman's voice broke into her thoughts.

'Zahra Ghafoori.'

'Thank you, and the full name of your husband and son.'

I must remember not to say Firzun's name! Firzun is Mahmoud. I must not slip up.

'Mahmoud Ghafoori and Ahmad Ghafoori.'

The questions came quickly. How long had she been married? What was her husband's job? Did they have any quarrels at home, fights maybe? Zahra felt nervous, not sure of how much they knew. Did they know about Mahmoud's violence? But how could they? They asked if he had another wife—she wasn't sure if they meant his previous wife. No, they wanted to know if he had two wives living in the same house.

'I am his second wife. His first wife died.'

'What I'm asking,' Sally said gently, 'is whether he has a wife here in Australia.'

'No, I'm sure he didn't ... hasn't.'

Well, that's the truth. But maybe Firzun has a wife here, not a fiancée.

She felt alarmed when they produced her passport and Ahmad's and flicked through them.

The hostel manager must have taken the passports out of the safe and handed them over. When they questioned the Russian stamps, she told them about the Soviet military checkpoint. They asked if she had ever been to the Soviet Union. Were they suggesting she was a communist? Should she tell them the truth? She was hiding in the back of the van with Ahmad when they crossed the border. How would that sound? She looked up; they were watching her, waiting for an answer.

'I've never been to the Soviet Union,' she said.

'And the other stamps?'

'We went through three checkpoints: Afghan, Iranian, and one manned by Soviet guards.'

Her questioners exchanged glances but said no more on the subject.

'So,' Sally pushed back her hair and consulted the folder, 'you arrived in Australia yesterday evening with your husband and son. When you got to the arrivals area at Sydney Airport. your husband ...' she looked down again, 'Mahmoud, walked away and you haven't seen him since. Is that correct?'

'Yes,' Zahra replied.

They asked again if she knew why he had left her. Had he met anyone at the airport? Did she know where her husband was? Sydney ... Melbourne? She repeated that she didn't know.

'Did he ever talk to you about friends in Sydney?' Sally asked in her quiet voice.

'No, I don't know if he has friends here.'

He has, but I don't know Nousha's family name.

'Are you sure?' Greg asked.

Zahra thought quickly. Firzun had mentioned once that Nousha and her family had lived in a migrant hostel for a time. Was it this one? Could they trace Nousha if Zahra told them about her? Greg repeated the question more sharply. Zahra lied to him. She didn't know if her husband had friends in Australia. They both regarded her silently across the desk. *They don't believe me,* she thought nervously. She took a sip of water from the glass. It felt slippery and her hand was still shaking. She put the glass down carefully on the desk as they continued to watch her.

'Zahra, how did you get to Iran from Afghanistan?' Sally asked.

'My husband hired a van and a driver. We crossed the border at night.'

Her voice wavered and her lungs contracted. She would never forget the man who had peered into the back of the van at the border. More memories came flooding back: Ahmad falling into a crater; Mahmoud's pale dead face; the shifty driver and the terror she'd felt when she found the drugs hidden in the apple boxes. These people had no idea. They could never imagine how awful it had been.

'Okay,' Sally replied brightly. 'Was your husband involved in any illegal activities in Tehran?'

What do they know?

'I don't know.'

'You don't know? But didn't you live together in the same house?' Greg affected surprise.

Zahra's stomach turned over. Had they caught her out? She was sure they knew something and were just playing games. They carried on with their questions, about friends in Tehran and why they'd gone there in the first place. They asked again about the border crossing. Finally, they got to the point.

'Were there any drugs in the van, Zahra? Opium for example, or hashish?'

Greg looked directly at her across the desk when he asked the question. Her stomach lurched. They suspected that Firzun had smuggled drugs into Australia. They believed he had left her because of that. She was sure he had, but did they know anything? She forced herself to stay calm, to act stupid.

They returned to their questions about drug smuggling across the border into Iran. Even when she told them she knew nothing, they came at the question from a different angle. Had she ever found drugs in their home? Had she seen her husband taking drugs?

'You know that the Australian government paid your fares to come here as refugees?' Sally said suddenly. Zahra shook her head.

'If your husband is convicted of importing drugs, he or you will have to repay your airfares,' Greg told her. 'He will also be imprisoned and may be deported when he's released. If you are found with drugs in your possession, you will also be arrested and charged by the police.'

She was terrified. Arrested and charged? If they put her in

prison, what would happen to Ahmad? Tears rose in her throat. They would take him away from her, put him in an orphanage. She'd had the same fears in Iran, and now she was in Australia still worrying about Ahmad being taken from her.

Greg was looking at her keenly. *He's thinks I'm a dumb refugee woman with a controlling husband,* she thought, trying to swallow her tears. *Let him think that.* They asked her why her husband had chosen to come to Australia.

'I don't know,' she replied nervously, reaching for a tissue and blowing her nose.

'I think she needs a break,' the welfare worker interrupted.

'All right, give her a minute,' Greg said impatiently.

Caroline handed Zahra more tissues and told her to have a drink. Zahra was too scared to ask what would happen to Ahmad if the police arrested her. They might think she was guilty.

'Look, why don't we get to the point?' Greg said irritably. He turned to Zahra. 'Mrs Ghafoori, we believe you may be involved in drug importation to Australia. Your hostel flat will be searched by officers from the Australian Federal Police Drugs Squad. You must be present when it happens.'

'Search my flat?'

'Yes. And everything you brought with you from Iran.'

'Why?' Zahra asked. She felt desperate, but also furiously angry.

'Drugs, Mrs Ghafoori. Isn't that why your husband disappeared at the airport?'

'I don't know!'

Oh my God! What if they find some? I've unpacked everything, there was nothing ...

'Look, let's get it over with,' Caroline said firmly. 'She's answered all your questions.'

Greg rubbed his chin. They hadn't got all the answers, he told Caroline. Mrs Ghafoori obviously didn't know where her husband was, and as for the drugs ... they were a police matter.

'Okay, Caroline,' Sally said. 'The police are over there now. We want to get this sorted. Listen Zahra,' she said, leaning forward, 'we are concerned that your husband abandoned you. You have a valid refugee visa and you can to stay in Australia with your son.' She paused. 'However, as we said, if the police find drugs in your possession, you will be arrested and charged.'

Zahra's fury toward her cousin turned into terror for herself. Within an hour she might be locked up and facing a prison sentence for herself and an orphanage for her son.

She heard chairs scrape on the bare floor as her questioners left the room. Caroline came back with a cup of tea. *My things are going to be turned over by the police. Please God, don't let them find anything incriminating.* She pushed the tea away, dreading the next half hour.

Caroline's words of comfort as they walked together to Zahra's flat made her feel worse. Angry tears blocked her throat. In her mind's eye, she saw Firzun pulling off his holy clothes and scurrying away from them at the airport. Did he have drugs with him? Maybe the police here assumed everyone from Afghanistan was a drug smuggler. Her shoulders slumped. *If only Karim was here, he could help me. I made the wrong choice, God help me. I should have stayed with him.*

She remembered how nervous she'd felt about going to breakfast that morning. That was nothing. Now the police were going to search her flat! The consequences of them finding drugs among her things didn't bear thinking about.

13

ANOTHER SEARCH

When she walked out of the administration block with Caroline, Zahra saw the Immigration officer, Greg, in the distance. He was standing outside the door of her flat with his back to her. She caught her breath; he was talking to two people, a man and a woman—blue uniformed police officers! Their police car was parked on the strip of bitumen near the units. As she and Caroline got nearer, Zahra strained to hear what they were saying. She was uncomfortably conscious of the police officers observing her as she walked toward them across the grass. Their voices drifted to her on the warm air.

'She says she doesn't know anything,' Greg said.

'We've had no sightings of him today,' the male police officer replied. 'Security here haven't seen him.'

'His bags were searched at the airport, apparently, but not hers.'

When Zahra got closer, she heard the female police officer say, 'Yeah, dumped it on his wife. She probably doesn't know.'

The comment frightened Zahra. Was Firzun's story about an assassin a total fabrication? What was worse: being followed by an assassin, or arrested for unwittingly importing drugs in her luggage? She hung back when Caroline went over to talk to the small group.

The air was warm and still, then a chorus of cicadas in the trees drowned out the police officers' voices. The noise unsettled her, and even the group on the footpath outside her door looked around and frowned. The high-pitched racket also alerted other hostel residents who were wandering about. A few of them stared across at the group of official-looking people outside her flat. Suddenly the door of the next flat opened and Zahra's humiliation was complete when a fair-haired woman came out.

'Ooh, sorry!' she said, giving the group a wide berth. When she saw Zahra standing on the grass, she flashed her a worried look.

Caroline beckoned Zahra forward and the female police officer gave her a half smile.

'I'm Sergeant Joanne Edwards. Pleased to meet you, Mrs Ghafoori.' She indicated her colleague. 'This is Senior Constable Ian Ross.'

The police officer pushed a stray strand of dark hair under her hat. Their blue shirts were a blur of badges and each of them had a revolver in a holster.

At least it wasn't a submachine gun, she thought. Greg the Immigration officer stood near the door of her flat, smoking a cigarette.

'Mrs Ghafoori,' the police woman began in a neutral voice, 'I have a warrant to search your flat. Do you understand?'

'Yes.'

'We need you to be present,' she continued. 'The welfare officer can come in with you if you wish. Open the door please.'

The woman didn't smile again or make eye contact as Zahra put the key in the lock. She fumbled with it, uncomfortably aware of the police officers, one standing at her side, the other behind her. When the door swung open, Sergeant Edwards touched Zahra lightly on the arm.

'Mrs Ghafoori, I must tell you that we have reason to suspect there may be drugs concealed in this flat. We will be searching through everything. Is there anything you would like to tell us before we go in?'

Zahra looked into the policewoman's blue eyes. 'I am sure there are no drugs in here.'

Although she tried to sound firm and resolute, she could hear the tremor in her own voice. If Firzun had hidden something, where was it? Certainly not in the things she'd unpacked this morning—but she hadn't been looking for drugs.

The police officer nodded and motioned her ahead into the small living room. Zahra was uncomfortably conscious of the huge bulk of the woman's colleague behind her. Caroline took Zahra's arm and led her to the yellow vinyl-covered sofa, motioning her to sit down. Through the window, Zahra could see the Immigration officials waiting in the sunshine. She clutched her hands together to stop them shaking.

'Is this your bag and suitcase?' Senior Constable Ross asked as he dragged them from the wardrobe.

'Yes.'

He exchanged a glance with his colleague, then ran his fingers expertly around the inside of her case. He turned it upside down and then did the same to her carry-on bag. At any moment, Zahra expected to hear a shout of triumph and a police officer holding up a small hessian bag. The policeman felt carefully in her handbag and extracted the roll of American dollars she'd transferred from her bra the previous evening. He put them on the dining table.

As she sat on the couch with Caroline, her mind raced frantically. If they found something, would they arrest her immediately and take her to prison? Tears welled up behind her eyes and she said she needed the toilet. The female police officer went with her, telling her to leave the door open. To Zahra's humiliation, the other woman stood with her back to her while she relieved herself.

The police officers worked their way quickly and methodically through the small flat. They took Zahra's few clothes off the hangers in the wardrobe one by one and rummaged through the drawers.

They shook everything out and then felt the hems of her skirt and trousers. The policeman slit the skirt hem with a sharp knife, releasing her gold necklace, earrings, and gold coins. He handed everything to his colleague. Zahra felt violated, as if the man had touched her body. Maybe they'd collect all her possessions and take them away. She'd heard about that happening in Afghanistan. Instead, they put everything on the dining table and counted the money carefully.

'One hundred and seventy US dollars in notes, one gold necklace, two pairs of gold earrings, ten gold coins ... and some foreign money, probably Iranian,' Sergeant Ross announced.

They asked Zahra if she'd hidden any other valuables anywhere. When she said no, they turned to the welfare officer and told her to advise Zahra to put everything in the safe in the office.

'She can understand English, you know,' Caroline replied.

Zahra looked at the small collection on the table. *This is all I've got in the world*, she thought wretchedly. She fingered the necklace Esmat had given her, which she wore under her blouse. It felt like the only thing she owned that hadn't been assaulted.

'There's a business card here in the coat pocket,' the policeman called out. He handed it to the other police officer.

'Mr Mehran Ashrani—accountant. There's an address in Sydney.' She read it out loud.

They questioned her about Mr Ashrani. Was he an associate of her husband? Was this who he met at the airport? Zahra managed to tell them that he was the son of a woman she'd befriended at Tehran Airport. They looked sceptical when she said they'd tried to help her find her husband. The female police officer copied the details from the card, then put it with Zahra's possessions on the table.

'She's telling the truth,' the welfare officer commented. 'Apparently a man who spoke Zahra's language did try to help her.'

'Well, we'll follow that up,' the female police officer said.

Zahra was overwhelmed with guilt. Because of Firzun, Leila's son, an innocent man, would get a visit from the Australian police. It wasn't fair, none of this was fair.

'It's nearly over, not long now,' Caroline assured her.

She could hear the police searching the bedroom and talking to each other.

'Turn up that mattress, Joanne. Can you manage?'

She heard them pounding the mattresses, then clanging things in the bathroom.

Sergeant Edwards came back into the room and addressed Caroline. 'We have to strip search her as well.'

Strip search me! Did they mean she had to take her clothes off? She was horrified; would they do it in front of the male police officer?

'Please go into the bedroom, Mrs Ghafoori.' The female police officer indicated the way with her head.

She walked behind Zahra, and once in the bedroom she closed the door firmly and drew the curtains across the window.

Will she make me strip naked with a man in the other room and another one outside?

'Are you okay?'

'I don't want to take my clothes off.'

The policewoman looked at her keenly. 'Do you have anything hidden on your body?'

'No.'

The other woman appraised her. 'I am going to search you to make sure you have not concealed any drugs on your person. Do I have your permission?'

'No!'

'Look, we can do this here, or I can take you to the police station and do it there.' Her voice softened slightly. 'It has to be done, Mrs Ghafoori. Let's get it over with.'

'I don't have any ...'

'I'll be quick. Take your clothes off and wrap yourself in this.' She handed Zahra one of the towels from the bathroom. 'The welfare worker will be in the room as a witness,' the other woman added.

'No!'

It was shameful enough to be searched, but watched by someone else!

'It's here or the police station. Just get undressed and I'll call her.'

Zahra undressed quickly, terrified that the people outside might be trying to look through the curtains. She tried to cover herself with the towel as she removed her clothes. She stood motionless, mortified, the towel pulled tightly around her body. When the policewoman came back into the room, Zahra backed into the corner. She was petrified that they would ask the policeman to come in as well. The female police officer ran her hands expertly over Zahra's discarded clothes.

'I have to do an internal search, in case you've hidden drugs inside your body,' the policewoman said. 'That means I have to insert my finger in your anus and your vagina. Do you understand?'

Zahra understood exactly what she meant. She backed against the wall in horror as the policewoman pulled on a pair of surgical gloves.

'No, you can't, *you can't ...*'

Caroline put her arm around Zahra's shoulder. 'Nearly over,' she said.

'Please turn to the wall and bend over,' the police woman ordered.

It was finished quickly, the pain, the humiliation.

'Thank you. You can get dressed now.' The police officer avoided eye contact and left the room.

Zahra sobbed against Caroline's shoulder. She could hear water running in her bathroom as the officer washed her hands.

'It's all over now,' the other woman said gently.

Zahra got dressed quickly. She could hear the group outside talking in low voices. She dreaded having to face them. She jumped when the female police officer knocked on the door and came into the bedroom.

'Well, we didn't find anything, Mrs Ghafoori,' the other woman began. 'However, we have to be sure your husband is not part of a drug ring with links to Afghanistan. If he contacts you, get in touch with me on this number.' She handed Zahra a card.

Zahra took the card, dumbfounded and scared by what the policewoman had said.

'Don't shield him, Mrs Ghafoori. He's already broken the law by deserting you.' Her blue eyes met Zahra's. 'Are you sure you don't know his whereabouts?'

'I have no idea where he is,' Zahra answered truthfully.

'Like I said, if he contacts you, you must call us.'

She touched her hat in a half salute and left the bedroom. Zahra heard the front door close and the voices outside got fainter as they moved away.

'Do you want me to stay? Make a cup of tea?' Caroline came into the bedroom. Zahra shook her head and followed the other woman into the living room. She sat on the couch, too embarrassed to look at Caroline's kind face.

'I'll come back later,' she said. 'And Zahra, it's a good idea to put your valuables and money in the office safe.' She closed the door quietly behind her.

Zahra stayed on the couch and sobbed with her head in her hands until there were no tears left. Her flat felt like an invaded, sullied place. She got up and scooped her money and jewellery into her handbag and put it in the wardrobe. In the bathroom, she stood under the shower, rubbing her body with the hard soap for a long time. She put on a cotton wrap that had once belonged to her friend Nasim.

She bundled up all the clothes she'd been wearing that morning and decided to dump them in the trash somewhere. She never wanted to see them again. She got dressed quickly in one of the cotton tops and pants from Karim's mother's shop. They still smelled faintly of rosewater—the smell of Karim's house—and she stifled an anguished sob.

The living room was stuffy and hot, but she couldn't bear to open the door or windows. People outside might want to peer in at her—the woman who'd had to strip naked for the police. She stood in the middle of the room trying to organise her scattered thoughts. She had seen officials searching Firzun's bag at the airport. Why hadn't they strip searched him as well?

A sudden sharp rap on the door startled her. Perhaps the police had new information and they'd come back. She stayed quiet.

'Cleaner! Anyone home?' a voice called out.

Before she could get to the door, the cleaner had put a key in the lock and the door swung open. A small woman stopped on the threshold.

'Oooh! You in here, I very sorry,' she said.

She paused on the step. Zahra couldn't see her properly because the light was behind her. 'Hello, I Lan, come clean you room,' the other woman said. 'Police gone?'

'I'm sorry, it doesn't need cleaning.' Zahra walked over to the door.

Lan, who only reached up to her shoulder, didn't move. She patted her long black hair, which she'd tied back. She wore a white top that reached below her knees over wide black pants. The pink apron over her clothes had the words 'Department of Immigration, Cleaning Service' embroidered on it.

'Police always here looking for tings. Don't worry, they gone,' she remarked.

Does everyone know everything here?

'My name Lan,' she repeated. 'I clean you room—get smell of police out.' She laughed.

Before Zahra could stop her, Lan picked up a metal bucket and clanged across the threshold. Zahra sat down on the sofa and put her head in her hands.

'No worries, you rest. How 'bout I make you cup o' tea?' Lan said cheerfully.

Zahra heard her fill the jug. The other woman came over and Zahra took the packet of tissues she handed her.

'Cup o' tea coming up,' she said brightly. 'You want fix up you face and hair in bathroom, make look better?'

In the bathroom, Zahra hardly recognised the person who looked back at her from the mirror. She had dark shadows under her red and swollen eyes, and her face had a haunted look. She took a deep breath, shook out her damp hair, combed it, and tied it back in place. She splashed more water on her face and dried it. After she'd dabbed on some make-up and lipstick, she went back into the living room. She was beginning to feel slightly better. She sat down on the vinyl sofa again and picked up her ruined skirt from where the police had left it. The sofa felt sticky from the rising heat of the day.

'My son's in the kindergarten. I've got to get him,' she told Lan.

'You relax. Have cup o' tea first, still early,' the cleaner replied. She fussed with the electric jug. 'My son there too.'

Lan opened the curtains and the window. The room was suddenly filled with warm air and bright light. She made the tea and handed the cup and saucer to Zahra.

'Drink you tea, no milk. Milk in tea make you sick. What you name?'

'Zahra,' she answered. Her hands shook as she drank the tea.

'Zahra, very nice. Okay, I tell you—police find nothing, leave you alone. Not come again.'

Lan dusted and tidied, humming as she worked. When she saw the skirt, she tutted and shook her head. When Zahra told her the police did it, Lan frowned. She took a needle and a bobbin of black thread out of her pocket and handed it to Zahra.

'You fix. Otralian people no understand,' she said with a firm nod of her head. 'Have easy lives.'

Otralian? Zahra was puzzled—*Australian!* She looked at Lan and smiled weakly.

'Where are you from?'

'From Vietnam. Things bad in my country. War. Lot of people die,' Lan said, smiling.

'It sounds terrible.'

'I here with my sister, she have three kids. I one son. Husbands dead, everyone dead. We come on boat. Dangerous. My husband die in water.'

Zahra stared at her; what a terrible story! Lan hardly looked old enough to have a child.

'You got husband?' Lan asked.

'He left me at Sydney Airport with my son.' Zahra bit her lip.

'Left? Ran away? Oh! Very *bad man*,' Lan exclaimed. 'No worries, Otralian government look after you, give you social security money, child support, help you get job. When leave hostel, help with rent. I clean, get money, save up, get sewing machine, make clothes.' She laughed and clapped her hands. 'Maybe get rich!'

Zahra concentrated hard on Lan's fractured English. She had learned more in five minutes with her, she thought, than in her dealings so far with the paid professionals.

'You be okay. It good place, Otralia, nice people,' Lan went on.

She moved into the bathroom. Zahra could hear water running and Lan humming as she worked.

'See you tomorrow. Cheer up!' She came back into the living room and smiled. 'I leave extra biscuits for you son.'

She waved away Zahra's thanks and clanged out the door with her cleaning gear. The brief contact with someone friendly had cheered Zahra a little, but it hadn't blotted out the humiliating memory of the body search. She rubbed her hands over her face, then stood up and threw the wardrobe door open.

Using Lan's needle and thread, she folded one of her scarves over and sewed several small pockets along its length. From now on she'd carry her money next to her body, just as she'd done when they'd escaped across the mountains from Afghanistan to Iran. She would leave her jewellery in the office with the gold coins but that was all. She wondered if Lan's local knowledge was right. The police had searched her once and wouldn't be back. As she sewed, she went over the events of the morning in her head.

Her flat had been searched and the police had found nothing. So there were no drugs and no need for Firzun to contact her. But where was he? Was he really escaping from an assassin? What's more, would the killer come after her if they couldn't find Firzun? She shuddered, glad there were security guards at the hostel gates.

The welfare officer had told her that she could eventually divorce her husband. What a ridiculous irony, she thought—divorcing a dead husband!

She finished her sewing, put her money into the body belt, and wound it around her body under her clothes. She looked cautiously out the window. The police car was nowhere in sight. She felt an overwhelming need to see her son, to hold him and hug him and be real and normal again. The sun was high in the bright blue sky and she opened the door cautiously to let in more fresh air. She looked across at the kindergarten and saw Ahmad through the wire fence. He was running around with another boy; he looked so happy that her heart lifted.

Ahmad. She frowned and tried to concentrate. Someone had said something that was related somehow to Ahmad—what was it? She stared unseeing at the kindergarten, then with a gasp she clutched the door handle. What had the Immigration people said?

'*Did you pack your own case, Zahra?*'

She'd nodded.

'*Did your husband ask you to put any packages in your luggage before you left Iran?*'

'No,' she'd answered truthfully.

Maybe he hadn't needed to, she thought. There wasn't anything in her luggage or his. But Ahmad had his own luggage—the backpack! The police hadn't searched everything. Ahmad's backpack was hanging untouched on a wooden peg in the kindergarten. She'd helped him hang it beneath the picture of a kangaroo that very morning. Her heart thumped in her chest. What if ...? Would Firzun stoop so low? She clenched her hands. Had he used Ahmad's backpack?

If he had, they'd been incredibly lucky not to have been stopped at the airport. Maybe Firzun had gambled that no one would search a child. Another terrible thought struck her as she stood at the open door. If he had stashed drugs in the backpack, they were still there! What's more, he, or *someone*, would return to collect them. Were the police still watching her? Even if they were, she had to get the backpack now, bring it here, rip it open ... and if she found heroin in it, what then?

14

IN AN ALIEN LAND

When he opened the apartment door to his mother Esmat and his sister Soraya, Karim's spirits lifted.

'It's *so* good to see you.' He hugged his sister hard.

'My mascara's running,' Soraya sniffed. 'We were so worried about you, Karim. Nadir still follows the politics back home. We thought you'd all be stuck in Iran and they wouldn't let you leave.'

'Well, we all got out and we're here—your husband had nothing to worry about, like I told him,' Esmat interrupted, giving her son a peck on the cheek. She shrugged off her leather coat and handed it to Karim. He took their bags and coats to the guest rooms.

'God knows what we've come to,' his mother was saying when he returned to the living room.

'Meaning?'

Esmat was sitting on the sofa opposite her daughter and patted the seat next to her. Karim sat down. She launched into a story of an incident that had happened to her in her daughter's street in Boston.

'One of Soraya's neighbours stopped me and asked if I knew anything about those poor diplomats held captive in Tehran.' Esmat sniffed. 'What was I supposed to say? I told her I had no idea!'

'Well, I guess she thought as you'd just come from Tehran, you might know something,' Soraya interposed.

Esmat ignored her daughter and continued. 'She had the nerve to say that she thought the US government should stop Iranian people getting asylum in the States. *Asylum!* As if *I* were a refugee! We've all been citizens for years, except you, Karim.' She frowned at her son.

'I've applied,' he said quickly. 'I've got a green card so I can still work.'

'Yes, well, get a move on. I can't see us going back to Iran in the near future.'

He was thankful that his mother lived in Boston, not New York. He was thirty-four years old, but he knew that now he was here she'd try to organise his life for him. She underscored his thoughts by telling him it was time he got married. She'd make it her business to find him a wife soon. She had plenty of Persian friends with single daughters. He told her to go ahead. There was no point arguing with her.

Brother and sister exchanged glances; his sister had kept her promise and never told their mother about his impulsive marriage to Nancy.

Over coffee he steered the conversation away from his private life. Esmat disappeared into the kitchen and Soraya leaned forward. She lowered her voice and confided that they might be in for a hard time as Iranians in the States. The woman who had accosted their mother had been full of righteous anger.

'Most of our neighbours have hoisted the Stars and Stripes in their front yards. It's a show of national unity, I guess.'

'What about the TV reports?' Karim interjected. 'Those student jailers in Tehran are giving interviews.'

'I know! It makes me nervous. They've got a worldwide audience.'

But what kind of message was it? Karim asked her. They had already held the hostages unlawfully for nearly a month. Although

Soraya thought they'd be out by Christmas as a goodwill gesture, Karim doubted it. They'd released a few for Thanksgiving and made a huge fuss about that, but more? He shook his head.

He didn't mention his own involvement fighting the radical students. But he hadn't forgotten their fanaticism. He couldn't see them giving an inch. They'd got the mighty United States backed into a corner. They were enjoying their power. His sister agreed that even though the shah was now in the United States, President Carter would never send him back to Iran. He would be tried and executed for what the new regime considered to be 'crimes against the people'.

'What a mess!' Soraya looked across at her brother.

Esmat appeared from the kitchen and changed the subject, telling Karim about their terrible flight from Tehran with Nasim. She was pregnant and newly widowed and wept most of the way. Nasim's parents had met her at the airport in New York and taken her with them to their 'wonderful' house in California.

'And that's where your father and I are going to live,' Esmat said conclusively.

She couldn't stand the winters on the East Coast and she was going to open a business. She'd been a businesswoman all her life. Karim and Soraya exchanged glances again—their mother was getting into her stride. She informed them that she'd shipped a lot of 'old stuff' from Iran. She could pass things off here, in the US, as antiques, she added. The items included his late grandmother's dresses—awful sequinned things. Karim was taken aback—who would buy them?

'You'd be surprised.' Esmat raised her eyebrows.

'Mom! You can't sell grandmother's clothes. What will Dad say?' Soraya objected.

'Nothing,' Esmat replied. 'He's lost his job and we both need something to do. I'm going to call the shop *Esmat's Persian Bazaar*. I shall refer to myself as Persian from now on.'

Karim congratulated his mother, impressed as ever by her

resilience. Esmat was going to distance herself from that 'awful regime,' she continued. *Persian* sounded better, softer—people would think of gardens and poetry, not war and madmen. She reminded them that their maternal grandparents were traders from Afghanistan. She'd inherited their entrepreneurial skills. The USA should be glad to have their family, she concluded briskly. She looked from Karim to Soraya, the light of battle glinting in her eyes.

'Well, you've earned a free lunch.' Karim laughed. 'We'll welcome ourselves to America!' he said, feeling happy for the first time in weeks.

Lauren O'Rourke sat in her apartment on West 57th Street, uncertain of what to do. Her ankle still ached even though her doctor had strapped it up for her.

'You've sprained it, Lauren. Rest, ice, and elevate is my advice,' he'd said. 'Try and keep off it for twenty-four hours.'

Lauren didn't want to do that. She looked down at the scarf she was holding. Karim Konari had secured the small ice pack with it in the restaurant yesterday and it had still been around her ankle when she got home. She had buried her face in it that night before she went to bed and its faint almond smell had stirred her senses. She had washed it reluctantly in her bathroom and dried it overnight.

She looked around the apartment, feeling suddenly very lonely. Only a month ago, she would have been out shopping or visiting friends with Max. Now he was gone forever and she still felt at a loose end on the weekends. She needed another man in her life, and Karim was nice. *I'll take his scarf back to him personally. Why not?* she thought.

She knew he lived a short cab ride away. If she telephoned he might put her off, but if she called round? She checked her watch; he might even invite her for lunch. She clenched her fists when she thought of Max. She'd had to cancel the wedding arrangements, while he had taken off for Europe. How humiliating! She knew who was behind it—his mother, Beatrice Jansen. Beatrice, who had married into the famous Wilhelm's family of art dealers. When Lauren had told Beatrice that her last name was O'Rourke, Max's mother had winced.

'Irish?' Lauren hated her condescending smile.

'My father's family was Irish, yes. My mother's family is from St Kitts in the Caribbean. We've got an estate in Antigua.'

'Oh, the Caribbean!' Max's mother had laughed quietly. 'I expect your mother's family are sugar traders?'

'They manufacture rum, ma'am.'

'Rum,' the other woman had said faintly. 'How very lucrative.'

'It sure is.'

Stuck up Puritan bitch!

Lauren dragged her thoughts back to the present. She stood up and flinched as her foot touched the floor. She took two painkillers and flexed the ankle carefully. She put the black and grey striped scarf into a Macy's lingerie bag. Might be a good vibe, she thought. She locked her apartment and headed for the elevator.

Lauren loved living in mid-town New York. She thrived on the buzz around her every time she left the apartment building—folks walking on the sidewalks, the sound of taxis honking, the small cafes, diners, and restaurants nearby. Besides, she was a short cab ride from Broadway. She was near the stores, the theatres, Carnegie Hall, museums, the Lincoln Centre—what more could she want? In addition, her block had a doorman and that made her feel safe. Her dad had bought the apartment for her after Max had left. She was a single woman now, not a fiancée. A twenty-four-year-old single woman. It sounded awful, like she was on the shelf. But she had to take a feminist view of it and start fending for herself, she knew that.

Her father had forbidden her to use the subway. He called it 'the muggers express'. He didn't even want her to walk far. She waited while the doorman called her a cab. Riding a hire-bike in Central Park on her day off had seemed a good idea at the time. If a mugger had shown up, she could have gotten away fast. Instead a really cool, good-looking guy had crossed her path—literally. Max had broken her heart, sure. But she wasn't going to live like a nun! Especially when there were guys around like handsome, exotic Karim Konari.

Karim had finally got his mother and sister into the lobby of his building.

'I'm not walking anywhere,' Esmat announced. 'This city is much too dangerous. Besides, I don't want to have someone push an "Iranians Go Home!" placard in my face.'

Soraya remonstrated that her mother was exaggerating. As usual, Esmat had a comeback. She'd seen a picture in the newspaper yesterday. A man was holding up a big sign: 'Deport Iranians'. It got airtime on the TV news channel last night. Hadn't she seen it? Soraya retorted that they should start speaking English in public from now on, in case someone recognised the Persian language and deported them on the spot.

Karim frowned at his mother and sister. As usual, they couldn't speak to each other without arguing. It was going to be a long lunch, he thought as they all got out of the elevator. He was manoeuvring them across the lobby when Lauren O'Rourke walked through the main door.

'Hi Karim, how are you?'

He was completely taken aback. Lauren, smartly dressed in jeans, calf-high boots, and a red coat extended her hand, shook his, and smiled. She'd coiled her auburn hair up but wavy strands of it escaped down the side of her face. His mother stopped mid-sentence and stared at the new arrival handing Karim a small bag.

'I ... you left your scarf.' Lauren blushed, obviously disarmed by Esmat's direct stare. 'I'm so sorry, I didn't mean to intrude.'

'Not at all,' Karim assured her with a smile as he took the scarf. 'I was looking for it just now.'

He took the scarf out of the bag and put it round his neck. His mother reached over and took the Macy's bag from him with a faint tut.

Karim's sister stepped forward into the uncomfortable silence and introduced herself and her mother. Within minutes, Esmat was interrogating Lauren about how long she'd known Karim. He interposed and quickly told the story of the bike accident.

'Well, I guess I'd better be going,' Lauren began, but Soraya invited her to join them for lunch.

'You're very welcome,' Karim added.

Lunches with his mother and sister, Karim recalled, often ended in heated arguments across the table. At least if Lauren was there they would have to control themselves. To his relief, Lauren thanked them and accepted. Karim glanced at his mother, who met his look with raised eyebrows and asked if he had booked anywhere. When Lauren suggested a Turkish restaurant further down West 57th, Esmat shrugged her acceptance.

To Karim's relief, his mother approved of the restaurant, mainly because the staff were ultra-polite and deferential. Esmat settled back in her seat opposite her son and asked if he had any more news from home. When she heard that Zahra's husband had survived the bomb blast and that they'd gone to Australia, she was astounded.

'Good heavens! Why Australia?'

'They got accepted as refugees, so why not?'

A waiter set down an entrée plate of lamb koftë, vine leaves stuffed with rice, white cheese, garlic yoghurt, and warm bread.

'I brought some photographs with me.' Karim frowned at his mother as she piled his plate with food. 'I can do that myself, Mother.'

'You need your hands free to show us the photographs.'

Karim turned to his sister. She and Lauren had something in common, she told him; they'd both graduated from the same university.

He returned Lauren's smile as he passed the prints around the table. He'd taken the photographs when the house looked as it always had. He didn't want their last sight of it to be the empty shell he had closed the door on only a few days ago. His sister held up a photograph of Zahra in the library and asked him who the beautiful woman was. Karim gave a brief history of what had happened to Zahra. To his relief, his mother was too busy talking to the waiter to interrupt. Once again, he wondered how his mother and sister would react if he told them how he still felt about Zahra and how much he missed her.

Esmat turned her attention to Lauren. Within ten minutes she had found out that Lauren's family owned a home in Darien, Connecticut and that Lauren had a horse on the property. She was impressed that Lauren's father had bought her an apartment in New York and that he had a large one near Central Park. She also discovered the Antiguan estate and that Mr O'Rourke was a wealthy businessman. She sympathised with the broken engagement, but then she opined Lauren was still young—twenty-three? Twenty-four? At the end of the interrogation, Esmat nodded approvingly and Karim saw her nudge Soraya. Lauren had passed the 'not a gold digger' test. Karim glanced at Lauren sitting on his right opposite Soraya. She was such a breath of fresh air, so uncomplicated, he thought. Her only baggage, it seemed to him, was a broken heart, which would mend eventually.

He couldn't help comparing Lauren with Zahra and the many layers of her life. Tehran, he reflected, was already beginning to feel like another planet. His mother met his eyes with an expectant look. He took the hint, called the waiter, and asked for the check. His thoughts turned again to Zahra while the women chatted amongst themselves. He had no control over what happened to her and no way of contacting her. *I've got to face it,* he thought as he paid the bill. *There's no way I can help her, even if she needs it. She's married to Firzun and she's out of my life forever.*

15

———

THE MICKEY MOUSE BACKPACK

Zahra stood in her stuffy flat in the migrant hostel feeling like a caged animal ready to spring at the bars. She had to get Ahmad's backpack from the kindergarten, *right now*. Suppose the teachers had already looked inside and found drugs in it? She frowned; Firzun wasn't stupid. If there was something there, it would be well hidden. But she still had to get it and find the stuff before anyone else did. She wrenched open the door, stepped out, and nearly collided with her neighbour on the path outside.

'Hello there! Remember me? We were on the same coach from the airport. I'm Julie, from England,' the woman said.

Zahra pulled the door shut and tried to focus. Before she could say hello, Julie rushed on.

'What a surprise, we're neighbours! How are you settling in?'

'Very well, thank you.' Zahra glanced again at the kindergarten.

'Excuse me for asking, but I saw the police here this morning,' Julie lowered her voice. 'Is there any news about your husband?'

So everyone knows?

'Who? Oh I ... no. Just questions.'

'Don't worry, the hostel people are absolutely wonderful and so supportive. We enrolled our daughter in school and our little boy in the kindergarten here.'

As Julie rattled on—about children, hostel meals, her husband's job—Zahra felt increasingly desperate. Every word the woman said was keeping her away from the backpack. Maybe the teachers had been suspicious and were peering inside it right now, exchanging worried looks. If they did find some drugs, Zahra imagined them standing back aghast. Would they call Ahmad in from the play area and ask him if Mummy had put anything in his bag?

Zahra's neighbour was still talking. There was a name, she said, *Sarah*—it was the English equivalent of Zahra.

'I'm sorry, I really have to go and collect my son,' Zahra interrupted.

Still Julie went on, about how good Zahra's English was, where did she learn it? Had she always—

She broke off suddenly and Zahra followed her gaze across to the kindergarten. A police car had stopped outside and two uniformed officers got out, pulling on their caps. Zahra put her hand on a nearby wall to steady herself. The police were walking toward the kindergarten. *No, no, no!* The teachers *had* found something in the backpack and they'd called the police.

'Oh,' Julie whispered. 'I hope everything's all right.'

Zahra could hardly breathe.

'It okay!' Lan appeared suddenly, pushing a cleaning trolley. 'They talk to kids 'bout road crossing safe.' She smiled at Zahra and nodded. 'Everything okay,' she repeated.

Julie told them she was greatly relieved. How awful if they started searching the kindergarten—what on earth would they be looking for? She looked quizzically at Zahra.

Lan took Zahra's arm. 'You go, get you boy,' she said firmly.

To Zahra's relief, Julie's attention was diverted by another resident who knew her.

'See you tomorrow? Want go shops?' Lan asked when Julie was out of earshot. 'I come nine-fifteen.'

Zahra nodded.

Her heart was thumping as she quickened her pace across the lawn toward the kindergarten building. She wanted to run, grab the backpack, and get home to her own place with Ahmad. She let herself into the kindergarten via the gate and rushed up to the door. A young woman in shorts and t-shirt, with blond hair tied up in a pony-tail, smiled at her and held the door open.

'Hello, you're Ahmad's mummy, aren't you?' she said. 'I'm Sharon, one of the teachers.'

Zahra forced herself to smile. Over Sharon's shoulder she could see the police officers kneeling down in the outdoor play area and talking to the children. She pulled her attention back to Sharon, who handed her a pen and asked her to sign Ahmad out. Zahra scribbled her signature next to her son's name just as Leanne appeared, holding him by the hand. He stopped suddenly, turned, and ran back into the playroom.

'He's forgotten his truck,' the teacher explained with a smile.

'I'll get his bag.' Zahra hurried toward the bag room and Leanne followed her.

She rushed forward and grabbed the straps of the Mickey Mouse backpack, but Leanne seized her wrist.

'Wait a minute!'

Zahra paused, her hand frozen on the bag. *She knows.* The police had searched it and told Leanne to keep the bag and Zahra in the kindergarten. She looked wildly at the teacher. She had to tell her the truth, that the drugs had been planted by her cousin.

'Oh, I'm so sorry.' Leanne looked startled. 'I didn't mean to scare you.' She took her hand away. 'It's just ... well ... we encourage the children to collect their own bags. You know, learn the picture on the peg. Ahmad chose the kangaroo ...' Her voice trailed away.

Zahra stood back as Ahmad came in clutching his truck. Every nerve in her body was on edge. It took an enormous effort of will not to snap at her son when he carefully unhooked his bag from the peg. She told him to hurry up in their own language, but he sat down on the bench under the peg and laboriously put his truck away.

'Well done, Ahmad!' Leanne said. She turned to Zahra. 'Are you all right? I'm sorry about before.'

Zahra forced herself to smile.

I'm not being watched. I've got to pull myself together or they'll get suspicious.

She told Leanne she was fine and only wanted to help her son. She remembered to mention that they were going to the shops the next day and he might not come to kindergarten.

'That's okay, bring him when you can.' Leanne smiled. 'He enjoyed himself today.' She kneeled down to the child's level and took his hand. 'Bye, bye, Ahmad. See you later.'

'Bye, bye! I'm happy,' Ahmad replied in English.

Clutching the backpack in one hand, Zahra hurried Ahmad out of the door. Her knuckles ached as she gripped the bag and her nails dug into her palm. She felt as if she hadn't breathed out for ten minutes. As soon as they were in their flat, Ahmad rushed to the bathroom, washed his hands, then helped himself to the extra packets of biscuits. Zahra hardly noticed what he was doing. She stood with the bag in her hand, testing its weight. Had Leanne suspected that she was acting oddly and said something to the police after she'd gone?

She stood irresolutely in the middle of the room still holding the backpack. What should she do? Supposing she left it here when they went to lunch and someone searched the room? Then she remembered that the police said she had to be there during a search. So she could leave it, couldn't she?

Ahmad was standing at the open door, hopping backward and forward from the outside to the inside, saying he was hungry. She stuffed the bag in the back of the wardrobe and joined him outside. In the dining room she felt as if people were watching as she collected their food. Maybe they were pointing her out to each other? The woman whose flat had been searched by the Australian police.

She saw Julie and chose a table as far away as possible from her. When they finished their meal, they left quickly, giving the other diners a wide berth. Back in the flat, she persuaded Ahmad to have a lie down. To her relief, he didn't object and within seconds he was fast asleep.

In the heat of the afternoon a soporific silence settled over the hostel. Zahra twitched the curtains aside. A couple of people came out of the administration block with sheafs of paper in their hands. There was no one else around, no officials, and the police car had gone. She drew the curtains closed and took the backpack out of the wardrobe. Her hands shook as she turned it upside down on the table. She'd forgotten about Ahmad's truck until it clattered loudly onto the floor. She waited, thinking it might have woken him, but there was no noise from the bedroom.

The backpack didn't feel as heavy now and she frowned. Had she imagined that Firzun had hidden drugs in it? She stood for a minute, feeling lightheaded. But when she felt around inside the bag, her heart sank. The bottom of the backpack was slightly raised. She put it down on the table. Why hadn't she noticed that before? But even the woman who had searched their luggage at Tehran Airport hadn't suspected anything.

Zahra felt around inside again, then stopped, wondering what she was going to do if she did unearth bags of heroin from the bottom of the backpack. She picked up her small scissors. If there was anything in the bag she had to get it out right now.

Damn Firzun for getting me into this mess!

She scooped the bag up by its straps and went to the empty second bedroom. The curtains were thicker here and she closed them quickly; no one walking by would be able to see into the room.

She picked up the reading lamp from the side of the bed and switched it on. Kneeling on the floor below the window ledge, she strafed the inside of the bag with the bright light. She could just make out the false base if she held the light steady. Both the material of the backpack and the thread had been carefully matched.

Zahra balanced the lamp at an angle and got to work, picking out the stitches one by one and keeping the thread intact. She worked carefully, afraid of damaging anything that might be hidden. When she prised up a corner of the material, her heart was beating so loudly she could hear it as she ran two fingers under the opening. Her fingers undulated over several soft, slippery plastic packets.

She leaned back on her heels and put her hands over her face. Tears slid through her fingers. How could Firzun have done this to her? He must have known how risky it was. He must have realised that she would have been arrested, not him, at Sydney Airport or at any of the airports they'd passed through.

Her hand shook as she adjusted the lamp and hooked out the rest of the thread. The white powder was in a neat, tightly packed row. She had unwittingly smuggled refined heroin, made from the opium poppies of Afghanistan, into Australia. Her head pounded with possibilities. If the police had found this, she would be in a jail cell right now. She wanted to laugh out loud at her good luck, then collapse in a heap with relief and fear.

She sat on the floor with her back to the bed. The story about an assassin was rubbish. Firzun had left them because of what was hidden in Ahmad's bag. She returned the lamp to the table and stood up with the backpack in her hand. A volcano of anger toward Firzun erupted inside her. She glared at the silly picture of Mickey Mouse with his big white waving hand and hurled the backpack at the wall.

'Oh my God!' She rushed across the room.

Had the powder spilled out? She grabbed the bag from the floor and felt around inside. Everything was still intact. She leaned against the door and spat out all the curses she knew in her own language. She stopped suddenly. She had to get rid of this stuff today—now! But how and where? Flush it down the toilet? No, it might clog up the drains. Call the police? They'd never believe her. Dumping it in the garbage on the hostel grounds wasn't an option either. Someone might see her. She went back to the living room and opened the wardrobe where her ruined skirt hung lopsided on its hanger. The police had already searched that. Why not sew the bags into the hem for now? She could throw the skirt in a bin tomorrow, maybe when she went to the shops with Lan. She took the garment out and got to work. As she sewed, she wondered if Firzun would show up tonight for the packets. After tomorrow, she thought angrily, he could search through the trash.

Zahra finished her sewing, found a garbage bag under the sink, pushed the skirt into it, and hid it at the back of one of the wardrobe drawers. Next she carried the backpack to the table and turned it upside down again just in case any of the powder had spilled. She felt as if she was working on automatic pilot as she fetched a wet cloth from the bathroom and wiped the bag carefully inside and out. Her neck and back ached with tension as she put the backpack in the bottom of the wardrobe. Ahmad would still want to take it to kindergarten.

Tiptoeing to the bedroom, she opened the door quietly. Ahmad was still fast asleep and she stood watching him for a minute as he lay on his back, breathing quietly. She touched his hair gently, then lay down on her own bed.

A persistent tapping on her face woke her from a troubled sleep. She blinked and checked her watch; it was evening meal time and Ahmad was standing next to her saying he was hungry. They had slept through the whole afternoon! As she pulled herself back into consciousness, she remembered her discovery with a shock and struggled to her feet. She tidied herself and Ahmad and, taking his hand, walked to the dining room. Lan was just leaving as she came in.

'See you nine-fifteen, you place tomorrow,' she reminded Zahra.

'Yes, thank you.' Zahra smiled, still feeling edgy.

After Ahmad had gone to bed, the evening stretched ahead empty and lonely, but she reminded herself that she had things to do. She transferred some of the American dollars from her money belt to her handbag. Maybe Lan would know where she could change them for Australian money. When she'd finished, she picked up the Persian poetry book Karim had given her and held it in her hand for a while. She stared at the cover with its picture of the beautiful mosque in Isfahan. She opened the book slowly and turned to the inside back cover and re-read the message Karim had written. *If ever you need me, Zahra, this is my sister's address in Boston, USA. Remember if you ever need my help please write to me.'*

Zahra studied the strange address for a long time, then sat on the hard sofa and indulged in melancholy thoughts about Karim. She had cared so much for him, but the timing was all wrong. Family loyalty had driven her to help her cousin—what a mistake that had been!

She picked up a writing pad Lan had given her from the cleaning trolley.

'Maybe you want write you friends,' Lan had said. 'I leave pen, envelopes too.'

Lan had mentioned that she had family in the US and that it took about a week for letters to get there. A week! A lot could happen in seven days, Zahra thought. She sat down at the small dining table and picked up the pen. The hostel address was printed across the top of each page.

After a few false starts she began to write. In her haste to tell Karim the truth she wrote quickly, returning to correct some words as they poured from her pen. She told him things she'd never told him before—her father's death when she was a child, her Iranian mother's life trapped in Afghanistan with her sister-in-law, Aunt

Mina, Firzun's mother. She spilled out the story of her marriage to her violent husband Mahmoud. She paused; she'd never forget the shocked look on Karim's face at Tehran Airport when Firzun had confessed to killing her husband. Would Karim really want to hear from her after that awful scene? But writing her story was cathartic and she pushed on. She had to tell him the truth.

'Please forgive me, dearest Karim, when you read the following,' she began. *'In spite of what I let you believe, I was never married to Firzun. As you know, he was a counter-revolutionary involved in anti-government activities in Afghanistan and Iran. The only way he could escape when things went wrong in Tehran was to take my dead husband's identity. When I promised to come with you to the United States, I truly believed Firzun was dead. I had no idea he was alive until he turned up in the middle of the night at your house. He said if I told anyone, he was finished.*

There were so many times I wanted to tell you the truth about the sham marriage. Please believe me, Karim. But Firzun swore me to secrecy. As long as everyone believed he was my husband, we could escape from Iran. He's my only blood relation apart from Ahmad. We were raised together as children, and although I'm sure you think he's abused my loyalty, please try to understand that he's family. You have a sister. Wouldn't you do anything for her if you believed her life was in danger? I can't say more, except that Firzun left Tehran and entered Australia as Mahmoud Ghafoori using my dead husband's passport.'

She wrote of what had happened at Sydney Airport, the police search and ... She stopped writing. Should she mention the drugs in the backpack? She shuddered when she remembered them. Even though Karim was one of the few people she trusted, she would wait for his reply before she told him.

She folded the two pages over, put them in the envelope, and copied Karim's sister's address carefully on the front. On the back she wrote her first name only and the address of the hostel. She would post the letter to Karim tomorrow. What did she have to lose?

Someone walked past on the footpath outside her window and she felt nervous again. But Firzun wouldn't make a noise, she thought. It was still only nine o'clock, too early for drug traffickers. She sat down on the sofa and listened again, afraid of looking out the window. She could hear a monotonous dull roar. Julie had asked her earlier if she'd noticed it. It was the sound of the surf pounding on the beach beyond the hostel fence and the distant trees.

Zahra picked up the poetry book again, but the words of the poems swam in front of her eyes. She thought of Karim settling into his old life in New York. He had probably shrugged off his memories of Iran and her, slipping back easily into his previous American existence. Perhaps she shouldn't post the letter after all, she thought.

She put the book down and looked around her room. She felt frightened—more frightened, if it were possible, than when Firzun had deserted her at the airport. There was a large amount of heroin hidden in her wardrobe. Firzun probably wouldn't risk coming here for the drugs himself. He'd send someone else—a stranger. But when would they come?

16

DECK THE HALLS

When Karim returned to the table at the Turkish restaurant, the three women were already on their feet. Lauren was supporting herself on the table. He took her arm and helped her walk out to the footpath. She leaned heavily on him.

'I guess I should have stayed home,' she said ruefully.

'Nonsense,' Esmat answered. 'Best thing is to have a bit of company, but put that foot up when you get back.'

His mother and sister said their goodbyes to Lauren. Soraya handed over a business card and told Lauren she was always welcome to look her up in Boston. After he had helped Lauren into a cab and whispered that he would call her, his mother turned to him.

'Not bad,' she shrugged, 'but not Persian.'

His mother and sister piled into a second cab with him and he suppressed a groan. They were determined to cram as much as possible into their New York weekend. His mother tapped him on the shoulder from the back seat.

'We'll drop you off at your apartment, as you requested, then we'll do our shopping and see you at your place around five,' she informed him. 'Then we'll go back this evening and look at the Christmas window displays with you. You've got to come with us—we don't want to go out alone at night. We might get mugged.'

The peace of his apartment settled over him as he checked a fax from his business partner Bahram. It didn't make good reading—the business might be in trouble soon. A few more clients had cancelled and there were only a couple of definite orders on the books. *It's because of the hostages*, Bahram had scrawled on the bottom of the fax in Persian script.

Even though he usually loved Christmas, Karim was totally fed up with it by the time they all returned to his apartment that evening. He had seen enough models of snowmen, tiny trains, mountain snow, and penguins in top hats to last him a lifetime. And now his mother wanted him to watch television with them.

'You must watch *The Love Boat*, it's wonderful!'

He excused himself and told them he had some business things to fix up.

Karim was reading the latest fax when his sister knocked on his office door to tell him supper was ready. Also, there was something he *had* to see on television.

In the living room, Esmat was on her feet, pointing at the television screen. 'Look! A British film crew is at the US embassy in Tehran doing interviews.' She sat down on the edge of the couch, riveted to the TV, and bit into her chicken sandwich.

'*The embassy has become a revolutionary theatre and the world's press are among the principal actors on the stage,*' the reporter's clipped British voice informed them. '*Every day reporters and cameramen assemble at the gates ... facts about the hostages are few ...*'

A young woman in a headscarf was sitting on the ground outside the US embassy. Behind her was a banner in English. Soraya read it out loud:

'*We differentiate between the United States corrupt government and fair honest Americans.*'

'What rubbish!' Esmat countered. 'And appalling English. What about fair honest Iranians like us?'

Someone held a microphone in front of the young woman and asked her a question.

'*The hostages are in our hands and we protect them strongly,*' she responded in her peculiar English. '*We cannot answer any questions about the security measures.*'

Karim watched in silence. If only his raid on the embassy had been successful, he wouldn't be sitting here now, in exile with his family. They would have struck a blow against the regime and brought the Americans home. In addition, Iran might now have a democratic government.

It looked cold in Tehran, and he knew exactly where the reporter was standing. He had met Firzun on that very spot, when the first blindfolded hostages had been paraded in front of the crowds.

'Stupid girl!' His mother's exclamation broke into his thoughts.

The students had allowed the press to interview them in a small courtyard.

'*The United States is an imperialist power and they have planted spy dens and spy networks all over the country ...*' the young woman was saying.

That's probably true, Karim thought. The US embassy in Tehran had once had a huge staff.

'*... they exploited our national resources, they exploited our oil. We don't say the hostages are innocent.*'

'*International law has been violated ...*' the interviewer cut in.

'Absolutely right! The embassy was on American soil in a foreign country,' Esmat opined.

'*The shah turned this country into a ruin. Do the Western people understand that?*'

The young woman's droning voice was beginning to get on Karim's nerves. The whole interview seemed to be going in circles.

The picture changed suddenly and they were looking at a run-down suburb of Tehran.

'Oh my God, what next?' Soraya asked.

Karim recognised Antaz, the place where the bomb had gone off only weeks earlier. The blast that he believed had killed Firzun. He had to admit it did look pretty bad. The contrast between the ultra-rich and this suburb meant the country was ripe for revolution, he reflected. The shah had been fabulously wealthy and families like his had benefitted. The people he was watching on the television looked grindingly poor.

'*These people missed out on the shah's dream of a new Iran,*' the BBC voice intoned.

Each man who jostled to the front to be interviewed looked poor and angry. Everyone blamed the country's woes on the Americans and the exiled shah, who was now an invalid and an exile in the United States.

Karim's mother was incensed. 'I provided plenty of work in my shops for people like that, men *and* women. I paid them well and their working conditions were good.'

The BBC was giving a one-sided view of the situation, she went on. Did these people think they'd be better under the rule of the Ayatollah Khomeini? Nasim's husband had been arrested, tortured and hanged! That's what would happen to anyone who disagreed with the new regime. Women were being forced to wear Islamic dress against their will. What kind of a country was that to live in? she asked her children.

Karim agreed, but reminded her that they were the lucky ones; they'd had enough money to leave. She gave him an irritated look and asked him what they'd come *to*. The whole of the United States was against Iran and Iranians. And that was just because of what some fanatics were doing in her beautiful country.

'So, we'll keep a low profile,' Soraya said soothingly. 'Something else will be in the headlines soon.'

'Ensh'allah,' Karim replied.

The following morning as his mother and sister were leaving, Esmat beckoned him to come around to the passenger side of the car.

'A word,' she said enigmatically, putting her hand out the window and touching his arm.

He guessed what was coming and ignored his sister's amused look.

'Be careful with that young woman Lauren,' his mother muttered. 'Nice enough, but she'll get her hooks into you. She obviously doesn't care where you come from.'

His mother wound her window closed before he could reply. He shrugged at his sister, who raised her eyebrows and smiled as she manoeuvred the large sedan onto the road. He waved, Soraya tooted the horn, and the car was soon swallowed up in the busy traffic.

He went back to his empty apartment and wandered into his study. He didn't care if Lauren 'got her hooks into him', he needed female company. He put his hand on the phone and paused. Whenever he was alone, he thought of Zahra. What was she doing now? Was Firzun taking care of her? Probably not. She was strong enough to manage him, Karim knew that, but he couldn't shake his niggling distrust of Firzun. The man always seemed to have a second agenda.

He shook his head and dialled Lauren's number. She picked up on the first ring.

'Hi!' She sounded really pleased to hear from him. 'Yep, the ankle is on the mend.'

'Are you free for lunch?'

'Sorry, I've got family business today and tomorrow. I can meet you at the French restaurant on Tuesday, twelve-thirty?'

'Sure,' he said, trying not to sound disappointed. The apartment echoed emptily, now his mother and sister had gone.

'Did you see the BBC interviews on TV last night?' she asked.

When he said he had, Lauren wrapped up the call. They'd discuss that over lunch, she promised.

He put the phone down. His mother was right, he reflected; Lauren couldn't care less that he was Iranian.

Karim was halfway to his office on Monday morning when he realised he had forgotten to bring Bahram's duty-free cigarettes with him. He stopped at a corner store and bought a packet of cigarettes as a small peace-offering. As he handed over the money, a display of red, white, and blue badges caught his eye. Each one had *Fuck Iran* printed on it in thick black letters. The bald statement was like a smack in the face.

'Hi Karim, welcome back,' the receptionist greeted him as he walked into the offices of *Konari and Yazdi*. His partner Bahram looked up from his phone call and waved.

'My wife,' he mouthed.

Karim smiled to himself as he looked around the shared office where he and Bahram had worked for the past few years. The white walls, light-coloured wood, and stainless-steel chairs reflected the ethos of their modern company. He wandered over to where a few models of buildings stood on a long table under the window.

'*Salaam*, Karim, how are you?' Bahram came in smiling, hand outstretched.

'Not so bad,' Karim replied, handing over the cigarettes with a quick explanation. 'I just saw some badges at the local corner store ...' he began.

'Yeah, I saw them too. Kind of insulting. I've changed my name to Bud Yates.' Bahram switched from speaking English to Persian. 'I might just get away with it. I've been here long enough to sound like a New Yorker.'

Karim thought so too. Bahram had been a high school exchange student like him and had graduated from college here in New York. He had dark hair and olive skin—he could have been from anywhere—and his English was perfect.

'So how are things in Tehran? Did you get anywhere near the embassy?' Bahram asked, lighting a cigarette.

'I was on the spot when they paraded one of the blindfolded hostages,' Karim admitted.

'Phew! Poor guys. They released the women and some of the African Americans for Thanksgiving. I guess you knew that.'

'Well, that's something,' Karim commented. 'So, Bahram, the cancelled jobs?'

'Things aren't good, Karim,' his partner answered.

Their eyes met, and for the first time Karim noticed lines around his partner's eyes and streaks of grey in his dark hair.

'The last four weeks ...' Bahram began, 'well, it's been a slow process, but there isn't much left on the books.'

He opened a folder and they pored over it together. He indicated a list of clients and the state of the work in progress.

'But we were so busy last year, we had to contract work out,' Karim said.

Bahram shook his head. 'I've taken most of that work over.' He ran a pencil down the list. 'I think we can salvage that one. It's well on the way, but this one's gone—Mrs Karth? Her son's a diplomat in the Middle East somewhere.'

Karim nodded. Things weren't quite as bad as he'd anticipated. But it didn't take much imagination to work out that if the hostage situation continued, their business would suffer.

'It's not just now,' Bahram said, echoing Karim's own thoughts. 'There could be anti-Iranian feelings in the US for years after this.'

'Even though we've got nothing to do with the government in Tehran.'

'Well, that's how it is. Look, Karim,' Bahram paused, then rushed on, 'I'm thinking of moving to the West Coast—Los Angeles to be exact. The lifestyle's easier going, the weather's good, and I think job prospects are better there. Lots of Iranians are moving to LA.'

'My parents are thinking of moving too,' Karim replied.

Why not sell the business outright and be done with it? he thought. There was barely enough work for two of them for the next six months. They wouldn't survive with so little work coming in. He knew he could find another job easily enough, he had plenty of contacts. Before he could say anything, his partner pushed a letter in front of him.

'It's a notice of audit from the IRS.'

'What? We've paid our taxes, haven't we?'

Bahram shrugged. 'Sure, sorry it's a surprise. Didn't you get one?'

'Maybe I did. I'm still going through my mail.' Karim looked at the official-looking document. It was dated November 8, four days after the hostage crisis had begun. Was this a coincidence? Was the IRS targeting Iranian-owned businesses to punish them? To see if they could get them for tax fraud? Surely not, he thought as he scanned the correspondence.

'It says we have to have everything ready by the middle of next week, Bahram!'

'Yeah, a guy called Gary Olson from the IRS called the other day.'

'So, have you been in touch with our accountant?'

'He's coming in tomorrow. He's been on holiday in Florida.'

'Doesn't give us much time.'

Karim was annoyed and frustrated with his business partner. Mention of the IRS had spooked Bahram, who seemed to be slipping into a catatonic state of denial.

Karim ran his hands through his hair. So it was up to him to sort out this mess. He decided to take the accounts with him to Boston on the weekend. His father was an experienced accountant; he'd be happy to look over them. Karim dragged his attention back to Bahram, who was muttering something about LA again and how his wife really wanted to go.

'Not till we've got this sorted, Bahram—*Bud*,' Karim said firmly.

* * *

'Have you ever heard of Stockholm syndrome?' Lauren asked as they took their places in the French restaurant.

'Vaguely, but first, how's the ankle?'

She extended her leg and flexed her ankle with a smile. She was wearing sheer black stockings and patent leather ankle boots. He felt a flicker of desire as their eyes met across the table. She looked away quickly.

'Well ... Stockholm syndrome,' she continued. 'The BBC interviewed a US marine guard—did you hear it? His name's William Diagos.'

'Yes,' Karim answered automatically, his mind on something else.

'Well, Diagos told the interviewer that the students were nice guys and looked after the hostages really well.'

Karim nodded.

'Stockholm syndrome,' Lauren repeated. 'It's when hostages develop a psychological alliance with the people who've captured them.'

'Yes, I've seen that myself—' Karim stopped abruptly.

'Tell me.' Lauren looked expectantly across the table at him.

'No, it was nothing. I remember seeing a documentary about it,' Karim answered hastily. She seemed satisfied and turned toward the waiter as he handed her a menu.

Karim took a deep breath. He'd remembered the night he'd

taken part in the raid to rescue the American hostages. Most of them had vocally resisted being released. When Firzun had shot and killed one of the guards in front of the Americans, a woman hostage had screamed in Karim's face. *'You've shot Sami, you bastards!'*

'Are you okay, Karim?' Lauren's voice broke into his thoughts.

He nodded. 'I'm fine.'

She reached her hand across the table for his and told him she was a good listener. He could tell her if anything was troubling him. When he told her that the IRS was going to audit his business, she laughed and replied that her dad's businesses were always being audited. Karim had nothing to worry about unless they'd broken the law.

'I thought it might be because we're Iranian—some sort of witch hunt.'

Lauren shook her head, then her green eyes held his. 'I like that you're Iranian,' she said softly.

He met her gaze, deciding not get too involved, if that was possible. He turned his attention to the menu and gave his order to the hovering waiter. While they ate, Lauren chatted about the horse she kept at 'Daddy's place' in Connecticut. He learned a lot about life in Antigua and the old friends she was getting in touch with now that Max was gone. He told her a little about Iran, the beautiful city of Isfahan, and the amazing ancient ruined city of Persepolis. She hung onto his every word, elbows on the table, her chin propped on her hands. He couldn't help but find her rapt attention flattering. After he'd paid the check, he helped her to her feet. Outside in the street, she pecked him on the cheek.

'Don't worry, honey. I'm sure no one's out to get you. Call me if you want to talk.' She smiled as she pulled on her gloves.

Karim walked back to his office feeling happier. His mother was wrong about Lauren. She hadn't pushed for another date. She seemed to have simply enjoyed his company over lunch. They'd arranged to meet for a drink before the concert at Carnegie Hall, but that was two weeks away. Lauren didn't seem to be in any hurry to start a new relationship, and neither was he. Zahra's rebuff had made him cautious. He didn't want to jump on another emotional rollercoaster just yet.

He was seriously worried about the IRS audit. Did they have the power to turn the place over and seize files? Yes, they probably did. But as far as he knew, his company had nothing to hide. Or was the IRS out to frame them? He tried to dismiss the idea, but it lingered in his mind.

Inside the building, he paused before he pressed the elevator button. He preferred to take the stairs, if he could—elevators always made him feel a tad claustrophobic—but he was in a hurry. While he waited, he turned over what Lauren had said about her father. What sort of business was he in that he attracted so much attention from the IRS?

The television footage he'd seen last night from Iran had revived thoughts of Zahra. He remembered kissing her the night he'd got back from the raid. She'd been shocked by his dishevelled appearance and the news that Firzun had been injured. He'd begged her to sleep with him, to comfort each other in a time of danger. She'd nearly given in. But then she'd pushed him away; she was married after all, and he respected that.

He got into the elevator still thinking about Zahra. In spite of everything, he desperately wanted to know how she was and what was happening to her. If she needed his help would she contact him? He doubted it—she was still married to Firzun. Writing to a man she'd known briefly in Tehran would be both stupid and dangerous.

17

NOUSHA

Zahra woke suddenly in the night and tiptoed into the living room, convinced she'd heard rustling outside her window. When she risked a look, the hostel grounds were deserted. A crescent moon floated in the clear night sky. She opened the window a fraction and the thin curtains moved slightly in the breeze from the ocean. She could smell a salt tang—was it the smell of the sea? She had never seen the ocean in her whole life. She promised herself she would take Ahmad to the beach soon. Through the open window, she could hear the dull rhythmic sound of the surf. A small animal scampered across the grass, startling her before it vanished into the trees.

The silence helped her to organise her thoughts. She would have some Australian money soon, thanks to Karim's earlier gift of American dollars. She opened the wardrobe drawer quietly; the skirt was still there in its plastic garbage bag. Tomorrow she'd get rid of Firzun's loathsome cargo and be free.

The following morning, Zahra shut her door and tested it to make sure it was locked. If it hadn't been for Ahmad, she would have skipped breakfast and stayed in her room to guard the drugs. She steeled herself for another public appearance as she stepped out into the sunshine. Ahmad ran ahead and she hurried to catch up to him. The winding path to the dining room took her close to the hostel gate and she glanced over nervously. *What if they search my room while I'm out?* But the security guards appeared not to notice her. They were chatting to a slim, dark-haired woman in blue jeans and white t-shirt. The woman turned suddenly and walked across to Zahra, falling in step alongside her.

'Hi!' the woman said in English.

Zahra returned the greeting hesitantly. The woman looked familiar. She could have been Afghan or Iranian, Zahra wasn't sure.

'I've been looking forward to meeting you, Zahra Ghafoori,' her companion said in *Dari*.

Zahra slowed and turned to her. Who on earth was she?

'I'm joining you for breakfast. I know the way to the dining room. Keep walking.' She took Zahra's elbow and propelled her forward. She lowered her voice. 'I'm Nousha. Have you looked in the kid's backpack yet?'

Zahra shook herself free, then stopped and faced Nousha.

'Yes, I have! Where's Firzun?'

'Don't stop, Zahra *djan*,' Nousha hissed. 'He's hiding out at our place ... Wait for Mummy, Ahmad!' she called out.

How does she know his name?

Taken by surprise, Ahmad halted as Zahra opened the door for him.

'This lady is Mummy's friend,' she explained.

Nousha pointed to an empty table and told her to sit there and wait. Zahra watched in stunned silence as Nousha headed for the breakfast counter. On her way she greeted several people—Afghans, Zahra noticed with a sinking feeling. Of course there'd be other Afghans here. People were escaping from Afghanistan ahead of the threatened Soviet invasion. Thousands of them were waiting in Pakistan for refugee visas like hers. Some were bound to end up here in Australia. News of Firzun's desertion had no doubt reached them already. They wouldn't be happy until they'd interrogated her, the deserted wife. It was a nice piece of juicy gossip.

Nousha returned with a tray of food. She unloaded sliced tomatoes, cheese, cucumber, yogurt, sliced apples, toast, mugs of tea, and a mug of milk for Ahmad. The woman remarked casually that the breakfasts were okay, but the other meals were 'crap'.

'You know some of the Afghans ...' Zahra began.

'Don't worry about them, they're villagers,' Nousha said dismissively as she sat down. 'They've got "yes", "no", and "thank you" in English and not much else. Firzun says your English is good. I guess that Iranian boyfriend of yours helped.' She smirked across the table.

'What? He was not my boyfriend,' Zahra retorted.

Nousha shrugged and, still smirking, buttered a piece of toast. According to Firzun, Nousha informed her, Karim Konari had nearly wrecked Zahra and Firzun's chance of getting out of Tehran in one piece. Wasn't he all designer clothes and high ideals? Nousha laughed out loud and helped herself to cheese.

Zahra was incensed. 'Mind your own business. How did you get past the hostel security?'

'Calm down, dear. I used to live here, everyone knows me. I was an unofficial interpreter for the Iranians and the Afghans.' Nousha leaned forward slightly, her black eyes hard.

'But I'm not here to answer your questions. Where's the stuff from the backpack?'

'In my flat,' Zahra answered hotly. 'What the hell was Firzun thinking?'

'Keep your voice down, would you? Some of those Afghans speak *Dari*.' Nousha glanced around. 'We want it today, but not here. I want you to ...'

'I've done enough!' Zahra cut in. 'I'm lucky I'm not in prison thanks to you and Firzun! I've been strip searched and my flat's been turned over. You can take it right now.' She pushed her chair back and stood up.

'Sit down and shut up, idiot. The security guards know who you are. The police told them to keep an eye on you.'

Her comment had the desired effect. Zahra sat back in her seat, feeling scared. But maybe Nousha was lying. Suddenly Nousha waved to someone on the other side of the room. She mouthed 'I'm fine! How are you?' Then she turned back to Zahra, her smile frozen on her face, and told her to listen.

'Bring the stuff to the shopping mall. It's too obvious here.' Nousha put her foot on Zahra's and pressed hard. 'Don't mess me around or you'll be sorry.'

'Get ... off ... me!' Zahra leaned angrily across the table.

'Wipe that look off your face, Zahra *Khanoum*,' Nousha snapped, releasing Zahra's foot. 'I'm going to say this once only. When I leave here, pick up the bag from the back of my chair. Be casual, act like it's yours. Put the stuff in the zipped compartment. Twelve packets. Don't try any games, like going to the police.'

She smiled sweetly with her head on one side while she gave the instructions. Zahra was to bring the 'stuff' to the local shopping mall at four o'clock today and sit on the bench near the Christmas tree. She waved away Zahra's protest that she hadn't been out of the hostel yet. She didn't know where the shopping mall was.

'Ask someone. There's a phone number in the bag. If you mess up, call it.'

'Mummy!' Ahmad tugged her sleeve.

'Shut up, Ahmad, I'm talking to your mother.' Nousha glared at him. Ahmad's lip trembled and he looked frightened. She pressed Zahra's foot hard again and told her to ignore Ahmad and listen.

'I'll come and sit next to you. Leave the bag on the seat and I'll pick it up.'

Nousha looked around the dining room casually. Most of the residents had gone. Zahra dragged her foot free, furious that Nousha assumed she'd do as she was told.

'Remember, don't mess us around,' the other woman repeated.

'Don't chuck it out either. The police aren't stupid. They'll lift fingerprints off the bags and be back here like a shot.'

Zahra stared at her, speechless. Why hadn't she thought of that?

Nousha eyes glittered. 'I'm warning you ...' she whispered. 'Get this right or I'll turn you in.'

'You're despicable!'

'Am I? What about your cousin Firzun? He dumped you at the airport.'

Ahmad was shifting in his seat and trying to stand up. 'Is cousin Firzun coming?' he asked suddenly.

'Can't you do something about him?' Nousha said irritably. 'Go and get us an orange from the kitchen, Ahmad,' she ordered. To Zahra's relief he did what he was told.

'Your dear cousin is staying with me and my brother, till we've got the consignment,' Nousha continued. 'After that, I'll be glad to see the back of him.'

'I thought you were engaged?'

Nousha laughed out loud. 'Why would I marry a stupid Afghan like him?'

'But he said ...'

'He's a loser like your wife-beating husband Mahmoud. Firzun had to kill him to get him out of your life. Think I want to marry a killer?'

Zahra was aghast. This woman knew all her business—thanks to Firzun!

Nousha stood up and leaned on the table. 'I'm on the lookout for a wealthy old Australian. Or maybe a flashy Persian, like Karim Konari.' Before Zahra could answer, Nousha repeated her instructions: 'Take the bag and don't mess up. Four o'clock at the mall.'

Zahra watched dumbfounded as Nousha walked slowly toward the door, swinging her hips in her tight jeans. She looked round for Ahmad; he was coming toward her holding an orange. She went over to meet him, then returned to the chair Nousha had vacated and casually picked up the bag left there. She slipped it into her own bag and headed for the door.

'Excuse me, Zahra!'

She stopped and turned, her nerves on edge. Her English neighbour was standing at her table. *Did she see me take the bag?*

'Hi, I'm Julie, remember? I'm sorry to interfere but ...'

Zahra held her breath. *She saw me. What's she going to do?*

'... you haven't cleared your table,' Julie went on. 'They get upset if people don't take their dishes back over there.' She indicated the kitchen area. 'Hope you don't mind me mentioning—'

'No, it's fine, thank you. I'll do it now.'

She went back to her table, hearing nothing Julie said as they loaded the tray together.

'I'm glad you've got a new friend,' Julie commented as they walked to the service area. 'Looks like there are more of your people over there too.'

Zahra glanced across the room to where the Afghan women were sitting, watching her intently. *Maybe I should talk to them, see what they knew about Nousha.* But that might not be a good idea. She was in no mood for questions right now. She ignored them and left the dining room with Julie, conscious of five pairs of women's eyes on her.

Back in the flat, she shut the door firmly and strained her ears, listening for a police siren. The only sounds were the carolling noise the magpies made as they called to each other and the chatter of people walking back from breakfast. She took off her sandal and rubbed her foot. The strong leather had protected it, but it was still sore. *Damn Nousha—damn all of them!* She stood at the side of the window behind the curtain. The Afghan women hadn't followed her, thank goodness.

While Ahmad crawled around the floor playing with his truck, Zahra unzipped Nousha's bag and found the note in an inside pocket. The message was terse: '*Phone me on this number only if you need to.*' She recognised Firzun's hasty script. What a nerve! she thought angrily. How dare he write that? What about an apology or an explanation?

A sharp knock on the door startled her. She opened it a fraction. Lan was outside, holding a small thin boy by the hand.

'All ready? We come in?' she asked as she stepped over the threshold.

'Tran!' Ahmad exclaimed when he saw his new friend. 'Kindergarten?' he asked in English.

The boy shook his head and said something in his own language to Ahmad.

'No kindy this morning. We go shopping, see Santa!' Lan said brightly. 'This my son Tran. You okay now, Zahra?'

At last, a normal person.

'I'm fine. We're going to the shops, Ahmad,' Zahra told him and turned to Lan. 'I have to phone someone, go to the bank ... and post something.'

'I show you everything at shops, no worries. Phone here in recreation room, but always busy.'

Zahra shoved Nousha's bag in the wardrobe. She folded Firzun's note into her own bag with the letter she'd written to Karim. When she shut the door, she tested it a few times before she followed Lan along the path toward the gate.

'Shops open nine clock, close five-ferty. My country, shops never close,' Lan announced.

As she walked out of the hostel, Zahra avoided looking at the security guards. Falling into step with Lan and the children, Zahra looked with interest at the single-storied houses they passed. The roses that twined around some of the veranda posts were already wilting in the hot sun.

'This way to shopping mall, take twenty minutes walk.' Lan pointed ahead. 'That way go to beach.' She indicated behind her at an empty road bordered on either side by tall trees.

Ahmad, who was running ahead of them with his friend,

stopped and ran back. He tugged at her hand. 'Mummy, that lady's got no clothes on!' He pointed across the road.

Zahra told Ahmad not to point, but she found it hard not to stare herself. A young woman was walking arm-in-arm with her boyfriend and she was in her underwear! A strip of blue material covered her breasts and another one barely covered her private parts. Her bright blond hair bounced on her tanned shoulders. She was chatting and laughing with her boyfriend, who wore nothing but a pair of patterned shorts and rubber sandals.

Zahra's companion followed her gaze.

'No shame. Look like bar girl,' Lan exclaimed.

More young women in underwear passed them and each time Lan tutted loudly.

'Phone box here,' Lan announced. 'You got twenty cents?'

Zahra looked askance. She had no local money.

'I give and show you.'

They all squeezed into the phone box. When her call connected and started ringing, Lan took the children out and waited on the footpath with them. It was stiflingly hot and the ringing at the other end went on and on.

'Hello?' A man's voice.

Zahra hesitated. 'Firzun?'

'Is that you, Zahra?'

Her legs felt weak when she heard his voice and she steadied herself against the glass wall of the box.

'Yes, Firzun!' She was furious with him. 'Did Nousha tell you about the police?'

She heard his quick intake of breath.

'You got the stuff?'

'I have!' she shouted. 'Is this why you dumped me, Firzun? How could you?'

He ignored her outburst. 'Yeah, Nousha said you weren't happy.'

'Of *course* I'm not happy!'

'I told you why I left. Remember Ali Esmaeili? He's here. Do you want him to kill me?'

'What about me? Do you want me to go to prison?'

'Okay, listen ...' he began.

Before he could speak, someone rapped on the phone box window. Zahra looked fearfully over her shoulder. Outside, a man in work clothes motioned her to hurry up. She nodded, then turned back to the phone.

'Be quick, someone wants to use the phone,' she urged.

'Did Nousha tell you what to do?'

'Yes, but what if ...'

The phone went dead. She shook it in disbelief.

The man outside banged on the glass. 'Come on, missus. Get a move on,' he called.

She grabbed the scrap of paper with the phone number and pushed past the man, avoiding eye contact with him.

'Over here,' her new friend called cheerfully. 'We go to bank and post office, then see Santa!'

Zahra joined Lan as she led them across a car park and into the air-conditioned shopping mall. Was this the place Firzun and Nousha meant? What a crazy idea to do a drug exchange here. Even at this early hour, there were throngs of people coming in and out of the busy shops.

'See Santa?' Lan sounded thrilled.

A white-bearded Santa in his red suit and hat sat on a huge chair near a glittering Christmas tree. Ahmad and his new friend backed away when he waved at them. Zahra looked around quickly. There was a bench near the tree. Was that it? She felt sick. *I've got to get back, check the packets are still there.* But Lan had other ideas; she was determined to show her around.

After she changed her American money at the bank, they went on a tour of the shops, including the post office. Zahra stood at the red post box and hesitated. *Why not?* She pushed the letter to Karim, bedecked with Christmas stamps, into the slot.

'Lucky country! Everyone never hungry here,' Lan commented as they walked back along the sunny road. Nearing the gates, Zahra's feeling of dread about the drugs nearly overwhelmed her. How was she going to get away with Nousha's plan? She looked behind her once or twice as they walked, wondering if they were being followed. Had the assassin found her? Was he watching her every move? No, Firzun had invented him to excuse his behaviour, she told herself.

After lunch with Lan and her son, she persuaded Ahmad to have a nap. Once he was asleep she drew the curtains and checked that the packets were still in the wardrobe. She moved silently to the window and looked out. A few people were walking back from the beach. The afternoon was hot, and she found it hard to believe that it was the end of November.

She put everything on the table. Trying not to fumble, she slit the hem of the skirt and took the packets out carefully. Using a damp face-washer from the bathroom, she cleaned each one before she spread them around the padded lining of Nousha's bag and zipped it up. She ran the face-washer over the inside and outside of the bag. Still using the cloth, she held the bag in her hand for a minute, trying to steady her breathing, then pushed it back into the dark recess of her wardrobe. She checked her watch: it was only one-thirty. She sat down at the small table feeling tense. How was she going to get away with it? She was about to leave thousands of dollars' worth of heroin on a bench in a busy, brightly lit shopping mall and run the risk of being arrested. Maybe she should throw the packets in the garbage after all. She shook her head; someone might find them and call the police anyway. She was in this up to her neck, thanks to her stupid cousin. But once rid of the drugs, she would be free.

18

———

THE SHOPPING MALL

Zahra sat on the couch in her hostel flat and checked her watch again. She felt relieved that she'd soon be rid of the drugs, but at the same time sick with fear. In two hours' time, she had to pass a bag of heroin to Nousha at a busy shopping mall. Surely someone would notice the transaction? Were the police still watching her? Maybe they were tracking her movements, hoping she would lead them to Firzun. What if they saw her pass the bag to Nousha? They'd arrest her on the spot, in public, and what would they do with Ahmad? Nousha had scared her about dumping the parcels. Her best bet was to get this over with as quickly as possible. She tried to steady her nerves and checked her watch for the umpteenth time.

At three o'clock she woke Ahmad and helped him get ready. When she took Nousha's handbag out of the wardrobe, she could feel the contents clearly through the vinyl. Only an hour to go and it would all be over! Nousha's instructions to leave the bag and walk away throbbed in her head.

She'd changed into a navy dress with small white spots, hoping the innocuous colour would help her blend into the crowd. She slipped her purse in her pocket. She wouldn't take her own bag—

carrying two bags might look odd. Instead, she'd leave Nousha's on the bench and go. At the last minute, she remembered the skirt. She grabbed it from the drawer, still wrapped in the garbage bag.

Clutching Nousha's bag to her side, she opened her front door. Ahmad rushed out immediately and ran around the lawn. She closed the door, called him over to her, and glanced round quickly. In the distance a few people were walking back from the beach. Another little group had gathered outside the administration block. They walked toward the gate. The security men were talking to someone in a delivery van. Hopefully no one would notice her or even be interested in where she was going.

The hot weather didn't seem to bother Ahmad as he ran ahead of her, jumping over cracks in the paving stones. A few cars passed them but she only saw one other person, a young mother with a toddler asleep in a stroller. Most of the houses had the blinds closed, and the flowers in the front gardens looked wilted and tired.

'Would you like to go to the beach this afternoon?' she asked Ahmad when she caught up with him.

'Surfing!' he said in English.

'Surfing,' Zahra repeated, trying to smile at him.

The huge signs for the mall loomed on the horizon and she felt sick with dread. They crossed the railway track and within ten minutes they were walking into the car park. With a deft movement, she dropped the wrapped skirt into a garbage bin. What a relief!

When the mall's automatic doors flew open, her stomach clenched. Once inside the air-conditioned space she felt better, but to her dismay the mall was busy. School was over for the day and the whole place echoed with the shouts of children. Her head throbbed. She checked her watch: three-forty-five. They were early.

She wandered around with Ahmad, looking vaguely in the shop windows. Her arm ached as she gripped the bag against her body. When people walked too close to her, she veered away. What if someone knocked the bag off her shoulder and the incriminating packets skidded across the polished tile floor?

Zahra checked her watch again: five minutes to four. She hurried toward the Christmas tree and looked around. There was no sign of Nousha. Santa was still sitting in his big chair listening to an earnest-looking child. She stood at the tree and pointed out the star and the angels to Ahmad. While she talked to him, she looked around covertly for Nousha. It was now exactly four o'clock. She sat down with Ahmad and slipped the bag strap off her shoulder, holding it casually on her left side.

'Can we go now?' Ahmad asked immediately.

'We've got to wait here for a minute.'

He wriggled off the seat and went back to the Christmas tree.

Nousha sat down so quietly that Zahra was startled when she spoke. 'Leave the bag, get the kid, and walk away.'

Zahra put the bag on the seat between them. She glanced around nervously, but Nousha nudged her arm.

'He sent a note.' She shoved it at Zahra. 'Now clear off, don't rush.'

Zahra pushed the note into her pocket and joined Ahmad at the Christmas tree. Out of the corner of her eye, she saw Nousha walking away with the bag over her shoulder.

'Ahmad, look at the star ...'

'Stop, thief!'

Zahra whirled round and nearly fell over Ahmad. *No, no, no!*

A heavy, sweating woman with yellow hair was holding Nousha's arm in a vice-like grip.

'Gimme that bag, you filthy wog!' she shouted as she wrestled it from Nousha's hand. Zahra froze—any minute the cheap bag would split open.

'See her?' The woman pointed to Zahra. 'She was looking at the tree ... and this mongrel nicked her bag.'

'Get to the toilets,' Nousha shouted to Zahra in *Dari*. She spat in the woman's face, kicked her hard in the shins, and bolted for the exit.

'Foul bitch,' the other woman yelled, wiping her face with the back of her hand. 'Here you! Look after your things.' She thrust the bag at Zahra's chest.

'Thank you.' The words stuck in Zahra's throat. She was rigid with fear. Had someone called the police?

The sweaty woman stomped away and the curious onlookers dispersed as fast as they'd gathered. Zahra sat down heavily on the bench. Ahmad looked petrified and she held him tightly. Was the woman going to come back with the police? Zahra wanted to sob out loud as she hoisted the bag full of drugs over her shoulder again. She expected that any minute she'd be arrested and escorted to a waiting police car. But to her amazement, everything had returned to normal. The incident had already been forgotten.

Her head was reeling. *I've got to get rid of it!* She stood up slowly. She had to get to the toilets and find Nousha. Reluctantly Zahra quickened her pace. She had no idea where she was, but she steered Ahmad in the direction Nousha had run. Finally, she saw a blue sign and hurried down a passageway. She pushed open a door with *Women* written on it. It was stuffy inside and she looked quickly at the cubicle doors. Only one of the three was occupied.

'Wee, wee, Mummy,' Ahmad said, heading for a cubicle.

He jumped violently and grabbed her hand when a voice from behind the closed door whispered in *Dari*.

'What kept you?' Without waiting for an answer, Nousha snapped out orders: go into the next cubicle. Pass the bag under the wall.

Zahra told Ahmad to wait outside. She held her breath in the cramped, smelly place and kneeled close to the toilet bowl. She managed to push the bag under the small gap.

Nousha snatched it and she heard her unzipping the lining. 'Firzun wants you to call him,' she muttered, fumbling and cursing as she unloaded the bag. When Nousha flung her door open, Zahra grabbed her arm.

'What's going on?'

'Filthy harlot,' Nousha spat as she shook her off. 'Mind your own business, whore!' She pushed Zahra against a washbasin and flung out of the stuffy room.

Zahra was too stunned to stop her. *Whore?*

A woman with a stroller reversed through the door and Zahra quickly steered Ahmad into the cubicle that Nousha had vacated. She picked up the bag from the floor and held it gingerly. The zipped compartment was wide open and empty. When she walked out of the cubicle, she glanced at the newcomer. The woman was fussing with her baby and had her back to her. Zahra pulled a bunch of paper towels out of the dispenser and wiped the bag down. She felt tainted and dirty. After she'd helped Ahmad go to the toilet and wash his hands, she jabbed several times at the soap dispenser. She covered her hands in soap and hot water, rubbing and rinsing until she felt clean. Before Ahmad could say anything, she put her wet finger to her lips. She didn't want the other mother to hear them speaking in *Dari*. It was obviously risky looking or sounding foreign here at the mall.

She opened the door and the cacophony of the shopping centre jarred her nerves. She let out her breath slowly. Thank goodness the place was air-conditioned, unlike the washrooms. At the ice-cream shop she bought Ahmad a huge cone. He cheered up and licked the ice-cream to a point as she hurried him toward the exit. She felt nervous, as if someone was watching her. When she saw an abandoned plastic shopping bag on the ground, she swept it up and slipped the handbag inside. They passed a garbage bin, into which she dropped the plastic bag.

Nousha's warning about fingerprints drummed in the back of her head. She'd wiped the bag down quickly with paper towels in the restroom. But had she got all her prints off it? Guiding Ahmad toward the exit, the only thought in her head was to get as far away as possible from the mall and the loathsome bag she'd disposed of.

When they got outside, the air felt like a blast from a hot bread oven. She scanned the car park for Nousha, but there was no sign of her. Cars passed them as she set off on the now familiar road to the hostel. Each time one passed, she felt edgy, fancying it might be the police. She risked a look at some of the drivers, but they were mostly women with children in the back.

The whole exchange in the shopping mall had left her feeling completely drained. Nousha had called her a whore! Why? Did she think Zahra had asked Firzun to kill her husband and pass himself off as Mahmoud? Or was it a reference to her friendship with Karim? She was furious with her cousin. Drugs! This was the last straw!

She looked down at Ahmad walking beside her in the hot sun, his ice-cream melting faster than he could eat it. Shame mingled with a deep-seated anger washed over her. Poor Ahmad had been through so much. She vowed that she would make a success of her life in Australia for his sake. She'd make sure he had a good education and a nice place to live. She'd get a job and work hard like she'd done in her own country. The fat blonde woman in the mall had scared her. She decided to speak English to Ahmad in public from now on, whether he understood or not.

Back at the flat, she cleaned Ahmad up before going to phone Firzun. Although she still felt shaky, a sense of freedom swept over her. The damning contents of the backpack had gone. After today, Firzun and Nousha could go their own ways. As she approached the recreation room with Ahmad, some of the other residents were coming back from the beach with their children. Julie, her neighbour, looked hot and pink like the other pale-skinned English people.

'You should take your little boy to the beach. He'll love it!' Julie called out to her.

'Yes, we're going soon,' Zahra answered.

All I have to do is phone Firzun and then I'm free.

To her relief, there was no one using the phone in the entry to the large room. She opened one of the glass doors for Ahmad and he ran over to the TV and sat down on the floor. She switched the television on and walked back to the pay phone. Turning the coins over to read the denominations, she slotted enough into the box and dialled the number. Someone picked up on the second ring.

'Who's calling?' Firzun's unmistakable gravelly voice asked urgently.

'It's Zahra.'

'Have you delivered the stuff?'

'Yes, an hour ago. Haven't you got it?'

'Not yet. Is everything okay?'

It was pointless going into details. He wouldn't be interested.

'Is anyone with you?' He sounded edgy.

'Just Ahmad.'

Is he going to thank me or ask after Ahmad?

'Listen,' Firzun lowered his voice, 'the stuff's a business investment. I'll cut you in later. We're going to send money home to fight the Soviets.'

So the Australian police had been right about him. He was here to peddle drugs. She told him she didn't want a cut or anything to do with their 'business'. The Australian police were still looking for him, or had he forgotten that?

'Please yourself about the cut,' Firzun answered nonchalantly. 'I'm not worried about the police. I've got another identity fixed up.'

She felt like slamming the phone down on his smug voice, but then he said casually, 'Remember that assassin I told you about—Ali Esmaeili? He's still around. Watch out for him.'

What next?

'How do you know?'

'On the grapevine. I'm leaving when I've fixed up the deal anyway.'

'Leaving for ...?'

'Afghanistan of course, to fight the commies!'

She was aghast. Although he was a useless nuisance, he was still family. Fighting in Afghanistan? Was he crazy? He really had dumped her in this country. She couldn't go home, she had no money. He rambled on about Afghan politics, informing her that their country was on the brink of war with the Soviet Union.

'Stay here, Firzun. Stay safe.'

'I don't do "safe",' he announced. 'Listen,' he added more kindly, 'you can call me on this number anytime. But once I've got the money, I'm off.'

He hung up and she stood with the buzzing receiver in her hand. He was going back home, back to Afghanistan, leaving her here at the other end of the world alone with her son. She felt abandoned and upset. She had imagined that Nousha's family would befriend and help her in the new country. Now she felt angry and cheated. The woman had called her awful names—why? She had forgotten to ask Firzun. She joined Ahmad and sat down in one of the jumbled collection of chairs arranged around the television set. Ahmad was entranced by a children's program about a kangaroo.

'He's called Skippy,' Ahmad told her seriously. 'And he can talk.'

I've heard everything now, she thought ... a talking kangaroo. She glanced around the big room. At one end there was a tennis table with paddles and balls left neatly on top. The windows looked out onto a wide expanse of grass toward a main road. She could see cars passing in a constant stream on the other side of the hostel fence. Julie had told her that the Pacific Ocean was just beyond the stand of trees across the road.

The program finished and Ahmad scrambled to his feet. She told him they were going to get some towels and walk to the beach. He hopped along next to her, like a kangaroo.

She found the way easily. As they got nearer she smelled the salt tang again on the light breeze. They walked across the main road to a stand of tall trees. Closer to the beach, they passed one of the near-naked girls they saw that morning. She was rubbing something on her arms from a bottle. Zahra squinted covertly at the label—coconut oil. The smell of the oil and the sea made her feel relaxed. She could already hear the regular booming sound from the breakers as they hit the shore.

They stopped at the top of a rise and she gasped. Ahmad squealed with delight when he saw the white sand and the magnificent dark blue Pacific Ocean spreading out to the horizon. Underfoot, wooden slats had been laid down a sandy slope to make it easier to walk onto the beach. On either side of the path, with its worn wooden handrails, stubby bushes swayed in the light breeze. The white surf from the sparkling water hit the beach with a roar. When it pulled back, it took shrieking children and bobbing people with it. Zahra stared at the blueness, her mind overloaded with brilliant images.

'Mummy, look! *Surfboard.*' Ahmad pointed and turned his delighted face up to her.

Zahra felt a rush of excitement herself at this, her first sight of the ocean. Ahmad took off his sneakers and she slipped off her sandals, feeling the warmth of the wooden slats under her feet. The white sandy beach stretched as far as she could see and she blinked in the reflected brilliance.

Ahmad raced ahead of her onto the sand, arms flung wide. He ran and twirled and jumped, shouting at the top of his voice, 'Yeah!' He chased the seagulls and they squealed as they flew away from him into the blue sky.

The sand felt hot under her bare feet as she ran toward the surf and grabbed Ahmad before he cannoned into the water. She dropped her sandals and his sneakers onto the sand and stretched her arms over her head, feeling the tension of the day seeping out of her. Ahmad ran back and pointed at the bronzed children on little boards, who were being washed in and out on the waves.

'Surfboard, look!' Ahmad shouted again in English.

She warned him not to go too near, then she sat down watching everyone. A young man waded out toward the arcs of water, then threw himself forward and swam toward the incoming breakers. He dived into a wave and disappeared. It passed over him and crashed onto the beach. Zahra screwed up her eyes; had he been washed out to sea? But he emerged above the waves, triumphant. He waded in again and waited for the next wave. It curved over him and she saw his arms reaching strongly as it swept him into the shore.

He stood in the shallows slicking his hair back with his hands. He wiped them over his face and returned to the incessant surf. She couldn't take her eyes off him. Then she realised with a shock that she was staring at a man, a bronzed man with a naked chest and wet blond hair. She would never have stared at a man like this in Iran or Afghanistan. She felt embarrassed and guilty as she took Ahmad's hand and walked further along the shoreline. She glanced back a couple of times, still spellbound by the man's careless bravery.

Ahmad raced in front of her as she strolled along the beach, carrying their shoes.

'You won't get me! You won't get me!' he shouted at the surf as it hit the sand and sucked at his small feet.

Ahead, rocky outcrops suggested more beaches and bays in the distance. Zahra looked around to get her bearings. The hostel was across the road to her left, hidden behind sand dunes and trees. She turned around and looked to the south. Behind them a small town spread out along low cliffs with a lighthouse at the end of a harbour. This must be—what had Julie called it—Wollongong? Further along the coast she saw thick smoke billowing into the air. Was this the steelworks where Julie's husband had a job? She looked at the town thoughtfully; maybe she could get work there? Living at the Fairy Meadow migrant hostel could not be a permanent arrangement for them.

Zahra turned back and followed Ahmad along the shoreline. The water felt cold and refreshing on her feet and the sun was warm on her back. Eventually she sat down on the sand and watched the surf as it broke on the beach.

Suddenly she remembered seeing a photograph of Karim in his grandmother's bedroom. He was dressed in shorts and t-shirt and standing on a beach with the sea in the background. Hands on hips, he was smiling straight at the camera. The image was so strong that Zahra almost felt as if he was here, sitting beside her on this beach. If only ... She blinked away a tear. None of this would have happened to her if she had trusted him and not her cousin. But Karim wasn't here and never would be. It would be Christmas in a few weeks and he'd be going to parties in New York. She belonged to his past in Tehran. Perhaps when he got her letter he'd read it, throw it away, and she'd never hear from him again.

Zahra watched the surf as it drew back and crashed again on the beach. What was the point of thinking about the past? She took a deep breath. She had to begin her life in Australia, without Firzun causing trouble. Orientation classes started in two days' time. She would meet the other refugees and migrants she'd managed to avoid so far. She wondered apprehensively if many of them knew her story. Thanks to Nousha the Afghans certainly did. As she stared unseeing at the ocean, a terrible thought occurred to her. What if Ali Esmaeili, the assassin, showed up in her class posing as a student? Maybe not in her class, but somewhere around the hostel? But was Ali another of Firzun's half-truths—something to keep her on edge and an excuse for his appalling behaviour? She called to Ahmad and they walked back through the shallows then up the beach toward the hostel. By the time she got to her flat, Zahra had convinced herself that Ali Esmaeili didn't exist.

19

A WEEKEND WITH THE FAMILY

Karim leaned both hands on Bahram's desk and surveyed the documents and receipts that they'd finally managed to organise into piles.

'My personal secretary left.' Bahram shrugged his shoulders hopelessly. 'Craig's on his way,' he added.

When their accountant, looking tanned and wearing a Hawaiian shirt, appeared in the doorway of the paper-strewn office, he raised his eyebrows.

'Well, hello y'all—yippee do!'

'Nice vacation in Florida, Craig?' Karim queried.

'Yeah, Miami. Great place! Man, am I relaxed. Looks like I got here just in time.'

'Love the shirt,' Karim commented.

They had till April to get the paperwork in order according to Craig, who flashed them a white-toothed smile. So they could relax! Craig sat at Karim's desk, smoking a cigarette and sifting through papers. His occasional 'uh-ohs' did little for Karim's nerves.

'Does he know what he's doing?' he asked Bahram in Persian. Before his partner could reply, Craig turned to them.

'Woah guys! Let's stick to English.' He stubbed out his cigarette and straightened up. 'You're not planning to make me a hostage, are you?'

'We need him too much for that,' Karim muttered in Persian to Bahram, who shrugged.

On Friday morning, Craig announced he'd finished.

'I'll get everything ready for you to sign,' he said from their office door. 'My invoice is in the mail. Next vacation—Mexico! *Hasta la vista*,' he called over his shoulder as he left.

Karim waved briefly, then told Bahram he was going to take copies of all the accounts to Boston that evening. He wanted his father to do a final check. Bahram nodded, but asked if they should tell Craig.

'Not necessary, Dad knows a lot about the IRS and audits.'

'Sure,' Bahram capitulated. 'Give your family my regards.'

Boston in winter—he'd forgotten about the chill factor in the wind. Karim turned his coat collar up as he left the airport and hailed a taxi. He settled in the back, hoping that his father would not find it too hard to go through the accounts now that the mess of papers and receipts he'd brought with him had been sorted. He glanced out the window at the familiar landmarks. He had started building a house here when he'd married Nancy. Both marriage and house had finished in the same month.

'Want me to drive slow so you can see the lights?' the taxi driver asked.

'Okay.'

He didn't really care, but as the driver meandered along streets blazing with lights, he had an idea. Maybe he should invest in a business that designed and set up Christmas lights on houses. He'd sure do a better job than some of the tacky displays they were passing. They drove past houses outlined in lights, the trees in the front yards wreathed in different glowing colours. Several houses had Santas, sleighs, and reindeer on their roofs. Porch uprights were festooned in greenery and silver lights, and holly wreaths graced front doors. By his estimation, most of the streets were using enough electricity to power an Iranian village for a year.

As the taxi stopped outside his sister's house in an exclusive suburb, he reflected that his brother-in-law Nadir's engineering business must be doing well. Their house was a two-storey Cape Cod style and stood on a rise with steps leading up to it from the road. The trees in the front yard were wreathed in lights and the porch and the upper storey glowed as well. A large brightly lit holly wreath sat under a small window below an apex on the roof. Nadir, being an engineer, refused to have Santa and a sleigh on the roof. The red front door flew open as he approached and his two nephews threw themselves on him, rattling the lights entwined around the entrance.

'Uncle Karim!'

He put his bags down and swung them into his arms just as his mother emerged, admonishing everyone to get inside. She collected his bags from the front porch and closed the door firmly.

'It's freezing out there,' she said dramatically, putting up her cheek for a kiss. She smelled faintly of garlic and cooking, and he smiled. The house was warm and full of happiness and light. As he followed his excited nephews into the living room, he took his accountant's advice and began to relax. His father was sitting in a chair near a log fire that crackled in the large fireplace.

'Hi!' His sister ran to greet him, followed by Nadir, who shook his hand. He wondered briefly whether Zahra would fit in here but knew in his heart that Lauren would be more at home with his Americanised family.

'Good flight, son? Everything okay at home?'

His father Abbas hugged him, and over his shoulder Karim exchanged a worried glance with his sister. The man seemed to have aged overnight.

'It was, thanks, *Baba*. We can talk later about Tehran, but I really need help with my business accounts.'

'If it's numbers, I'm your man!' his father said with a hint of his old vigour.

As Karim followed them into the main living room, he commented on the outside decor.

'It's not a good idea to be the only house in the street with no Christmas lights,' Soraya explained. 'You know, the Iranian neighbours who don't like Christmas?'

After the noisy family meal was over, Karim excused himself, glad to be alone with his father again. He gave Abbas a wry look and dumped his collection of files on his brother-in-law's desk in the study. He was relieved that his father had agreed to double-check Craig's figures. Abbas had been chief accountant in his last job and had never thought much of Craig's skill.

Late Saturday afternoon, Abbas closed the final folder. He'd double-checked everything and was sure the firm had nothing to worry about, he told his son. Karim stretched his arms above his head and thanked his father. They weren't being targeted because they were Iranians, his father told him as they packed the books into Karim's bag. The IRS chose different types of businesses each year to audit—bad luck that it was architects this time round.

'I still feel uneasy about it,' Karim answered.

'No need. I worked for an American oil company in Tehran and the IRS investigated it here in the States many times.'

'Well, if they did that to their best money-spinners ...' Karim commented.

He watched his father pour them a drink, reflecting that he seemed a whole lot better already. Abbas had always been there for them all. In spite of his mother's blustering, it was his father who had got everyone out of Iran. Over a drink, his father confided that he'd never wanted to leave Iran, that he was too old for change—yet here he was.

They talked about Karim's friend Rashid and his untimely death, and that all he'd wanted was democracy. Abbas mentioned that Esmat had spoken to Nasim, Rashid's widow, recently and mentioned that Nasim's baby was due in May. Karim felt overwhelmingly sad; Nasim and Rashid had been his friends for as long as he could remember. He'd loved going to their house to visit, the house Rashid had been dragged out of before being executed two days later, the house Firzun had camped out in. He wondered what was Firzun up to in Australia—probably nothing legal.

His father's voice broke into his thoughts. 'It's better not to dwell on the past, son.'

'That's true, *Baba*. Apart from the IRS, my life isn't so bad,' Karim replied.

Abbas told him, with a wry look, that his own life might be full of lady's clothing again. Had Karim heard his mother's latest plans? They were going to move to Los Angeles and Esmat was definitely planning to open *Esmat's Persian Bazaar* as soon as she could.

Abbas swirled his whisky around in his glass and asked if Karim knew about the 'freeze'. The US government was starting to freeze Iranian assets in the United States.

'Would that apply to us?' Karim asked.

'Who knows?' his father replied. 'There's a lot of uncertainty. I'm glad you've applied for citizenship. Green cards can be revoked, you know.'

'I feel nervous enough about the IRS ...'

'Anyway,' he father grinned, 'your mother's on the lookout for a wife for you. She thinks your new girlfriend might be okay.'

'Please, *Baba*, don't you start.' Karim drained his whisky.

'Well, did you get it sorted out?' his mother demanded. She turned from drawing the heavy drapes carefully across the glass snowflakes in the window and hugged her son. 'Your father is much better since you arrived,' she whispered. She frowned and admonished her grandchildren as they whooped past. 'Isn't it time they were in bed? They'll be too excited to sleep.'

'Mom, they are permanently excited.' Soraya clapped her hands and rounded the children up. Karim hugged his older nephew Reza goodnight. The boy reminded him of Ahmad, and for a second Karim felt a pang of pure sadness. Reza's obsession with Mickey Mouse had waned and been replaced by Superman. Reza had loved the Superman movie they'd seen together in the summer. Karim was sure that Ahmad would have loved it too.

Before he left late Sunday afternoon, his sister motioned him to one side.

'This came for you, from Australia,' she whispered. 'I grabbed it before Mom could start asking questions. 'It's from Zahra. That's all she wrote, *Zahra*, and an address in Australia.'

His heart flipped and he pushed the letter quickly into his jacket pocket.

'The woman in the photograph?' His sister's perception startled him and he nodded.

'Thanks for getting it before *Madar djan*. Zahra used to work for us. You know what Mom's like about that.'

'Sure.' His sister gave him a mock frown. 'I hope you didn't ...'

'Hand on heart, absolutely not.'

'Good. She's still furious with you after what happened to poor Yasmin in Ramsar all those years ago.' She raised her eyebrows. Before he could ask her what she meant, she nudged him. 'Here she is. Tell her we've been talking about old friends.' She squeezed his arm. 'Love you, bro!'

Worried that he might drop it somewhere, Karim waited until he was on the plane before he carefully removed the letter from his inside pocket. The address puzzled him; so Firzun wasn't staying in a hotel with his family. During the short flight he read and re-read what Zahra had written. He sat back in his airline seat feeling completely drained. What an awful story and what a bastard Zahra's cousin was. He decided to phone Zahra as soon as he got home.

His apartment was eerily quiet after the busy house in Boston. From where he stood in the entrance, he could hear the intermittent ping of the answering machine in his study. He dumped his briefcase on the desk and listened to the messages.

The first one was from Lauren, inviting him to Christmas drinks at her father's apartment the following Friday. As he wrote down the address he realised that it was only two blocks from his own place. The second message was from Bahram. He sounded worried. The IRS auditor, Gary Olsen, was supposed to be coming on Monday but he'd cancelled and wouldn't be there until a week from Monday. What did Karim think? Were they digging up more dirt? Karim returned Bahram's call and reassured him that everything would be fine, they now had a bit of breathing space. His father had said they had nothing to worry about.

Karim got Zahra's letter out again. Without hesitating, he dialled the international operator and read out the phone number from the top of the lined sheet of paper.

A young-sounding female clerk answered. She was taken aback when he asked to speak to Zahra. She couldn't bring a resident to the phone, she told him. When he asked why not, she explained that they had over five hundred people living in the hostel, from all over the world. Karim hesitated; he hadn't thought of that. He asked her what he should do if he wanted to speak to Zahra.

'I can take your details, leave a message for her, and she'll call you back.'

'I'm in the United States. Can you ask her to call me collect?'

'Of course, I'll write that on the note. We call it "reverse charges" in Australia,' she added. She assured him she'd walk over to Zahra's flat and deliver his message personally.

When he asked whether she knew if Zahra was all right, the

clerk apologised and told him she couldn't comment on individual residents. He dictated his phone number and address in New York carefully. He reminded her that the time in New York was fourteen hours behind Sydney.

'Yes, sir. It's midday here.'

'And who am I speaking to?'

'I'm Helen McIntyre, Mr Konari. I'll make sure she gets your message.'

Karim said goodbye and put the phone down, then sat for a moment thinking about Australia. It was hard to imagine on this dark winter's night in New York, that it was midday tomorrow where Zahra lived.

Before his mind started to wander any further, he unloaded the account files from his briefcase and flicked through them quickly. He frowned when he recalled his sister's comment about 'poor Yasmin in Ramsar'. What had she meant? He and Yasmin had dated, they'd parted, and she seemed okay when he'd seen her a few days ago. Maybe Soraya was sorry that Yasmin had married so young, but why had his mother been involved? He shrugged; he would ask his sister next time he saw her.

He hesitated before he returned Lauren's call. If Zahra got the message immediately, she might phone him back at once and he needed to keep the line free. He called Lauren on the fax phone and she picked up on the first ring. As soon as he heard her voice he relaxed—why not go for Christmas drinks next Friday? What else was he doing except worrying about the IRS and now Zahra? Then he called his sister's house to report his safe arrival in New York, sent a thank you message via his sister's husband to his father, had a quick word with Nadir, and said goodbye. Now he was free to take Zahra's call when she rang back.

He wandered into the living room and flicked on the TV news. The newsreader was sitting in front of a scowling photograph of the Ayatollah Khomeini. Above it were the words *Day 35*. Karim was about to switch off when the newsreader said: *'Tuesday President*

Carter will be lighting the Christmas tree outside the White House. But fifty-three candles will remain unlit around the periphery of the building. They'll be lit again when the hostages come home.'

He poured himself a whisky and raised his glass to the Ayatollah's image on the screen.

'You should try some,' he said aloud in the empty room. 'Loosen up!'

Karim flicked through the channels, looking for something bland. He couldn't cope with any more news, good or bad. He put the phone next to him on the coffee table, expecting it to ring any minute. As he sat in his silent apartment, his thoughts were full of Zahra. She was a single mother and stuck in a migrant hostel in a foreign country with her son. After the IRS audit, providing everything was okay, he had no commitments.

He sat down and wrote a long letter to Zahra, assuring her that he would apply for a visa immediately and come to Australia to help her. He folded four fifty-dollar notes inside it and sealed the envelope. *My God! I wish I'd hit her stupid risk-taking cousin when I'd had the chance.* Firzun and Zahra were lucky they hadn't been arrested at Sydney Airport on identity theft charges. A surge of relief swept through Karim—she was free! He longed to hear her voice, but although he stayed up until past midnight, she didn't call.

20

———

ALI

Zahra was glad that the orientation week was over, even though it had been an interesting introduction to life in Australia. During a couple of long hot days, representatives from banks, government agencies, and the police had talked to the new arrivals. She'd opened a bank account, learned how the government worked, and heard about the social security system for single mothers. She learned she could stay in the hostel for a year, and a woman from the employment service discussed career options for her. She suggested Zahra could take a course and sit an exam to become an interpreter.

Along with other parents of young children, she'd taken Ahmad to the local primary school and enrolled him. He was disappointed that he'd have to wait until the new school year started in February. She was given a student rail and bus pass, and her group had done an orientation trip to Sydney, seventy kilometres away by train, with two teachers from the hostel.

She felt relieved though when the weekend came around and she was able to go to the mall. She exchanged a few more American dollars, banked some, and bought a school uniform for Ahmad. He'd been given a second-hand uniform at the school, but she wanted to buy him new things for their new country. *If I ever write to Karim again, I'll tell him I spent the money he gave me in Tehran on Ahmad. He'd like that.*

The mall was busy and crowds of hurrying people milled around her. They all looked so purposeful, she thought. Everyone had somewhere to go, a place in the world. They had families to shop for, homes full of their own things. *All I've got is stress and worry. Will I ever leave the hostel, get a job, and live a normal life again?* She felt lost in a sea of busy English-speaking strangers. She was in a foreign country, but she felt as if she had landed on another planet.

Ahmad wanted to revisit the Christmas tree and she took him over reluctantly, the memory of Nousha still fresh in her mind. She looked at him as he gazed up at the Christmas tree, then to her surprise he waved at Santa. He was already as obsessed with Christmas as he had once been with Mickey Mouse. *How will I be able to teach him about his own religion and culture? He's already being absorbed into this one. Once he goes to school and starts speaking English, will I lose him? Will there be an ever-widening gap between us?*

She'd found his school uniform in a big clothing store and promised him he could try it on when they got back to the hostel.

'Can I ride the fire engine?' he asked plaintively.

She usually said no to the tiny carousel with its child-size police car and fire engine. Ten cents seemed very expensive for a sixty-second ride. But she had hardly seen him this week—he deserved a treat.

'All right, Ahmad, just one go.'

He whooped and ran toward the carousel. When she caught up with him, he was already sitting in the fire engine, ringing the bell. She slotted a ten-cent piece into the machine and the carousel turned slowly. He waved as he passed her each time and she smiled and waved back. She was so absorbed that she didn't notice the stranger standing nearby until he spoke.

'I wonder if I may have a minute of your time, Zahra *Khanoum*?' he said in Persian.

She spun round, alarmed both by hearing her name and the familiar language. How had he snuck up on her like that? She glanced at the short dark man fearfully. He looked completely out of place among the casually dressed shoppers in his business suit, white shirt, and striped green tie. Before Zahra could stop him, he leaned forward and deftly slotted more coins into the carousel.

'I'm so pleased to meet you at last, Zahra Ghafoori. My name is Ali Esmaeili.'

She backed away from him, terrified. Ali Esmaeili, the assassin Firzun had warned her about. He was a real person, and he was here! He was saying something—that he represented the Islamic Republic of Iran and his government was wondering where her husband was.

'Rather, the man who was posing as your husband, your cousin Firzun,' Ali concluded.

His words took her breath away. She clenched her trembling hands together.

'I don't know where he is,' she said, trying to control her shaking voice.

'Oh, I think you do, Zahra *Khanoum*. You left Tehran together and arrived here as a family. I saw you at Sydney Airport, but then Firzun disappeared. I've spent a long time looking for him. I've been watching you, though. I thought you might lead me to him, but so far you haven't.'

She felt cold inside. How long had he been following her? Had he seen the drug exchange with Nousha? She repeated that she didn't know where Firzun was and if Ali didn't leave her alone, she'd call the police.

He told her to go ahead and that he was sure the Australian police were looking for her 'husband' as well. He laughed derisively, then lowered his voice. What a nasty business that was, here in this very shopping mall, he continued. He had retrieved the handbag from the garbage bin, just in case.

Zahra was too stunned to reply. When he moved closer, she could smell his sickly cologne, or maybe it was the oil he'd put through his wavy black hair. Both the moustache above his full lips and the dark beard that outlined his jaw were carefully clipped. She stepped back, but she was now trapped between him and the edge of the carousel, which grazed her legs as it moved around slowly.

'I'm not interested in the handbag you threw away,' he went on. 'I'm looking for your cousin. That *whore* you passed the drugs to got away. So now you're the only person who can answer my questions.'

Zahra felt a prickle of fear run down her back but pulled herself together. She looked Ali straight in the eye. 'Firzun's gone back to Afghanistan,' she told him firmly.

He said he didn't believe her. He had contacts in the Australian Department of Immigration and believed that Firzun was still in the country.

He's lying! He knows nothing and he doesn't have any contacts.

'He's gone back to Afghanistan,' she repeated.

Ali Esmaeili ignored her. 'I know he hasn't left the country,' he insisted. His deep set dark eyes searched her face. 'Just tell me where he is and I won't bother you again.'

'Leave me alone!' She tried to move away from him, hoping he wouldn't see how frightened she felt.

'Look at you,' he said, changing tack. 'No scarf, short sleeves. You'd be arrested and whipped for indecency in Iran,' he sneered.

'We're not *in* Iran,' she replied sharply. 'I'm protected by the law in this country. Stop harassing me or I'll call the police.'

He reminded her that he still had the handbag. If she didn't cooperate he would personally deliver it to the police station. They would find her fingerprints all over it.

I wiped it clean, he's got nothing on me—or has he?

Ali leaned around her to put more money in the carousel. But before he could slot in the coins, a woman Zahra hadn't even noticed tapped him on the arm.

'Excuse me, sir. Your son's had a long ride and my little girls have been waiting for ages.'

Ali was completely taken aback by the interruption. He turned around and looked with astonishment at squirming twin girls who were trying to get out of their stroller. Zahra leaned over and pushed a red button. The carousel slowed and she ordered Ahmad to get off.

'No!' he yelled.

She half-dragged him out of the fire engine. He resisted and hung on to the small steering wheel. He yelled that it wasn't finished, it was his turn. Eventually she managed to pull him off. When she finally got him on his feet, Ali had gone. Zahra rushed past the apologetic mother and dragged her protesting squealing son to the exit.

'Stop it, Ahmad! We've got to go *now*.'

She was desperate to get back to the safety of the hostel. She took his hand and ran out to the car park, scanning the parked cars for any sign of Ali. A taxi slowed down next to her and stopped. She wrenched the rear door open and pushed Ahmad into the backseat.

'The hostel,' she gasped. 'Be quiet!' she snapped at Ahmad, who was still wailing loudly.

The taxi moved off and she looked round again. Would Ali be waiting for her outside her flat? She had to warn Firzun! The taxi stopped at the administration building and she pushed money at the driver. She scrambled out, pulling Ahmad and her shopping bags with her.

There was no one waiting outside her flat. She struggled with the key in her haste and finally pushed the door open. She dropped onto the sofa, feeling safe in her sanctuary with its locked door. Ahmad recovered quickly and scampered to his room. She tried to pull herself together as she relived the encounter, then got up to check Ahmad. To her relief he was playing quietly with his cars. She fumbled through her purse for Firzun's phone number. What if he wasn't there? Angry as she was with her cousin, she had to warn him about Ali. She told Ahmad he could watch TV and hurried to the recreation room with him. There were a few children watching cartoons and Ahmad sat down with them. She watched him from the entrance as she dialled Firzun's number. It rang for a long time and she was about to hang up when a woman's voice said hesitantly, 'Hello?'

Zahra asked in *Dari* if she could speak to Firzun. The woman said nothing.

'Hello?' she repeated. 'I'm Zahra, his … wife. It's urgent.'

'He's gone to Sydney,' the woman whispered. 'Quick, write down this number. Don't let Nousha know I told you.'

Damn Firzun and his cloak and dagger life, she thought as she dialled the new number. When Firzun picked up the phone, she poured out the story of Ali Esmaeili. He said nothing for a minute.

'Firzun!'

'Zahra, I've hidden more stuff. You've got to get it to me.'

'*What?* More stuff! Where is it?'

'In Ahmad's toy truck where the batteries go.'

She gasped out loud. 'How *could* you?'

'I need it now. I can sell it and get a flight out tonight. Bring it to Sydney and I'll give you some money.'

She couldn't believe what she was hearing. It was bad enough to be stalked by one of Firzun's many enemies. But this! And now he wanted her to get drugs out of a toy truck, travel seventy kilometres to the city of Sydney, and deliver them to him.

'No, Firzun, I am not coming to Sydney now.'

He started shouting, telling her that Nousha and her brother had cheated him. He needed money for the plane fare. She had to get a taxi at once and bring the stuff.

When she refused again, he continued to rant about her ingratitude, her lack of family feelings, her … She interrupted and repeated that he would have to wait. When he said he didn't want to, she told him it was just too bad. He calmed down quickly when she threatened to throw the drugs down the toilet.

The phone she was using was in the entrance to the recreation room. She looked quickly through the glass door into the room itself, fearful that someone might understand what she was saying. But the people who were playing table tennis or watching TV were Europeans. She tuned in again to Firzun, who was still complaining on the other end of the phone.

'I'm a dead man if you don't help me, Zahra.'

'Like I said, I'll come tomorrow, Sunday,' she said firmly. 'You're lucky I got your phone number!'

She ignored the oaths he spat down the phone. 'Shut up and tell me where to meet you, Firzun.'

'Sydney Opera House steps, ten-thirty tomorrow morning,' he said sullenly. 'Make sure Ali doesn't follow you.'

'If he does, that's your problem, not mine.' She hung up before he could say anything else.

When she got back to her flat, she told Ahmad he could play outside with the other boys, who were kicking a soccer ball around. She moved quickly, pulling the black gloves she'd worn in Tehran from the back of a drawer. She collected a plastic bag and then the truck from the bedroom floor. She glanced out the window—Ahmad was still playing soccer. In the bathroom, she spread a handtowel across the basin. Using her scissors and a nail file, she undid the battery compartment of the truck. Biting back her fury, she took out the four packets of white powder Firzun had concealed and dropped them in the plastic bag. She ran to the wardrobe and stashed them in her handbag. When she returned to the bathroom, she cleaned out the truck and was replacing the screws just as Ahmad ran in to use the toilet.

'I'm fixing your truck,' she told him, but he wasn't interested. He washed his hands, wetting the towel in the sink, and ran outside again.

She wiped down the whole bathroom area carefully with the

damp towel. She was on the other side of anger now, an icy calm. It was the space she had often got to with her violent husband Mahmoud. She was thoroughly disgusted with her cousin. Family or not, after this she never wanted to see or hear from Firzun again. True, he had given her a new life in Australia—but at what cost?

Before Ahmad came back she checked the train timetable for the following day, glad she had a rail pass for both of them. *After I deliver the drugs to Firzun, this is my final involvement with him,* she told herself with resolute calm. If she unwittingly led Ali Esmaeili to him, then the two men could sort out their differences themselves. It was not her problem. She bit her lip; she did have a problem, she thought. She had to go out in public again with a bag full of heroin. This time the handover was in an even busier public place—the Sydney Opera House. How on earth could she do that?

21

THE SYDNEY OPERA HOUSE

Zahra double-checked the timetable when she woke early Sunday morning. There was one express train on Sundays, and it left at eight o'clock from the main station in Wollongong. She and Ahmad were the first people in the dining room that morning at six-thirty, followed by a few others in beach gear. After a quick breakfast, Zahra shut her door firmly at seven-fifteen. She didn't feel nervous anymore. *It's the calm of inevitability*, she told herself, *I just want this over with.*

Loaded up with water, bananas, and biscuits they set off for the station. As they hurried toward the gate, her heart sank. A hot day was forecast and some hostel residents were already walking to the beach. A couple of children called out hello to Ahmad as he ran ahead of her. The last thing she wanted was to be seen leaving the hostel so early. She decided to get a taxi from the main road to the station. She couldn't really afford it, but at least no one at the hostel would remember her leaving in a taxi.

She clutched her handbag close to her side, trying to look casual as though they were going for a walk or taking the long way to the beach. One of the security guards nodded and said good morning as they walked out of the gate.

She had fifty Australian dollars in her purse. Maybe she shouldn't waste money on a taxi, she thought; she might need it for something urgent. As they walked across the railway line, the bells at the level crossing started ringing. From reading the timetable she knew that this train was an all-stops to Sydney. Should she catch it? At least it was going the right way. No, better go into town for the express, she decided.

Another group of near-naked young people was waiting at the bus stop on the main road. Even though they were all wearing t-shirts, the girls still had bare legs. Zahra stood as far away from them as possible so that she could flag down a taxi. But Ahmad was fascinated by the teenagers and edged closer.

'Surfboard,' he tried out his favourite English word on the nearest youth.

The long-haired teenager shifted his surfboard and grinned at Ahmad. 'Yeah, mate. You a surfer, are ya? Got a board?'

Ahmad shook his head and ran back to his mother. 'He spoke to me,' he whispered. 'What did he say, Mummy?'

Before Zahra could answer, one of the girls smiled at Ahmad and said to her friend: 'Hey, the wog kid likes ya, Ben.'

Zahra moved further away from them, pulling Ahmad with her. The teenagers, oblivious of Ahmad's delight, lost interest in him and chatted among themselves. The road was already busy and cars passed them with music blaring from open windows. She wondered if Ali had a car and she tried to see into each car that passed. Was he circling the hostel looking for her, waiting for her to make a move? In spite of the warm morning, she shivered. She was already feeling thirsty and stressed.

When a city-bound bus stopped, she decided to take it. Thanks to her orientation trip last week, she knew where to get off. The young people stood back to let her get on, then struggled on themselves with their surfboards. The driver grumbled at them, but eventually the bus moved off. Zahra found a seat, but the windows were grimy and she couldn't see out very well. The bus was grindingly slow and stopped frequently. She checked her watch, feeling anxious and wishing she'd waited for a taxi after all, or taken the slow train.

Finally, the bus turned into the railway station. Her heart leapt with fear as she hustled Ahmad off the bus. The eight o'clock express train was already waiting at the platform. She couldn't afford to miss it! And there were stairs to climb, a bridge to cross, and other stairs to run down.

'Hurry up, love,' a man in uniform called out as she ran down the final flight.

She fumbled for her student pass and showed it quickly. The whistle blew just as she was helping Ahmad onto the train. She jumped aboard, but when the train started to move a terrible thought struck her. She hadn't double-checked that it was going to Sydney. What if it was going the other way? She looked out the open door as the train moved off, but she couldn't see the destination board. Her glance took in a man running across the railway bridge. He stopped, exasperated when he saw that he'd missed the train. She recognised him—Ali Esmaeili!

Her legs felt like jelly as she walked behind Ahmad down the aisle, then collapsed into one of the vinyl seats. To her relief, an announcement came over the loudspeaker: *This is the Sydney express train to Central. One stop only at Hurstville.* Ali had followed her, hoping she would lead him to Firzun, but he had missed the train. She sat back in her seat and closed her eyes. She had given Ali the slip, but would he catch up to her? He probably had a car and could beat the train to Sydney. In spite of her jangling nerves, she dozed fitfully as the train rushed through the small stations and eventually lumbered into the terminus at Central Station.

When they got off, Zahra scanned the platform. Thank God, Ali wasn't there. She hurried along with Ahmad, trying to remember how they'd got from the main station to the Opera House and Circular Quay with the hostel group. A notice pointed her to an escalator and the City Circle trains. The hands on a large clock nearby clicked forward to nine-forty-five. She was in good time and hopefully so was Firzun, she thought as she hurried through the station. She helped Ahmad on to the escalator and then up the stairs to the City Circle trains. She looked over her shoulder once or twice, but there was no sign of Ali behind her.

She had to concentrate to understand the announcements. According to the destination board, there was a train in five minutes. When it glided in and stopped, people pushed ahead of her but she managed to help Ahmad on. Before she could stop him, he ran up the stairs of the double-decker train. It raced through tunnels, then suddenly they were in bright daylight. Circular Quay sparkled with sunshine and she saw the Sydney Opera House floating like a large meringue at the water's edge.

They got off the train and she grasped Ahmad's hand again, following the crowd down the escalator and out of the station. The breeze from the water fanned her hot face. They hurried past the ferry terminals to the wide pathway that led to the Opera House. Ahmad started to whimper and said he needed a toilet. She stopped, followed the signs, and took him into the ladies' toilets with her.

They set off again quickly, oblivious of their surroundings. Her one thought was they had to get to their destination as fast as possible. The crowds made Ahmad nervous and he gripped her hand as they hastened along the waterside.

She checked her watch: nearly ten-twenty. Firzun had said ten-thirty, but what if he wasn't there? Or what if Ali had got there before her? She glanced over her shoulder; was that him in the crowd behind her or was she imagining things? She quickened her pace and almost broke into a run. The other day when she'd come with the group, the Opera House had seemed much nearer. The road round the quay seemed to go on and on. The water slapped against the harbour wall on her left and Ahmad wanted to stop and watch the ferries as they sailed past, but she hurried him along.

'No, keep moving. We'll do that later.'

She dodged around the crowds of strolling people, dragging Ahmad with her. He slowed down pointing at the Harbour Bridge. Again he wanted to stop, but she urged him forward. She had to get this over with, free herself from the drugs—and Firzun—forever. All along the walkway, lengthy flags attached to poles belled out in the breeze with their Christmas themes of Santa and snowflakes and holly. Ahmad slowed down again, pointing at Santa.

'On the way back,' she promised.

The graceful shell-shaped roof of the Opera House, perched on its plinth at the entrance to the quay, revealed itself as they approached. She'd forgotten there were so many steps up to the building and that it was huge. But now, finding one person on the long stairway that led to the main doors seemed impossible. Firzun had told her to wait at the bottom of the steps, but each one looked about a hundred metres long. People walked, lounged, or posed for photographs all over them. Then, to her relief, she saw him.

He was leaning on a rail, dressed in a denim jacket, jeans, and t-shirt and had pulled a dark blue cap over his thick hair. He still had a beard and moustache, but both were neatly clipped. He hadn't noticed her and Ahmad yet and she slowed down, observing him from a distance. She had never noticed before that he was the image of her father, his uncle. Her father had been Firzun's age when he had died. She stopped in the middle of the swirling busy crowds and sighed. *This is why I put up with him,* she thought. He's family, the only family I've got besides my son.

She pointed out Firzun to Ahmad. He'd been too excited about his surroundings to notice his second cousin. When Firzun saw them, he pushed himself away from the handrail at the side of the steps. His injured leg still wasn't very strong, she thought, and he wasn't using his cane.

'Zahra, Ahmad, thank God you made it.'

He grasped both of her hands in his and asked if she'd brought 'the stuff'. When she nodded, he told her to start walking with him as if they were out for the day. He leaned down and picked up Ahmad, staggeringly slightly under the child's weight.

'How are you, kid? Are you happy?'

'Yes!'

To Zahra's surprise, Ahmad put his arms around Firzun's neck. Firzun hugged him and carried him for a while. Her anger began to melt away and she was overwhelmed with sadness. Was this the last time she would ever see her cousin?

'My leg's hurting,' Firzun said as he put the boy down.

He scanned the crowds, then jerked his head to the left. Zahra followed him around the base of the building to the front concourse. She asked him about his injured leg, but he shrugged and told her he could manage. Ahmad was busy staring across the water at the big grinning face on the entrance to Luna Park. The Ferris wheel had started to revolve slowly. He had his back to them and shrieked when the wash from a ferry slapped against the low wall he was leaning on.

'Better give me the stuff now, while he's not looking,' Firzun muttered.

Zahra passed him the small plastic bag and he slipped it into the inside pocket of his jacket. He put his hand on his heart, thanked her, and indicated for them to walk. He asked her again if she thought Ali had followed them. She told him what had happened at the station and that the man might not be far behind her.

'I can sell the stuff today and be on a flight out tonight,' Firzun told her decisively.

So that's it, he's finally going, she thought with a mixture of sadness and relief.

'I've done the best I could for you, Zahra.'

'You abandoned me, turned me into a drug smuggler, and now you're leaving me alone with my young son in a foreign country,' she reminded him, her anger rising to the surface again. 'I could have been in New York with Karim if it hadn't been for you.'

She wondered why she'd bothered saying anything at all when he answered, 'Yeah, well, blood's thicker than water, isn't it?'

At least, she thought, he had the grace to look sheepish. He didn't apologise but thanked her for saving his life—yet again. Now he could save the lives of others in Afghanistan, he continued. He could get out of Australia using his other identity, not Mahmoud's. He would join the fight against the Soviets in Afghanistan. And no, before she asked, she couldn't come with him. She had to look at the bigger picture. He was a revolutionary soldier again. He had done her a favour, he told her, although she might not realise it now. She was out of Afghanistan and it was going to be a long war. Life in the USA wasn't too good for Iranians right now, what with the hostages and all that, he told her.

'Remember the bigger picture, cousin,' Firzun repeated.

The bigger picture! She felt like grabbing his shoulders and shaking him.

'I'm going to make a go of it here, no thanks to you,' she retorted.

'Sure, sure,' he answered. 'You'll thank me one day, when our country's been bombed out of existence.'

He took her hands in his, touched them to his forehead, and asked her to wish him luck. He swept Ahmad in his arms again and hugged him. He said goodbye and told Ahmad to look after his mother, that he was going away now. Ahmad was upset and asked why he couldn't stay with them. To Zahra's surprise, Firzun looked upset too and she touched his arm, all anger spent.

'*Khodāfez,* cousin. Write to me at the hostel. Let me know you're safe.'

'Of course,' he promised. His eyes met hers. 'Goodbye, Zahra. Give me a few minutes to get ahead of you.'

She held Ahmad's hand tightly and watched her cousin limp away toward the Royal Botanic Gardens. When he disappeared around the side of the Opera House, she felt bereft and terribly alone. She turned around and told Ahmad they were going to get the train again. He shook his hand free and ran ahead of her, back the way they'd come. She had to hurry to keep up with him as he skipped along the harbour walkway, his fear of crowds apparently gone. Zahra felt her spirits lifting slowly. Her cousin had been in her life, making demands on her for as long as she could remember. She had always felt indebted to him, especially for her freedom from Mahmoud. But now she had repaid all her obligations.

This is the day my new life begins, she thought. She looked down at Ahmad, who was smiling and waving to people on passing ferries. She vowed that everything she did from now on would be for him. She alone would give her son a better life. She took his hand and walked back toward the railway station at Circular Quay. Firzun hadn't given her the money he'd promised. How typical! Maybe it was just as well, she thought. If there ever was a police investigation, she could honestly say she had given, not sold, the drugs to her cousin.

Up ahead she saw a large sign advertising pizza. On an impulse she went into the shop and ordered one. When it was ready, she carried the big box to a bench near the water. With the pizza box open between them, she and Ahmad ate the hot slices and watched the ferries come and go on the harbour. A sense of elation swept over her. *I'm free at last from my obligations to Firzun!* A new chapter in her life was about to begin and it was going to be a good one. The cathartic letter she'd written to Karim the previous week had cleared her mind, and she was ready for whatever the future had in store for her.

From the top of the Opera House steps, Ali Esmaeili watched the Afghan woman and her child disappear around the bend in the quayside. He shifted his gaze to the left and watched his target walk through the high gates of the Botanic Gardens. Ali congratulated himself on his assassin's skills, particularly how he'd picked up the woman's trail at the station, how he'd driven and beat the train, and how he'd been rewarded as the woman had led him to his quarry. Now he had Firzun Khan in his sights and would keep him there. He would bide his time until the opportunity arose for the final act.

22

A CASE OF IDENTITY

On Monday morning, Zahra was halfway through her first English class when, glancing out the classroom window, she saw a police car coming through the hostel gates. Her heart missed a beat. *They've come for me!* She risked a covert look at her classmates, but they were all busy writing in their books. Zahra found it hard to concentrate. The events of the previous day were still playing like a tape in her brain. When she looked down at the questions on her paper, the words swam in front of her eyes. Was Firzun really out of her life forever? Maybe he was halfway home already. She looked at her watch: it was nearly midday. If he had taken an overnight flight, he would be well on his way to Bahrain by now.

Yesterday had exhausted her emotionally and physically. What if Ali had followed her and then tracked Firzun down in the Botanic Gardens? She was shocked to realise that she didn't care. Firzun was a survivor; he'd have given Ali the slip, met his contacts, and sold the heroin. The deal would have been done before she got off the train in Fairy Meadow. She looked nervously out the window again. The police car was parked a short distance away.

The teacher's voice from the front of the class brought her back to the present. 'So, how did you all go with the newspaper article about koalas?' Susan asked. 'Did you use the new words *endangered* and *species* in your answer?'

Zahra looked down at her blank page. *Endangered species —that's me!*

The teacher smiled as she scanned the classroom. 'Can I have a volunteer to answer the first question? Thank you, Phuong.'

The student was stumbling through his answer when the door opened. Caroline the welfare officer beckoned Susan outside.

'Keep going, Phuong,' the teacher called over her shoulder. 'I'll be back in a minute.'

As she closed the door behind her, the student's narrative ground to a halt. Zahra had glimpsed a police officer outside the classroom when Caroline opened the door. *They've come for me!* She half rose in her seat, wondering how quickly she could get out of the classroom, collect Ahmad from kindergarten, and run away. But where could she go? Maybe she could lock herself in the flat and refuse to open the door. She sat down again and tried to collect her thoughts. *I must calm down. I'm not the only person here. They've come for someone else.* She looked down at her English book, feeling nauseated as the words swam in front of her eyes.

Some of the other students commented on the police car, but then starting chatting to each other in their own languages. They stopped when Susan came back into the room looking flustered. She walked over to Zahra's desk and asked her quietly to come outside.

'Bring your handbag. You can leave your books here, Zahra. I'll see to them.'

Zahra stood up slowly, feeling as if her body was made of lead. A tangible silence fell over the class as she picked up her bag. Without looking at the other students, she followed the teacher out the door. Outside in the corridor, the welfare officer and the principal of the English Language Centre were waiting for her. In the background, she saw a uniformed police officer and another woman, their faces solemn.

'The police would like to speak to you, Zahra,' the principal told her quietly.

'Is Ahmad all right?' Her voice came out in a high-pitched rush.

'Ahmad's fine,' Susan reassured her.

Thank God! But what do they want? Are they going to arrest me?

Caroline took Zahra's arm. 'Let's go to the office. The police can talk to you there.'

The other woman steered her toward the administration building. As they walked, Zahra's mind was in turmoil. *Ahmad took his truck to kindergarten this morning. Why did I let him do that? I should have thrown it out and bought him a new one. Have they found traces of heroin in it?*

When they walked into the office area, one of the clerks got to her feet with a piece of paper in her hand. She offered it to Zahra and started to say something, but the other clerk interrupted.

'Not now, Helen, she can call him later.'

Both clerks gave her a sympathetic look. *What on earth's wrong? It must be Firzun. They've found him and he's been arrested!*

She was ushered into an office where she'd been interviewed the previous week. When she saw the police officers, she felt faint. Only the male officer was wearing a uniform. Maybe they were from the Immigration department *and* the police force. Were there more police officers waiting outside her flat? Her body sagged as the welfare officer guided her to a chair.

'Good morning, Mrs Ghafoori.' The female police officer sat down on a chair opposite her. 'I'm Detective Sergeant Frances White and this is Sergeant Barry Ascot from the New South Wales Police Force.'

Zahra looked at the young female detective. She was wearing a bright summer dress and her brown eyes were full of concern.

'I'm afraid we have some sad news,' the police officer said.

So they are the police! The woman was one of those high-level people who didn't wear a uniform. They were the police who followed people. They blended into the crowds, like the crowds near the Sydney Opera House on Sunday. *Sad news. What did she mean?*

'Mrs Ghafoori ... Zahra, have you seen your husband recently?' the uniformed police officer asked, taking a seat next to his colleague.

She shook her head. *Had they seen her with Firzun?* She raised her eyes. Like the teachers, the people opposite her looked serious but sympathetic.

The female detective hesitated, then she added, 'Not since he deserted you at the airport?'

Zahra gripped the sides of the chair, convinced now that they'd arrested Firzun. 'No.'

The detective shifted slightly in her seat. 'Mrs Ghafoori, a man's body has been recovered from Sydney Harbour. We believe it's your husband Mahmoud Ghafoori, and that he drowned, probably late Sunday night.'

The police officer glanced at the welfare worker, who put her hand on Zahra's arm.

Zahra stared at them, unable to take in what the woman had said. 'My husband, Mahmoud is dead?' she blurted.

'Yes, I'm afraid he is,' the other police officer answered. 'We found his passport and his wallet on the body. That's how we identified him.'

'We're very sorry for your loss,' Detective Sergeant White added. 'Zahra, we need you to accompany us to the morgue to make a positive identification.'

Zahra's mind was in turmoil. Who were they talking about? It couldn't be Mahmoud—he was buried in Afghanistan. They were talking about Firzun! What had happened after she left him on Sunday? He was going to sell the drugs and leave the country. Had someone killed him? Ali? If she had led Ali to him, she would never forgive herself.

She put her hands over her face. *He can't be dead. He was so alive and hopeful when we met.* She kept her head bowed. *They've found his body, have they found the drugs? Will they trace them back to me?*

'I'll come with you,' Caroline said.

'Where to?' Zahra felt confused and trapped.

'We need you to identify his body. It means you have to look at him and say whether he is your husband or not,' she explained.

'But I can't leave Ahmad!'

'He's in the kindergarten, we'll take care of him,' Caroline answered. 'After you've identified the ... his ... body and answered some questions, the police will bring you back here.' She touched Zahra's arm again. 'I'm so sorry, Zahra.'

Zahra stood up, feeling dazed as they led her to the police car. She was dimly aware of Caroline sitting next to her in the backseat as the car swung out through the gates. Eventually she was helped out in front of a modern brick building, then led inside through several corridors. Someone opened the door to a small room. An overwhelming smell of disinfectant made her cough and catch her breath.

Next to her, Caroline patted her hand. 'It won't take long.'

Zahra looked down at the floor, dreading seeing Firzun's body. Tears welled in her eyes as she remembered how he'd looked—was it only yesterday? He'd been worried but confident he could get back home and carry on the fight. She tried to remember what she'd said to him. Had she been mean and angry? Yes, she had! She blew her nose and Caroline handed her another tissue.

The detective came back into the room and explained what she had to do. Zahra nodded, keeping her eyes on the polished wood floor. The disinfectant smell was making her feel nauseated.

When the detective asked if she needed an interpreter, she shook her head.

'All right. They're ready for you.'

When she got up, her legs felt weak. Caroline and the female detective held her arms and led her into a bigger room, bare except for a few chairs. Sergeant Ascot was standing near a curtain that covered the bottom third of the room. They explained that when she was ready they would open the curtain and ask her to come forward.

The police officer opened the long curtain slowly and Zahra gasped when she saw the covered outline of a body lying on a hospital trolley. She moved nearer reluctantly with Caroline's help.

'We're going to uncover his face. I want you to look at him and I'll ask you if he is your husband Mahmoud Ghafoori,' the detective told her.

She nodded and the police officer drew the sheet back slowly.

'Oh no! God help me,' Zahra cried out in *Dari*. 'It's him—he's dead.' She put her hand across her mouth, staring in horror at the pale face.

'Mrs Ghafoori, we need you to answer in English. Is this your husband? Is this Mahmoud Ghafoori?' the detective asked.

Zahra turned to her. 'It's him. He's dead,' she repeated in English. Zahra felt as if her brain was going to burst. How had this happened?

She looked down in disbelief at the dead face of Ali Esmaeili. Her stalker had been alive on Sunday. How could he be dead? Her mind was in turmoil as she stared at the inert body, unable to tear her eyes away from his waxen face. Where was Firzun? Did he have something to do with this?

Of course this wasn't her husband. But if she told the police the truth, what would happen to her and Ahmad? They believed the body was Mahmoud. They'd already told her they'd found his passport and wallet in the jacket pocket. In one crucial minute, she could free herself and officially become a widow.

'Zahra, he's been in the water for a while, but is it him ...?' Caroline prompted.

Zahra took a deep breath. She held her cupped hands out in front of her, bowed her head, and murmured, *Please God, forgive me* in her own language.

She turned to the policewoman. 'Yes,' she said quietly. 'This is my husband ... Mahmoud Ghafoori.'

Her legs felt weak. *What's the punishment in this country for telling such a terrible lie?*

'How ... how did he die?' She looked up at the police officer.

'He drowned,' she replied. 'We can talk about it in the other room.'

Caroline guided her to a chair and she heard the policeman closing the curtains on their noisy track. She sat down, breathless, unable to process what she'd seen. Had Ali really drowned? What had happened after she'd said goodbye to Firzun? She sat stunned, head down, eyes focused on the tiled floor. Her mind reeled with questions as she tried to piece everything together. There was no doubt in her mind that there had been foul play. This couldn't have been an accident, could it?

'It's always a terrible shock for people,' the detective said quietly.

As she was led out of the room, she tried to think clearly but couldn't. She heard them talking about forms and about returning her husband's possessions. She felt as if she was in a strange dream. At any minute, she expected to wake up in her room in the Konari house in Tehran.

Caroline held her arm firmly as she walked along a corridor. Without her help, Zahra was sure she would have slid to the floor. The social worker led her to a comfortable chair in another room. The two police officers were sitting across from her and the female officer was holding a file on her lap. Someone put a cup of coffee on the small table in front of Zahra, and after she'd drunk some of it she began to feel better.

'Take some deep breaths,' Caroline advised.

'Mrs Ghafoori, could your husband swim?' the uniformed officer asked.

She shook her head and told them he couldn't.

'Zahra, it appears that your late husband had been drinking heavily at a harbour-side pub,' the female police officer continued.

'When he walked out along the wharves, we think he slipped, fell into the water, and drowned. There's a mark on his temple where he might have hit his head as he fell.'

A mark on his temple? That's how Firzun had killed Mahmoud, with a sharp blow to the temple. Had he done the same to Ali?

Zahra pulled her attention back. The police officer said they were treating his death as an accident at the moment, but until the post-mortem report was completed they were keeping an open mind.

'Was your husband a heavy drinker?'

'Yes, he drank alcohol,' she replied automatically.

Had Firzun plied Ali with alcohol, suspecting a weakness? Had Ali, a devout Muslim, been tempted?

The female police officer consulted the open file. She asked Zahra if she'd had any contact with her late husband since he'd deserted her at the airport on 27 November. Zahra shook her head. She felt nervous, hoping no one had seen her at the Sydney Opera House. They asked her again if she knew why he'd left her. She shook her head, trying to remember what she'd said in her first interview at the hostel.

'I haven't seen my husband since he left me.'

The officer pressed the point. Had he said anything to her before he'd abandoned her? Zahra shook her head and repeated that he had just walked away before she could stop him.

'Did he have any friends in Sydney? Someone he might have stayed with?'

Zahra's mind raced with possibilities. Maybe the hostel authorities had told the police about her talking to Nousha. They'd be able to trace her, wouldn't they? But that had all happened over a week ago, when she'd first arrived. Nousha and her brother would be long gone from Fairy Meadow by now. Zahra tried to look relaxed, as if every word she said was the truth. She reminded herself that she must appear to be a well-educated, confident woman and a distressed widow. They wouldn't question her too hard, would they? And she did feel genuinely distressed.

'I don't think he knew anyone in Sydney.'

She looked up. The police officer was regarding her with a mixture of sympathy and enquiry.

'You see, Zahra, the barman remembered your husband. He was drinking with another man of Middle Eastern appearance. Do you know who that might have been?'

'No, I don't.'

Zahra tried to gather her thoughts together. The only logical explanation was that Firzun had got Ali drunk, then pushed him into the water. Or maybe Ali fell. How thoroughly would they investigate this 'accidental death'?

Her answer seemed to satisfy her interlocutors and they both nodded. Detective White pushed a plastic envelope across the table and asked her to identify the wallet and passport they'd found on the body.

'We were unable to get any fingerprints from the items, unfortunately. They've been in the water too long.'

Zahra glanced reluctantly at the passport in the bag, which was open at Mahmoud's photograph. The picture was blurry because of the water damage. No wonder they'd mistaken Ali for her husband. They were both dark skinned, brown eyed, and had a beard. She picked up the plastic envelope containing Mahmoud's wallet. She had never expected to see it again. So Firzun had kept the wallet as well as the passport, she thought. She had seen him leaning over Mahmoud's body and going through his pockets that terrible night in the mountains.

The police had removed Iranian and Afghan notes from the wallet as well as over two hundred dollars—American and Australian, they told her. They would dry them out as best they could and return them to her. They didn't mention a weapon, so they must have thought it was an accident, Zahra told herself. Or had Firzun relieved Ali of what? A knife ... a gun? Maybe the weapon was at the bottom of Sydney Harbour. She wondered nervously if Firzun was still in Australia or whether he'd finally gone. Her head whirled with unanswered questions.

'Mrs Ghafoori, is this your husband's wallet and passport? We need a positive identification,' the detective's voice cut across her thoughts.

'Yes, they both belonged to him,' she said, trying to keep her voice steady.

The police officers asked whether they needed to contact anyone in Afghanistan. She told them she would write to his family.

'We'll leave it there, while you fill out the forms,' the detective told Zahra. 'We're sorry for your loss.'

'I can help her with the paperwork,' Caroline offered.

The police officer closed the file and she and her colleague stood up.

'Thank you for your cooperation. There will be an inquest, of course.' She looked at Caroline, who nodded. 'There may be a few more questions, but they can wait.'

Zahra looked up and thanked them. Someone brought her another cup of coffee. She desperately wanted to get back to the hostel and her son, but with Caroline's help she completed the documentation. She managed to answer the questions about Mahmoud easily. After all, she'd been married to him for seven years. Caroline explained what the papers were, but she didn't care; she just answered the questions and signed her name.

When the police officers returned, they explained about the post mortem report. His body could not be released for burial until it was complete.

'But he's a Muslim. He must be buried the day after he died.'

I owe him a Muslim funeral at least, Zahra thought. He was someone's son. Would that be possible here?

The police officers exchanged glances and repeated that his

body couldn't be released yet. They had to wait for a final report. She might be able to arrange a funeral in a few days' time.

'Just one more thing,' the detective said to her. 'We have the name of someone who helped you at the airport ...'

'Leila Ashrani?'

'Maybe her son?' She squinted at the note in her hand. 'Mehran Ashrani?'

Zahra nodded.

'Would you like us to contact Mr Ashrani, tell him what's happened?' She consulted her note again. 'When we visited him after the airport ... thing ... he was very concerned about you.'

Caroline supported the idea. Zahra would be able to talk to someone in her own language, she said. Mr Ashrani might be able to help with the funeral arrangements too.

Zahra thought for a moment. Even though it meant telling more lies, she needed to speak to someone in her own language. 'Yes, it would be helpful.'

'Once again, we're sorry for your loss, Mrs Ghafoori,' the detective sergeant told her. 'We'll get in touch with Mr Ashrani.'

Zahra couldn't remember how she got back to the hostel. She politely refused Caroline's offer to sit with her. She needed to be alone.

'There's a note from the office here,' Caroline said, picking up the folded scrap of paper. 'It looks like a phone message. Maybe it's from your friend Leila. You can deal with it later.' She smiled and put it on top of the pile of leaflets the police had handed to Zahra.

After Caroline had left, Zahra glanced at the papers and leaflets she had placed on the coffee table. She didn't feel like calling Leila at the moment. The papers would have to wait for a few days while she got her head around what had happened. She was beginning to confuse Ali's death with Mahmoud's. She'd have to bury Ali as

Mahmoud Ghafoori, and she wasn't sure she could go through with it. *At least I'm not burying Firzun.*

When Leanne brought Ahmad from the kindergarten, she said a quick condolence and left. As soon as the other woman had gone, Zahra got Ahmad to sit on the sofa with her. She told him that his daddy had gone to Paradise with the angels. She had to cover all her bases, she thought wretchedly, in case someone mentioned it to him. He asked if that's where cousin Firzun had gone too. She paused, wondering whether to warn him not to say anything about Firzun. *I'm sick of all these lies.*

'Cousin Firzun's gone back to his old house,' she said.

Ahmad looked pleased. 'What about Uncle Karim? Can we see him again?'

'Maybe one day.' Poor Ahmad, she thought, there are no men left in his life now.

They went to dinner as usual and she wondered how soon her news would get around the hostel. She smoothed her black dress carefully. It wouldn't be too hard to look distressed after all that had happened.

Leila and her son arrived at the hostel the following afternoon. Leila folded Zahra in her arms and wiped away a tear.

'God give you patience, Zahra *djan*.' She fussed around as she made tea. She'd brought homemade Persian pastries and arranged them on a plate. Ahmad was delighted with the visitors and happy to kick a soccer ball around with Mehran in the sunshine.

'We're coming to the funeral, of course,' Leila said. 'Mehran will arrange everything at the Sydney mosque.'

Leila heaped promises on her when they took their leave. She would support Zahra at the funeral and visit during her days of mourning. After that she wanted Zahra to visit her at her son's place, every day if she wanted to.

After they'd gone, Zahra took Ahmad for a walk on the beach. It had been a relief to speak Persian again and to express exactly how she felt. Let them think her husband was dead! He was. She was a genuine widow. Fending for herself in her new country would be much easier now, she reflected. Her drug-dealing cousin, his corrupt friends, and an assassin from Iran were no longer a threat to her new life.

Ali's body was finally released and the funeral took place on Friday, Muslim holy day. She was grateful to the imam at the Sydney mosque for arranging the funeral to suit them at one o'clock in the afternoon. She didn't take Ahmad, but left him at the kindergarten. There was no point. It wasn't his father who was being buried. Leila said she totally understood; funerals were no place for young children.

Afterward, Leila and her son took Zahra back to the small flat where they lived with Mehran's young wife and their two children. She sat on the sofa in their comfortable living room, relieved it was all over and grateful to be in a home again.

'You must come for a proper meal, after the mourning period,' Leila insisted, plying her with sandwiches, cakes, and tea.

When they drove her back to the hostel, Leila accompanied her to her flat.

'I'll take care of you, Zahra,' Leila told her, picking up a small piece of paper from the floor. 'Don't stay inside though,' she added as she secured the paper under a brochure on the coffee table. 'When I visit, we can walk on the beach each day and I'll keep you company.'

Zahra grasped the older woman's hands, overwhelmed with gratitude. She'd had no one, and now God had sent Leila back to her.

After Leila and her son left, Zahra collected Ahmad from the kindergarten and went to the recreation room. When she called the number Firzun had given her, it rang unanswered until the line cut out.

The evening was warm and after dinner she walked slowly back to her flat with Ahmad. When he was in bed, she glanced at the sheaf of papers and leaflets still on the coffee table. Most of them were duplicates of forms she had already filled out and brochures about how to handle her grief. She swept everything up and threw the pile in the bin.

23

CHRISTMAS DRINKS

'I can't promise that this will be processed before Christmas, sir.'

Karim was slightly disappointed that the person who dealt with his visa application at the Australian consulate was a young American woman. He had looked forward to a chance to hone his Antipodean language comprehension. He handed over his completed forms and passport for photocopying.

'It might take at least four weeks, sir,' the young woman added.

'Seems a long time for a tourist visa,' he commented.

She smiled sweetly. 'I guess you'll have to blame Santa for that.'

He felt edgy. 'Would the visa got sorted by, say, the first week in January?' he asked.

The clerk told him she really didn't know. But Zahra needed help—*his* help, he thought anxiously as he hailed a cab. As he stood waiting to cross the road, an icy wind cutting through his jacket, he found it hard to imagine Australians celebrating Christmas in the middle of summer.

By Thursday evening, Zahra still hadn't returned his call and Karim felt both piqued and worried for her. The woman at the hostel had assured him that she would deliver the message personally and that had been Monday, Australian time. He drummed his fingers on the desk in his home office and decided to put another call through. He checked his watch. It was twelve-thirty am in New York and he calculated that it was two-thirty on Friday afternoon where Zahra lived in New South Wales. On Monday, the clerk had said something about English classes finishing at one o'clock, so Zahra should be around by now.

He went through the usual lengthy process of calling Australia. The same clerk, Helen McIntyre, took the call. He identified himself and when he asked if his previous message had been delivered, she told him it had.

'I haven't heard from Mrs Ghafoori,' he continued.

'Just a minute, please.'

She put her hand ineffectually over the phone and he heard her say, 'It's the American gentleman again asking about Zahra Ghafoori.'

Another voice said, 'Okay, I'll take it.'

'Mr Konari? My name's Caroline Parks. I'm the Migrant Women's Liaison Officer. Are you related to Zahra?'

He was taken aback by the direct question. 'No, I'm not. She used to work for my family, in Tehran. I just wanted to know how she is.' He frowned; why the question? Should he tell this woman about Zahra's letter? He didn't wait for a reply but rushed on. 'Is she all right? Is Ahmad okay?'

There was a slight pause.

'Erm, I'm sorry, Mr Konari,' Caroline answered slowly. 'I'm not at liberty to discuss personal matters concerning the hostel residents, or their families.'

What the hell is going on over there? Karim thought. The liaison officer sounded cagey.

'Can't you at least reassure me that Zahra is all right?'

'Yes, she is. I really can't say any more, unless you're a member of her family.'

Why didn't I say I was her brother instead of her employer?

'Did she get my last message?'

Caroline assured him that all phone messages were delivered. They were slipped under resident's doors if they were not at home. It sounded pretty inefficient to him, but if that was their system, what could he do? He asked to leave another one, and Caroline said she would make sure Zahra received it. He gave his phone number, address, and instructions for Zahra to call him back collect.

The woman assured him she would take it over personally.

'Erm ... Mr Konari, she might not call back today. She has some personal business to attend to. I'm sorry to sound so vague, but I think she would rather tell you herself.'

'Thank you, I'll wait for her call. You've been very helpful.'

'I *will* get the message to her,' Caroline assured him before she hung up.

It all sounded mysterious and frankly annoyingly incompetent to him, Karim thought as he put the phone down. *Personal business,* what was that about? All he could do was write to her again and hope to God she called him. He had a feeling that something was seriously wrong. He had no doubt that this mysterious business concerned Firzun. Maybe he'd shown up!

He turned on the television. NBC were re-running the lighting of the White House Christmas tree from Tuesday. He sat back in his chair, trying to forget about the phone call, and watched the news broadcast.

'*Tuesday night President Carter, his wife and daughter lit fifty small Christmas trees outside the White House,*' the newsreader intoned solemnly. '*He will not light the National Christmas tree until all the hostages come home. Here's some of what he said ...*'

President Jimmy Carter looked weary as he spoke into the microphone:

'*Around the periphery of this crowd are fifty small Christmas trees,*' the president began. '*One for each of the American hostages. On the top of this great Christmas tree there is a star of hope. We will turn on the other lights on this Christmas tree when the American hostages come home.'*

There was total silence when the president's daughter Amy threw the switch and the huge tree was lit only by the star of hope. Karim leaned back on the sofa and thought about the situation in his homeland. Negotiations for the release of the hostages, it seemed, were at a standstill. The American press had now been banished from Iran, according to the latest news bulletin, and only 'independent observers' were allowed to see the hostages. As if that wasn't bad enough, things were getting worse for people in the US. Gas was running out; hopefully time wasn't also running out for the hostages.

On a prosaic level, he remembered the invitation to Lawrence O'Rourke's Christmas drinks tomorrow night. In addition, he'd been invited to several of his Persian friends' houses over the weekend. No doubt his Persian friends would spend their time in endless discussions about Iranian politics. And they'd all have plenty to say about the hostage crisis. Still, it would be good to sit around speaking his own language and eating familiar food. On Monday the IRS officer was coming to start on their accounts. Next thing it would be Christmas!

What the hell is happening to you over there, Zahra? he thought anxiously as he got ready for bed. *Why haven't you returned my call?*

'Oh my God! You look like Sean Connery when he was James Bond,' Lauren exclaimed when she opened the door to her father's apartment the following evening.

He smiled and raised his eyebrows in a Bond-like gesture. If only she knew! Less than a month ago he'd been running for his life under fire at the US embassy in Tehran.

'Come and meet my folks.' Lauren signalled to a hovering butler, who took his coat.

As he followed her, he couldn't help but admire her slim body in its shimmery gold sheath dress. She wore her auburn hair loose and had straightened it, so it fell in a long curtain over her bare back. He looked around, curious to see what sort of people had arrived to share Christmas drinks with her family. The guests stood in groups, some by a huge glittering Christmas tree that almost touched the high ceiling, some near a discrete bar where a bartender was shaking cocktails. Lauren turned and he took her arm with a smile.

The groups were an interesting cross-section of New York society. There were slender blonde women accompanied by short swarthy men, and several tall men and women, possibly African-American, Karim thought. Like him, the men all wore tuxedos, the women cocktail dresses. As they passed each group, people smiled and greeted Lauren.

Above the discrete hum of conversation, she leaned into him and said, 'Let me introduce you to Daddy.'

Karim had only half-expected another redhead, but the man making his way toward him with outstretched hand had startling ginger hair. Everything about him was ginger-coloured: his bushy eyebrows, his receding frizzy hair, and the stubble on his chin. Even though Karim reckoned Lauren's dad must be about sixty, his hair had stubbornly maintained its colour.

'Karim, this is Daddy, Lawrence O'Rourke. Daddy, this is Karim, the guy I hit with my bicycle in the park!'

Karim shook the other man's hard bony hand. The pelt of ginger hairs on the back of it felt more animal than human.

'Pleased to meet you, sir.'

'Well, hon, you've got yourself a real looker this time!' Father turned to daughter. 'I-ranian, that right?'

'Yes, sir.' Karim struggled to place the other man's accent.

'Some heavy stuff going on over there. You're better out of it,' Lawrence commented in his strange voice. 'So, you're a New Yorker now. Where'd'ya live?'

When Karim told him, Lawrence's pale blue eyes flickered with interest.

'Round the corner from John Lennon. I knew his mother Julia, nice girl.'

'Daddy's from Liverpool in England,' Lauren explained. 'The whole family migrated there from Northern Ireland during the Depression.'

'I was born in Emdale, near Drumballyrooney in County Down. Betcha can't say that after a few drinks! No one's ever heard of it.' He waved his hand dismissively. 'Best thing I ever did was getting work on the banana boats from Liverpool to the Caribbean. The worst thing was marrying your mother!' He grinned a crooked-teeth smile at his daughter, making his gaunt face look ghoulish. 'Hope you like a drink, Karim—I've got plenty of good Irish whiskey here.'

Before Karim could respond, Lawrence nodded and moved to another group. His ill-fitting brown suit looked totally out of place amongst the smart tuxedos and black ties, but he obviously didn't care.

'He doesn't mean it when he says that about Momma,' Lauren told Karim quietly. 'She couldn't make it tonight. When Daddy drinks he ... Anyway, what can I get you?'

'Whiskey sounds good,' Karim said.

A waiter paused politely, and as Lauren ordered their drinks, Karim felt a wave of sympathy for her. She'd looked down and bitten her lip when her mother was mentioned; her father's comment about his wife had obviously stung. Karim wondered for a minute if Lauren's former fiancé Max had changed his mind after he'd met Lawrence.

A white-coated waiter materialised quietly at his side.

'Oh! I love these Champagne flutes,' Lauren exclaimed. 'They're Venetian glass. Daddy and Momma bought them years ago in Italy. Look, they've got little Christmas angels engraved around them.' She twirled her glass carefully on its stem as the bubbles rose in rapid lines to the rim. 'I asked for Champagne for you too.' Her green eyes met his. 'You can have whisky any time.'

He picked up the glass carefully from the tray and clinked it with hers. As he took a sip, a movement across the room caught his eye. Someone was signalling to him. He looked closely—surely not! But yes, it was. Hamid Ashrani from his old school in Tehran was standing at the bar.

He hadn't set eyes on the other man since he'd left school. He remembered that the boys at school used to call him 'the peasant' because of his lowly origins. What was he doing here? What possible connection could he have with Lawrence O'Rourke and the *beau monde* of New York? *I'm about to find out,* Karim thought as he watched Hamid, drink in hand, making his way toward him with a knowing smile on his face.

'Hi,' the other man greeted Karim warmly. 'Ashton, Harry Ashton.'

Karim was tempted to say, 'Bond, James Bond,' after the compliment Lauren had given him, but he was feeling more surprised than flippant. He smiled as he shook the other man's hand.

Harry grinned and said in Persian, 'Hi Karim Konari. It's me, Hamid Ashrani.'

'I recognised you, but ... what are you doing here?' Karim asked.

He remembered everything about the Ashrani brothers. At Karim's exclusive private school in Tehran, all the kids knew that they were the poorest kids there. Hamid's mother had worked as a seamstress for Karim's mother in her department store. Karim remembered standing at the top of the stairs once and seeing Mrs Ashrani and her younger son waiting in the atrium of his house. Hamid was staring open-mouthed at the opulent decor. Mrs Ashrani was 'pushy and a bit above herself', according to Esmat. The father was a minor public servant. Now here was little Hamid in New York, wearing an expensive-looking tuxedo and sipping a martini.

'Good to see you ... Harry,' Karim replied in English. 'Have you been in New York long?'

'Harry works for my dad,' Lauren said. 'You two know each other? How great is that?'

'We were school buddies in Tehran,' Hamid told her.

'What a small world!' Lauren was thrilled. 'Why don't I leave you to catch up while I go circulate?'

'She's a real looker, isn't she?' Karim's companion commented quietly in Persian as they watched Lauren greet her father's guests. 'I guess she's your date?'

'Well, sort of,' Karim replied.

'Drink?' Hamid asked, raising his eyebrows at the empty Christmas Champagne glass Karim was still holding.

'Scotch, thanks.' Karim followed the shorter man to the bar in the corner of the room.

'Still a Scotch drinker,' Hamid commented.

Karim nodded, glad to get rid of the girly glass and surprised that the other man remembered his preferred drink.

'So, you work for Lawrence O'Rourke, eh?' Karim picked up the crystal tumbler. 'What do you do?'

'I'm his real estate development manager,' Hamid said with a touch of hubris. 'Mr O'Rourke is into real estate in a big way these days. He owns several clubs too, mostly in the southern states and one in Antigua.'

'The Caribbean?' Karim raised his eyebrows.

'Yes, that where his wife, Lauren's mother Beulah, comes from. She's part Creole,' he added. 'Mrs O'Rourke's family was in the rum trade. They had properties and businesses on a lot of the islands. I think Mr O'Rourke has bought most of the family shares out by now. See those people over there?' He indicated the couple Karim had thought were African-American. 'They're from St Lucia. They're in the rum business too.'

Karim hid his surprise and wondered why Lauren had never mentioned her mother's ethnic origins. But then, he hardly knew her.

'So how come you work for Lawrence O'Rourke?'

'Ah!' Hamid smiled. 'Well, you know I studied business management here? It cost my family a fortune. I got bartending jobs in clubs while I was studying. At one point I was so poor I had to sleep in my car for six months. Anyway, I was keen to stay in the States, since things have been bad in Iran for years, as you know. I had a job in one of Mr O'Rourke's clubs and he asked me if I could handle a weapon. I've done my National Service in Iran, so I thought, why not?'

Karim wondered how many martinis Hamid had put away already. He was talking pretty freely about Lawrence's business. But then, they were speaking quietly in another language.

'So, go on, did he want you to "rub someone out"?'

'Not quite,' Hamid replied seriously. 'He owns a gentlemen's club in Charleston—South Carolina. A few new girls there—dancers —were being harassed by the patrons. He wanted me to go to the club and escort them back to their hotel rooms. That sort of thing.'

That sort of thing? What kind of operation was Lauren's dad running?

'So, I did, and he paid me well. There wasn't any trouble. When the stage door hangers-on saw me, they cleared off.'

Karim wasn't surprised. Hamid had always been a stocky, thick-set kid. As an adult, he'd bulked out. He was swarthy and had never managed to totally get rid of his stubble, even as a teenager at school. The other kids didn't dare tease him about it. Anyone who got in a fight with Hamid Ashrani always came off worse.

'So, you were a bouncer for Lawrence?'

'Security. He trusted me never to get fresh with the girls. Ladies are not my scene.' Hamid paused. 'If you get my drift.' He looked away, then back at Karim.

Another surprise, Karim thought. How many more this evening? No wonder Hamid had worked out at the gym. There were plenty of intolerant people around and the Hamids of this world had to protect themselves. As for Iran, someone of his sexual orientation would have been arrested, thrown in jail, and beaten up. Karim was keen to hear more about Lawrence's clubs, but this wasn't the place. Instead he asked a bland question.

'And now you're into real estate?'

'I am. I have a friend, Nigel—we live together. He's an interior designer.' He paused. 'He's a great help. Sometimes we have to furnish the houses and apartments for the boss.' Hamid finished his drink and ordered another. 'What about you, Karim, still working as an architect? Have the IRS bothered you at all?'

Karim was taken aback. Was Lawrence checking up on him?

'We're being audited,' he admitted.

He regretted confiding the information as soon as he'd said it. But maybe Hamid would tell him why the IRS audited Lawrence's businesses regularly.

'It's not uncommon.' Hamid shrugged without mentioning Lawrence. He sipped his drink and asked Karim casually if he'd be interested in getting into real estate himself. Mr O'Rourke was into property development. He was planning to build in South Carolina near Myrtle Beach and they needed an architect.

'I might be interested,' Karim said cautiously.

'Well, it's apartments and condos, mainly. He's looking south of Myrtle Beach. He's buying land like it's going out of fashion.'

Karim thought about his business in New York. Work from Lawrence O'Rourke, even though the actual build was a thousand miles from here, might mean that his company Konari and Yazdi could stay afloat until the hostage crisis was over. Yet, and he wasn't sure why, he felt uneasy about having any dealings with the man.

'Can't really talk about it now,' Hamid said quietly. 'Let's meet for lunch next week. I'll give you the lowdown then.' He handed Karim his business card. 'Mr O'Rourke pays well, as long as you keep your mouth shut. He doesn't like people knowing what he's planning till he's finished it.'

Lauren touched Karim's elbow, reached over, and adjusted his bow tie slightly. 'Harry, I'm going to drag your old buddy away to meet some new buddies.' She smiled.

'Ciao, Karim. Call me.' Hamid raised his martini glass.

Lauren took Karim's arm, holding it firmly as they went from group to group. He had a creepy feeling that his future was being decided for him. He felt like a chess piece being moved around a board. If he wasn't careful, he might lose control of his own life and become a pawn in someone else's. He tried to shrug off the sensation as he smiled and chatted, but it was still with him when he let himself into his apartment later that evening.

He went straight to his office and checked the answering machine. Zahra hadn't called. He was disappointed again, disproportionally so. He sat at his desk, his hands clasped in front of him. Why? After sending him such an overwhelming letter and saying how much she missed him, why hadn't she called back? Had something awful happened to her? Or maybe to Firzun?

24

CARNEGIE HALL

Bahram was waiting for Karim in the office when he arrived on Monday morning at eight o'clock.

'The IRS guy called. He'll be here at nine,' Bahram announced after a hasty good morning.

'Okay, this is it.' Karim followed his partner into the office.

The large table that usually held their scale models of building projects now had their files and envelopes full of receipts stacked at one end. The rest of the long table had been cleared in readiness. They pored over the figures together for a final check. Bahram organised the receptionist to re-type a couple of pages.

'The others are fine. It's these last two years that really needed some work. Dad decided to keep them for a couple of days and he couriered them back to me.' Karim sighed, wishing he'd paid more attention to the business side of Konari and Yazdi. Instead, he reflected, he had either been out on site visits, sorting out his life with his ex-wife, or rushing back to Iran.

'I wish the IRS assessor would take the stuff to his own office.' Karim frowned. 'Why does he have to hang around here all day?'

'So he can ask us questions, I guess.' Bahram's phone buzzed. 'Okay, thank you.' He turned to Karim. 'He's here.'

A tall man in his late thirties, with a blond crew cut, was waiting at reception. He stepped forward with a smile, his hand outstretched. 'Hi, I'm Gary Olson, IRS. Good to meet you.'

A tense atmosphere settled over the office. Despite this, at the end of the day, Gary looked up from his scrutiny and smiled.

'Seems okay so far.' He stretched and said yes to a cup of coffee.

'Do you need to come back tomorrow?' Karim asked.

'No, I'll take your accounts to my office. I can finish them there.' Gary picked up his cup. 'You're both Iranian, aren't you?'

'Is that a problem?' Bahram snapped before Karim could stop him.

'No, not at all ... I was with the Peace Corps in Turkey for two years in the sixties. On the way home, I travelled overland through Iran and Afghanistan. Ended up in India. Some vacation that was! Your country is beautiful—I loved Isfahan.'

A thought, a half-remembered comment he'd heard somewhere, niggled in Karim's brain. '*Some of the Peace Corps volunteers were working for the CIA. Brilliant cover.*' Who had said that to him? Could it be true?

'*CIA, CIA, CIA*' was what the students had chanted as they rounded up the Americans at the back of the embassy on 4 November. Was Gary checking up not on their tax liabilities but on them? Had he been asked to report back to someone about Bahram and him? Iranians in America. Gary was saying something to him.

'So, did you live in Tehran, Karim?' Gary repeated with a smile.

'Yes, we sold up everything and escaped here.'

'There's some pretty heavy stuff going on.' Gary was piling their documents into a serious-looking brown case. 'You must be glad to be out.'

'Sure am,' Karim replied.

'I guess you didn't support the new regime.' Gary smiled his bland smile again. Their eyes met as Gary drank the rest of his coffee.

'Not at all.' Karim glanced round for Bahram, but he was taking a phone call.

'Do you think they'll release the hostages soon?'

'I sure hope so.' Karim tried to sound non-committal.

'Well, I can't see President Carter returning the shah to his country,' Gary went on. He glanced up sharply as he shut his case. 'What do you think?'

'I guess not.'

Am I being questioned? Or am I being paranoid? Karim told himself that Gary was simply making conversation. He was obviously interested in the Middle East. Why imagine something sinister that wasn't there? He accompanied Gary to the reception area.

'The accounts look fine. You've done a good job,' he told Karim. 'Can't say more, but if there's a problem you'll hear from us before Christmas.'

He extended his hand.

'*Khodā hāfez, Karim Agha.*' Gary's penetrating blue eyes met Karim's.

He knows some Persian! Karim was too astounded to reply.

No, he doesn't, he only knows how to say 'goodbye, sir.' Only goodbye.

On Wednesday evening, Karim ran his hand over the narrow ochre-coloured brickwork of Carnegie Hall while he waited on the foot-path for Lauren. Snow had finally begun to fall in New York and the flakes whirled around the ornamental lamps on the old building. A northerly breeze ruffled the flags suspended on poles above the awning. He had no idea why she had suggested meeting him outside rather than let him collect her from her apartment, or even meet him inside, he thought. He didn't have the mental energy to second-guess women anymore. He moved closer under the awning out of the wind.

'Does this Roman-style brickwork gladden your architect's heart?' Lauren tapped him lightly on the shoulder. 'I thought you might like to take a closer look while you waited for me.'

He turned and smiled at her, still unused to her being on his eye level. Snowflakes were swirling around her and some had caught in her hair. He kissed her lightly on the cheek. She looked very elegant, he told her, and she pulled her white coat up around her chin and thanked him. He took her arm and they walked into the brightly lit foyer.

'I haven't been here since summer.' Lauren shook her head sadly and her diamond earrings caught the light. There was a hint of nostalgia in her voice, he noticed. Maybe the last time she'd been here was with Max.

'Though I like it better in the winter,' she rushed on. 'I'll have to ask Nigel, Harry's guy, how yellow can be a warm colour.'

'You know Nigel?' Karim asked.

'Of course,' she answered as she shrugged off her coat. 'He's a great guy.'

As he waited for their coats to be checked, Karim ruminated on this latest crumb of information. Harry, Nigel, Lauren, and Lawrence—one big happy family. He turned from the cloakroom and walked toward her. *She's a stunning looking woman. I should be glad she's my date.*

She took his arm and they made their way through the foyer. He saw several people stare at them as they passed. Her sleek red dress was as amazing as her auburn hair, which she wore loose, caught back by two diamond pins. He wondered uneasily if she expected him to sleep with her tonight.

He settled her at a small table in the bar and ordered Champagne from the hovering waiter. Across the table, Lauren glanced quickly at her small diamond-studded watch. She apologised and told him she got a tad agitated if she wasn't seated at least fifteen minutes before the performance started.

As he nodded, he felt slightly guilty. She was attractive, interesting, loved music ... but he was in love with someone else. He thought of Zahra and how he had longed to spend the night with her. How every time they were together, he'd wanted to touch her. It just wasn't there with Lauren; there was no sexual spark. Maybe a ten-year age gap was too much, he thought. As the waiter fussed with mats and drinks, Karim's mind wandered again to Zahra. Why hadn't she called? The gut feeling that something was wrong still lingered. He decided to go back to the Consulate and hurry up his tourist visa.

'Hello there! Where are you?' Lauren trilled as she raised her glass. 'Let have a toast to ...'

Please don't say the release of the hostages.

'To freedom, pure and simple.' She smiled at him.

'We'll drink to that too!'

Karim turned to the speaker. Hamid Ashrani, or rather Harry Ashton, was standing behind him, accompanied by a tall slim man. His fashionably cut blond hair almost touched his collar and he brushed it off his lightly tanned face. He gave Karim a dazzling smile.

I am being followed, Karim thought as he struggled to his feet.

'So, you found a park, wonderful,' Lauren remarked. 'Harry and Nigel drove me here,' she confided across the table to Karim.

For God's sake! She's got more chaperones than an Arab princess, Karim thought. *Good thing I don't want to sleep with her. No chance of that with the bodyguard and his boyfriend hanging round.* Lawrence either didn't trust him or didn't trust his daughter. Either way this was going to be an interesting evening. He wondered if they would all be sitting in a row during the concert.

After Lauren had introduced Nigel, the other couple excused themselves. Before they moved off, Karim exchanged a look with Harry—he guessed he should call him that from now on. Harry raised his eyebrows slightly and said he hoped they would enjoy the concert.

'Lucky you booked so well in advance, Lauren, honey,' Nigel said in his British accent. 'It's *packed* in there, darling!'

No mention was made of Max, the man Karim had obviously replaced. He returned the other couple's '*Ciao!*' and watched them disappear into the crowd.

'Daddy's a little overprotective,' Lauren said apologetically as Karim resumed his seat.

'I'm not surprised, you're a beautiful woman,' he replied automatically.

She smiled her thanks and consulted her program. 'So, we start with Bach, "The Goldberg Variations." After the interval he's going to play a couple of Chopin *etudes* before he hits us with Schumann's "Carnaval". Oh wow! The beginning of that is so *intense* ...' She passed him the program. 'I'm sure you'll love it all, especially the Bach. Youri, the soloist, is *so* Russian and *so* talented!'

The Bach piece brought back memories of Tehran that Karim would rather forget. He'd been playing that same music the day the Religious Police had called at his front door and tried to shove their way into his house. He'd never forget the fear he'd felt when he'd opened the door and been questioned by the seemingly innocuous young men. He pushed the memory to the back of his mind, hoping he could sit through the first half of the concert without getting edgy.

When they took their seats in the huge auditorium, there was no sign of Harry or Nigel. The stage was empty except for a grand piano. Karim was glad someone else was performing and not him. He'd played the piano on several occasions at soirées organised by his mother. Once when he was a teenager, he'd even performed at the American embassy in Tehran. Hard to believe that now, he thought, as he scanned the program.

The Russian pianist Youri Egorov delighted the audience. He was twenty-five and looked ridiculously young. His thick black hair almost obscured his vision as he leaned over the piano, and when he took a bow before the interval he pushed it back with a boyish grin. Karim had glanced sideways at Lauren a few times during the recital. She obviously loved music as much as he did. At least they had that in common, he thought.

During the interval Lauren told him that the Carnegie main concert hall was going to be refurbished soon. He nodded; it did look a little shabby, but that didn't detract from the performance. He glanced around again, but there was no sign of Lauren's minders.

'Oh, Daddy asks if you'd like to spend Christmas with us in Darien. I guess you don't celebrate ... but we're not a religious family. You can stay over. There's plenty of room.'

He thought quickly. Why not? He was curious to see Lawrence's other house and to meet Lauren's mother.

'I don't celebrate Christmas, but thank you, I'd love to come.'

He told her he was spending the weekend with his folks and would drive down on Christmas morning and back to New York the following day. She looked pleased and said that Harry and Nigel were coming too, as well as her brother and his girlfriend Magda.

'You'll get to meet Momma too,' she added. 'I'll write some directions for you.'

Karim was curious to meet the rest of her family, and her place was an easy drive from Boston. He looked at Lauren across the table. She smiled at him and pushed her hair back over her shoulder. He wondered vaguely why she hadn't mentioned her brother before.

The audience went wild at the end of the recital. Shouts of *Encore!* echoed around the concert hall. Youri Egorov returned to the stage to take a bow, looking slightly fazed. Karim knew exactly how he felt; Egorov had been in another place for the last hour. The applause must seem to be coming from a long way off, slowly bringing him back to the world. The dark-haired Russian resumed his seat at the piano. He placed his fingers on the keys and the haunting notes of the first movement of Beethoven's 'Moonlight Sonata' hung on the air. Breath left Karim's body in a long slow sigh.

He was immediately back in his parents' house in Tehran a couple of months ago. He remembered coming home tired one afternoon and wandering into the library. This particular piece of music always helped him unwind. He had hardly got through the first six bars when Zahra, concealed behind a bookcase, had dropped a book on the floor. He'd stopped playing and gone to investigate. She was in tears and he'd put his arms round her. He'd realised immediately that he should never have touched her. She'd pulled away but he'd wanted to hold her tighter and kiss her hair and her trembling lips.

The applause for Egorov brought Karim back to the present. He collected their outdoor coats and then handed Lauren over to her bodyguards, who were waiting in the foyer. He accepted a lift back to his apartment from Harry and joined Lauren in the backseat. The snow was getting heavier. When they stopped outside the apartment block, Lauren leaned over to him and kissed him lightly on the lips. She told him she was going to Connecticut the next day to be with 'Momma'.

'So, I'll see you on Christmas Day. Here's the address.' She smiled and handed him a page from her small notebook. 'Thanks for a lovely evening.'

Karim felt a tad guilty; he'd spent most of their date thinking about Zahra.

He wished Harry and Nigel goodnight and got out of the car. The snowfall had deadened the city noise and he stood for a minute on the footpath after Harry had driven off in the Lincoln Continental. Then he hurried under the awning of his apartment building. The 'Moonlight Sonata' played in his mind as a background to his thoughts of Zahra as he lay in bed that night. He was worried that maybe something awful had happened to her. Whatever it was though, he couldn't do anything. He had no business to even be thinking of her.

Karim knew his mother was pouting while he spoke to her on the phone the following day. He studiously ignored her faint tuts when he told her his plans for the coming weekend. She asked him why he wasn't spending Christmas Day with his family. When he pointed out that they were not a Christian family and it shouldn't bother her, she tutted again.

'Well, your father and I will be babysitting,' she informed him. 'It's not my favourite occupation. Your sister and brother-in-law will be out doing good works. Serving Christmas dinner to the homeless.'

'Like I said, *Madar djan*, I'll be there on Friday and stay till Tuesday—Christmas morning. Won't that make you happy?'

His mother sniffed; he could almost see her shrugging when she said, 'If that's what you want.'

The phone went silent for a minute and Karim frowned. 'Are you still there?'

'I am. I've been making enquiries about the O'Rourke family.' She paused dramatically longer than necessary. 'My advice is that you shouldn't get mixed up with them, especially the father.'

'And why is that, Mother?'

Lauren might be all right, his mother went on—she'd seemed nice enough. However, she didn't know if Karim knew about Lauren's broken engagement earlier this year. He said he knew and he didn't want to hear any gossip.

'Well,' she said, ignoring his interjection, 'a *very* prestigious New York family forced their son to break off his planned wedding with Lauren O'Rourke. She was a totally unsuitable match. Well, maybe not her, but her *family*.'

Karim wasn't totally surprised; this was his mother's usual *modus operandi*. But she'd only been in the country four weeks. How did she know all this? She lived in Boston, for goodness sake, not New York. When he asked her, she said she had plenty of friends in 'the big apple' *and* a telephone.

'Okay, I'll see you Friday,' he promised.

'Don't do anything rash with that young woman, Karim. You know what I mean,' Esmat added darkly.

Before he could answer, she hung up.

Karim put the phone down. How did his mother manage to remind him of his chief failing—impulsiveness—while at the same time letting him know she knew something he didn't? It was a finely finessed skill and it never failed to annoy him. Besides which, the call had added to his own uneasy feelings about Lauren's father.

When he had mentioned Lawrence O'Rourke in passing to Bahram, the other man had raised his eyebrows.

'He pays his bills on time, I know that,' Bahram had said. 'Not sure about the other stuff.'

Before Karim could ask about 'the other stuff', Bahram had disappeared into the main office to take a phone call.

Karim pushed thoughts of Lawrence to the back of his mind and checked his watch. He had enough time to take a cab to Bloomingdales on Third Avenue and pick up a few gifts. Lauren would certainly expect one. He didn't relish the idea of fighting his way through the Christmas rush, especially in the snow. Still, it had to be done.

It was getting closer to Christmas, and even from his cab the city was beginning to look frenzied. Huge tides of people swept along the sidewalks. Blow-up Santas looked down from every awning and shop lights glittered on newly fallen snow. He got out of the cab and felt a rush of excitement. He actually loved Christmas—not dragging around shops with his mother and sister, but the sense of anticipation and bonhomie. He loved the decorations, the lights, the feeling of excitement. Even though Bloomingdales was more restrained in its decorations than most of the other stores, the display windows glowed in various hues of green, red, purple, and yellow. Inside each were Christmas scenes. The yellow window was a mock-up of a small clapboard house. Yellow ribbons were tied around the trees in the front yard. He got the message: *bring them home—release the hostages.* Above him as he plunged into the store, the flags of nations hung on poles and blew in the chilly breeze. The Iranian flag wasn't amongst them.

He wondered if Iranians in Australia were feeling as bad as he felt here in the United States. He remembered that Harry had mentioned his brother lived there. He decided to ask him more about his brother on Christmas Day. Karim might be able to get in touch with the brother, see if he could track down Zahra. He dismissed the thought almost immediately. Sydney was a big city. Chances of the Ashranis ever meeting or finding Zahra were very slim.

25

LEILA ASHRANI

Zahra stood with Ahmad at Fairy Meadow station waiting for the train to Sutherland. Leila had been very persuasive and eventually Zahra had agreed to get on a train and visit her new friend.

'We live right near the station. It will only take you about half an hour,' Leila had told her. 'I know you're nervous about leaving the hostel, but you're living in Australia now.'

Zahra would never be able to tell Leila the real reason it took all her courage to get on a train. The fearful memory of Ali running across the railway bridge as her train had left the station was still with her. Tomorrow it would be a week since his funeral, and remembering it still made her shudder. She had heard nothing from Firzun.

She tried to think of something else while they waited. Tomorrow was Friday 21 December, and it was the final day of kindergarten before the Christmas break. There was going to be a children's party and a surprise visit from Santa. She was actually looking forward to it.

The train slid slowly into the station and Zahra watched Ahmad as he jumped on then ran down the aisle and got them a seat. Her son loved everything about Australia. Firzun had been right about something: he'd given both her and Ahmad a wonderful opportunity to live safely in a new country. It was even because of him that she knew Leila. But it would still take her a long time, she reflected, to forgive Firzun for all the other things.

The train lurched along slowly and stopped at the small stations the express had rushed through before. Sometimes the ocean and beaches were close to the railway line and Ahmad waved at the small figures who ran into the surf. Then the line began to climb upward and she almost shrieked like Ahmad when a windsurfer glided from the top of the cliffs, down through the blueness, to the beach below. Gradually the ocean and beach disappeared behind them as the train began to manoeuvre slowly along the winding track bordered by sandstone cliffs. A few little houses surrounded by trees came into view, then the vast green expanses of the National Park. How immense this country is, Zahra thought. Although she had pored over maps of Australia in the Konari library when she lived in Tehran, actually being here was daunting. Their train was a slow-moving dot in a tiny corner of a vast, ancient land.

Leila was waiting for her at the station with her nine-year-old granddaughter Lili and Lili's six-year-old brother Darius. They were thrilled to see Ahmad and shouted 'hello' as soon as he got off the train. Leila rushed up and hugged Zahra and asked how she was.

'Zahra! How are you, my dear?'

'I'm well, how are you, Leila?'

Zahra assured her friend that she was feeling good. What a relief it was, she thought, to speak the familiar language.

'It's the school holidays,' Leila told her. 'My daughter-in-law is at work, so I'm on grandmother duty. I'm so glad to see you!'

She linked her arm through Zahra's as they ushered the children out of the station. As they waited at the traffic lights, Zahra looked around curiously. The suburb was newer than Fairy Meadow. Most of the houses were brick, not wood, and there were more apartment blocks like the one where Leila lived. She stole a sideways glance at

Leila. As usual, the other woman was smartly dressed, this time in a tailored cotton dress with matching jacket.

'I make all my own clothes.' Leila had noticed the look and she smiled at Zahra as they crossed the road. 'I was a seamstress in Tehran. I'll tell you more when we get to the flat.'

They walked down a leafy road with apartment blocks on either side. *Maybe Ahmad and I could live somewhere like this one day.* The thought no longer filled Zahra with dread. She would definitely enrol for the interpreter's course in January. Hadn't Nousha worked as a casual interpreter in the hostel? *If she can do it, so can I,* she thought. *Nothing in the future could be as bad as what I've just been through.*

Inside the ground floor apartment, Leila fussed over her. She made Iranian coffee and managed to stop the children eating all the sweet cakes and pastries she'd put on the coffee table. While Leila's grandson and Ahmad played soccer outside, her granddaughter sat at the table with pencils and a colouring book.

After she'd enquired about Zahra's health and how she was coping, Leila indicated the flat with a slight shrug. There were only two bedrooms, she told Zahra, and she was sharing with the children at the moment. But they were very excited; her son had put a deposit on a house and they hoped to move at the end of January. *A house! How permanent,* Zahra thought. Leila confided that she had brought some money with her from Iran and she was hoping to get a job as a seamstress again. She had worked in a big department store in Tehran called Arezoo. Maybe Zahra had heard of it?

'It was way out of my price range.' Leila laughed.

Arezoo! Karim's mother Esmat had owned it. Zahra was stunned by the coincidence. Before could say anything, Leila rushed on.

'It was owned by Esmat Konari. She was a good enough boss, but very exacting. I went to their house once in Elahiyeh with my younger son. The place was like a palace! Esmat Khanoum and I had a few run-ins though. She was a very forceful woman, but I wouldn't let her push me around.'

Zahra smiled; she remembered Karim's mother very well. She hesitated, wondering whether to tell Leila that she too had worked for Esmat Konari as a companion to her mother-in-law Rezvan. Why not? She was unlikely to hear from Karim again. After all, he hadn't replied to the letter she'd sent him. When she told Leila, the other woman was amazed.

'We have so much in common, Zahra! Esmat's mother-in-law was a real lady. Of course, you know Esmat's grandparents were from Afghanistan. They made their money running market stalls to begin with.'

'So I believe.'

'Esmat was the first of her family to marry an Iranian—Abbas Konari—from an upper-class family,' Leila continued.

She told Zahra that Esmat was a real beauty when she was younger. Did Zahra remember her green eyes? Her son Karim had unusual eyes too, a sort of honey-coloured hazel, with gold flecks.

'Did you meet Karim?' Leila asked.

'Yes, he was around.'

Leila told her that all the women in Tehran were after Karim Konari, but he still wasn't married three months ago when Leila gave her notice.

'So, did they all go to the States?'

'Yes, I helped pack up the house.'

'I am truly amazed, such a coincidence!' Leila shook her head.

Although Zahra longed to hear more about Karim, she didn't want to pique Leila's curiosity.

'Esmat found it hard to deal with my boys being at the same school as her son Karim.' Leila laughed. 'We had to save very hard, but my boys won part scholarships,' she said proudly. Leila's husband, she told Zahra, had been a public servant with a low salary.

'Where does your other son live?' Zahra asked, but before Leila could answer, Ahmad and Darius rushed in. Leila got up and fiddled with the television set. She had a video of a program called

Skippy about a talking kangaroo. It might keep the boys in one place for half an hour.

'My other son lives in the United States,' she told Zahra as they prepared lunch together. 'He's not married, but we live in hope. We know a few families in Sydney with single daughters, so we hope he'll visit soon.'

Zahra smiled; she might have to look for a wife for Ahmad one day.

'Hamid, my son in the States, has changed his name,' Leila added. 'He calls himself Harry Ashton now.'

Walking back from the station to the hostel, Zahra felt happy for the first time since she'd arrived in Australia. She liked Leila and it had been relaxing to speak Persian all day. The next two weeks would be very quiet at the hostel, her neighbour Julie had told her. English classes finished before Christmas and wouldn't resume until the new year. Susan, Zahra's teacher, had given her some extra study sheets to work on over the holiday period.

The kindergarten was closed over Christmas and a lot of families had moved out so they could spend Christmas in their new homes. Even Lan was leaving.

'Family come by boat, uncle and brothers,' she'd told Zahra. 'It very terrible, like how I come. They live in hostel in Sydney. Me, sister, and kids, we go live there too, later get house together.' She smiled. 'I very happy, very happy.'

Zahra had held her hand and thanked her for helping her through her first three days.

'No worries, be happy, maybe you meet rich man one day! I wish you good luck.'

As they neared the hostel, Zahra felt a few specks of rain on her face. She took Ahmad's hand and told him to hurry. They had just run through the hostel gates when someone called out to them.

'Hello, Zahra and Ahmad!'

Caroline, the welfare officer walked over to them and asked if she'd received her second phone message. Zahra shook her head. *Phone messages? Surely Firzun hadn't called the hostel?*

'From a gentleman in America?' Caroline went on. 'Erm, Mr Konari. He said he was Iranian, but I'd never have guessed from his accent.'

Karim!

'I didn't know anyone had phoned,' Zahra answered. Then she remembered the note Caroline had given her on the day she'd identified the body. But where had she put it?

'Well, he was very insistent the second time. All we can do is take a message and the number and put it under your door. He wanted to know how you were. He's not family, is he?'

'No.'

'Look, I've got to pick my children up from school. I copied the number and put it in your file. Helen should be in the office for another half an hour or so. She can give it to you. Sorry, I've got to run. The rain's getting heavier!'

Zahra hurried toward the office in a daze. Karim had called! She felt as if a huge weight had lifted from her shoulders. Ahmad squealed with fright as a sudden flash of lightning forked through the sky, followed by a crack of thunder. She took his hand, then turned and ran to their flat. She would go to the office after the storm passed. By the time they got to the front door, the summer storm had soaked their clothes. She helped Ahmad get changed and dressed hastily herself. They were both shivering and she made a cup of tea. She looked out the window at the administration block. The rain streamed down the glass and blew in sheets across the lawn. At each clap of thunder, Ahmad whimpered and clung to her.

Another sizzle of lightning and crash of thunder convinced her that she would never get him to go outside. She couldn't leave him, but she was desperate to get to the office. She checked her watch: four-fifteen. It was the middle of the night in New York, but she had to have Karim's number. Suddenly she remembered throwing a pile of papers in the bin. Had the notes from the office gone out with the trash? There was another huge crack of lightning, then a thunder-clap exploded overhead. When on earth would the storm pass?

The flat seemed gloomy and dark because of the lowering clouds and she switched on the overhead light. Nothing happened. The storm must have hit the power lines. How long would the power cut last? In Tehran they'd lasted hours! Maybe the phone lines had been affected too.

Eventually the storm weakened and blew out to sea. Behind it were clear skies and sunshine. The power was still off and the grass sodden, but she could get to the office on the paths. She knew it closed at four-forty-five—she'd just make it. Ahmad wasn't keen on going outside in case the storm came back, but she promised he could watch TV for a while in the recreation room.

Water was still pooling on the concrete paths as she hurried along. She pushed open the door of the administration building. It was eerily quiet in the foyer and all the office doors were shut. A handwritten notice on the front counter said: *We apologise but the office is closed due to the power cut. We will open again at nine am tomorrow.*

Zahra stood in the foyer with Ahmad and swallowed back her tears. Just to hold a message from Karim ... As she turned to walk back to her flat, Clive the hostel manager emerged from another door. When she asked him if he could get her file and find a phone number for her, he shook his head.

'I'm sorry, Mrs Ghafoori, residents' personal files are confiden-tial. I don't have permission to access them. I'm just the hostel manager. Cheer up, the power'll be back on soon.'

She took Ahmad's hand and walked toward the recreation room but stopped halfway. The power was off, so no television. Ahmad was desperately disappointed and close to tears as they returned to the flat. When she flicked the light switch, the power was back on. But another day would pass before she could phone Karim. If only she'd got the number today … She could have called him later that evening.

Zahra swallowed her disappointment and started planning. Tomorrow morning, she would get the number before the kindergarten Christmas party started at ten. She might even have time to phone him. When she called Karim, she would tell him everything that had happened so he'd understand why she hadn't returned his calls.

She gave in to Ahmad's entreaties and took him back to watch TV. By the time she got to the recreation room and settled her son in front of the television, she'd decided not to mention Firzun or Ali to Karim. Yes, he'd been interested enough in her welfare to phone her. But if she told him everything, he might just give up on her altogether. She stared straight ahead; he had called twice. Did that mean he still cared about her? That he hadn't met another woman in New York and that maybe, just *maybe*, she would see him again one day? She might even hear his voice again tomorrow! The thought lifted her spirits and for the first time in a very long time she was looking forward to the following day.

26

A FAMILY BUSINESS

As he walked along Broadway for the lunch appointment he'd fixed up with Harry, Karim loosened his scarf and opened his jacket. The snow from last night had cleared to slush in the sunshine and the temperature felt mild for December. Steam rose from gratings and hung on the air. He glanced up at the gathering clouds, wondering if more snow was on the way. The city, for all its Christmas decorations, looked a tad shabby, he thought. Large slabs of tar had been spread in patches on the roadway and the sidewalks were uneven in places. At times he was forced to walk through the residue of building rubble. There was a constant noise of banging and drilling, interspersed with thumps, while concrete mixers revved up and reversed off the roadway across his path and into building sites.

Karim was carried along by the tide of pedestrians on the crowded footpaths. Scaffolding around several buildings narrowed the space, making it hard to get anywhere quickly. Grey clouds had trapped in the smells of the city—hotdogs, diesel fumes, and wet concrete. He wished it would snow again and clean the place up, or rather, hide the mess. He'd considered taking the subway for the few stops. But he'd taken it the other day and hadn't enjoyed sitting in the dirty, graffitied carriages on an uncomfortable seat with torn upholstery.

He'd arranged to meet Harry at his favourite diner and he'd asked the other man to get a booth for privacy if he got there first. He wasn't surprised to see Harry waiting for him when he arrived. Harry stood up and shook Karim's hand and they took their places opposite each other on the high-backed brown leather bench seats. Diners were one of the things he loved most about New York, Karim told Harry.

'This one's been given a make-over,' Karim remarked as he looked around. Harry nodded with a smile.

The new fittings were first-class, Karim noticed. The orange fabric in the decor and toning orange lamps over the bar matched the backs of the chairs and the bar stools. He ordered a beer and was surprised when Harry ordered a soda.

'I have to keep sharp, no alcohol during the day. I hope you don't mind me sitting facing the door,' he went on. 'That way I get to see who's coming in,' Harry explained in English, adding quietly in Persian, 'Let's stick to English okay?'

'Fine by me.'

Karim paused while the waiter served their drinks. Another waiter handed each of them a huge menu, which he put to one side. 'So, how are you?'

'I'm well, and you?' Harry answered, unfazed by the formal start to their conversation.

'I'm good. Tell me more about South Carolina.'

'Okay, Mr O'Rourke owns land between the beach and the wetlands.' Harry leaned forward slightly as he got down to business. 'As I mentioned, he wants to build apartment blocks and some condominiums.'

'Are we talking sand dunes?' Karim was already calculating the cost of concrete footings.

'Yes, and he wants every apartment to have ocean views.'

Karim mentioned the storm surges that often hit the South

Carolina coast. Harry was aware of that, he said, and that's why Mr O'Rourke wanted Karim to see the land and give his opinion. Karim was mildly surprised. So Lawrence and Harry—he had to remember to call Hamid by his adopted name—had already been discussing him.

'I'm going to Myrtle Beach between Christmas and New Year,' Harry told him. 'Why not come with me? Mr O'Rourke will pay your expenses.'

A waiter appeared and they gave their orders—a tuna steak for Harry and a t-bone for him.

Harry continued that Mr O'Rourke wanted him to check out things at Cassandra's, the gentlemen's club he owned on the peninsula in Charleston.

'Cassandra's?' Karim raised his eyebrows slightly. He remembered Harry mentioning a club at Lawrence's drinks party. 'Wasn't she the prophetess of doom?'

Harry smiled but didn't comment as he sat back and drank his soda.

'Is "gentlemen's club" a euphemism for something else?' Karim probed.

When pressed, Harry was cagey, saying only that the club was many things. Karim frowned, wondering again how much Lauren knew about her father's businesses.

'I'm certainly interested in having a look at the land,' he told Harry. Why not? he thought.

'Yes, it's a good proposition, I've heard a lot of Iranian-owned businesses are losing clients.'

'How do you know that?'

Harry smiled briefly and told him that his friend Nigel, who was British, had picked up a lot of interior design work recently. People were boycotting Iranian-run companies. When Karim quipped that maybe Lawrence had been checking up on Konari and Yazdi, his own business, Harry laughed.

'Of course not,' he replied, his face a blank mask.

'So, if I do come to have a look at the land, what then?' Karim asked.

Harry's answer was delayed by the arrival of the food.

'Well, we need another survey—a detailed one. I can organise that, and then you could start drawing up plans.' Harry smiled across the table. 'Mr O'Rourke pays well.' He helped himself to wasabi from a small white dish.

'Okay,' Karim said slowly as he cut into his steak. 'I'm free from twenty-eight December.'

'I'll let Mr O'Rourke know,' Harry answered.

Karim decided to change the subject before he rashly agreed to anything definite. When he asked about Harry's family, he learned that his father had died of a heart attack. It had happened shortly after Khomeini had declared Iran to be an Islamic Republic in April that year. His mother was now in Australia, living with his older brother and his family. The Ashrani parents had planned to go together, but his father hadn't made it. After expressing his condolences, Karim asked where the Australian Ashranis lived.

'Sydney. My brother's doing well—he's a self-employed accountant. He was always marginally better than me at numbers.' Harry allowed himself a brief smile.

Karim couldn't remember Harry's brother's name, but before he could ask the drinks waiter reappeared. Taking a cue from Harry, Karim ordered a soda. He, too, needed a clear head before he agreed to anything other than a reconnaissance trip to South Carolina. Having got Karim's agreement to check out the site, Harry was happy to make small talk. He and Nigel had recently seen a fantastic show called *Evita!* he told Karim.

'There's a song,' Harry suddenly waxed lyrical, '"Don't Cry for Me Argentina!" Goosebumps! You've got to go see it.'

Karim continued to eat his steak. A glitzy show like *Evita* put a piano recital in Carnegie Hall in the shade, he thought. Harry carried on chatting about art events, gallery openings, exciting new clubs, and restaurants. He wanted to talk about anything, it seemed to Karim, other than the political melt-down between the USA and Iran. Or, for that matter, details about Lawrence O'Rourke's business interests. When they finished their meal, Harry insisted on picking up the check. As they left the diner, with its polished vinyl tiled floor and efficient staff, Karim hoped that Harry wasn't going to pin him down for a definite answer on the sidewalk. Instead he kept everything general.

'South Carolina and Myrtle Beach—it's a good proposition, you'll see when we get there,' Harry said. 'There's some heavy stuff going on at home. None of us can go back.'

It was the first time either of them had mentioned the hostage situation, or the impact it was having on their expatriate lives.

'I know,' Karim replied in their own language. 'People think the hostages will be out by Christmas.'

Harry shook his head. 'The US government doesn't have a clue about the guys holding them. They're fanatics!' He extended his hand. 'Let's hope no one in the Tehran embassy gets trigger happy.'

'*Ensh'allah*, that won't happen,' Karim sighed.

Harry released Karim's hand. '*Ensh'allah!* I'll check flights for 28th. Call me by tonight if you change your mind, okay? *Khodāfez*, Karim.'

Harry crossed the road and hailed a cab. Karim was mildly surprised to see the other man going downtown, away from where Karim had assumed Lawrence had his office. But then, what did he really know about Harry *or* Lawrence?

Back in his own office Karim asked the receptionist to find out all she could about building codes in South Carolina. His business partner, she told him, was out having a long lunch with some clients. Probably trying to persuade them not to cancel a project, Karim thought gloomily.

Bahram wasn't back by the time Karim left the office at five. After a few circuits at the gym, he settled himself in front of the television with a sandwich and a coffee.

'Oil has increased today by six dollars a barrel,' the NBC news reader intoned.

Karim sat up straight in his chair—six dollars was a massive increase! Exports of Iranian oil to the United States had been disrupted since the revolution in Iran, but now the shortages were beginning to bite.

The next story showed a gas station in Queens, New York. One woman said she'd been in line since four o'clock that morning. A few angry scuffles had broken out and the gas station manager told the reporter he needed extra security. The shot widened. 'We're outa gas!' the man announced. He was greeted with jeers of disbelief from the motorists waiting in their cars.

A picture of the Ayatollah Khomeini emerged behind the newsreader. The cleric looked pinched and angry in his dark clothes and white turban. Above it: *Day 45—20 December*, below it a single word: *KHOMEINI*. 'Independent observers will be allowed to see the hostages in Tehran,' the newsreader began. There were no details about who the observers would be. Karim shook his head sadly; the situation was terrible. Harry's proposition could be a lifeline, he thought. He estimated that the income from his own business would dry up by the middle of next year. If they didn't sell, both he and Bahram would be chasing work. He wouldn't change his mind; Harry could go ahead and book a flight for him on 28 December. Why not go to South Carolina? He had nothing to lose by just taking a look.

His thoughts turned again to Zahra in Australia. He would write one more time and ask if the hostel had a fax number. There wasn't one on the letterhead. Phoning the place seemed pretty useless; maybe she hadn't got any of the messages he'd left. He checked his watch, it was close to seven-thirty. He'd promised to call his mother and tell her what time to expect him tomorrow. He reached for the phone and was just about to pick it up when it started ringing.

27

SANTA

Ahmad could hardly control his excitement on Friday morning as he skipped alongside his mother on their way to the dining room. During breakfast he talked non-stop about his kindergarten Christmas party. He wanted her to be there to see the snowman he had made and the Christmas card with a tree.

Zahra ran over her calculations again in her head. The party started at ten o'clock and the office opened at nine. She had time to take Ahmad to the kindergarten, collect the phone number from the office, then go to the recreation room and call Karim. If she called him at nine-thirty this morning from Australia, she knew it would be seven-thirty the previous evening in New York. But what if he wasn't home? She pushed the thought to the back of her mind and checked her watch again. It was only eight-thirty—in an hour's time she might hear Karim's voice. She clutched the collar of her blouse, remembering how he'd tried to pull her away from Firzun at Tehran Airport. Would he still feel the same, though, after returning to America?

As she walked Ahmad to the kindergarten, she allowed herself a twinge of pleasure about her phone call to America. She signed him in and reassured Ahmad that she'd be back for the Christmas party at ten o'clock. She hoisted her handbag over her shoulder. The coins she'd collected for her call were heavy, but she was still not sure if she had enough. When she got to the administration block she waited impatiently while the clerical assistant dealt with another enquiry. Finally, the young woman turned to her.

'So sorry about yesterday,' she said. 'Caroline told me you came over for your phone number. Anyway, I found it in your file.' She handed Zahra a piece of paper. 'The gentleman asked you to "call collect". It means he'll pay for the call,' she explained.

'I don't have to put coins in the phone box?'

'No, you dial the international operator in New York.' Helen wrote another number on a piece of paper and handed it to Zahra. 'Tell the operator the number, and that you want to reverse the charges. In America they say "call collect".'

Zahra felt frazzled. Why were there so many words for the same thing in English? The phone number for America seemed particularly long too—suppose she didn't pronounce it properly. If the operator couldn't understand her, he or she might ring the wrong number. She glanced at the office clock; the time had crept to nine-twenty and she was due in the kindergarten at ten.

She hurried across to the recreation room. *Khoda!* One of the English residents was chatting on the pay phone.

Another English woman, one of Julie's friends, said brightly, 'Hi, Zahra! Sorry, there's a queue. I just want to say hello to my Mum in London before she goes to bed. It's past midnight over there. She's waiting up for me, I won't be long.'

Long enough to make me late to speak to Karim, late for Ahmad's party, late for Santa!

Zahra turned away. There just wasn't enough time to talk to Karim and go to Ahmad's party. She would have to phone later or maybe tomorrow and hope Karim was there.

'Hello Zahra,' Caroline approached and touched her arm. 'I'm so sorry about yesterday. Helen told me she closed the office early. Have you got the phone number now?'

Zahra nodded and told Caroline the public phone was busy.

'Look, it was our fault you didn't get those other messages. I shouldn't do this, but you can use my office. I'll help you. The gentleman insisted he wanted to speak to you as soon as possible and he repeated that he'd pay for the call.'

'Insisted!' Zahra felt a frisson of hope. After all she'd told him, he still wanted to speak to her.

'You've been through a lot in your first few weeks here,' Caroline commented as she opened her office door. 'I'm sure you'd love to talk to someone in your own language.' She indicated a chair and smiled as she picked up the phone.

Zahra sat upright in the chair, clenching her hands in her lap, and tried to control her pounding heart. She listened carefully to the English phrases Caroline used as she spoke to the operator.

'... make a reverse charges call ... thanks, I'll wait.' The other woman nodded at Zahra and mouthed *not long now*. Turning her attention back to the phone she thanked the operator and passed the phone across the desk to Zahra.

'He's agreed to accept the call. He's on the line now.' Caroline smiled.

Zahra's legs felt weak and she was glad she was sitting down. She heard the office door click shut and at the same time Karim's voice came on the line, as clear as if he were in the next room.

'Zahra? Thank God, you called back! How are you? I was so worried when I got your letter.'

In an instant, the tension of the past weeks drained away from her. 'Karim, it's so good to hear your voice ...' She faltered.

'I've applied for a visa—I'm coming to see you, Zahra.' His voice was calm and reassuring. 'Just tell me everything.'

She took a tissue from the box on Caroline's desk and blew her nose quietly, then she began her story, unable to hold anything back.

Karim listened with mounting alarm as her narrative unfolded.

At one point he interrupted her and asked if there was anyone listening who could understand Persian. When she told him she was alone, he urged her to continue.

He sounded furious with her cousin Firzun for what he'd done to her. Not only had he deserted her at the airport, he'd made her do a drug exchange—twice. And now, because of him, she'd lied to the Australian police and mis-identified a body as her dead husband. What a mess!

When she repeated that Ali Esmaeili was a trained assassin and would have killed her cousin, Karim believed her. No wonder Firzun had been hiding out in Tehran; he had plenty of enemies. It didn't surprise Karim that someone wanted him dead, or that they'd followed him overseas. He had Zahra to thank that he was still alive. She told Karim, though, that the egocentric scoundrel had finally cleared off. When she then said she just wanted to start a new life in Australia, Karim repeated that he'd join her as soon as possible. He had a business project and by the time that was finished he expected his visa would be through.

He mentioned the South Carolina development and why it was important. He was going with another Iranian man, he said, to check it out. She'd never heard of Myrtle Beach or Charleston, but it sounded like a good business proposition.

'I'll be back in New York on 31 December. Promise you'll call me then on this number, Zahra. You've got my sister's number too and you can always leave a message with her.'

When she agreed to stay in touch, he sounded relieved and asked her about Ahmad.

'He's really happy here, it's a beautiful country. I've made some new friends and a really nice Iranian family helped me with the funeral.' She glanced up at the wall clock. 'Karim, I'm sorry I've got to go. Santa's coming to Ahmad's kindergarten!'

'Try to send me some photos of the two of you.'

'I promise. Ahmad hasn't forgotten his Uncle Karim.'

'Stay in touch,' he urged again. 'I've sent you a letter with my New York address. Take care, Zahra.'

'I miss you, Karim. *Khodāfez.*'

'Miss you too. *Khodāfez*, Zahra *djan*. Love you.'

Zahra put down the phone and a wave of relief washed over her. He'd said 'love you'. Did he mean it? She brushed away a tear, took a deep breath, and opened the office door. She thanked Caroline, who was waiting outside.

'It's the first time I've seen you look happy since you got here.' Caroline smiled. 'Enjoy the kindergarten party and Santa!'

Zahra hurried along the path to the kindergarten. She felt exhilarated and overwhelmed with relief. *He still cares about me!* She'd forgotten to mention that her friend Leila had a son in New York and ask whether Karim had met him. But in a city the size of New York, she reasoned, he was unlikely to run into Hamid Ashrani.

At last, I've got something to look forward to, she thought. *I've lied so much to Karim in the past to help my cousin. But he's still coming here, to Australia, to see me.*

Karim sat back in his office chair and shook his head. As soon as he'd heard Zahra's voice, he realised how much he missed her. What a mess her idiotic revolutionary cousin had dropped her in. Karim felt impatient, wishing he could go to Australia tomorrow. He couldn't, so there was no point in changing any arrangements. He'd still spend Christmas Day with Lauren's family and go to South Carolina with Harry. He felt uncomfortable when he thought of Lauren; there was definitely no future for them together now. He wouldn't tell her yet though—why spoil her Christmas?

In the kindergarten, Ahmad could hardly sit still and he jumped up when Santa arrived complete with red suit and bushy white beard. He winked at Zahra and Julie, who was sitting next to her.

'My husband's a good Santa, isn't he?' Julie whispered. 'Our little boy hasn't recognised him.'

The children lined up for their gifts from Santa's sack. When Ahmad got a boogie board for riding in the surf, Zahra thought he would die of excitement. Who had bought him that? All the parents, including her, had brought a small gift to go in Santa's sack. Ahmad's from her was a car. She looked at Julie, who was beaming at Ahmad.

'Happy Christmas from us.' Julie smiled and patted her arm. 'We'd better make sure he learns to swim soon. Please sit with us for Christmas dinner next week, Zahra.'

When she got into bed that night, Zahra thought of Karim thousands of kilometres away, waking up to a cold Friday morning in New York. He'd promised to come to Australia and she had absolutely no doubt that he would.

On Christmas Day, a traditional Christmas dinner was served at lunch-time in the hostel dining room. Zahra would have been happy to avoid eating the roast turkey and vegetables, and instead go for a long walk on the beach with Ahmad. This was something she had done every day since Ali's funeral, almost two weeks ago. However, for Ahmad's sake, she joined in the festivities. The meal was better than usual, she thought, as she shared a table with her neighbour and her family. Julie reached across and patted Zahra's hand, telling her that she missed her family in England.

'Perhaps 1980 will be a better year for all of us—especially you.' Julie smiled.

Zahra smiled back. *It couldn't possibly be worse.*

Ahmad scrambled out of his chair and shrieked. 'Santa's here!'

She took his hand and went up with him to collect another Christmas gift—a new truck in a box. All the gifts had been donated by a local charity, Julie told her. Zahra smiled across at Ahmad as they returned to their seats. Julie had brought her a dessert and

Zahra looked apprehensively at the lump of black cake covered in yellow sauce.

'It's Christmas pudding!' Julie said joyfully as Zahra took a tentative bite. Ahmad loved it and ate hers as well.

After Julie left, Zahra risked a look across the dining room to where a large group of Afghan women were finishing their meals. Ever since she'd arrived at the hostel, she'd managed, sometimes with difficulty, to avoid the other Afghans. They all had large families and lived in the bigger family units further away from her. They usually ate their meals later than her.

Today though, they were here on time and in force. Right now, they were staring across the room at her. There was no way she could avoid them, she realised when the forerunner of the group rushed across to her vacant table and sat down. Five more women, surrounded by a cohort of children, headed purposefully toward her. They settled themselves in the places Julie and her family had vacated and dragged more chairs across from the next table.

After the usual greetings and exclamations of *Mashallah!* when they saw Ahmad, they shooed their own children away. Zahra knew what was coming and steeled herself for it. They'd heard about her husband's death, one of them said solicitously. May God give her patience.

They were from her own region of Afghanistan and spoke *Dari*, but she was wary. She listened attentively to their stories of escape, hardship, and eventual resettlement in Australia. She waited them out. She knew the questions and comments about her own circumstances would start soon, but she said nothing to encourage them. She was just getting up to leave when one of the women grabbed her arm and told her not to leave so soon.

Zahra sat down reluctantly. *I might as well get this over with now,* she thought.

'We heard about your husband abandoning you at Sydney Airport,' the woman remarked almost gleefully.

'Of course, we weren't surprised. A lot of Afghan men do that to their wives,' another woman added. 'The Australian Immigration people don't like it.' The woman rubbed her thumb and second finger together. 'Costs too much in social security money.'

A couple of the others nodded their agreement. One of them added that a lot of men ran off with younger women when they got to Australia. Zahra put up with their comments and made the right noises for a few more minutes. But she was already running out of patience. The women were taking a nice long time to get to the point —her husband's death.

'You know the Soviet Union's going to invade our country, don't you?' a woman called Fatima asked her. 'I bet you're glad your late husband brought you here.'

'Yes,' Zahra answered.

'I heard your husband was drunk when he fell in the water,' Fatima continued with a sly look.

Who on earth told her that? Then Zahra remembered Nousha saying that the Afghan women didn't speak much English. They couldn't have read about the accident in the paper. Obviously Nousha had filled them in on the gossip. She felt nervous—did Nousha know that Firzun was still alive? He said he'd cut off all contact with her family, but Zahra still felt vulnerable.

'It's hard to be a good Muslim in this country,' another woman was saying. 'With so many vices and temptations. And you alone, with a young son ...'

'Ahmad loves Christmas already. I saw him go up and get his gift,' someone else added.

'Even though you're in Australia, you'll have to see he keeps the faith,' Fatima instructed. 'Especially now he hasn't got a father to guide him.'

Zahra was fed up with them. She was getting to her feet again, when one of them said, 'You're in the top English class. We've got a few documents we need translated.'

'You'll have to wait till I'm a qualified interpreter,' Zahra snapped, pushing her chair under the table.

'Nousha was happy to do it. She wasn't above herself,' Fatima sneered.

So Nousha had been talking to them.

'You met Nousha Kashani, didn't you?' a sharp-nosed woman in a headscarf asked Zahra. 'I saw her the other day in a flashy car with an older man.'

Zahra was even more determined to escape her countrywomen.

'Our husbands got good jobs in the steel works,' Fatima informed her. She then asked Zahra if she'd be looking for another husband after the mourning period was over? Maybe an Australian or, she paused, an Iranian?

Zahra was turning toward the door but whipped round. This was too much. 'I don't know what lies Nousha's been spreading about me,' she said, 'but my personal life is my own business, thank you.'

The other women were taken aback. The sharp-nosed one looked at the others, pulled a face, and shrugged.

Zahra took Ahmad's hand, said goodbye, and left them gossiping. She felt their eyes on her as she walked away. She could guess what they were saying about her: *Loose woman ... widow ... a bit above herself, all that English ... fancy letting her husband drink like that ... Nousha Kashani had told them a thing or two about Zahra Ghafoori and some rich man in Iran ... no wonder the husband left her! He probably killed himself ...*

Outside the dining room, Zahra seethed with irritation. The Afghans had told her they intended to stay in the hostel as long as possible. She made up her mind that if she got an interpreting job, she'd move to a hostel in Sydney if she could. The people here knew too much about her.

It was too hot to join Julie's family at the beach, but she didn't want to sit in her small flat alone with Ahmad either. She headed for the empty recreation room. The only sound was the click of the over-head fans as they stirred the warm air round the room. She turned on the television and watched a Christmas cartoon with her son.

When it finished, a news flash made her sit up straight in her chair. She leaned forward, straining to understand the newsreader's rapid English. Soviet troops were already in her country, like the Afghan women had said. She stared at the screen, watching the footage of Soviet tanks rumbling across the mountains and deserts in northern Afghanistan. In Kabul, large planes flew overhead. The communists that Firzun had fought against all of his life had finally occupied their country, just as he'd predicted. A deep sense of despair washed over her.

'We can never go back to Afghanistan!' she said out loud.

Ahmad turned around from the TV screen. 'We can stay here, Mummy. It's *really* nice!'

28

AN AMERICAN CHRISTMAS

Karim still had a couple of projects to tidy up at work that kept him busy until the late afternoon. It was already dark when he got back to his apartment. His housekeeper had found his note and packed a case according to his instructions. But before he went away, he was due at Bahram's that evening at eight o'clock. He'd just put on his outdoor coat when the phone rang. He checked his watch—seven-thirty—Zahra again? He grabbed the receiver, expecting to hear the operator's voice.

'Hi, gorgeous. How are you?' Lauren asked.

Disappointed, he thought, and immediately felt guilty. 'I'm good. Looking forward to Christmas Day.'

'Okay, you've got our address. I guess I should give you some directions,' she went on.

Greencastle, their home in Connecticut, was actually between Stamford and Darien. Once he got to Apple Tree Point Road, he was to look out for a mailbox with a metal shamrock on the top—Daddy's idea! Then turn up the track. They were expecting him at two o'clock, was that okay? He assured her it was, making a mental note that he'd have to leave Boston at about eleven. He'd already warned *madar djan* that he would be leaving mid-morning.

'See you on Christmas Day,' he said, hoping he sounded cheerful.

'Can't wait,' she whispered. 'Bye, hon.'

He hung up the phone and put the bag of toys he'd bought for his nephews next to his case. While shopping for them he'd also picked up a Superman model with flashing eyes for Ahmad. He paused and smiled. *Ensh'allah,* he would be there when Ahmad unwrapped it. Maybe it was time to replace Mickey Mouse. He fastened his coat and left the apartment.

Karim enjoyed Christmas morning with his family in Boston, and as soon as he could, he took his sister to one side. He hurriedly arranged for her to keep *madar djan* away from the phone around seven in the evenings for a while. Soraya was taken aback when he told her he was planning a trip to Australia and why. He swore her to secrecy—the less his mother knew about his private life, the better. When Soraya asked about Lauren, he blustered a bit. They'd only had a few dates, he told his sister. It was nothing serious. Soraya frowned. Lauren was a really nice woman, she opined, but she was a tad young for him. What was she, twenty-four? As for being a psychologist ... Soraya raised her eyebrows.

'Well, tread carefully, bro,' Soraya warned. 'Mom thinks Lauren's family is bad news.'

'And what does that mean?'

'Well, she says she's heard that Lawrence O'Rourke's business dealings are only just on the right side of the law.'

'Look, I hardly know Lauren or her family,' Karim assured his sister. 'I won't get involved with them—or her.'

As he said the words, he felt like a worm. He was pretty sure Lauren would love him to be a member of her family. He didn't mention his business trip to South Carolina either. His sister might crack up under interrogation from their mother. He would tell them about it when it was a done deal and he'd got a contract.

'Okay, as long as you make that clear to her, bro,' his sister said. 'And take it easy with her folks.'

Karim was relieved to be alone in his car away from his sister's boisterous family. His mother's information about Lauren's family was mostly hearsay, he thought as he headed down the freeway toward Connecticut. Still, he decided to tread carefully with Lauren from now on. With Zahra back in his life, his future might be headed in a completely different direction.

On an impulse, he decided to leave the freeway and drive through some of the picturesque towns before he got to Darien. Outside one particular single-spired church in a small town, the congregation had gathered after morning service. Snow still stuck to the church roof and blanketed the small gardens around the building. Had the worshippers prayed for the safe release of the hostages in far-away Iran this Christmas morning? He hoped so.

Following Lauren's directions, he turned off the main highway. The roads soon became country lanes. He passed huge New England-style houses with attic windows and deep porches. Several of them were set back from the road with front yards the size of soccer pitches. Christmas trees shone in windows and Santa balanced on roofs in his sleigh. He passed trees with yellow ribbons tied round them. It reminded him of the dark days of the Vietnam War—*bring our boys home.* In every second yard, the Stars and Stripes flapped from flagpoles. The hostage crisis was reuniting the country.

He had made good time along the narrow roads bordered by snow-dusted skeletal trees. He passed a couple of walkers in thick coats and hats, their dog scampering ahead of them on the frosty lane. They waved and smiled at him. After that, he saw no one and eventually turned right onto Apple Tree Point Road. The mailbox with its enormous green shamrock was hard to miss. Within half a minute, he'd pulled up in front of *Greencastle*.

Oh my God! I'm in Disneyland.

He parked the car, got out, and surveyed the fortress-like structure. This was certainly not traditional local architecture. It looked more like the Tower of London than a house, with its long windows on either side of the four towers. He took his bag from the car and shrugged on his overcoat. As he headed for the arched wooden front door, he wondered if anyone was watching from the windows in the towers. Or was there a marksman observing him from the rooftop battlements? He shook his head, admonishing himself for such fantastical thoughts.

He walked across the snow-dusted gravel to the front door with its two huge holly wreaths. Before he reached up for the bell-pull, Lauren threw the door open. *Someone had been watching.*

'Merry Christmas! Come in. We've got eggnog and an open fire.' She hugged him and stood back, tugging at her long loose plait of hair, which hung over her right shoulder. 'Like my sweat shirt?' She spread her arms wide.

He read the message, *'I kissed Santa—lots of times!'* which undulated across her breasts.

'Love it!' He smiled at her. 'Merry Christmas, Lauren.'

She was like a breath of fresh air, he thought guiltily.

A silent butler took his bag and coat, and Karim followed Lauren across the wide oak-panelled entrance. Directly opposite the front door, an elaborately decorated fragrant Christmas tree touched the ceiling. Tiny bells tinkled in the draft as the butler shut the door. Karim turned around slowly, trying to take in the huge space and absorb all the Christmas paraphernalia.

'Sorry, I should have warned you about the decorations,' Lauren trilled, lifting her arms out wide again. 'This is the baronial hall with fireplace ...' She indicated a roaring fire in a large grate that was reflected in a long mirror on the opposite wall. 'Over there are two sets of stairs depending on where you're going. Daddy loves wood panelling.' She indicated the walls, then the furniture. 'Genuine Tudor settles from England.'

Karim glanced at the uncomfortable-looking pieces with their wooden bench seats and high backs.

'It always looks brighter here when we put the Christmas decorations up,' Lauren went on, promising to give him a tour of the house later. She took his arm and leaned against him. 'Mmm, I love your jacket—corduroy, right? It feels so soft,' she whispered.

The butler ushered them into an enormous room. Another fire burned in a grate that was large enough to roast an animal. Lawrence, sitting opposite the door, rose from his wing-backed chair, hand outstretched.

'Merry Christmas, lad.' He shook Karim's hand.

'And to you, sir.'

Lauren introduced him to a dark-haired man, who got to his feet upon seeing Karim.

'My brother Seamus—he likes to be called Shea, like the stadium. This is Magda, his girlfriend, and my Momma, Beulah!' She beamed as Karim shook hands.

'Sit down, lad. Like an eggnog?' Lawrence asked.

Before Karim could answer, a maid dressed in black with a white apron appeared at his side with a large glass on a silver tray. He drank it slowly as he answered questions about his journey and looked around the group.

Beulah O'Rourke sat quietly on the fringe of the gathering, sipping her drink. Occasionally her thick dark hair fell forward over her face and she pushed it back absentmindedly. Karim felt her deep-set dark eyes on him as he spoke. He couldn't help glancing at her as he talked. She was stunningly beautiful and he reckoned she was at least fifteen years younger than her husband. Her diaphanous white dress complemented her light brown skin and a string of small diamonds glittered at her throat. She didn't join in the lively conversation between the others, just watched silently from beneath her curtain of hair.

Lauren's brother Shea had his mother's colouring, but his girl-friend Magda was his total opposite, with shoulder-length blond hair and light blue eyes. She reminded Karim of his former wife Nancy, especially when the conversation turned to Christmas customs. Magda began a long story about being a Polish-American Catholic. On Christmas Eve, she told them, her family kept the Polish tradition of looking for the Christmas star before they went to midnight mass.

Lawrence interrupted her impatiently. 'Okay, we know you're a papist, honey,' he said sharply. 'Let's keep religion outa Christmas, okay?'

Shea's girlfriend gave him an odd look and shrugged.

'Daddy!' Lauren admonished. 'That's crazy.'

Lawrence grinned at his daughter, showing his crooked teeth. When he indicated Karim with his head, his ginger hair glowed in the firelight.

'Why don't you show your new guy to his room, honey?' he suggested. 'Then take him to the garage and show him what Santa brought you this morning.'

Lawrence smiled indulgently at his daughter as she stood up. She took Karim's hand and led him across the cream wool carpet to the large wooden door.

Out in the hall, she spun around with arms up and open and told him Nigel had done all the Christmas decorations. She smiled at Karim, reached up, and kissed him quickly on the lips. Karim saw them both reflected in the long mirror: a tall dark-haired man in a tan corduroy jacket, open-necked blue shirt and black corduroy pants. In the refection, Lauren stepped back and he saw himself in the mirror. He looked worried. He smiled at Lauren in an attempt to look more relaxed.

'I'm *so* glad you're here,' she said as she took his arm. 'Do you like the decorations?'

They're totally over the top.

'They're beautiful,' he told her.

Large glass snowflakes hung against the windows and thick garlands decorated the mantle across from the mirror. Glass reindeer were perched in alcoves next to small glittery branches. Lauren led him to the stairs; the handrail was out of action, festooned as it was with masses of silver flowers and leaves. At the top of the stairs, more glass snowflakes hung from the high ceiling.

'Every room has a different Christmas wreath on the door,' Lauren said over her shoulder. 'Yours has *Happy Christmas* in Gaelic on it—you're in the Irish room.'

Karim groaned inwardly. Not another themed room! When Lauren flung open the door, he stifled a gasp. The room was awash with Irish tartans, green cushions, and shamrocks. The carpet was a green, black, and sand-coloured tartan. If anything, it was even worse than his mother's Scottish room in Ramsar.

'I should have said to bring a tweed jacket!' Lauren laughed.

If I wore one, I'd disappear into the carpet, he thought.

She pushed the door shut behind them, reached up, and kissed him deeply. She tasted of eggnog and nutmeg and he felt obliged to fold his arms around her and pull her closer.

'Our first real kiss,' she whispered.

Alarm bells rang in Karim's head. Should he tell Lauren now that he was committed to someone else? Just seeing her father again had made him uneasy, especially after his conversation with Soraya. Zahra was back in his life again, he thought guiltily as Lauren kissed his neck.

'Lauren,' he began, but she put her finger on his lips. She told him she couldn't sleep with him here, in this house. They'd have to wait until they were back in New York.

That's never going to happen.

'Sure, I understand,' he said, feeling like a rat. He made up his mind not to drink too much alcohol while he was here. He needed to keep a clear head.

'This is Daddy's favourite room. He even sleeps here sometimes,' Lauren told him. 'He says it reminds him of Ireland.'

'It's Santa time,' Karim announced, changing the subject. He released her and crossed to where his overnight bag had been placed on a stand.

Her exclamation of delight when he handed her an elaborately wrapped packet made him feel guilty again. He knew he would never spend another Christmas with this woman. She tore off the paper like an impatient child and opened the box.

'A charm bracelet, I love it!'

He helped her fasten the delicate gold bracelet around her slim wrist.

'One of the charms is a bicycle,' he pointed it out.

'Karim, I *seriously love* it,' she repeated.

He wanted to tell her right now that everything had changed. That he was leaving on a jet plane, just like the song from the 1960s. That there was this other woman, brave and sophisticated and well-read, who had suffered more than Lauren could ever imagine. A woman who needed him.

'Lauren,' he attempted again, but before he could speak, she wrapped her arms around his neck and sought his lips, opening his mouth with her tongue. He felt aroused by her, in spite of his plans to leave, and returned her kiss. She manoeuvred him closer to the bed. She deftly slipped his jacket off and tossed it on the tartan counterpane. She eased his shirt up and he shuddered when she ran her hands up his bare back. She was athletic and ten years younger than him, he tried to remind himself. Any second now he'd be flat on his back with her straddling him.

'No, honey, not here,' he whispered.

'I want you. I want you real bad.' Her voice was hoarse with desire. She kissed him deeply again, her hair falling around him in a scented cascade.

It took a huge effort of will to push her away as gently as he could. He had he tell her right now about Zahra. But wouldn't that wreck Christmas Day for her? He tried to smile as she stepped back, looking slightly puzzled. *She's the one who said we couldn't 'sleep' together here*, he thought, trying to gather his scattered wits.

'We'll wait till we're in New York,' she told him breathlessly, then twirled round. 'I got you a gift too. It's under the tree in the hall.'

He hurriedly tucked his shirt back into his pants.

'First though, come see what Santa brought me!'

She waited as he slipped a dark sweater over his shirt, then she took his hand and led him to the door, down the stairs, and into a cavernous garage. Her new Mercedes coupé was still festooned with red and green ribbons. She explained how Daddy had made sure it was automatic; she didn't like driving stick shifts. She looked sideways at Karim, smiled, and ran her tongue over her lips. He made a mental note to lock his bedroom door.

Daddy was a hard act to follow, he thought as she showed him all the wonderful things on her new car and the diamond bracelet she'd found 'by accident' in the glove box. He followed dutifully on her guided tour of the house. The main feature upstairs was a long gallery full of mirrors and large canvases of castles. Two of the towers served as individual guest suites, she said. They often had visitors from the Caribbean. He was about to ask her about the Caribbean connection when she danced ahead of him down the stairs. She was waiting at the Christmas tree with his present when he joined her. She'd bought him black leather driving gloves.

'It's not very original, but they'll match that gorgeous leather jacket you've got.'

He kissed her cheek; it was a thoughtful gift.

Karim was tempted to tease her and ask if guests were locked up at night in their towers, but the doorbell clanging interrupted him. The butler padded across the entrance and swung open the outside door. Harry Ashton, dressed in a calf-length camel overcoat, stepped over the threshold. He brushed off a few snowflakes as he looked around. His friend Nigel, wearing a fashionably long brown leather coat, followed him into the house.

Nigel, with his British accent, proved to be an entertaining and amusing guest at Christmas lunch in the wood-panelled dining room. There was no end to his hilarious anecdotes from his former life as a theatre set designer. Everyone, except Lawrence, plied him with questions as the butler and a maid served the traditional Christmas turkey and ham on to their plates. Beulah, Lauren's mother, appeared uninterested in hosting the table. She watched wordlessly as her daughter passed dishes of food to the guests. Throughout it all, Nigel kept up a stream of witty theatrical tales. He was mid-sentence when Beulah, sitting opposite her husband at the end of the long table, stood up. She swayed slightly on her feet.

'I wanted to be on the stage. But *he* wouldn't let me,' Beulah hissed. She pushed back her chair, grabbed a long carving knife, and pointed it at Lawrence.

'Oh, Momma, it's Christmas.' Lauren got up and moved slowly toward her mother. Before she could get to her side, a plump black woman in a dark dress appeared next to Beulah. She took the other woman's hand and guided the knife back to the table. It clattered against a plate as Beulah let go.

'Take her to her room, Cynthia,' Lawrence said wearily. 'I'll be up later.'

Beulah shook off the restraining hand. 'I can walk thank you, Cynthia,' she slurred the woman's name. Then she turned to Lawrence. 'You haven't heard the last of this. I could have been famous,' she spat as she was led away.

Karim met Lauren's eyes across the table. She was wearing a bright green dress with shimmery sequins on the bodice. She wore her hair loose, tied back with the diamond pins she'd worn at Carnegie Hall. In spite of the beautiful clothes and the diamond bracelet that flashed on her wrist, Karim felt a wave of pity for her. She smiled faintly at him as she wiped away a tear with her Christmas napkin.

'Sorry about that, everyone.' Lawrence rang a small bell next to his plate. 'I think it's time for good old English plum pudding and pumpkin pie.' He nodded toward Nigel. 'Did you work with my namesake Laurence Olivier? I guess he was a piece of work.'

'Oh my *word*!' Nigel expostulated in his British accent. 'Was he ever! Larry loved the ladies—*and* the boys, some people said.'

Karim watched Lauren thoughtfully as she made a huge effort to look cheerful. He was glad that he hadn't mentioned Zahra earlier; Lauren had enough to deal with here. He tuned in again to Nigel's exuberant chatter as the equilibrium around the Christmas table was re-established.

After lunch Lawrence made his apologies.

'Business' he said tersely. He jerked his head sideways at Harry, who got up and held the door open for him. After the door closed, Nigel suggested a game of charades.

'It's an English game—you have to guess whether I'm miming a book, a film, or a proverb. Ready?'

Magda, Shea, and Lauren all joined in enthusiastically, but Karim was relieved when the butler whispered in his ear, 'Mr O'Rourke will see you now.'

The evening had closed in and the maid was pulling the thick drapes across the windows. He excused himself and followed the butler across the hall, now bathed in light from the Christmas tree and several ornate coach lamps. The man opened a door in the panelling and announced his arrival.

Lawrence's study was almost as large as the living room. Harry, looking urbane and relaxed, was sitting opposite his boss in an armchair, sipping whisky. A huge fire burned in the grate between them. Harry had changed from his smart suit into a casual black zip jacket over a white polo neck shirt. Lawrence was still wearing the baggy green sweater with a huge red Santa on the front he had worn all day. Karim took a seat on the couch opposite the fire and accepted a Scotch from the butler. The man asked if 'Mr O'Rourke' needed anything else. When Lawrence shook his head, the butler left, closing the door quietly.

'We've been talking about South Carolina. Seems you might be interested?' Lawrence began. He took a long drink from his full tumbler.

'I might, but I have to see the land first,' Karim answered cautiously.

'So you can get there on the twenty-eighth?' Lawrence looked up at him as he put the glass on a small side table.

'Yes, sir,' Karim answered. With an effort he pushed his family's negative comments to the back of his mind.

'Good.' Lawrence smiled his crooked-teeth smile at Harry. 'You were right, he's a no-nonsense kind of guy.'

'I'm going tomorrow,' Harry said. 'I'll stay over New Year—it's warmer than here.'

'Sure is!' Lawrence cut in. 'Accommodation is fixed up at the apartment in Myrtle Beach. My secretary will be in touch about the flight time.' He stood up and motioned Karim to a long table under the window. 'Basic plans my former architect drew up,' he said, giving no explanation for the word 'former'.

He unrolled some drawings and laid them out on the table with Harry's help.

'Well, here it is!' Lawrence announced, standing back so Karim could get a closer look.

Karim examined the drawings of what looked like an enormous development: condominiums, two high-rise apartment blocks, and single dwellings in their own 'village'. A contract like this could keep Konari and Yazdi in work for years.

'Will you want a residence for yourself?' Karim asked.

'Hell, no!' Lawrence laughed. 'This is for the snow-birds from the north. I've got a place on St Lucia and one in Antigua in the Caribbean. You can keep South Carolina—that's just business.'

When Karim asked for more details, it seemed Lawrence's plans were further ahead than he'd expected. He already owned all the land and he'd 'fixed up' the compliances. He told Karim to take the rough plans with him, work out some details. First though he wanted Karim to see the land, check that his idea had legs.

This is a dream come true, Karim thought. His business was haemorrhaging money, he was being investigated by the IRS, and suddenly his life had turned around. He wondered if part of his payment would be the ogre's daughter's hand in marriage? Well, that wasn't going to happen, he thought.

'I'll need you to report back, say, late January.'

Karim said nothing about his planned visit to Australia. He could manage both if he started work immediately. Besides, he had no idea when the visa would come through.

'I'm taking Beulah home to her folks for a while, they can manage her,' Lawrence announced.

Before either Harry or Karim could respond, Lawrence took a large swig of his drink and waved the glass at them. He told them how he'd been tricked into marrying her. Her family had known about her drinking—*bastards*. They'd thrown money at him and got him to take her off their hands and get her away to New York. They didn't want a slur on the 'good name' of their old island family. Lawrence laughed out loud and for a minute Karim thought he was going to spit in the fire.

'When Beulah gets her hands on alcohol, she goes crazy. Same as that old colonial family of hers—drunks, the lot of them! They're drinking rum as fast as they make it. Old colonial, my arse!' Lawrence's beady gaze strafed Karim and Harry.

'She got her hands on a steak knife last week,' Lawrence muttered. 'Coulda killed me, the stupid bitch.'

Karim glanced at Harry and raised his eyebrows slightly.

'Lauren's the best thing I got.' Lawrence sat hunched over and looked into the fire. 'My son, Shea—what a useless piece of shit. Only happy if he's sitting on a bed in Vegas, with a whore on either side of him, a bucket of fried chicken in his lap, watching game shows or playing the slots.' He laughed again, then frowned.

'How about that other stuck-up old family of art dealers in New York and their son Max Wilhelm—what a spineless goof. Didn't want my little girl, not good enough! You're the only decent guy she's ever brought home.' He looked at Karim. 'You got baggage—wife and kids back in I-ran? Not bankrupt, are you?'

'No, sir.'

I'm a liar, Karim thought. *I'm not bankrupt, but I have baggage, and ... there's no way I'm marrying into this family. My mother would have a fit.*

'So, you want me to check out the club?' Harry asked, deftly changing the subject.

'Sure, plenty of people in Charleston would like to see it burn to the ground. Make sure it's all above board and those guys in the State Legislature get fixed up for the building compliances. Okay?' Lawrence rubbed his thumb and forefingers together.

'Sure.' Harry's face was a mask of compliance.

Karim lay on his back in the Gaelic bedroom, wishing he'd stuck to his plan and hadn't drunk so much. Drifting between waking and sleeping he thought he heard the bedroom door open. He opened his eyes and his blood ran cold. A white-robed figure was standing next to his bed.

'Lawrence honey, I'm here ...' The voice was female and seductive.

'Lauren?' Karim said, struggling to sit up.

The figure strafed his face with a torch.

'Oh my God, I'm sorry. Wrong room!' the woman gasped.

Karim found the lamp switch just as the door closed behind the intruder. Fully awake, he leapt out of bed, rushed across the room, and into the corridor. Coach lamps burned dimly in the wide space, but no one was there. But the interloper had left a faint perfumed scent behind her. He recognised it—*Opium*. His sister used it. And so did Shea's girlfriend, Magda.

He was just closing the door when Lauren emerged from

another room further down the passage. She was dressed in a flowing pink satin gown. *What next?*

'Karim,' she whispered. She looked over her shoulder and hurried toward him.

'Not here ...' he began.

She grasped his hands in hers.

'Karim, I've been watching television. There's footage of Soviet tanks. The commies have invaded Afghanistan!'

It took Karim a moment to absorb Lauren's words.

'The Soviet Union has invaded Afghanistan,' she repeated slowly. 'You've got a television in your room,' Lauren reminded him. 'I can't come in ...'

'I know,' he said.

She reached up and kissed him on the lips.

'Not here, too public.' He pushed her away gently.

'Sure is.' She moved her head in the direction of the ceiling. When he saw the small camera tucked away high above the oak panelling, he felt slightly sick. He wanted her gone now—and quickly. He didn't mention the nocturnal visit from Magda. That would make interesting watching for someone tomorrow, he thought. He gave Lauren a brief hug and turned her toward her own room.

He wondered if there was a camera in this room too. He guessed not, if Lawrence was in the habit of entertaining his son's girlfriend in his Gallic hideaway. But was every movement in the public spaces being recorded?

More pressing, though, was the news about Afghanistan. He fiddled with the television controls and finally got a news channel showing grainy footage of helicopters flying over Kabul. The Soviets had invaded from the north as well, with tanks—hundreds of them. He watched as they rolled across the rough roads and wondered if Firzun was watching them from a dug-out in the mountains with his co-fighters and an arsenal of weapons. He wouldn't have joined the

Mujahideen though, Karim thought. He'd probably formed his own splinter group.

Karim flicked off the television. This meant that Zahra was stranded in Australia, she could never go home. He was even more determined to get there as soon as he could.

29

SOUTH CAROLINA

As Karim walked down the stairs the next morning, he glanced covertly around the huge hall. Sure enough there were two cameras, one trained on the front door, the other over the door itself. He felt uncomfortable as he crossed to the small oak table under the mirror and selected *The New York Times* from the collection that someone had laid out.

He read the front page as he walked toward the dining room. The hostage story was still the lead with a couple of photographs of the hostages, shabby and bearded, shaking hands with Catholic and Protestant clergy. *'Four clergymen meet 42 hostages in Iran. New doubt on total,'* the headline read. The account detailed how the hostages and clergymen wept and prayed together. The visiting clergy could only tell the State Department that there were between forty-two and fifty hostages. There was still no exact number. There was a brief mention further down the page of the Soviet invasion of Afghanistan with a full report on page two.

Karim felt depressed as he sat down at the breakfast table. Those poor guys, he thought as the maid poured his coffee. The hostages' main concerns, according to the newspaper, were for their families. They wanted them to know that they were safe and being well treated.

If only our raid had been a success, I'd have been awarded the Presidential Medal of Freedom or something. Instead I feel like an illegal immigrant in the USA. He re-read the report about Afghanistan. It was much as he'd seen on television: an aerial bombardment of Kabul, followed by thousands of ground troops. The commies weren't taking any chances.

Harry joined him looking as urbane as usual. He, too, had picked up a newspaper and he raised his eyebrows at Karim as he wished him good morning. Magda, Shea, and Lawrence didn't make an appearance at breakfast, so Karim was spared the embarrassment of seeing the nocturnal wanderer in the daylight. Lauren was bright and cheerful and kissed Karim on the cheek before she sat down next to Nigel. Over breakfast they discussed the hostage story and the invasion of Afghanistan.

'1980 isn't going to be an easy year for Iranians if this hostage thing drags on,' Harry commented, helping himself to toast.

'Will our government do anything about Afghanistan?' Lauren asked.

'Probably arm the resistance—the Taliban, they call themselves, and the Mujahideen,' Karim suggested.

'If they've got any sense,' Harry added, 'the US will keep out of Afghanistan. They'd be crazy to arm those guys—they're seriously *wild.*'

The news about Afghanistan buzzed at the back of Karim's mind as the talk moved on to South Carolina. Karim admitted that he'd never visited Charleston but Lauren was enthusiastic when she heard their plans.

'All that antebellum architecture and Southern manners! I'd love to come, but I'm working tomorrow.'

Karim drove away that morning from *Greencastle* feeling

relieved. Although he'd enjoyed himself, he also felt as if he'd been holding his breath for twenty-four hours.

Harry was waiting for him in the small terminal at Myrtle Beach Jetport.

'The Defence Department still uses the main runway,' Harry told him as he put Karim's bag behind the seat in the pick-up truck. 'There aren't many commercial flights at the moment. When that changes, just watch those land prices go up!'

'So, Lawrence is ahead of the game,' Karim remarked as he got into the passenger seat.

'Always ...' Harry smiled. 'We're staying over in Charleston tonight,' he added. 'We'll call in at Mr O'Rourke's apartment here first. You can freshen up, have a quick coffee, then we'll get going.'

Karim checked his watch. It was already nine-forty-five. 'Feels a hell of a lot warmer here than New York,' he commented.

'You should become a Snowbird,' Harry quipped.

Karim glanced sideways at Harry as they drove along a broad highway with very little traffic toward the township of Myrtle Beach. He was the original company man, Karim thought. He always referred to Lawrence as *Mr O'Rourke* and he never gossiped. Harry had transformed himself from the underdog at the rich kids' school to the right-hand man of a millionaire. Lawrence was lucky to have Harry as an employee, Karim reflected. He wasn't a time-waster, he'd done his homework, and brought another copy of the drawings with him as well as the surveyor's report and the county regulations. He'd smoothed the path for Karim to get down to the business of checking out the land. When that was done, Harry would let Mr O'Rourke know if his dream was a possibility.

Myrtle Beach was being developed at a rapid rate, Karim realised, noting the apartment blocks under construction on either side of the highway. Lawrence's penthouse in the block he had recently bought was hardly six months old, Harry told him. After he'd freshened up, Karim had a minute to admire the commanding view over the Atlantic Ocean before Harry ushered him back to ground level. They picked up a coffee to go and got back into the truck. Within twenty minutes they were standing above a long, yellow sand beach. The sky was a clear blue and the Atlantic Ocean lapped quietly on the shoreline. Karim smiled to himself; it felt good to be doing a site visit again. He'd dressed in his usual site visit gear: lightweight black tracksuit, t-shirt, and sneakers.

'Up ahead,' Harry indicated as they turned away from the ocean. Karim looked at the land in front of them. *This is going to cost a fortune!* he thought as looked from left to right.

The beach rose gently to sand dunes on which tufts of sage-coloured grass swayed in the slight breeze. They climbed up the low dunes, then looked across to where the sand sloped toward salt marshes. Both men stood quietly and stared across the wilderness in front of them. A couple of large birds rose, screeching, from the coastal scrub around the marshes and whirled overhead. Nearby, some boats were tied to stakes that had been driven into the ground. In spite of the sunshine and clear skies, the area looked bleak and desolate. There wasn't another soul in sight.

It's beautiful, Karim thought. Why would anyone want to build on it?

I'm the person tasked with building on it, he reminded himself.

How had Lawrence managed to buy these marshes for development? Karim knew from his studies that humans changed the ecology of dunes and marshes at their peril. If there was a storm surge from the ocean, anything built on the dunes would be flooded. He knew that marshes often absorbed storm surges and protected the land. Lawrence was intending to pour concrete and lay roads here close to wetlands, which should never be touched. Who was allowing this to happen? Or didn't they care?

'Remember I mentioned hurricanes and storm surges?' he asked.

'The last one was twenty years ago in 1959. Hurricane Grace—

it was a category four,' Harry replied. 'Luckily it made landfall at low tide. Since then, building codes have been much stricter. We just have to build so that a storm surge doesn't knock our buildings down.'

'Or blow off a roof and kill people,' Karim added as he followed Harry to a long wooden bridge beyond the tied-up boats.

'Quite a place isn't it?' Harry smiled. 'Mr O'Rourke wants to share it with everyone.' He leaned on the bridge rail and looked out over the marshes. 'He's going to build round the marshland, make it a feature of the village complex. Can you do it?'

'I have to take photographs,' Karim answered, avoiding the direct question as he took out his camera. 'It's not going to be an easy build. The houses will have to be built on stilts ...'

'Seems a shame to build here at all, really,' Harry said quietly.

Karim nodded, surprised that Harry was expressing his own opinion about something his boss was doing. Maybe it was because they were speaking in their own language, he thought. They walked around the whole area together. As the day got warmer, they returned to the vehicle and threw their tracksuit jackets onto the backseat.

'We can go to the Dead Dog Saloon for lunch,' Harry suggested.

'Dead Dog?'

'It's a steakhouse—devoted to people's deceased pets. You can look at photographs of them on the wall,'

'As long as we're not eating them!' Karim quipped and Harry permitted himself a short laugh.

The outside of the saloon was plastered with advertisements promising live music from bands with names like Heart and Soul of Country, Jack and the Rippers, and Loula-May's Song Boys. Harry eased the new-looking truck into a parking space, seemingly unaware of the stares they were attracting from the locals. *He's been here before and he's used to it*, Karim thought as they walked up the wooden steps to the restaurant.

'Looks like a happening place, even at lunch time,' Karim said in English. As he opened the door, raucous music assaulted his ears.

Harry indicated a wall to the right of the reception desk. It was plastered with photographs of dogs in various stages of life and decline.

'Not much happening for them,' Harry commented. 'They do a good fried chicken here though.'

Over lunch, Harry told him it would take a couple of hours to drive to Charleston. The club was in a quiet street in the downtown area, he went on. Mr O'Rourke rarely visited himself; he left that to Harry.

'Have you ever been to Charleston, Karim?'

'Never.'

'It's got an interesting history dating from the Civil War. They pride themselves on being a classy town. Wait till you see some of the houses. It puts Elahiyeh, Tehran in the shade.'

'Careful, that was my suburb!' Karim smiled as he sipped his beer.

'Yeah, I know. Your suburb had a couple of fancy streets. Charleston is one big fancy street,' Harry replied.

During the drive down the broad highways to Charleston, Karim had a chance to familiarise himself with the landscape. The flatlands of South Carolina were broken up in places by palm trees, and Karim lost count of the number of golf courses on either side of the road.

When he mentioned them, Harry turned his head slightly. 'That's Mr O'Rourke's next venture, after the village.'

'A bit easier to design,' Karim suggested.

'He's got a professional golfer lined up for that.'

The outskirts of Charleston had the usual scattering of light industrial buildings that didn't seem to promise anything particularly stunning.

'Prepare to be amazed,' Harry commented as they left the factories behind. 'I'll drive you down Battery Street. You'll see the best antebellum houses there. Some of them were built before the Civil War.'

Although Karim had studied antebellum architecture at college, seeing the real thing was something else. Harry drove along slowly, and when they got out, Karim was surprised at how close the waters of Charleston Harbour were to the street. He could hear the slap and retreat of the tide against the concrete bulwarks.

'Is that Fort Sumter?' Karim asked, pointing to a lump of buildings that guarded the entrance to the enormous harbour. He could just see a flag flapping in the breeze from the top of a tower.

'Sure is,' Harry answered. 'What do you think of the houses?'

'Architectural indigestion!' Karim laughed.

Each enormous three-storey brick house had a clear view across the water. They were like plantation houses but cheek by jowl on the long street. Huge porticos sheltered large front doors. On the upper levels, wide verandahs had been built to catch the sea breezes on sultry summer days. Most of the houses were painted brilliant white, their long, low windows outlined in the same shiny black as the metal balustrades of the verandahs. Smaller flat-roofed houses were squeezed among the large ones. Although it was December, the sub-tropical gardens bloomed with winter flowering plants.

'I'm going to buy one of these eventually,' Harry commented. 'I'll be near Mr O'Rourke's club in Chain Street, then.'

'Odd name for a street.'

'Charleston was a big slave port,' Harry replied evenly.

Karim opened the car door, holding it steady against the cool wind blowing across the water. As the sun sank behind the houses, the castellated roofs and circular verandahs cast eerie shadows across the footpaths. Karim shivered and looked out to sea. The late sun caught the walls of Fort Sumter. He'd read that Confederate forces had opened fire on Fort Sumter and bombarded it—the first offensive in the American Civil War. Countrymen fighting countrymen—he knew how that felt.

'Okay, let's go!' Harry said, cutting across his train of thought. 'We'll drive down the main street.'

Karim was captivated by the three-storey pale brick buildings in King Street with its palm trees that had been planted at intervals next to the footpaths. On the lampposts, holly wreaths and twined Christmas greenery already looked past their use-by date. Staff from the bay-windowed cafes were bringing in their blackboard menus. As they drove down the street, the sun finally set.

'We'll have dinner at the club,' Harry told him. 'Mr O'Rourke wants me to check out a few things there. That's why he suggested we stay overnight.'

'Fine by me.'

Karim wondered curiously what Lawrence's club was like. Would it be leather Chesterfield sofas, cigar smoke, and old men dozing gently in winged chairs? He doubted it—hadn't Harry said something about 'the girls'? He looked around with interest as Harry manoeuvred the large vehicle off the main road, turned left, and then sharp right. He slowed down and pointed to a house that looked similar to the ones on Battery Street.

'That's it. Pretty impressive, eh? Mr O'Rourke wanted it to look more like a residence than a club.'

Probably a good idea, Karim mused. He speculated that given its size, Cassandra's might offer much more than a bar, restaurant, and overnight accommodation. The white-painted building stretched over two blocks in the quiet street. From the outside, though, the three-storey edifice did have the appearance of a large residence. Long windows with green painted shutters led out onto deep porches. Everything was curved, from the first-floor bay windows to the terraces on the upper floors. On the left-hand side, the roof was flat with a low Italianate balustrade. As Harry drove slowly past the building, Karim noticed a pitched roof with tiny French-style dormer windows in it. Probably the original servant's quarters.

Harry eased the truck round the side of the palm-filled gardens and stopped in a car space marked 'Management Only' at the rear of the building. A tall, dark-skinned man opened the vehicle doors, greeted them, and told Harry quietly that he would see to the bags.

Karim glanced up at the building as they followed the man. All the drapes on the second floor were closed, but here and there a chink of dim light filtered through. Harry waited for him in a rectangular area paved in black and white tiles. To his left, Karim could hear the clatter of pans. The smell of barbecued steak drifted through the partially open kitchen door. He followed Harry and the man with the bags up a wooden staircase at the rear of the kitchen.

'Half an hour?' Harry suggested, and Karim nodded. 'This is Vernon, by the way—he's from St Lucia in the Caribbean. Vernon ... my friend Karim Konari.'

Vernon smiled. 'This way, Mr Konari, sir.'

He opened a door to a room furnished, as Karim had expected, in the antebellum style. The highly polished wooden floor was mostly covered by a Turkish carpet. Vernon crossed the room and released the green drapes from their silk ropes, adjusting them carefully against the floor-length windows.

'Shall I unpack for you, sir?' Vernon asked as he hung Karim's dinner suit in the closet.

'Later, thank you.'

'The bathroom, sir.' He indicated a door. 'Enjoy your stay.' He left the room silently.

After he'd showered and changed, Karim joined Harry on the landing.

'We can go down the main stairs, now that we're suitably dressed.' Harry smiled briefly as he led the way down a wide, polished wood staircase.

Karim sensed a wariness about the other man. He was like a bodyguard, his dark eyes constantly on the lookout for trouble. Karim caught a glimpse of a gun strapped under Harry's dinner jacket, which reinforced his impression that Harry was on the alert for trouble. The staff near the main door nodded deferentially as they stood in the entrance. The club manager appeared and conducted them to the main lounge. He drew Harry's attention to the chandelier, which had been adjusted as 'Mr Ashton' had requested.

Karim looked around with interest during the muted conversation. He recognised the genesis of the Turkish carpet that covered the floor—*Hereke*, from the carpet makers to the former Sultans of Turkey. Karim knew that a carpet this size, mostly silk, would cost a fortune. The leather armchairs, Chesterfield sofas, and dark crimson drapes had the effect of making the large room look homely and welcoming. He was surprised that several of the men chatting together looked younger than he'd expected. Some seemed to be hardly fifty. A few looked up when they came in and acknowledged Harry, who excused himself and went over to talk to a small group. A waiter showed Karim to a comfortable leather armchair.

'Scotch, I believe, sir?' the man said. He returned quickly and placed a crystal tumbler on a small white mat and a tumbler of soda on the other side of the table. Karim sipped his drink slowly, waiting for Harry to join him.

'So, what do you think?' Harry sat down opposite him and lifted his glass in a mock toast.

'Very impressive. Is that all there is?'

Harry's eyes met his. 'We'll go down to the basement club after dinner and watch the show, if you like.'

'Should be interesting,' Karim murmured.

Karim watched Harry as he ordered from the menu. Harry, urbane and good-looking, was the perfect front man for his boss. Lawrence, Karim surmised, would actually have been out of place in his own club with his shabby clothes and rough manners. He wondered if Harry ever brought Nigel here, but he guessed not. Nigel would have loved the white tablecloths, heavy silver cutlery, gold-rimmed white crockery, and Italian glassware. But would the patrons have felt uncomfortable with Nigel around?

Another thick Turkish carpet served to mute the conversations at the various tables. In a corner near the bow window, a young male pianist played Chopin nocturnes on a baby grand piano.

The service was five-star and the food excellent. Harry had suggested a seafood entree and a speciality of the restaurant, crusted duck breast, for the main. Although Harry had ordered a bottle of French Chablis, which was a perfect choice, he stuck to soda for himself as he had in the New York diner. Over a pecan pie desert, Harry talked again about his family in Australia—he was planning to visit them for Persian New Year in March. When Karim asked why his mother hadn't come to New York, Harry shook his head.

'She doesn't know about Nigel, and she loves being with her Australian grandchildren.' He took a breath. 'Better she lives in hope that I'll find a nice woman to marry one day.'

Karim nodded. His own mother was in no doubt that he liked women. She'd thrown enough of his girlfriends out of their various houses over the years.

'So,' Harry said, 'would you like a nightcap?'

As the waiter moved Harry's chair out, Karim again glimpsed the gun in its holster under Harry's dinner jacket. Harry didn't miss the look.

'Most people follow the second amendment here: " ... *the right of the people to keep and bear arms shall not be infringed ... *",' he quoted as they left the dining room. He led Karim to another back staircase tucked away to the left of the dining room. At the bottom of the stairs, they were greeted by a tall, well-built man with an accent Karim was beginning to recognise as Caribbean.

'Your table is ready, Mr Ashton, sir. Mr Konari.' He ushered them through a saloon-style door that swung shut behind them.

'Thank you, Raymond.' Harry inclined his head as they took their seats at a table facing a small semi-circular stage. The gold curtains, which were closed, shimmered in the slight breeze from the ineffectual air-conditioning.

I'm in a strip club! Karim thought as he looked round. In the dim light from the small table lamps, several of the club patrons lounged on sofas or slouched in chairs. They'd loosened their bow ties, giving them an air of dissipation. A small group of musicians—a guitarist, pianist, drummer, and double bassist—played quiet jazz numbers in the background.

Karim had never liked confined spaces. He would always take the stairs rather than the elevator if he could. He excused himself both to visit the bathroom and to have a closer look at the exit points in the stuffy room. He discovered a small kitchen, where two chefs were preparing hot snacks. Beyond the kitchen was a metal spiral staircase. Probably the original back stairs of the house, he reflected. He ran up the steps quickly and stopped at a fire door, which he pushed open and closed again. Easy access to ground level made him feel more secure. As far as he could make out, the staircase continued up to the top of the house. It seemed to lead eventually to the flat roof. He returned to the table, stepping around several beautiful women in red satin leotards who were taking drinks orders.

He nodded to Harry as he sat down. 'Just checking out the exits,' he explained. 'I'm a tad claustrophobic.'

'The fire department insisted Mr O'Rourke put in the metal spiral staircase.' Harry paused. 'A few of the clients take it to the second floor ... where the ladies are.'

So, Karim thought, the club did offer more than fine dining, comfortable lounges, and a floor show.

A drum roll announced the start of the entertainment. The shimmery curtains rolled back and five young women emerged from the gloom. Their dance routine was to the song 'YMCA'. It was lively, upbeat, and professional. The dancers pointed and pouted at the audience, who joined in enthusiastically. Karim had to admit that each long-legged dancer was stunning, from the blondes to the Caribbeans. Each girl wore either a tiny police uniform or a bikini made from the Confederate flag. When the loud applause had died down, a couple of women did a modern dance piece together.

Harry whispered in Karim's ear. 'If you don't want to sleep alone tonight, let me know. I can organise female company for you.'

Are you kidding? Karim thought, shaking his head. Or had Lawrence told Harry to test Lauren's boyfriend?

Another upbeat number followed. Between the flashing lights and patches of dark, Karim noticed a couple of men being ushered toward the spiral staircase by the male waiters. He wondered if Lauren knew about her father's business interests in the south. He sipped his whisky and watched the show. The alcohol had relaxed him, and he didn't react immediately when Harry jumped to his feet and yelled.

'*Son of a bitch!*'

Karim saw him reach for his gun, but it was too late. The bottle had already smashed on the ground, sending a stream of burning gasoline across the floor toward the stage. Another one exploded behind Karim. The flames reached the shimmery curtains, and in an instant they became a wall of fire. The girls on the stage screamed and ran. Suddenly everyone was yelling and rushing in different directions. The stairs they'd come down were already on fire and Karim realised he was trapped between two rapidly spreading blazes. His only escape was to get to the spiral staircase. He saw one of the waitresses frozen in terror. He stuffed his wallet in his back pocket, tore off his jacket, and flung it round her.

'Move! Over there!'

She put her arms through the jacket sleeves then staggered on her high-heeled shoes. She reached down to pull them off.

'Leave them on! Run!'

He grabbed her round the shoulders and propelled her toward the staircase. Behind him, the waiters were spraying the flames with small fire extinguishers. He took his chance and pushed through the burning river. The girl screamed as the flames caught her ankles.

Harry was already at the bottom of the spiral staircase, yelling at people to move faster. There was another smash and an explosion. People who hadn't been injured turned around.

'Get me out!' a man's voice yelled.

Karim pushed the girl ahead of him. He held her round her waist, propelling her up the stairs.

'The fire door's locked!' someone yelled. For a second Karim froze. Since he'd checked it, someone must have locked the exit to street level from the outside to stop gate-crashers. When he got to the door, several men were throwing their weight against it. It didn't budge.

'Keep going up!' Harry shouted. 'The whole building's on fire.'

30

FIRE

Karim stepped onto the bottom rung of the metal staircase and glanced back. Behind him the small club was engulfed in flames and black smoke. He held the waitress firmly round the waist and half dragged, half helped her upward. She waved her arms around in front of her.

'I'm scared! I'm scared!' she sobbed.

He heard Harry yelling, 'Keep moving! Go up!'

The woman with Karim leaned heavily on him; she seemed hardly conscious. He threw his head back and inhaled, gulping in fresh air. As he staggered upward, he heard an explosion, then another and another. Glass shattered in huge bursts of sound. The windows were already blowing out with the heat. At the top of the steps near ground level, it was pandemonium. On the other side of an exit door people banged and yelled.

'It's locked! It's locked!'

'Let me out!' a woman screamed at the top of her voice.

Harry pushed his way through and shoved a key in the lock. Someone inside flung it open and a mass of people fell out onto the stairs.

A sweating man confronted Harry. 'Some asshole locked the exit door.'

Harry ignored him. 'Get up there,' he ordered. 'Don't stop.'

'You son of a bitch. We're all gonna die!' The man's large frame blocked everyone's exit onto the small landing.

Harry levelled his gun at him. 'Move,' he snarled.

The man swore then pushed his way onto the stairs.

Harry raised his voice. 'Keep going! Get to the roof!'

With a deafening roar, something collapsed inside the club. Karim pushed on, dimly aware that Harry had gone back down the metal stairs and was urging people up. More of them were stumbling over each other, pushing and shoving in their desperation. There were short periods of silence followed by explosions of glass as the fire roared through the old building. Someone shoved open the fire door from the second floor and staggered onto the staircase. They stood disorientated, blocking everyone's way. One of the scantily clad women had singed hair.

'Get outa my way!' a man growled. He pushed the survivors against the handrail and elbowed past them. The woman with the singed hair collapsed, but no one seemed to notice as everyone surged upward. Someone stopped and dragged her up. She twirled like a rag doll, then clung to her saviour, slowing him down.

The door was still open, and the fire inside roared with the injection of oxygen. Flames shot out onto the stairs.

Karim pushed the woman he'd helped toward another man. 'Look after her!'

He threw his shoulder against the open door. He smelled burning cloth and looked down at his smouldering shirt sleeve. He hit at it as someone else helped him to force the door shut against the inferno.

'Hallelujah! Lord, save us. Have mercy, oh Lord!' a voice cried out.

As Karim helped another woman, he was pushed against the

scorching wall of the building. The heat seared through his shirt again, making him gasp.

'Go, go!' he urged her. From somewhere in the distance he heard the sound of sirens.

A voice from above yelled, 'Fire Department's here!'

The announcement caused a stampede. Women in high-heeled shoes were shoved to one side and overtaken by burly men. People ran or stumbled up the stairs. Some tripped, grabbing the overheated handrail and screaming in pain.

'Someone help us!'

Above the shouts, Karim heard another rending crash from inside the building. Was that the staircase or the old ceilings falling in? Got to get to the concrete roof, he thought desperately. If the outer walls were destabilised, the staircase he was on might collapse. Thick smoke fanned down the stairs, enveloping everyone as people coughed and gasped for breath around him. Karim fumbled for a handkerchief and tied it over his nose and mouth. The waitress he'd helped had disappeared. Had she got to the roof? He assisted more women as they tripped and staggered up the stairs. He looked back. No one was behind him. He was the last person out.

There was little sanctuary on the roof. Flames leapt up from the floor below and billows of white, then thick black smoke swept over the huddled survivors. The fire was beginning to lick at the edges of the roof balustrade. The air was full of shrieks, screams, and curses.

Women hung on to each other, weeping and calling on God to save them. Smoke and flames fanned upward and threatened to engulf everyone. Karim heard a massive explosion. The windows immediately below the roof had blown out. More flames soared toward them all and everyone jumped back.

'Christ, have mercy. Save us with Your Grace!' someone sobbed.

For a second, the smoke cleared and Karim saw a crowd of onlookers in the street, their faces turned upward. Fire engines, lights turning, stood below. The fire crews trained hoses on the lower floors and more smoke billowed up. To his relief, he saw firemen on the roof with breathing apparatus attached to their backs, moving people quickly to the ladders.

Karim couldn't see Harry and he scanned the crowd anxiously—he'd thought he was the last person out. Suddenly the roof door flew open. A tall woman in a spangled leotard burst out. Her hair was on fire. Her piercing screams tore through Karim like a knife. Before he could move, Harry cannoned through the doorway after her. He had his jacket off, ready to throw over the woman, but she raced screaming to the edge of the roof. He reached her and raised the jacket. Simultaneously, the low balustrade that edged the roof peeled off like lace from the hem of a skirt, taking part of the roof edging with it. In an instant, Harry and the woman disappeared from sight over the edge. A black plume of smoke billowed across where they'd fallen.

'HARRY!' Karim yelled. He tore his handkerchief from his face and ran into the smoke.

31

A FAMILY TRAGEDY

There were fewer people in the dining room at meal times in the week between Christmas and New Year and the hostel grounds were quiet. The kindergarten was closed for two weeks, and English classes resumed the week after that. It was as if Christmas had cast a soporific spell over everything, Zahra thought one morning as she looked out at the deserted lawn and silent classrooms. Even the administration block seemed to be working at half speed and would close early. The Christmas season had been a watershed for many of the residents who'd been anxious to move into their own homes by then. So far, no new ones had taken their places.

The frenzy of Zahra's first weeks in Australia had passed and she now felt hollow and sad. She often went into Wollongong and wandered round the large shopping mall there. There was a small harbour with fishing boats and Ahmad loved to walk along the harbour wall and gaze up at the lighthouse. They went to Sydney once or twice, and walked from the Sydney Opera House and through the Royal Botanic Gardens. Someone told her about a place called Paddy's Market. When she went there, it reminded her of the bazaars at home. Each night she lay awake going over what had happened and wondering how she could have changed things—stopped Firzun leaving or prevented Ali's untimely death.

The days between Christmas and New Year stretched ahead, empty and humid. The only bright light on the horizon was an invitation from Leila to visit them the coming Sunday, 30 December. Leila promised that if there weren't many trains, Mehran would drive them home. Zahra was looking forward to the visit; it was always good to get out of the hostel and be in a real home again.

She wondered many times if Karim might change his mind and not come to Australia. After all, she'd confessed about lying to the police and misidentifying a body. But between Christmas and New Year, two of Karim's letters from America had arrived. The first expressing disappointment about not being able to speak to her and the second about the pleasure he'd felt after their phone call. In each letter he'd enclosed four US fifty-dollar bills. *Thank you, thank you, Karim!*

There were no admonitions in the second letter, as she'd feared, just concern for her welfare and Ahmad's. Karim was eager to see her as soon as possible, he wrote, and his visa application was going through. He told her more about his plans to visit South Carolina and a city called Charleston before the New Year. His business wasn't going too well, as he'd mentioned. The Iranian man he was checking out the site with was called Hamid Ashrani, and by a strange coincidence they'd gone to the same school. Zahra stared at the name. Was this Leila's son? Surely not. Wait till she saw Leila on Sunday! She wondered if Hamid had told his mother that he'd met Karim. Such strange serendipity. But then, Zahra thought suddenly, would Leila wonder why Karim was writing to her, a former servant in the Konari household? Maybe she shouldn't say anything.

She often took Ahmad for a late walk on the beach. The sand was warm under their feet and the water fresh and cool. Susan, her teacher, had visited her in her flat just after Ali's body was found and mentioned the interpreter's course that Zahra could attend. It hadn't meant much to her at the time, but she'd found out more from

Caroline recently. Zahra was determined to find work for herself, in spite of Karim's promises. There was definitely no certainty in this world—she'd known that since she was a child.

Money was a constant issue in her life, but Karim's gifts had made a huge difference. The money might be enough for a bond on a rented apartment and she still had gold coins that she could sell. During the beach walks, she imagined a future when she and Ahmad would live outside the hostel in a small apartment block like Leila's. But if she moved to Sydney she might have to stay in a hostel there for a bit longer. She'd heard rents were higher in the city. She hardly dared to hope that Karim might be with her in the future.

Both she and Ahmad were eagerly anticipating their next visit to Leila's apartment. She dressed carefully in the calf-length flowered dress and new sandals she'd bought at the market. She disliked her old sandals now, with their association of Nousha's foot pressing on hers. Ahmad wore his new Superman t-shirt, and she looked at him proudly. He was happier now than he'd ever been in his short life, she thought.

As usual, Leila met her at the station in Sutherland and commiserated with Zahra about the invasion of her country. They were both in the same boat now, she said sadly. Neither of them could go home.

'We shouldn't be walking in the hot sun at midday,' Leila said, holding a white umbrella over them. 'Anyway, we've got a couple of fans in the apartment, cold drinks, and lots of food!'

Once in the apartment, they chatted about what Zahra had done on Christmas Day and about Afghanistan and Iran. The children played outside in a tiny paddling pool that their parents had set up. When the food was ready, they all sat at the small table and Leila and her daughter-in-law, Tula, passed around dishes of chicken kabobs, rice, salad, and eggplant.

Zahra looked round the apartment; it was so much bigger than her flat. *When I'm here, I feel as if my life is getting better,* she thought as she helped the women clear up in the kitchen after lunch.

Leila's son suddenly put his head round the door, looking worried. 'The police are here, Mother,' he said quietly.

Zahra's heart plunged and she nearly dropped the glass salad bowl she was drying.

'The *police!*' Tula exclaimed. 'What do they want?'

'They wouldn't say. They just want to talk to the family.' He turned to Zahra. 'Could you watch the kids outside please, Zahra?'

Zahra followed Leila and Tula into the living room. She glanced quickly at the two uniformed police officers, a man and a woman, who were sitting on the edge of the couch. They flicked their eyes over her as she passed. She felt alarmed by the serious looks on their faces. She stepped quickly outside into the afternoon heat and rolled the patio door closed behind her. The boys were kicking a soccer ball round on the grass area and Lili was sitting quietly in the paddling pool with one of her dolls.

When Zahra heard Leila scream '*NO, NO, I don't believe you! NO!*' she clutched her hands to her throat. What on earth had happened? An accident? But all the family was here. Maybe it was someone in Iran? The boys stopped playing soccer, and Leila's grandson Darius ran to the patio window and tried to open it. Zahra took hold of his hand and Ahmad's. She walked the boys over to the paddling pool where Lili was standing, looking frightened.

'Your nana has had a shock, but it's all right,' she reassured them. 'We'll just stay here until your daddy or mummy come out.'

The patio door opened slowly and Tula emerged, her face blotchy with tears.

'Terrible news,' she said, wiping her face. 'It's about Mehran's brother, Hamid—he's been killed in a fire, somewhere called Charleston,' she blurted. 'Mother-in-law is devastated. Oh, Zahra, it's awful!'

Tula's frightened children ran over to their mother and clung to her. Zahra stood holding on to Ahmad, totally shocked by the other woman's news. *Leila's son—dead. Killed in a fire.* In a rush, Zahra remembered what Karim had written. He was going to Charleston with Hamid Ashrani. Her legs felt weak. Was Karim dead too?

She walked slowly into the living room. The police had gone and Leila was sitting on the couch, her face buried in her son's shoulder. She looked up when Zahra came in.

'The police said Hamid's dead.' She shook her head in disbelief. 'I'll never see my boy again!'

'God give you patience.' Even as she uttered them, the words sounded empty and meaningless to Zahra. She turned to Mehran and Tula and told them she would go back to the hostel on the train. They needed to be together as a family.

'I'll phone tomorrow,' she told Mehran as he walked her to the end of the road. 'I'm so sorry ... God give you patience.'

Mehran apologised for not taking her back in the car. 'Hamid only called a couple of days ago ... I can't believe it!' he stammered.

Zahra sat on the hard wooden bench at the station with her restless questioning son and waited nearly an hour for a train. Her thoughts were in overdrive. How would she ever learn if Karim, too, had been killed in the fire? Maybe she could get in touch with his sister in Boston, even if it meant running the risk of Esmat answering the phone.

***

There was something covering Karim's face and he put his hand up to pull it off.

'No, Karim. It's helping you breathe,' his sister whispered.

He opened his eyes. His sister was sitting at the side of his bed. No, not his bed ... a hospital bed. He was propped up on big pillows. He tried to pull himself upright.

'They said you had to stay like that.' Soraya pushed him back gently. 'You're in Saint Florian's hospital in Charleston. They carried you off the roof, unconscious.'

A nurse came in before he could speak.

'We can take the mask off now.' She looked keenly at him. 'Hello there, Mr Konari.' She removed the mask and replaced it with a small breathing tube and deftly attached it to his face. 'How do you feel?'

'Thirsty.' His voice was hoarse.

'Okay.' The nurse helped him drink some water through a straw.

'The fire,' he said, struggling to remember.

'The place was gutted. You were so lucky ...' Soraya's eyes filled with tears. 'They called us on Saturday. We've all been here since then. You've been in the intensive care unit for a few days. They had to intubate you. They told me you couldn't speak, so I asked Mother not to phone today. She'll be here tomorrow with Dad.'

He turned his head; the drapes were drawn.

'It's Tuesday evening. Happy New Year,' she said ruefully. 'Lauren's coming to visit later.'

'What happened?' He winced and put his fingers to his throat.

'Someone threw Molotov cocktails into the club.' She looked at him sorrowfully. 'Harry didn't make it, Karim. May God give you patience.'

Karim closed his eyes. He couldn't speak. *Harry, the company man—dead? Damn Lawrence O'Rourke! Damn everything!*

'He was buried yesterday. They found a Muslim cleric from somewhere. I went to the service with Nigel, his partner. He's devastated,' she added.

'His family?' Karim managed to say, and she told him the Australian police had broken the news to them in Sydney.

Harry—Hamid gone? He shuddered, remembering his last sight of Harry as he fell over the rooftop and into the flames.

'He was my age.' Karim started coughing, unable to say more.

'I'm so sorry, big brother.' Soraya took his hand gently in hers.

She told him he had to rest; he was suffering from smoke inhalation and burns to his shoulder and back. He vaguely recollected being pushed against a wall. He flexed his back and winced.

An orderly helped Karim sit up and to eat the tepid clear broth he'd brought. While he ate, Soraya talked quietly. She told him that Lawrence O'Rourke was seriously bad news. He had a turf war going in Charleston—all about development and bribes. He had brought women from the Caribbean to work in the club as ... Soraya raised her eyebrows; she was sure Karim could guess. News of the fire was all over the local television stations. The police wanted to interview Lawrence, but he'd gone to ground. Karim listened wearily as Soraya poured him some water, wishing she didn't look so worried.

'I guess Mom was right about the family. Lawrence is a big-time crook ... You might be called to testify at some point.'

Poor Harry. He closed his eyes, remembering how they'd tramped over the sand dunes together. When was that? Only days ago? And now Harry was dead.

His sister told him that Lawrence's company would be paying his medical bills. That's if the IRS hadn't frozen his bank accounts.

'You could have died.' Soraya brushed away a tear. 'I'd never get over that, Karim, never!'

He reached up and patted her face. What a fool he'd been! He'd never really trusted Lawrence, but his own business problems had made him turn a blind eye.

'I'll leave you to rest,' his sister said quietly, then left the room.

When she'd gone, he closed his eyes. *For God's sake, why was I worrying about money? I can sell the New York apartment. I've nearly been killed twice in the last two months. It's time I valued my own life and the people I care about.*

Thinking exhausted him. His throat hurt, and if he breathed deeply his chest hurt too. He drifted off to sleep. When he woke, Lauren was sitting at his bedside.

'I'm so sorry!' She burst into tears. 'Oh Karim, I thought you were dead.' She controlled her weeping and laid her hand on his arm. 'Harry's gone! It's all my family's fault. Please, *please* forgive me.'

'Harry's a hero,' he managed to say. 'He tried to save people.'

'Don't speak.' She stroked his arm. 'You're in shock. It might take you a while to get over this.' She was failing miserably at being a professional psychologist, he thought. She couldn't stop crying.

'Nigel's devastated.' She wiped away the tears with a handkerchief, then put a letter on the table next to his bed. It was the latest one from Harry's mother in Sydney, Lauren told him. Nigel asked if Karim could write to her in Persian when he was feeling better. How awful that her son was buried in a foreign country!

Karim shook his head slowly. "'... *Nor does anyone know in what land he is to die ...*'" He gasped for breath. 'They say that at Muslim funerals.'

'Happy New Year by the way.' She smiled faintly and held Karim's hand. 'Karim ... I'm going to turn my life around. I'm leaving for Europe to be with Max, away from his mother. I'm sorry, honey.'

Their eyes met. Well, that's it—it's over, he thought. When he wished her all the best for her new life, she looked away.

'Nigel's at the Myrtle Beach apartment,' she went on. 'He said he couldn't find your bag. I guess you took it with you to Charleston?'

Karim nodded; he couldn't even remember what he'd had in it. He squeezed Lauren's hand as she kissed him lightly on the cheek and whispered goodbye.

'I thought we could ... you know ... I'm so sorry,' she repeated. 'I'm leaving tonight.'

He wished her good luck in Europe, told her he hoped she'd find happiness. She avoided his gaze, then stood irresolutely at the door for a couple of seconds before she walked out into the corridor.

His head ached and he felt his eyes closing. A nurse came in and gave him some medication. When he woke, he wondered if he'd imagined Lauren's visit. The drapes were open and daylight filtered through the blinds. An orderly arrived wearing a name badge: Luke. He put Karim's breakfast down with a cheery greeting and asked how he was.

'Better, I think.'

'I put your letter away.' Luke indicated the bedside chest.

Karim's next visitor was a young doctor in a white coat, who told him the burns to his back and shoulder would heal soon. He would probably have permanent scars but they would fade in time. When the doctor listened to Karim's chest, he frowned.

'It'll take a couple of weeks for you to recover from the smoke inhalation,' he said in his faint Southern drawl. 'You were lucky to get out alive,' he added. 'The whole building was gutted.'

'How many dead?'

'A few,' the doctor answered evasively. Karim didn't miss the look that passed between the doctor and the nurse who was assisting him. *They probably think I was a client at Cassandra's.*

'You'll be here a couple more days—you're still coughing,' the doctor said. 'You need rest and oxygen.'

After the medical staff had gone, he lay staring out of the window for a long time. The sub-tropical winter sky was a pale milky blue with scattered clouds. He didn't want to go back to New York, to the cold weather and his huge empty apartment. He drifted in and out of sleep and was startled awake by the phone next to his bed.

'How are you?' His mother sounded worried.

He was relieved when his sister, dressed in a smart business suit, walked into the room. She raised her eyebrows and he mouthed, *'It's Mother.'* She took the phone from him, pushed back her short dark hair, and relayed their mother's message. Their parents were on their way to see him. They'd rented an apartment for a few weeks in Myrtle Beach so they could look after him. His mother wanted to discuss his future when she saw him. After the call, brother and sister smiled at each other.

'Will you be able to stand it?' Soraya asked.

'No choice.' He coughed. 'I guess you're going back to work.'

'Yes, my flight to Boston leaves in a couple of hours.'

She stayed a while, then kissed him on the cheek. At the door, she turned and looked at him again and bit her lip, her eyes moist.

'Thank God you escaped, Karim.'

Outside his room he could hear the hum of hospital life—steps going along the corridor, the clatter of the food trolley, and people talking quietly. Karim reached into the drawer for the letter. He felt slightly uncomfortable at the thought of reading personal correspondence between a mother and her son. But it was what Nigel wanted. It might give Harry's partner an idea of the family he would never meet. The unopened mail was postmarked ten days ago. Karim held it in his hand for a long time before taking the fruit knife from the top of his bedside cabinet and sliding it under the flap.

He took out the folded blue paper and a newspaper clipping fell onto the bed. He picked it up carefully. After he had read the first few lines, he leaned back onto his pillow. Strangely, the contents of the envelope concerned his life as well.

32

FOREIGN CORRESPONDENCE

Karim stared at the slim piece of newsprint that had been carefully cut from an Australian newspaper. The letter bore a Christmas stamp. It must have been delayed by the Christmas mail.

He read the headline quickly, though he already knew the story. Zahra's confession about misidentifying a body had shocked him. And here was a report of Mahmoud Ghafoori's death in newsprint. He knew that the victim was certainly not her cousin Firzun. He would have been on a plane out of Australia before the body was discovered. Karim shuddered, knowing that the deceased man was Ali Esmaeili. The man Firzun had, rightly or wrongly, believed to be an assassin sent to kill him.

Karim turned his attention to the newspaper clipping.

BODY OF AFGHAN REFUGEE FOUND IN SYDNEY HARBOUR

The body of an Afghan refugee was retrieved from Sydney Harbour late Sunday evening. Documents found on the body identified him as Mahmoud Ghafoori, a refugee from Afghanistan. According to police sources, Ghafoori drowned after apparently losing his footing near the wharves at Walsh Bay. Police say there are no suspicious circumstances, but a post-mortem examination revealed that the victim had been drinking heavily prior to the accident. NSW police are asking for anyone who witnessed Ghafoori leaving the Old Wharves pub, Walsh Bay, late Sunday afternoon, 7 December, to come forward. Ghafoori apparently left the pub in the company of another man. So far, the police have been unable to establish the identity of the dead man's companion. Mahmoud Ghafoori is survived by his wife and young son, who are living in a migrant hostel near Wollongong.

The letter from Harry's mother to her son was in precise Persian script and easy to read. Karim scanned it hungrily for more information about what had happened to Zahra. It was clear from the first sentence in Leila Ashrani's letter that Zahra had not told anyone else about the dead man's true identity.

15 December 1979

    My dearest son Hamid,

    I'm enclosing a cutting from the newspaper about an incident that has shocked us all. Mahmoud Ghafoori was Zahra's husband, the young woman I met on my journey here to Australia. You may remember I told you how he abandoned her at Sydney Airport. Your brother Mehran helped her find the immigration people and they took her to the hostel. As I mentioned in my last letter, we had a visit from the police shortly afterwards, asking us if we knew anything about Zahra's husband.

    Well, the police got in touch with us again because of this latest tragedy. Zahra was terribly upset and Mehran arranged her husband's funeral, which was a couple of days ago when they released the body. I went with her, and Mehran stood at the graveside to say the prayers for the dead. She looked terrified and was very distressed during the service. She's still living at the migrant hostel with little Ahmad. She was devastated, though I don't think he was a satisfactory husband. I visited her during the three-day mourning period and I'll certainly stay in touch. She's a very brave woman, and I feel so sorry for the little boy.

Karim let the letter fall onto the bed cover and stared at the opposite wall. Firzun, the cat with nine lives, had escaped again, thanks to Zahra. God knows how he got out of Australia! He probably organised a forged passport. Risk-taker that he was, he might even have used the assassin's passport to leave the country. Leila obviously had no idea about the true identity of the person they had buried.

And what about poor Leila? She had the tragedy of her son Hamid's death to deal with now. The Australian police had probably already visited the family again. He continued to read how proud she was of Hamid and how she thought she'd found a suitable wife for him. Harry's mother obviously had no idea about his relationship with Nigel, Karim thought. He scanned the rest of the letter for another mention of Zahra but it was mostly family news and Harry's brother's plans to buy a house.

Karim re-read the first paragraph. His head ached when he tried to imagine what had happened when the body was found. It was bad enough hearing Zahra's account, but to read in the newspaper that there were 'no suspicious circumstances' was both reassuring and alarming. He started to cough and a nurse appeared at his door. She tidied his bed, told him to relax, and gave him something to make him sleep. His last thought before he drifted off was of Zahra, thousands of kilometres away. He had to write to her again, tell her that he was alive. She told him the Ashranis had helped her. He hadn't even had time to mention the coincidence to Harry before ...

'He needs rest and he mustn't be upset.'

Esmat's voice woke him up from a deep sleep. She was sitting on his bed and his father was in the chair next to it.

'How are you, son?' they asked in unison.

'Recovering,' he croaked.

His mother helped him have a drink, then insisted on checking the burns on his back and shoulder. Not too bad, she told him—just like a sunburn. He nodded, trying to look compliant. What was he thinking of before he before he'd fallen asleep? Zahra! He had to call her.

His parents stayed while he ate his lunch and Esmat told him that they were definitely moving to California as soon as she'd nursed him back to health. Karim thought about Lawrence's development plans. No chance of them ever getting off the ground now. Maybe he should move to California as well, he thought. As usual, his mother was a step ahead of him.

'You should get rid of the apartment in New York and move to LA!' Esmat enthused. 'I take it your relationship with the gangster's daughter is over?'

What could he say but agree? He didn't have the energy for an argument with his mother. He was grateful that they had come; it meant he would be discharged from hospital sooner. He wondered whether to tell Zahra's story to his mother—not a good idea! Zahra had been his grandmother's companion in Tehran. If he said anything, his mother would start niggling about her late mother-in-law. He told her instead that he was going to write to Harry's mother in Australia. Esmat nodded her approval. He didn't mention that he was going to Australia as soon as he could. Forget California!

Nigel finally visited him mid-morning Thursday. He looked like he'd lost weight and hadn't slept for days. His fair hair hung limply on his collar and his eyes were red-rimmed. He wanted to know exactly what had happened. When Karim had finished talking, he felt exhausted.

'Harry was very brave,' he told Nigel.

'Thank you, Karim.' Nigel was close to tears. 'I wish I could meet Harry's family,' he said wistfully. 'I'd like to tell them how much he meant to me.'

'I made plans to go to Sydney to ...' Karim hesitated, '... to see someone, before Lawrence's development came up. I even applied for a visa—still waiting,' he went on. 'When I get out of here, I'm going to Sydney. I can take some of his things if you like.'

Nigel told him about his friend Jason, who worked in the Australian consulate.

'I'll call him and get him to hurry it along,' he promised.

After Nigel left, Karim lay back on his pillows. He frowned as he tried to remember. He was certain they'd left a folder full of drawings and site plans on the table in the Myrtle Beach apartment and taken another set with them to Charleston. The second ones were lost in the fire, of course, he thought. When he'd mentioned it to Nigel, the other man said he hadn't seen anything like that when Lauren had let him into the apartment to collect some of Harry's things. So, where were they? Had Lauren taken them when Nigel wasn't looking—to protect her father?

Karim was discharged from hospital into the care of his parents in a large rented beachfront apartment. He was surprised at how debilitated he'd felt once he'd left the hospital. He wrote immediately to Zahra and told her what had happened, then he wrote to Leila and her family. He took slow daily walks along the ocean boardwalk with his father Abbas. The weather was pleasantly mild with sunshine and pale blue skies. Most of the cafes, donut stalls, and pizza places were still open, even though it was winter.

As they walked, father and son talked quietly in their own language.

'I get homesick for Iran,' Abbas began.

Instead of a pleasant retirement, his father told him he felt stranded in a foreign country. Karim turned to him; he was only sixty-five years old and yet he looked shrunken and defeated. His job as the chief accounts executive in the Tehran office of an American oil company had finished within three months of the revolution.

He'd take the doctor's advice to live in a warmer climate if he could, at least for a year or so. Cold air would be very bad for his lungs. He longed for the visa to come through so that he could get to Australia. Most days he sat near the patio window, reading or staring out across the Atlantic Ocean. One morning, his old friend Nasim called.

'Oh, Karim, how are you?' she asked.

Her voice was so familiar, so reminiscent of home, that he felt a sudden rush of emotion.

'Better than I was,' he managed to say.

He told her he'd nearly recovered and asked what life was like for her now. She was a pregnant widow in a foreign country, but she sounded reasonably happy. She was living with her parents in a large new house in Los Angeles, she told him. She'd met up with old friends from Tehran too. Her baby was due in May and if it was a boy she wanted to call him Ahmad, after Zahra's little boy. It was the opening Karim had been waiting for. When he told her that he knew Firzun and Zahra weren't married, he heard Nasim sigh.

'I'm so sorry we all lied to you about that, Karim,' she said quietly. It was for Zahra's own protection, she explained. They knew Karim's mother wouldn't have allowed her to live with them if she'd been a single mother. And of course, it was too dangerous for her and Ahmad to stay with her and Rashid. It certainly was, Karim thought; their house had been a hotbed of counter-revolutionary activity and Zahra's cousin was up to his neck in it all.

Nasim wasn't surprised when Karim had told her that Firzun was alive. She'd got a terrible fright, she said, when he'd called her from her old house in Tehran. She sighed when she learned that Firzun had gone back to Afghanistan leaving Zahra in Australia.

'Poor Zahra. At least she's safe. But Firzun always looked at the bigger picture, didn't he?' she said.

Karim didn't trust himself to reply politely. Instead he mentioned his plan to go to Australia and find Zahra.

'You're very kind, Karim. I know you always had a soft spot for her. If you come to LA, be sure to visit. I have to go. Please stay in touch, Karim *djan*.'

Karim returned the phone to its cradle and leaned back in his chair. He scanned the local newspaper, relieved that news of the fire had finally moved to the inside pages. Even though it was weeks since the event, the paper was still running salacious stories about Cassandra's.

The local police had been cynical when they'd interviewed him. They clearly didn't believe that he knew nothing about Lawrence O'Rourke's business. He was told that he'd be called as a witness at a coronial enquiry later in the year and to make sure he was available. The newspapers had dredged up witnesses who had reported seeing Harry and him walking round on the sand dunes—'checking stuff out'. In Hicksville, Karim thought, a couple of foreign-looking men walking round the dunes and wetlands was bound to attract attention.

A sudden squall rustled the pages of the newspaper where he'd left it on the coffee table. He glanced out the open window to see a thin cloud of sand rise above the beach. He closed the patio window, picked up the paper, then dropped it back on the coffee table. He was ready to go home to New York and reconnect with his life. He wanted to phone Zahra, but it was too awkward with his mother around. She had a habit of listening to his calls on her bedroom extension. He wrote another letter to Zahra.

It was already dark by the time Karim arrived at his New York apartment. As he'd expected, New York in a January snow storm was not an inviting place. The cold hit him hard after his time in the south. The concierge had turned on the heating in his apartment, so it was warm, if not welcoming. He put his bag down in the entrance and looked around. His mother had told him it was too big for him, and she was right. He'd sell it, get out of New York, and move somewhere else.

The doctor had advised him to stay out of the cold as much as possible. His lungs were still not one hundred percent. He ordered a take-out meal and turned on the television. *Crisis* was the main word on the news broadcast: the Oil Crisis, the Hostage Crisis, the Weather Crisis. His television viewing in South Carolina had been mainly game shows and his mother's favourite, *The Love Boat*. Now, back in New York, he was once again pitched headlong into world news.

The first story on the news was about the weather—snow and more snow was forecast. So, it's January. Is that news? he thought. Then behind the newsreader a picture of the Ayatollah Khomeini emerged and above it the words 'Day 72'. He shook his head in disbelief; had the hostages really been in captivity for that long? There was footage of American news crews arguing with protesting students outside the embassy. *'US reporters and cameramen have been banned from reporting about the crisis,'* the studio anchor reported. *'They all left Tehran, Iran today.'* Why wasn't the government doing more to get those guys released? Karim thought, shaking his head. He'd had enough of the United States for a while, he thought. Tomorrow, he'd go to the office and tell Bahram he wanted to sell his share of the partnership.

Before he left the following morning, he called the Australian consulate. His tourist visa was ready—*thanks Nigel!* By the time he got to his office with the new visa in his passport, it was ten o'clock. He had rugged up well, but still the cold air made him cough. Bahram was concerned and asked if he should be out at all.

'I'll go crazy if I stay inside,' Karim told him, thankful for the coffee the receptionist put on his desk.

When he told Bahram that he wanted to sell his share of the partnership, the other man wasn't surprised. In fact, it seemed he already had a buyer in mind because he was definitely going to California and he'd guessed that Karim might want to sell.

'Okay, let's sort out some meetings,' Karim replied, then asked what had happened with the Internal Revenue Service and their tax audit.

'Everything's gone quiet,' Bahram said.

Karim frowned. 'Gone quiet, what does that mean?'

Bahram shrugged and told him he hadn't heard another word. Their firm must have passed the test, whatever it was.

'Hey, what about Lawrence O'Rourke?' his partner said with a grin. 'The papers have been full of it!'

Bahram reassured Karim that he hadn't been mentioned by name, but the New York newspapers had done plenty of investigative stories about Lawrence's business. There'd been photographs and footage of the burning building in Charleston all over the newspapers and on the television news.

'You were lucky to get out alive, friend,' his partner commented.

And without being named, Karim thought.

Bahram took a lighter from his pocket. When he lit the cigarette that had been dangling in his mouth as he talked, Karim waved away the smoke.

'Sorry, Bahram, would you mind not ...'

Bahram stubbed out the cigarette with an apologetic smile

'Why don't I start clearing my desk?'

'Yeah, okay.' Bahram put his hand on Karim's shoulder. 'I guess this is it.'

As Karim sorted out his office desk, he felt despondent. His life in New York, just like his life in Tehran, was coming to an end. It was 1980 and New Year's Eve had come and gone while he was in the intensive care unit at St Florian's hospital. He'd turned thirty-four last November and was looking at starting a new life again, but where? He'd lived and worked in Tehran, Boston, and New York. He was going to visit Zahra, but dare he pin his hopes on a future in Australia?

'I've fixed up a meeting with a prospective buyer.' Bahram's voice cut across his thoughts. 'Day after tomorrow, okay?' he asked as he helped Karim carry his bag and a box to the elevator.

'Sure, I'll be there,' Karim told him. 'You'll have to speak English in California. No more swearing in Persian.'

Bahram laughed, then looked serious.

'Who would have thought it, eh? We had a such a great business, Karim. I'll miss you.'

Karim smiled and shook his former partner's hand.

'Thanks, Bahram. *Khodāfez.*'

'*Khodāfez,* old friend! See you at the meeting.'

The late afternoon temperature had dropped below zero and Karim pulled his scarf over his mouth. He hailed a cab and sat back feeling deflated. Although the snow had brightened up New York a little, it still looked drab without the Christmas decorations and bright lights. He paid the cab driver and walked into the foyer of his building. The concierge wasn't around—pity, he could use some help. He shifted the weight of his box and managed to press the elevator button. The concierge appeared from the other elevator just as the doors of his were closing.

'Oh, Mr Konari. There's ...' the man started to say.

The doors closed and his words were lost as the elevator moved up. The man had looked extremely agitated. Outside his apartment, Karim slid the box to the floor. He straightened up and his breath caught in his throat. His door was partly open. Was this what the concierge had been trying to say? Had someone broken into the apartment? Impossible! This was a totally secure building. He frowned; the lock hadn't been forced or the door damaged. Someone had used a key.

A burly man looked up as Karim stopped in the entrance.

'What the hell?' He dropped his bag on the floor.

'Mr Konari? Karim Konari?'

'Who wants to know?'

Karim looked around quickly. His office door was open and another man was going through his desk.

'What the hell's going on here? This is private property. How did you get in?'

He turned back, intending to get the concierge, but the man who'd spoken stepped forward and took hold of his arm.

'I'm Agent Hank Lanzarote and ...' he indicated Karim's office, '... that's Agent Jay Polito.'

Polito and Lanzarote? Was Lawrence involved with the Mafia as well? Whoever they were, they had no right. Agent ...?

The man was saying something.

'Pardon me?'

'FBI, Federal Bureau of Investigation, Mr Konari.' Lanzarote held up a card. 'May we speak with you?'

33

UNWELCOME VISITORS

The man's identity card looked genuine enough. There was no mistaking the huge letters FBI, a photograph of the agent, and his signature. Karim shrugged off his overcoat and scarf and threw them on a chair.

'FBI? What are you doing here?'

'We have a warrant to search this apartment, sir. It concerns your association with persons of interest to us,' Hank Lanzarote began.

'What?'

'Mr Lawrence O'Rourke and his assistant, the late Mr Harry Ashton ...' the agent continued. He consulted a notebook. 'Ashton is also known as Mr Hamid Ashrani, an American citizen of Iranian descent.'

'How dare you come in here and search my place!'

Lanzarote handed Karim a folded document and told him it was an official search warrant. The other agent wandered into the room, acknowledging Karim with a curt nod. He introduced himself as Agent Jay Polito, FBI, and held up his card.

'Listen,' Karim said firmly. 'Mr O'Rourke asked me to check out some land in South Carolina. I hardly know the man.'

Both agents regarded him silently and then Lanzarote indicated a chair and asked him to sit down.

'You hardly know Mr O'Rourke?' Agent Lanzarote repeated as he settled his bulk into another armchair.

How long were they staying?

'I've met him a few times,' Karim answered, trying not to sound evasive.

He frowned; somehow the agents had managed to position themselves on a chair and the couch in such a way that he wouldn't be able to leave the area without passing both of them.

'Are you aware, Mr Konari, that Mr O'Rourke is involved in money laundering, prostitution, people trafficking, and drugs?' Polito asked.

'No!'

'So, you can't shed any light on his business dealings?' Polito continued.

'Like I told you, I hardly know him.'

'You knew Lauren O'Rourke pretty well,' Agent Lanzarote ventured.

When Karim said that Lauren had nothing to do with her father's businesses, Polito raised his eyebrows. Then he asked if Karim knew where Lauren was.

'Europe. She's gone to join an old boyfriend.'

'She said that, did she?' Lanzarote smirked. 'Well, we have confirmation of Miss Lauren O'Rourke and her brother Seamus leaving Charleston Airport in a private jet bound for Antigua in the Caribbean on ...' he consulted his notebook again, '... the evening of 1 January this year.'

'We just missed them,' Polito added.

January first? The day Lauren had visited him in hospital. He remembered her wishing him a happy New Year. So, she'd lied about going to Europe. She'd run home to Daddy, taking his private jet to Antigua. She must have known the FBI would question his associates. And what about Lawrence? No doubt he'd be able to dodge the law easily by island-hopping to the French and Dutch islands in the Lesser Antilles.

'So, Mr Konari,' Lanzarote's voice cut across his thoughts, 'where do you fit into O'Rourke's vice ring ... girls ... drugs ... money laundering ... cheap rum ...?'

'How about bribing State officials to fix contracts for land deals?' Polito added.

'Nowhere,' Karim snapped. 'I had nothing to do with any of that.'

Thank God Nigel hasn't brought Harry's bag round yet. God knows what's in it!

They asked if he was an American citizen, though they obviously knew he wasn't. They seemed unimpressed when he told them he had a green card, but he *had* applied for citizenship.

'So, you're an Iranian citizen, correct?'

'As, no doubt, you know.'

They ignored the sarcasm. Polito reminded him that his country's leaders were unlawfully holding US citizens in the American embassy in Tehran. Had he been involved in that? He'd arrived in the United States shortly after the hostage crisis began ...

What the hell!

'You know what, Mr Konari?' Lanzarote continued. 'We Americans don't like Iranians at the moment.'

'You can't think I support that crazy regime in Iran?' Karim replied hotly.

'Well, we don't know what to think, Mr Konari.' Polito shrugged.

'You want us to believe that you don't support the government that is illegally holding American citizens?' Lanzarote raised his eyebrows.

'Although you're not an American citizen yourself,' Polito added. 'You're I-ranian?'

They returned to his involvement in Lawrence O'Rourke's business dealings. When Karim said he hadn't any, Lanzarote reminded him of a few things. Hadn't he spent Christmas Day at O'Rourke's house in Connecticut? Then there was the visit to the gentlemen's club in Charleston with Mr O'Rourke's fixer, the late Mr Hamid Ashrani—Harry Ashton. Plenty of witnesses had seen them wandering around the wetlands south of Myrtle Beach. People at the Dead Dog Saloon would swear on the Bible that they looked 'pretty shifty'.

'I'm an architect, that's what I *do*. I check out development sites.'

The men looked at each other and laughed.

'Good try, Mr Konari. So, what's happened to the plans—your drawings? They're not registered at City Hall.'

Lanzarote leaned forward and stared in Karim's face. He said quietly that in their opinion he was what they called an 'undesirable alien'. Not only did he consort with criminals in the USA but his own country, Iran, was holding the United States to ransom. Before Karim could answer, Polito told him bluntly that he wasn't welcome in the USA. Karim brought his fist down on the arm of his chair and told them that he had come to the United States because he loathed the regime in Iran. The two officers continued to stare at him.

Their next question threw him completely off balance. They asked why he was going to Australia. Was he still conducting business for Mr O'Rourke? He denied it and told them he was going to visit a friend in Sydney.

'Harry Ashton's brother?' Polito sneered. 'You were lucky to get a visa—friends in high places?'

Karim was shocked but kept quiet. How much more did they know? They'd be investigating the death of Zahra's 'husband' in Sydney next! They told him it was lucky for his family that they were all US citizens.

'Leave my family out of this, dammit!' Karim growled.

'You see,' Lanzarote said, ignoring his outburst, 'we think you are loyal to the Ayatollah Khomeini. That's why you're still an Iranian citizen. We think that you're playing by a different set of rules.'

'What the hell does that mean?' Karim shouted. 'I detest the Ayatollah Khomeini and all he stands for. You people are crazy. You've got everything wrong.'

The outburst brought on a fit of coughing, which the agents ignored. They informed him they were revoking his green card. Agent Polito looked around and commented that judging by his apartment here, he probably didn't need to work anyway. He had two weeks to leave the country, Agent Lanzarote told him. If he didn't leave voluntarily, he would be served with a deportation order and he would never be able to come back into the United States of America. They were actually being very lenient, they commented. Most people were put in detention, then deported.

'I—am—innocent! I was a *counter*-revolutionary. We tried to free the hostages.'

'You and whose army?' Lanzarote asked cynically. 'Can you prove that?'

'Of course I can't! But when the hostages are released they'll be able to identify me.'

I was wearing a balaclava. Identifying me would be impossible.

'Did any of the hostages give you a message while you were trying to release them?' Polito looked at him scornfully.

'We'd sure like to pass it on to someone's family,' Lanzarote added.

When Karim didn't answer, Polito leaned forward slightly and looked straight at him.

'So, you admit that you were a political activist in Iran. Since you returned to the United States you've consorted with known criminals. In addition, your business has been investigated by the IRS and you are making plans to travel overseas. It doesn't sound good does it?'

'If you could give us a release date for the hostages,' Lanzarote sneered, 'we might reconsider your case.'

'Telephone the Ayatollah. I'm damned if I know.' Karim's voice was almost hoarse.

The two men stood up. Lanzarote put his coat on slowly and regarded Karim.

'I'm serving you with an order to leave the United States within two weeks, Mr Konari.' He handed him another folded document. 'If you do not leave by the date on that order, you'll be arrested and deported.'

'How can you do this? I haven't broken the law.'

'As I said, the Internal Revenue Service are examining your business accounts, Mr Konari,' Lanzarote said quietly. 'You might have broken the law.'

No wonder Bahram hadn't heard from the IRS—they'd been instructed to bide their time.

'Good evening, Mr Konari.'

Both men touched their fingers to their temples in a half-salute. They left quietly, closing the door behind them.

Karim poured himself a whisky but before he could slump on the couch, the doorbell rang. It was the concierge, holding the box he'd dropped in the hall. The man was full of apologies. The agents had shown him their badges, he said, and insisted he open the apartment. Karim assured the man that he understood he'd had no choice. He closed and double locked his door and walked back into the living room. It felt tainted and dirty. He got a can of room freshener from the kitchen and sprayed it round, which brought on a coughing fit.

'Damn!' He coughed. 'Damn, damn, damn!'

He put the spray can back and sat on the couch. He was halfway through dialling Nigel's number when he had a thought. Had the FBI bugged the phone before he got there? He got up from the couch. He could use the phone at the concierge desk—but maybe that was bugged too. He shrugged on his coat, intending to phone from the corner store. He was about to open the door when his intercom rang.

'A gentleman named Nigel Palmer would like to see you, sir,' the concierge announced.

'Okay, fine, send him up.' He pushed aside the box and brief case he'd dropped on the floor, opened the door, and waited for Nigel to arrive.

When Harry's partner heard what had happened he looked scared and asked if Karim thought the FBI had been watching him too. Karim shook his head and told Nigel he was lucky he was British—at least he could go back to the UK if he needed to. He poured them both a drink and they raised their glasses.

'Here's to Hamid Ashrani, aka Harry Ashton.'

'He was a great guy ... and I loved him!' Nigel bit his lip.

They clinked glasses. *I'll never understand that,* Karim thought, *but who am I to judge?*

'I've brought this ...' Nigel said, pointing to a brown leather satchel. 'It's personal stuff for his family.' He passed a business card to Karim. 'I've written the Ashrani family address and phone number in Sydney on the back.'

Karim promised to deliver the bag personally when he got there. He'd call the Ashranis before he left.

'Tell the family we were friends ... no need for details,' Nigel said. 'He left them a lot of money. The lawyers are sorting it out.'

'Harry was a good guy, Nigel. Lawrence didn't deserve his loyalty.'

'Lawrence didn't judge us, though. He was always polite to me,' Nigel added. 'But I've got some good news for you too.'

Nigel's friend Jason at the Australian consulate had rushed the tourist visa through, but had also come up with another idea for Karim—a business migrant visa. He handed Karim an envelope. Inside were forms for a business visa application. All Karim had to do was deposit a certain amount of money in an Australian bank account and agree to start up a business in Australia within a year. Jason would make sure the visa would be granted quickly. If the business was successful, Karim could eventually apply for citizenship.

'Jason will get it through, don't worry,' Nigel assured him.

Karim was immensely relieved—*I've been thrown a life belt.* He told Nigel he'd like to thank Jason personally.

'Better not, I'll do it,' Nigel said. Jason, he told Karim, had had a rough time recently. His partner Kevin had died from an immune deficiency disease. The doctors were completely baffled.

'Can I get you another drink, Nigel?'

'No thanks, got to go ... people to see, things to do,' Nigel said with forced brightness. 'It's been good knowing you, Karim. Good luck in Australia.'

Karim walked with him to the elevator, then returned slowly to his apartment and sank on the couch with his whisky. He flicked the television on ... the first news item was *Day 73 of the Hostage Crisis.* He switched the TV off and closed his eyes.

A year ago, I believed I had the world at my feet. Now I'm being treated like an undesirable alien in my adopted country. Thank God for the Australian visa. The next step was booking a flight. Still convinced that his phone was bugged, he decided to call Zahra from the phone in the local diner. If he couldn't get through, he'd ask the Ashrani family to pass on a message once he had some dates.

I've got two weeks to get out of America! It was nowhere near enough time to pack up his past life, let alone work out a future.

34

FOG AND A REUNION

Was it really three weeks since Hamid died? Zahra wondered. She'd visited Leila regularly and each time her friend's distress had upset her. There seemed no end to the grieving in the Ashrani house.

Her own life had taken on a routine of sorts. Every day, she bought a couple of newspapers from the local shop, then took Ahmad to the beach before it got too hot. He spent the rest of the day in the kindergarten, while Zahra read the papers with the help of a dictionary. In the late afternoon they returned to the beach and walked along barefoot in the shallows.

English classes were due to begin again tomorrow and she was determined to pass the interpreter's exam and forge a new life for herself. But sometimes the days dragged. She was enormously relieved when a letter had arrived from Karim, but reading about the fire and his time in hospital had shocked her. She wrote back straight away and told him about the astonishing coincidence of her knowing the Ashrani family.

Today another letter from Karim was in her mailbox. He was on his way back to New York, he wrote, and would call her from there. His visa had come through, he said, and he was determined to get to Australia soon to see her and especially Hamid's family. He would give her a definite date as soon as possible. He might arrive, she thought, just as Ahmad starts school in early February. The next day there was another letter in her mailbox telling her that the interpreter's exam was on the following Friday, 25 January.

'That's wonderful news, Zahra,' her teacher Susan said. 'Look, I've put a vocabulary list together for you. It might help. Good luck.'

Perhaps by the time I've sat the exam, Zahra thought as she walked to the dining room for lunch, *I'll know when Karim will get here.* A sudden doubt crossed her mind; perhaps he was just coming to see the Ashrani family. But he'd told her before Christmas that he wanted to see *her*. Maybe now he knew everything about her, he might have changed his mind.

'So, you sat the exam all day on Friday. How was it?' Tula Ashrani asked when she got to their house the following Monday.

'Quite hard. I'm really not sure if I've passed.'

'*Ensh'allah* you have.' Leila took both of Zahra's hands in hers. 'We're celebrating the Australia Day weekend *and* success with your exam.'

Zahra smiled at her friend. Leila had lost weight, she thought, and although the other woman tried to be bright and cheerful, her eyes still looked sad.

Leila's family was curious to hear the sorts of questions she'd had to answer and she gave them a brief outline.

'It sounds quite hard, Zahra. If you pass, where would you get a job?' Mehran asked.

'In banking, law, health, or social and community services,' Zahra answered. 'I've learned those off by heart! If I pass, I'll have to do a course to become a professional interpreter and translator.'

'I'm sure you will,' Tula commented. '*And*, more news, Karim

Konari phoned yesterday. He's arriving in Sydney next Saturday. He's got some of Hamid's things.'

Zahra's heart flipped and she felt a mixture of emotions. Why hadn't he called her? Maybe he'd tried today, thinking it was a weekday, unaware that the hostel office was closed because it was a public holiday.

'He asked if we would let you know,' Tula told her. 'He sounded such a nice person. We've got a new phone with a speaker so we all listened to the call.'

Leila told her that Karim had said he'd like to see Zahra. He'd read the newspaper clipping she'd sent to Hamid about Zahra's husband's death. She'd received a lovely letter of sympathy from him about Hamid's passing. Leila patted Zahra's hand.

'The Konari family was always good to their employees,' she added.

Zahra tried to hide her sting of disappointment. Leila was probably right; Karim wanted to see her because she was a former employee. A servant who had got herself mixed up with the police in a foreign country. He hadn't written anything about his feelings in the letters he'd sent her. He'd said 'love you' at the end of his last phone call, but maybe he always said that to women.

The promises he'd made to her in Tehran, to take her and Ahmad away with him to America to a new life, now seemed like a fairy tale. People often said things in desperate times, she thought. He'd rashly promised to visit her in Australia after she'd told him what had happened to her. He was only coming now to visit the Ashranis, because he was the last person who had seen Leila's son alive. Leila had told her, too, that Karim was bringing important legal documents for them to sign.

By the time Mehran drove her back to the hostel, Zahra's initial euphoria at the thought of seeing Karim again had evaporated. He wasn't coming as a lover after all, she thought, but as a man she had known briefly in Tehran. He was the son of her previous employer.

A wealthy upper-class man who felt it his duty to be concerned about the welfare of his former staff.

She opened the door to her flat and as usual Ahmad ran in ahead of her. *I'm not a servant anymore, I'm a survivor. I'll make my own future in Australia. If I don't pass the interpreter's exam this time, I'll take it again. I can manage anything now. I will always love Karim, but I can deal with it if he really doesn't care about me.*

The taxi driver manoeuvred his cab carefully through the New York streets.

'You'll be lucky to get out today, pal,' he told Karim.

His journey to JFK hadn't been without incident. The snow storm had got worse as they'd neared the airport and the driver had skidded a few times on the icy roads.

When he checked in at JFK, he was assured that the flight was still scheduled to leave in spite of the weather. The young woman at the counter gave him a flirtatious glance that took in his well-cut overcoat, jacket, and open-necked white shirt. He'd seen her check his hands, bare of rings. He handed her his passport and watched her expression change to frosty politeness when she saw that he was Iranian.

'You're in a non-smoking seat in first class.' She managed a smile as she took the top copy of his ticket and returned his documents. 'Enjoy your flight, sir.'

'I'm sure I will.' He raised his eyebrows at her slightly, feeling a tinge of satisfaction when she blushed.

It was already day thirteen of his order to leave. If he didn't get out of New York that morning, he would miss his connecting flight to Sydney and be served an official deportation order. He checked his ticket again; his flight would leave at ten that evening from LA and refuel at Honolulu in the middle of the night. He couldn't help feeling annoyed with himself. It had taken him much longer than he'd expected to sort out his affairs. He patted his briefcase again. He had a wad of traveller's cheques and two airline tickets in there, as well as plenty of cash and a credit card in his wallet. Above him in the luggage compartment, Harry's brown leather bag was on its way to his family. Karim felt an enormous sense of relief as the plane began to taxi down the runway after a short delay and he relaxed back into his seat. He glanced out the window at snowbound New York and wondered if he would ever come back.

At Los Angeles, the attitude of the emigration officials bordered on hostile. He handed over his passport and was told to wait while his name was checked against a list. He reluctantly stepped to one side as other people were called forward. *I'd expect them to get me out of the country as fast as possible,* he thought irritably as he waited. *I'm an undesirable alien after all.*

The official beckoned him forward and reminded him that he would not be eligible to return to the United States for at least five years. He said nothing.

'Did you understand what I said, sir?' the man enquired.

'I did.'

He bit back a comment about the amount of tax he and his family had paid during the years they'd lived and worked in the US. But what was the point of saying anything?

'You're free to leave the United States,' the emigration official informed him as he returned Karim's passport. 'You won't need an exit stamp in Honolulu. You'll be in transit. Have a good flight, sir.'

The man's final words were almost inaudible as he turned away.

Hour after hour in a plane, with nothing beneath them but the Pacific Ocean. Karim pushed his seat back, glad no one was sitting next to him. The plane took off on a cool wet Los Angeles night. He sipped the alcohol he'd been given, reflecting that there was little for him to celebrate. His brain was still in overdrive from all the goodbyes. Predictably his family had been shocked and his mother outraged by his treatment at the hands of the FBI.

'After all the money we've poured into this country! And I knew Lauren O'Rourke was bad news the minute I saw her,' Esmat announced. 'You're well out of that friendship.'

When he'd protested that it was her father who was the bad guy, Esmat agreed vociferously. 'That man nearly killed you—my only son!'

He finally got his mother to agree not to mention the O'Rourke family during the time they had left together. Esmat was deep into her plans for moving to LA and it made her feel better that she and Karim were at least 'on either side of the Pacific Ocean'.

Maybe it was the champagne or his own exhaustion, he thought, but deep inside he felt the hard stone of misery returning to its familiar place just below his heart. He knew his family would come to see him in Australia eventually. But he still felt as if they had been torn apart. He tried to prepare himself to talk about Harry to his grieving family. It had been hard enough when he'd called them from his office. Seeing them face-to-face would be very distressing.

And then there was Zahra. He'd tried to phone the damned hostel again, but once again he'd been frustrated. No one had answered at all this time. He relayed his message to Zahra via the Ashrani family, trying to sound casual when he'd mentioned that he would like to see her again. He repeated his reason, that she'd worked for his family. Mehran told him they knew the hostel where Zahra lived. They'd driven her there several times.

Karim was desperate to see her and at least apologise face-to-face for making a scene at Tehran airport and ... and what? Was he really in love with her? Had his feelings for Zahra been heightened because of the trauma and conflict in Tehran at the time? Had he been attracted to her simply because he'd believed she was unavailable? She was married to her cousin Firzun, or so he had thought. In retrospect, he reflected, it was like a war-time romance. Relationships such as these often melted like ice when peace came. Then he remembered how he had felt when he'd heard her voice on the phone—this was no fleeting romance, this was the real thing.

The meal service had finished, the cabin lights were dimmed, and he reclined his seat. He was woken in the middle of the night and staggered into the deserted Honolulu airport where he waited in the first-class lounge with other bleary-eyed passengers. Finally, he fell wearily into his seat for the last ten hours of his journey.

The sharp light woke him as the cabin crew raised the window blinds. The sun was coming up, turning the sky and the ocean below into a blaze of red and gold. Breakfast was served and cleared and the captain's voice came over the loudspeaker, welcoming everyone to Sydney. The local time was 5.45 am and the temperature was 26 degrees Celsius, 79 Fahrenheit, clear skies ...

Karim stood at the window of his hotel suite. From here he could see Sydney's spectacular harbour, the Opera House, and the Harbour Bridge. He checked his watch: it was still only eight in the morning and he'd already showered and changed his clothes. It was too early to call Harry's brother, so he went for a walk, marvelling at the relaxed atmosphere in the city and the bright sunshine. He sat in an open-air cafe at Circular Quay and had several cups of coffee. Although he felt like he hadn't slept for a week, the coffee made him marginally more alert. He returned to his room and phoned Mehran Ashrani.

Karim was surprised that it had taken over forty minutes to get to the Ashrani family apartment. The day was soporifically hot, and the grass round the three-storey red-brick building looked yellow and parched. A wonderful smell of cooking greeted him when Mehran threw open the scratched front door of apartment number one.

'*Khosh omadid,* Karim *Agha!* Welcome!' He hugged the visitor while his wife, Tula, took Hamid's bag from him.

They asked how he was and did he have a good journey? The weather in New York? Things in Iran? He managed eventually to enquire about them.

'We're well,' Mehran answered in English.

Tula, standing with Hamid's bag in her hand, blurted, 'We're all devastated—especially my mother-in-law.' She sniffed. 'It's so good of you to come. No please, you're a guest,' she added as Karim started to remove his shoes.

'*Madar djan!* Come out of the kitchen. Karim's here,' Mehran called.

Karim glanced round quickly, wondering how three adults and two children managed to live in such a cramped space. The windows were all open, but the air hung heavy inside as well as out. Two large fans balanced precariously on a dresser and a coffee table only served to move the heat around the small living room.

When Leila emerged from the kitchen wiping her eyes, she looked exactly as he remembered when he'd seen her and Harry waiting in the atrium of his house in Tehran all those years ago. She was as neat and regal as ever in her flowery summer dress, her dark hair tied back in a bun. Karim smiled as he shook her hand, liking her instantly.

'Thank you so much for making such a long journey,' she said, and her eyes filled with tears. 'Please sit down and we'll get you some tea.'

Their eyes met and both knew that between them was an unbreakable, unspoken bond. Karim was the last person who had seen Leila's son alive. He had shared the final day of Harry's life. He sat on the worn couch and while he drank his tea and ate the refreshments the women insisted he try, they talked of Hamid.

'We will always think of him as Hamid, not Harry,' his brother said.

They were still talking about Hamid and what had happened in Charleston when Tula served lunch. Karim took his place at the dining table. It seemed cramped to him with six of them round it, but no one seemed to mind. Nigel wasn't mentioned, and Karim thought it best to arrange lunch with Mehran soon and raise the subject of Harry's partner then. After lunch the conversation turned to Zahra.

They told Zahra's story from their point of view—she'd been devastated at the airport and then distraught when she'd had to identify her husband's body.

'She's a wonderful woman,' Leila added. 'She's picked up the pieces and even sat for an interpreter's exam on Friday, which sounded really difficult.'

As Karim listened, he felt an overwhelming need to see Zahra at once. The family had already mentioned that the hostel was less than an hour's drive from their suburb. *How could I have doubted my feelings for her?* Karim asked himself and he made a move to leave.

The Ashrani family offered to drive him and protested when he thanked them and refused. He pointed to Harry's bag, which Tula had left beside the television set.

'I think you need to open it together,' he told them. There were personal things in there, he went on, and documents to sign. They called a taxi and let him go, but not without repeating that he was welcome to stay and telling him he must come back and visit soon.

'Fairy Meadow Migrant hostel—you okay with that?' Karim asked the cab driver.

'Sure, I know, I live there before!' the driver answered.

'Good, let's go.'

The other man cranked up the air-conditioning. 'Is hot day, too much humid. Where you from?'

'Iran.'

'Oh, you got bad government like my country, Chile. Crazy people take over, everyone leave. Australia no bad. Wife and kids, we happy here.' He looked across at Karim and introduced himself as Julio.

What a contrast from the American attitude, Karim thought.

The driver told him that the temperature had already reached thirty-three degrees celsius and the humidity was eighty-five per cent.

'Maybe thunderstorm later, clear the air,' Julio said.

As they drove down a wide freeway, Karim found it hard to pay attention to Julio's chatter. Just the thought that he would see Zahra soon made his head ache and threaten to burst through his skin. Would she look the same? Would she be happy to see him? How on earth had she survived these last two months? Had Ahmad grown?

Julio was forced to slow down as they travelled further south. Low grey clouds loomed ahead of them and wisps of mist swept across the windscreen. The driver explained that the freeway was on the top of an escarpment. The cool air from the sea met the warm land air creating fog. Through the thickening mist, Karim could just make out dense forest stretching to the left and right of the wide road.

'We go slow now,' Julio commented as they passed a flashing warning light.

To Karim's dismay, the mist suddenly changed into a thick fog. Visibility was reduced to about twenty metres, and he gripped the side of his seat when tail lights appeared ahead of them through the gloom.

'I think we should slow down a bit more,' he told Julio.

The driver glanced at him briefly. 'Is okay, I know this road.'

Karim had just relaxed when he heard a car overtake them. Then without warning, it pulled across in front of them. Julio braked, swerved, and skidded onto the side of the road, throwing them both against their seat belts.

'Is too dangerous,' Julio said. 'Maybe turn back to Sydney.'

It was a sensible suggestion; the fog was getting thicker by the minute. He wouldn't see Zahra today after all, Karim thought, and he suddenly felt overwhelmingly tired. After all the events that had led him here, all the dangers and set-backs, it seemed that fate was dealing him yet another blow. The driver manoeuvred the taxi into a slow u-turn and through the fog Karim saw a sign directing them to Sydney. He closed his eyes and leaned back against his seat.

Late that same afternoon, Zahra collected their beach things and locked up the flat. She hadn't heard from the Ashrani family all week, but she knew they'd been away for a few days. She wondered if Karim had arrived in Australia yet. He'd promised to call when he had a definite date, but he hadn't. Maybe he was here already, she thought, and he'd had second thoughts about getting in touch with her.

She walked slowly along the road to the beach, tipping her wide-brimmed hat lower to shield her face. The temperature and humidity were almost unbearable even now in the late afternoon. She was glad she'd bought a beach dress at the market, the light material was perfect for a hot day like this. She threw their towels and bags down and followed Ahmad for a paddle in the surf. As she walked up the beach to where they'd left their things, she saw clouds gathering on the escarpment blotting out the trees. She looked over the top of her sunglasses—they weren't clouds ...

'Foggy up there,' an English woman from the hostel called to her. 'I wouldn't like to be driving along that top road.'

Zahra squinted up at the thick fingers of mist that shrouded the top of the hills and frowned. She had a strange feeling that there was something she should know. The air was oppressively hot and she knew she'd find it hard to sleep tonight in the small bedroom. She took the towels to the water's edge, keeping an eye on Ahmad as he splashed in the shallows and lay on his boogie board.

As she watched him, she was suddenly overwhelmed by a deep feeling of hopelessness. Her son was about to start school, he had no father and no extended family—just her. She knew she could bring him up on her own, but he was a boy and in the future he would need a man's guidance. The bright future she'd imagined as an interpreter, so recently, now seemed crushingly difficult to achieve. Maybe she would fail the exam and be forced to take a job in a shop or a factory. Either way, it would take her forever to earn enough money to leave the hostel and rent a small place for them.

Always at the back of her mind was the niggling worry that someone would find out about Ali, the man who had been buried (*God forgive me*) using her husband's name. She stared at the ocean, thinking about Firzun. He'd sent her a card from the transit lounge in Singapore Airport. '*It was an accident, cousin. Wish me well.*' It was written in his usual florid script and since then she'd heard nothing. She was certain now that he had used Ali's passport to get out of Australia the night Ali drowned.

She watched the surf as it rolled onto the beach and was sucked back, leaving small crabs skittering on the wet sand. *I'm lonely and isolated, like those little creatures.* Would another wave crash into her life, rolling her this way and that? The surf hit the beach again and took the sea creatures back with it. She stared unseeing at the water. *Firzun has gone forever. I'm finally free of him.*

'Look, Mummy, there's a rainbow,' Ahmad shouted above the sound of the ocean.

She followed his gaze. A spectacular rainbow arced through the mist from the escarpment, then over her head and disappeared into the sea. At the same time, a cool wind picked up and rattled the umbrellas on the beach. She called Ahmad and told him to get out of the water. The temperature was dropping and the fog on the top of the escarpment was breaking up under the onslaught of the wind. Clouds rolled in from the south and she felt a spot of rain. A couple of women called out to her as they ran past with their children.

'Better get back—there's a storm coming!'

Ahmad ran up to her and she wrapped him in a towel. He was already shivering. A couple of minutes ago they could hardly move for the heat; now the raindrops were falling fast and there was a clap of thunder. Ahmad shrieked with fright. She pushed their things into her bag, grabbed his hand and ran up the beach with everyone else.

By the time she got to the hostel grounds, the rain was sweeping across the lawns.

'I'm c-c-old!' Ahmad chattered.

Zahra's hair and clothes were already drenched and she was shivering like her son. When she got to the edge of the lawn, she looked across at her flat. A man was standing outside it, sheltering under the eaves, his jacket collar turned up against the rain. It couldn't be! Was it a trick of the light?

'Uncle Karim!' Ahmad yelled and ran toward him.

Karim picked up Ahmad in his arms and hugged him.

Zahra stood stock still with rain pouring down her face, then she ran to Karim too.

'Karim, you found me! *Thank God*, you found me!'

He folded her in his arms and hugged her. She pulled away, laughing, and fumbled with the door key.

Karim helped her inside, struggling to walk with Ahmad clinging to him.

'I can't believe it! I'm overwhelmed ...'

'We drove into fog,' he said. 'The taxi driver turned back to Sydney, then he found the coast road and the weather cleared. Oh, Zahra, you're shivering.' He hugged her again.

She pushed back her damp hair and turned to him. 'I don't know what to say ...' She bit her lip, on the verge of tears.

'Say you're happy, Zahra. Say you're glad to see me. But you must get dry.'

'I'm happy, believe me, I am. Stay here,' she told him. 'Stay here, I'll be back.'

Karim watched as she hurried Ahmad ahead of her down a tiny hallway. He could hear Ahmad's excited voice and a shower running. He, too, could hardly believe he was actually here. When he'd seen her running across the grass in the downpour, holding Ahmad by the hand, he knew with absolute certainly that Zahra was the woman he was meant to be with.

He looked curiously around the room. What a dreadful little hot box of a place, he thought. It was far worse than the Ashranis' apartment. His gaze took in the worn-looking yellow vinyl sofa with scratched wooden arms. On the plastic-topped coffee table in front of it, Zahra had left a notebook and an English dictionary. She must have been studying before she'd gone out. A small dining table was pushed against the brick wall and on it was what looked to him like an Iranian table runner, all sequins and embroidery on a blue background. Maybe it was an unwanted item his mother had passed on to her. It was the sort of thing *Madar djan* wouldn't have in the house. Zahra had balanced a small vase of flowers in the middle of it and it gave the room a personal touch.

He walked over to one of the windows and moved the thin curtain aside. There was a view of what looked like a utility block. Through a half-open door, he could see a washing machine. He turned around. The other window looked over a lawn of sorts.

The internal walls were *brick,* for God's sake! At least someone could have plastered them. The place was so small! But even though the furniture was cheap and worn, the flat was clean and it had obviously been a sanctuary for Zahra and Ahmad. At the little sink setup in the corner, he picked up a cumbersome ceramic jug. They'd both looked so cold that he was sure they'd need a hot drink. There were teabags and strips of instant coffee and sugar in a small basket next to some packaged biscuits. He filled the jug with water and switched it on. While he waited for it to boil, he sat down on the sofa and wondered where to begin his own story.

His reverie was interrupted by Ahmad running back into the room wearing shorts and a Superman t-shirt. He dropped the hoard of toys he was clutching at Karim's feet and started to show them one by one to his visitor.

In the bathroom, Zahra showered quickly and dried her hair with the hairdryer she'd bought that week—with Karim's money, she thought suddenly. She smiled at herself in the mirror. *He came back!* Although he'd promised to come, it was still like getting a huge unexpected gift. *He found me!* The words repeated in her brain. She switched off the hairdryer, and in the silence she remembered how much she had told Karim. Then other thoughts crowded out her pleasure. *What does Karim want? Why did he come looking for me? Is he just visiting 'a servant'? Should I tell him about Firzun's postcard from Singapore?* Doubts overwhelmed her as she changed into a summer dress and sandals and tied her hair back. One thing she knew for certain, having him back in her life felt absolutely right.

As Karim talked to Ahmad and admired his toys, he had his own doubts. Zahra didn't know anything about the FBI and his banishment from the United States. He wasn't in the same position he'd been in when he'd offered her a new life in the States a couple of months ago. *I'm no longer a partner in a successful architecture firm in New York. I can't live in the States for at least five years. There will be no wonderful life in New York. Although I've still got plenty of money, I'm practically a stateless refugee. And like her, I can't return to my own country.*

She came back into the small room where he was kneeling on the floor with Ahmad. He went to pour the tea, but she shooed him away and poured a cup for both of them. He sat next to her on the couch and took her hand.

'Like I said, I nearly didn't get here today,' he told her.

He had truly believed that Fate had been conspiring against him when Julio had turned the car round and started heading back for Sydney, he told her.

'I think I fell asleep, then when I opened my eyes the sun was shining and we were passing a sunny surf beach. The driver said we were only twenty minutes away. I had no idea if you were still here. It's been so difficult to phone.'

Fate had been on his side in the end and brought him to Fairy Meadow.

'Fairy Meadow, what a strange place to live.' He laughed and turned her to face him.

When her dark eyes met his, he saw that she'd lost the hunted wariness she'd had in Iran. He knew that of all the women he'd ever known, Zahra was truly his soul mate. She smiled at him.

'How long are you going to stay, Karim?'

'I've got a six-month visa,' he answered honestly. 'I'm expecting to be granted another visa soon, so I can stay longer and find a job.' He sighed. 'Zahra, I once offered you a wonderful life in New York, but I can't promise that now.'

He told her briefly what had happened in South Carolina and when he'd returned to New York. She listened in shocked silence.

'So, I can't live in the States and I can't go back to Iran,' he concluded. 'I'm a refugee of sorts, but I want to stay in Australia.'

She looked down at her hands and he noticed she'd removed her wedding ring.

'I'm sure I've got a future here in Australia with Ahmad, Karim. I can get work ... I ...'

'*We've* got a future here, Zahra. The three of us together ... if you want me to stay,' he told her.

When she looked into his eyes she felt as if a huge weight had fallen from her shoulders. She shook her head slightly in disbelief.

'I'd *love* you to stay with us, Karim *djan*.' She smiled and took his hand in hers. 'Welcome to Australia, dearest Karim. Welcome home.'

GLOSSARY

Ensh'allah
God willing

Mashallah!
Sometimes used in Iran, especially by older people when first meeting a child. Literal meaning is 'God protect him/her'.

Khoda
The Persian word for God

Haji (Persian spelling)
A Muslim who has been to Mecca as a pilgrim

Shalwaar Kameez
A man's long shirt

Khoda Hafez/Khodafez
Goodbye (literally translates as 'God be with you')

Dari
A language that is close to Persian and is spoken by people in the Iranian border regions of Afghanistan. Both languages are written in the Arabic script.

Khanoum
Translates as 'Madam'. It is used after someone's first name—*Zahra Khanoum*, or to attract someone's attention: *Khanoum!*

Agha (pronounced *Aya*)
Translates as 'Sir'. Also used after someone's first name, eg. *Karim Agha*. More formally it is put before a name, *Agha Karim*=Mr Karim. Can be used alone to attract someone's attention: *Agha!*

Djan
Term of endearment often used after a name: *madar djan*—dearest mother.

Baba
Daddy/Dad

Chador
A woman's long cape worn over her outdoor clothes that ties at the collar with strings made from the same material. Although it is usually black, some village women wear flowered capes. It is usually worn with a black headscarf and the hair is pulled back under a band.

Hijab
A headscarf that completely covers a woman's hair.

ACKNOWLEDGMENTS

I'd like to acknowledge the following people who read, corrected, and commented on the early manuscript of *The Revolutionary's Cousin*: Debbie Lewis-Bizley, Louise Cox, and Mal Davies. Thanks so much for your time, and Carolynn Davies for all your help. Many thanks to Fran and David Lyon for providing me with a quiet space to work in the Illawarra region so that I could visit the site of the former migrant hostel. I'm indebted as ever to my husband Harvey for always being available to read parts of the manuscript and for his insightful comments. I'm also grateful for the encouragement from our daughter Emma and sons Adrian and Mark.

Thanks must go to my writer's group for their input: Vivien Wilson, Flick Pulman, Helen Lyne, Margaret Zanado, Bea Yell, and Jacques Horeg. Finally, of course, my publisher, Michelle Lovi at Odyssey Books, for her excellent editing of the final manuscript.

ABOUT THE AUTHOR

Cindy lived in a small town on the Black Sea coast of Turkey for two years where she taught English. This was the beginning of a life-long interest in Middle Eastern culture and language. Born in the UK, she emigrated to Australia in 1975 with her family. She's been an English language teacher, freelance travel writer, and tour guide in Turkey and Sydney, Australia. Her first novel *The Afghan Wife* is a love story set against the background of the Iranian Revolution in 1979.

The Afghan Wife was placed third in the New York Chapter of the Romance Writers of America in the romantic thriller category.

Since its publication, Cindy has been busy giving talks to a variety of groups in the Sydney and Illawarra area in NSW about the history of Iran and its modern day politics. Her second novel, *The Revolutionary's Cousin* follows the same characters from the first novel, as they try to establish themselves as migrants in both the United States and Australia.

Cindy is currently working on a third novel set in Australia and the UK. Its working title is *The Family Tree.*

www.cindydavies.com.au